HEART
OF THE
GAME

Praise for Rachel Spangler

Timeless

"*Timeless* is unusual. It is a sweet romantic tale of girl going home to find that thing she didn't know she wanted was there all the time. But it is much more than a simple romance…Ms. Spangler's characters are always deep and multidimensional."—*Curve* magazine

Does She Love You?

"Spangler has given us well developed characters that we can love and hate, sometimes at the same time."
—*Lambda Literary Review*

Spanish Heart

"Spangler's novels are filled with endearing characters, interesting plot turns, and vivid descriptions. Her readers feel immersed in the worlds of her novels from the start."
—*The Observer*

LoveLife

"Rachel Spangler does a wonderful job creating characters that are not only realistic but also draw the reader into their worlds. The lives these women lead are so ordinary that they could be you or I, but it's the tale Spangler weaves between Elaine, Lisa, and Joey that is so beautifully written and extraordinary."—*CherryGrrl.com*

The Long Way Home

"Rachel Spangler's third book, *The Long Way Home*, explores how we remake ourselves and the consequence of not being true to our real selves. In the case of Raine, her perceived notions of small-town life may have been tainted by being 17. The reality of what she finds when she returns as an adult surprises her and has her wondering if she'd been wrong about her home town, her parents, and her friends. Spangler's story will have you staying up very late as you near the end of the book."—*Lambda Literary Review*

Trails Merge

"Sparks fly and denial runs deep in this excellent second novel by Spangler. The author's love of the subject shines through as skiing, family values and romance fill the pages of this heartwarming story. The setting is stunning, making this reviewer nostalgic for her childhood days spent skiing the bunny hills of Wisconsin."—*Curve* magazine

Learning Curve

"Spangler's title, *Learning Curve*, refers to the growth both of these women make, as they deal with attraction and avoidance. They share a mutual lust, but can lust alone surpass their differences? The answer to that question is told with humor, adventure, and heat."—*Just About Write*

By the Author

Learning Curve

Trails Merge

The Long Way Home

LoveLife

Spanish Heart

Does She Love You?

Timeless

Heart Of The Game

Visit us at www.boldstrokesbooks.com

HEART
OF THE
GAME

by

Rachel Spangler

2015

HEART OF THE GAME

ISBN 13: 978-1-62639-327-1

This Trade Paperback Original Is Published By
Bold Strokes Books, Inc.
P.O. Box 249
Valley Falls, NY 12185

First Edition: March 2015

Credits
Editors: Lynda Sandoval and Stacia Seaman
Production Design: Stacia Seaman
Cover Design by Sheri (graphicartist2020@hotmail.com)

Acknowledgments

I was born October 20, 1982. Down the road I may regret putting that in print since it will always mark my age, and I admit it now only in order to make a point. You see, most people see their birthdays as important to their lives for obvious reasons, but for me something else happened on my birthday, something important, maybe even more important than my birth: the St. Louis Cardinals won the World Series. When I say I have been a Cardinals fan since birth, I'm not exaggerating. What's more, I was born almost a month early. I like to think it's because I didn't want to miss seeing that game. I don't remember a time when baseball wasn't a part of my life. The game has taught me so many lessons about life, loss, and human nature, and even love. This book is my attempt to give a little bit back to the sport that has given so much to me.

Still, baseball, like life, is a team sport, and I've been blessed with one of the best support teams in the world. Jenifer Langosch, sportswriter for MLB.com, answered countless questions about the day-to-day life of a sportswriter over the course of the last year. I am sure there are a few details I still managed to boot, and those mistakes are mine alone, but Duke is a much stronger, more realistic character because of Jenifer's patience and willingness to share her expertise. Thanks to my friend Teresa Grettano, who let me use her last name when, halfway through the book, I still didn't know what to call Molly. And thank you to Will Banks for continuing to keep me updated on great things happening in Queer studies. Toni Whitaker and Barb Dallinger once again served as beta readers. They are kind and gentle and caring, and they are always the first people who get to hold my new babies. They also make the book stronger by letting me know if I've actually done what I set out to do.

As usual, the Bold Strokes team has done a bang-up job of making this book better than I could ever make it on my own. Sheri's cover is another eye-catcher that fully captures the mood of the story. Toni Whitaker is the woman to thank for making it available to you in a multitude of eBook formats. Stacia Seaman did the hard work of copy-editing for an author who to this day has no idea where the commas really go. Ruth Sternglantz made sure those of you on social media knew when the novel was finally available for purchase, and a myriad of proofreaders checked and double-checked to make sure none of us missed anything along the way.

My good friend and substantive editor, Lynda Sandoval, despite her lack of interest in sports, stood by me from start to finish. Lynda is the editorial equivalent of the best catcher in baseball. A good catcher is not just the brains of the team. She actually makes the pitchers better by giving them the confidence to throw the pitches they really want to. I trust Lynda to block any pitch I may accidently bury in the dirt, then pick it up, toss it back, and say, "I've got your back. Go ahead, try that one again." Whatever the writerly equivalent of an ERA is, mine is better because I knew I had Lynda behind the plate.

I'd also like to thank two other groups of people who don't normally make an appearance in these sorts of things. The first is my parents, who taught me to love the game. They let both me and my brother miss school every spring training so we could see live games, and they let us stay up late to watch big games on TV. They paid money they likely didn't really have to get us to Busch Stadium on vacations; they taught us about the fundamentals and hard work and never giving up on your team even when they were down in the count or in the standings; and no matter what hardships our relationships have endured over the years, we have always been able to talk about the Cardinals. The second group is made up of the kids I've gotten to coach in Little League. Many of their names have appeared in this book as a way to honor their pure joy in playing a sport. The last few years of working with them reminded me that all the finest parts of baseball will always be best understood by children.

And speaking of children, I once joked that one of the main reasons I had one of my own was that I needed an excuse to keep playing ball. Jackson has never let me down in that sport. Teaching the boy I love the game I love has been one of the great privileges of my life, and I already see ways in which the student is surpassing his teacher. Jackie, you remind me of everything that is right, and pure, and good in the great American pastime.

Finally, there are never enough words to thank Susan Spangler. How do you thank the person responsible for giving you the courage and the freedom to live a life you love? There's no better teammate, no better batterymate, and no one I'd rather have hitting behind me in the lineup or waiting for me at home plate. You are the heart of my team, and I couldn't do any of this without you.

I am abundantly blessed with such a large and amazing team, not through my own deserving, but through the grace of God. Soli deo gloria.

For Susie.
There's no one I'd rather have with me during a long season,
and even after so many of them, it's still all your fault.

Pre-Game

The crowd pushed around her, a mass of denim and skin blocking the sun and even, at times, the air. Tall trunks of legs rose past her line of sight, a solid forest uprooted, flowing and shifting like a river and carrying her along. Everyone towered impossibly high and swift around her, a legion of giants, but such is the worldview of every four-year-old. With her small hand engulfed securely by her father's, she found nothing disconcerting about her inability to see beyond the blue jeans in front of her. She allowed herself to be pulled along in his wake, content to be part of this stream of people with him for once. She even looked like him now, almost. Her overalls were only a shade lighter than his pants, and they covered her legs the same way even if they did come up higher and have silver buckles. They also said "OshKosh." She liked that word. Her mother had said it when she pointed to the blue label. Her father didn't have a blue label, but he wore a red shirt like hers. Red like a fire truck, red like a crayon, red like the little bird on her hat. It wasn't her hat, though. It was Aidan's, but Aidan was sick, so she got to wear it.

She also got his ticket. "Ticket." She said the word loudly enough to be heard by her own ears, then float away on the sea of moving trunks behind her. She liked the word as much as she liked the slip of paper protruding from her tight fist. She'd seen it at home but hadn't been allowed to touch it until they'd come into this cavernous hallway. Once in the dim night and the forest of knees, her father had handed it to her. She sensed its importance without understanding its purpose and silently hoped to prove herself worthy of this thing, this ticket.

She felt more than saw their path change. There was a pause, then a step to the left, a few more steps forward, then over. Soon they were near a wall, close enough she could have touched it, but she didn't. She followed only the denim knees she recognized as his as they turned down another smaller hall. This one wasn't as crowded. Light slipped in among the legs ahead, and the gray slab walls on either side offered shelter from the pushing, grinding river of bodies. Her father slowed, allowing the tension in their joined arms to slacken, and she scooted up even with him. Gradually the layers of legs before her stepped away, each one leaving more slivers of sunlight for her eyes to adjust to until finally the last of the legs stepped away, revealing the most beautiful sight her young eyes had ever seen.

The enormity of the view seeped in slowly, like the gentle warmth of the setting sun against her cheeks. The path before her descended steeply to a low wall, separating this plain of cold, gray concrete from a vast open field of colors more vibrant than anything she had in her box of crayons. The dirt was a rich shade of orange, but not like an actual orange, burnt, crumbled, and cut through with stark, bold white lines. They offered a dry contrast to the lush green of the grass, which stood bright and deep, rippling into patterns. Rows crossed one another in the faintest shades, lighter or darker, like those left by her mother's vacuum across their living room carpet. If someone had vacuumed the field, it must have been God. Surely no person could have done something so big and so perfect. Even though the concept of the divine hovered foggy and uncertain in her mind, she knew God lived in the stained glass and tall pipe organ of her church, and she knew instinctively He lived here, too.

Men, or rather, big boys occupied the field. They dotted the richly colored grass, the brilliant white of their clothes signaling to her they were part of the field, or maybe the field belonged to them. They ran about, back and forth, or swung bats. Some of them simply sat in the grass, arms and legs outstretched, bending and straightening languidly. They were playing. The formality of gods blended with the youthfulness of children to draw her closer.

A group of younger children brushed past her, their hands clutching cotton candy, popcorn, snow cones, but her eyes remained locked on something more compelling than any petty treat. The men on the field had birds on their shirts, red birds, bright and definitive against the white, the same little bird she had on her hat. She drew steadily nearer now, slowly but purposefully inching closer, over the lip of each stair. She'd let go of her father's hand, but still felt anchored, as if tethered to him. He had brought her here. He wore the red bird, so did those boys in white, and so did she. Her mind made connections loosely, rapidly, freely, but her feet moved to a rhythm set to a reason she could only sense.

She stepped to level ground, the last of the gray concrete beneath her feet, before the low wall, and saw her opening. A little door, a small gate, towering bodies of men shifted all around, but they were dull and faded compared to the sharp pull beyond. She strode with an unnamable confidence now, threading her way nimbly around obstacles too big to pay her any mind. Her foot struck out, both of its own accord and of her deepest wish, then hovered, suspended over the burnt orange clay. Inches from Eden, she halted, then was whisked backward and upward as her father scooped her swiftly into his arms.

"You scared me to death, Sarah. Don't ever wander off like that again." The harshness of his words was undercut by both relief and exasperation as he carried her slowly back up the muted gray stairs.

She struggled against his hold, squirming around to see the field over his shoulder, her face scraping against the dark stubble of his beard. "I want to be out there, Daddy."

"So does everybody else who's ever picked up a baseball," he snapped, then sighed. "We all want to be out there, but we're not allowed."

"Then why are those boys out there?" She pointed to the players.

He turned slowly toward the direction indicated by her outstretched hand. He stared at the men on the field, his blue eyes seemingly focused on something bigger or farther away than the players in his line of sight. He didn't speak, and she waited, captivated by the pensiveness in his gaze, the sag of his shoulders, the slight crook at the corners of his lips. He'd always been a giant in her eyes, but for a moment he changed in a way a mythical creature may be timeless, or boundless. They stood, transfixed for what felt like a long time before he sighed heavily. His shoulders dropped and the deep creases along his mouth returned as he turned back to her and said, "Some of those boys are blessed, some of them work harder than all the others along the way. Most of them are both. Either way, they earned the right to go on that field. The rest of us are just lucky to be able to see them play."

He set her down on the stadium seat, then with a smile even a child could tell was fake asked if she'd like a hot dog.

She ignored the question and tried to focus on the feeling slipping away. "Blessed," she repeated as she stood on her bright red chair and looked out once more on the field, the colors, the boys, and their play. She didn't know if she was blessed, but she did understand hard work. If that was what she needed to do to get closer to that game, then that was what she'd do. Somehow those men with the bird on their shirts had earned their spot in this place. She turned to her dad one more time and said, "Someday I'm going to earn it, too."

Top of the First

You Can't Win 'em All If You Don't Win the First One

Sarah Duke stood in the first row of the stands with nothing but a low green wall separating her from the edge of the field. She could have easily stepped over if she'd had to, but she didn't. Instead she ran her fingers slowly over the press pass hanging from a lanyard around her neck. The little badge was her ticket to virtually any part of Busch Stadium. The small, laminated index card granted her access to even the field itself during batting practice. A thrill coursed up her spine as the security guard swung the gate open wide. She nodded gratefully in his direction, but the emotions clogging her throat prevented her from actually saying "thank you."

Taking a deep breath, she stepped through the doorway. Her foot hovered only a second on the rising cloud of old memories before landing firmly on the clay of the warning track. She stepped slowly forward until she was almost directly behind home plate, enjoying the crunch of the dry ground beneath her feet. Then looking down, she kicked up a little cloud of burnt orange dust simply because she liked the way it settled across the toes of her shiny black shoes. It didn't matter that she'd polished them earlier that morning. Nothing ever looked as good as it did with a thin sheen of ballpark on it.

She playfully scuffed up another little cloud of dirt, then glanced over her shoulder, still half expecting someone to scoop her up and carry her away, but no one paid her any attention. Not security, not the trainers or the grounds crew working at the edge of the field, not even the players gathered around the batting cage. Everyone was right where they were expected to be, diligently performing the task they'd been assigned, playing their part in this magnificent play, and now she was one of them. It might have taken her twenty-six years from that first game with her father, but she'd earned her spot on this field. No matter what anyone else said or thought, she belonged here.

The crack of a bat drew her attention long enough to confirm the ball would land safely away from her, but, like a child, her focus wandered quickly to the next amazing detail. Stepping forward a few paces to the side of the batting cage and into foul territory, she crouched down between the dugout and the backstop pretending to eye the pitcher or the batter. Then, hiding another smile, she bent low and ran her fingers through the short grass. She relished the prick of the soft blades against her palms and wondered if there was any scent in the world more invigorating than freshly cut Kentucky bluegrass.

Behind her, the crowd filed into beautiful Busch Stadium. She could hear them now, their jubilant, anticipatory sounds filtering in through her sense of awe as they all clamored to get a better view of the last batters to warm up. Those masses she'd waded through so many times were to her back now, and every person in the crowd would love to be in her shoes. The glee was almost too much to contain. She snatched up a single blade of grass, then, standing, released her grip and watched the grass flutter to the ground. She wanted to do it again, but press pass or not, she shouldn't play around out there so close to such an important game.

Shielding her eyes from the afternoon sun, she turned and took in the mammoth stands of the stadium rising red and gray until she had to tilt her head back so far she almost toppled over. Expected attendance for the Cardinals' home opener was over forty-two thousand people, teeming mobs of fans decked out in a sea of red and white. Already, hordes of young, and young at heart, stacked five or six deep around the wall closest to the dugout, each one jostling for a better position. They held hats and balls, trading cards and jerseys, in their outstretched arms as they called to the players still warming up. An autograph wasn't likely forthcoming at this stage, since the players were as keyed up as the kids, but she didn't blame the fans for trying anyway. She'd been covering the club every day for the last four weeks of spring training, and she still got the urge to ask for an autograph when one of her favorites brushed past on his way to the clubhouse. Of course, it wouldn't do much for her credibility as a serious sports journalist to ask an interviewee to scrawl his name across her notebook, but she still thought about it occasionally.

Members of the grounds crew bustled around her as they began to clear the field. The final players and coaches had cleared out, and the crew was hauling away the batting cages. She recognized her cue to leave. Glancing at her notepad once more, she confirmed again that she already had everything she needed. She'd been at the park for six hours already. She'd submitted her pre-game comments half an hour ago, and they were likely already up on the website. The clubhouse and players were now off-limits to the media as everyone entered their final warm-ups. She had nothing left to do until she started her in-game Twitter feed once the Cardinals took the field. Maybe she'd comment on the Opening Day ceremonies, but even those wouldn't officially begin for another thirty minutes. Eschewing her formal seat in the press box for the excitement down below, she decided to spend a few minutes being a spectator.

She flashed her badge, and once more the security guard swung the gate open wide. Ambling into the stands, she threaded her way through the crowd of boys around the dugout. Their numbers had dwindled significantly with the end of batting practice, but a handful of enthusiastic holdouts remained. They leaned on the rail and called out, "Hey, mister! Hey, mister!" at the batboy or the trainer or the security guard, anything to get a leg up on the competition. She admired their commitment. They all went after what they wanted, ceaseless in their efforts.

All except one of them.

A few feet back, a lone child sat in the seat closest to the dugout, but didn't seem to pay any attention to the scrum gathered there. He was dressed like the rest of them in his white jersey and blue jeans. His red baseball cap and round glasses shaded his face, nearly covering the smattering of freckles across his nose. He chewed lightly on the end of his pencil while he balanced a notebook on his knees, a steady look of concentration creasing his otherwise youthful features. Why wasn't he clamoring to be noticed like the others? He didn't even glance in their direction when their noise level rose at the sight of a player entering the dugout. Instead his eagle-eyed focus remained centered on the outfield, or perhaps something just beyond.

She scooted closer and scanned the direction he was watching.

There were no players in the outfield. Had something on the Jumbotron caught his eye? No, he wasn't looking up quite that high. Was it the fans over the outfield wall? Curiosity got the better of her. She crept closer and bent down behind him, trying to match his line of sight. Maybe it was her reporter's instincts, or maybe she was nosy, but she had to find out what could hold a little boy's focus in such a chaotic environment.

His shoulders tensed and he turned slowly, suspiciously to look up at her, his little brow furrowed. "Am I in your seat?"

"No." She straightened quickly and stepped back, embarrassed to have been caught trying to scoop a child. "You're fine."

"Are you sure?" he asked, uncertainly. "I can move."

"No, really." She laughed nervously as she realized how creepy she probably seemed to him. "I'm sorry. I should get back to work."

His eyes widened in sudden recognition. "You're Sarah Duke."

"Yes, I am." She squared her shoulders, inordinately pleased at having been recognized publicly for the first time and surprised that it came from a kid. Some of the players didn't even know her yet, and she'd covered them for weeks. Of course some of them ignored her on purpose either because she was new or a woman, but her response remained the same in both cases. Hard work, dedication, and raw skill had answered every question ever raised about her over the years. It would prove the naysayers wrong here, too. This boy didn't seem to require any convincing, though.

"I read your column on MajorLeagues.com this morning," the boy said with a seriousness exceeding his age.

"Yeah? What did you think?"

"I think Molina is going to have a good year, too. Maybe MVP kind of stuff."

She chuckled. "Glad we're on the same page."

"It's bad luck to have to start against Cary Pistas, though, with the wind blowing in from right field."

Duke glanced out to the outfield wall. While the flags on the third base side were barely stirring, the ones on the right side of the field were blowing harder, directly back toward the pitcher's mound.

"Huh. You're right, and it's chilly, too, which will deaden the ball."

He nodded thoughtfully, then flipped open his notebook and scratched a few marks in the top corner.

She peeked over his shoulder to see him add "game time temp" to an already elaborate heading with the date, start time, and opposing team. All things she'd already made note of on her own tablet.

"That's not an autograph book." She stated the now obvious.

"No, it's my game notes."

"Then you better add starting pitchers, too," she said, amused once again by his seriousness. "When you review it next time the Pirates come to town, you'll remember who started each game."

"Thanks." A sparkle of light shone in his dark eyes beneath lenses a little too big for his face. "Do you think Ben Cooper will have his good stuff today?"

She considered the question and then glanced at her watch. "You know, now actually might be a good time to get some inside info. Maybe I should head out to the bullpen and do some scouting."

His shoulders slumped slightly, and a frown pulled at his smooth face. "Yeah, okay. Thank you for talking to me."

He looked like a sad little puppy who'd been told to sit and stay. She wanted to pat him on his head. Instead, she arched an eyebrow questioningly. "You wouldn't want to put a few notes in your book, would you?"

He hopped up eagerly. "I could come, too?"

"Well, it's too late to go down on the field, but I know a good place out of the way where we could peek into the bullpen and make our own assessment of warm-ups if you want."

"Yes ma'am." He jumped up and grabbed his things eagerly, his excitement magnifying hers. She remembered being that age and loving the game so very much, but not being seen as part of it, or even worthy of having an opinion on the subject yet. She would've loved to talk baseball with anyone who would listen, much less someone who had inside information. Okay, maybe she was showing off a little bit, too, but she'd finally earned her dream job, with the access every kid craves. Who could blame her for wanting to flaunt that to someone who could appreciate it? She indicated a direction and happily loped on alongside the boy as he moved excitedly toward the end of their section.

She was about to steer him into the tunnel under the stadium when a voice sent her skidding to a stop.

"Joseph Landon Grettano, freeze right there."

And freeze they did. The hair on her arms stood on end and the muscles in her neck tensed instantly as if a cold blast of artic wind had raked across her back. The boy whirled around, and his profuse apologies starting to flow immediately.

"I'm so sorry. I didn't mean to run off. I got excited. It won't happen again. You can trust me to sit closer on my own. I promise. I just, I met Sarah Duke."

Way to throw me under the bus, kid. She turned around slowly to see a young woman raise her hand, cutting the boy off mid-sentence.

Her sun-kissed skin stood out against her white jersey, a bold contrast to the dark hair flowing freely down her back. Her stunning brown eyes smoldered, making her look older than she probably was. The curly-haired child perched on her hip didn't do anything to highlight her youthful features either. Still, in another place, a beach, or a bar, she might have passed for a co-ed if not for the expression on her face, which couldn't be mistaken for anything other than that of an angry mother.

The boy, Joseph Landon Grettano apparently, shifted quietly from one foot to the other as he awaited his sentencing.

"I trusted you, and you broke my trust. It's time for you to come back with us until you can prove yourself to me again."

"Yes ma'am," he mumbled, hanging his head.

Duke felt guilty for getting him in trouble. She hadn't thought her offer through, but how could she know he wasn't supposed to run around the stadium? It wasn't her fault he didn't ask his mom first.

She quietly slid back, hoping to fade unnoticed into the crowd.

"And you," the woman said, slowly, deliberately turning her focus. "Who do you think you are?"

"Um," she glanced down at her press pass, suddenly unsure of the answer to that question, "I'm Sarah Duke. I'm a sportswriter."

"A sportswriter who lures little boys into dark tunnels?"

"No. I mean, yeah, but"—that sounded horrible—"not like that."

"Seriously? You try to abscond with my child without telling me, then lead him into the underbelly of a sports stadium to some place I don't have access to and cannot see." She waved her free arm so wildly it flipped her hair over her shoulder dramatically. "And all you can say for yourself is, it's 'not like that'?"

"Uh, well." She squirmed much the same way the boy had. Could anyone in the world stand a mother's scolding when they knew she was right? "Look, I'm sorry. He was sitting alone and—"

"He was not alone," she snapped. "I was ten rows back, and I had my eye on him the whole time."

"Okay, fine. I didn't know."

"You didn't know anyone was watching him, so you thought you could take him?" She shifted the younger child to her other hip while giving Duke a moment to realize how bad that sounded. "I should call the police on you."

That was just what she needed on Opening Day. "I said I'm sorry."

"When it comes to my kids, sorry doesn't cut it. What were you thinking?"

"I wasn't thinking, obviously." She shrugged. "I'm a massive moron who wanted to do something nice for a kid who seemed, I don't know, smarter, or more together, or just better than the rest."

The woman's expression softened, so Duke plowed on. "He asked me some intelligent questions about pitching, so I wanted to show him where the pitchers warmed up. Clearly that was stupid of me."

"No." The woman sighed exasperatedly. "*That* was nice of you. You were stupid not to think he had a mother somewhere who would worry herself sick if he disappeared. You were stupid to think it would be okay for a stranger to take a nine-year-old boy into a tunnel at a sports stadium. You were stupid to—"

"Stupid's bad word," the child on her hip said around the two fingers in his mouth.

"You're right, honey." She paused to kiss him on the forehead, and for one second, her entire being transformed. The tension in her face relaxed. Every line softened as she closed her eyes and pressed her lips tenderly to his smooth skin. Then, as if exhaling all her anger, she blew out a heavy breath and asked, "Sarah Duke, do you have children?"

"No," she said quickly.

"Then you have no idea what it feels like."

"What does it feel like?" she asked, captivated by the change in the beautiful woman before her.

The woman raised her eyes, deep, dark eyes awash with fear. "Like I watched you pick up my heart and carry it into a place it might not return from."

Duke thought she'd been sorry before. She'd certainly felt sorry while getting yelled at, but now with her stomach clenched and her breath caught in her throat, she understood true remorse. "I am so sorry."

"Fine." She sounded exasperated and tired.

"Fine?"

"Does this mean we can go now?" The older boy asked in a tone that suggested he already knew the answer.

"No," his mother said. "You're still ballpark grounded. You're not to leave my side. Got it?"

The kid looked absolutely crestfallen but managed to mumble, "Yes ma'am."

"It's hot dog time?" the younger boy asked, clearly immune to the trouble his brother was in.

"Not until the third inning, honey." His mom handled the non sequitur gently before she turned back to Duke. "Don't you have work to do?"

"Yes ma'am," she replied, then waited, unsure of what she should do. Had she been dismissed? Should she apologize once more? Offer to make it up to them somehow? Or run? Clearly getting out of there was the best option. Something about the woman's disapproval and her son's disappointment constricted Duke's chest. "Okay, then I guess I'll go. Really, I'm very sorry, to both of you."

The woman said nothing. She didn't even acknowledge her retreat. She'd clearly returned her focus to her family, leaving Duke on the outside of the circle.

❖

Nothing in sports compared to Opening Day at Busch Stadium in St. Louis. In some ways, the fanfare was the same all over Major League Baseball with the ceremonial first pitches thrown out by politicians, the grandstand announcers calling the names of the Opening Day rosters, the local-kid-made-big singing the national anthem, and the sonic boom of fighter jets cutting low in formation over the infield. The Americana of it all could soften the most hardened cynic, but St. Louis had something few other teams shared, and that was a true tradition of excellence. Former players wheeled around the warning track in red convertibles waving to the crowd with their World Series rings glistening in the springtime sun. The World Series banners snapped proud and high in the wind above the scoreboard, eleven of them in all, making the Cardinals the gold standard of the National League.

Then came the Clydesdales. If the red bird was the symbol of the franchise, the Clydesdales were the symbol of the city, strong, proud workhorses that could pull more than their own weight and who worked best when they worked together. The gloriously regal draft team of behemoth horses decked in gold trimmings pulled a grand wagon carrying the official game balls. Their heavy footsteps offset a light jingle of bells as they neared home plate and echoed loud enough to be heard over the din of the crowd all the way to the press booth. History was on parade, and the future of the organization was on the field in their iconic red and white. The birds on the bats shone boldly across the chest of every man blessed enough to play in this city, on this day.

As the pageantry faded, the energy level crescendoed, and a race of chills broke out across Duke's arms when the lead umpire shouted, "Play ball!"

This was what she'd lived for every minute of every day for as long as she could remember. At thirty-one years old, she had her dream job. She had unfettered access to the game she loved, and someone actually paid her. All she had to do was watch a sport she would have watched for free and comment on the proceedings occasionally. She would've laughed at the absurdity of making money for that if she'd actually been doing her job, but after tweeting out the first pitch, a knee-high curveball from the Cardinals' ace, she found herself scanning the crowd, wondering where the young mother and her two boys sat.

The woman had said she'd been only about ten rows behind her son, which would put her almost to the back of the first section behind the home dugout. Nice seats—probably too nice for a single mother of two. There must've been a father somewhere she'd missed.

The writer next to her blew out a low whistle and shook his head, causing Duke to realize she'd made a horribly sexist stereotype. She didn't need a man to make money for her, or to get her to the ballpark. Why assume that about another woman?

"LeBaron is dealing," the writer said.

"Huh?" She looked up to see a big "K" flash across the scoreboard, indicating their pitcher had recorded his first strikeout. So that was what'd caused his reaction, not some ability to mind-read her decidedly unfeminist thoughts. Maybe the mother was a hotshot lawyer and her husband was a loser. Maybe he was a total deadbeat. Maybe she didn't even have a husband.

No, Duke couldn't go there.

She tweeted the strikeout and marked it down in the score-keeping app on her tablet. Instead of returning her focus to the game, however, she continued to scan the crowd. Why was she so fixated on finding them? Sure, she still felt embarrassed about her mistake, but that should've been a reason to avoid them. Looking for them now only added to her creepy child-stalker credentials. She didn't want to do anything to incur that kind of wrath again. She didn't want to disappoint the kids, either. She'd hated the look on the older boy's face when his mom told him he couldn't go see the pitcher. No one should be sad on Opening Day. Opening Day should feel like a clean slate, a first impression, a time of hope and belief. They had a long season ahead, inevitably full of ups and downs, but today set the tone for everything to follow. Then again, maybe she wanted to see the family one more time. Whatever the reason, she missed the next two outs looking for them.

Pulling herself together long enough to tweet "three up, three down," she turned to the man next to her. Cooper Pachol was in his forties and had a beer gut and a bald spot. His red tie already had mustard on it.

"You got a problem, Rook?" he asked, around a bite of his hot dog.

"Nope." She didn't mind the nickname. It was her rookie season, after all, and while he often greeted her presence with mild disdain, she chose to consider the mild hazing as paying her dues. "Just wondering if you ever get up and walk around the park during the games. Maybe get quotes from fans or view things from different vantage points?"

He rolled his eyes. "Aren't you the eager beaver?"

She grinned and turned back to the field. "I guess that's a no."

They watched in silence as the lead-off hitter popped up and the second batter struck out swinging. Then Yadier Molina stepped to the plate.

"This is his MVP year," Duke said.

Cooper grunted and shook his head.

"He's going to live up to his new contract."

"He's not. He's got nothing left to play for. He's locked up for the rest of his career. Now he's going to phone it in or wreck his knees."

She disagreed. An image of Joseph Landon Grettano once again flooded her mind, and she smiled, because whether anyone believed it or not, these players had a lot to play for.

As if validating her sentimentality, Molina pulled a double down the right field line, and the crowd roared. The rumble of it shook the stadium, and she found herself enthusiastically clapping along with the masses. A few of the other sportswriters looked her way, some with amusement, others with disdain.

"Tough crowd," she muttered, and bent over her Google Nexus tablet to blast the hit on social media.

The reverie was short-lived as the next player grounded out, but she smiled down at the section where the young family sat and wondered if they'd enjoyed the hit.

❖

The second inning passed uneventfully, and the air in the press box had grown heavy and stale. The room had a buzz of its own. The energy there hummed, dedicated, focused, busy. She found plenty to love, but on Opening Day she wanted fresh air, she wanted to jump to her feet over a good play, she wanted to high-five a stranger. Besides, the third inning seemed like a good time for a snack. Someone had said that recently…

Right, the mother had promised her boys hot dogs in the third inning.

Why did her mind keep returning to them?

She had an idea, and before she examined it closer, she rose and scooted around several colleagues.

"Where you going, Rook?" Cooper called. "Ladies' room?"

She ignored the jab. "Hot dogs in the third inning."

"Bring me one," he called out.

She jogged down a back stairway and onto the open concourse before weaving her way through the crowd and out into the stands. The press corps had food catered in for them, and it was a pretty nice spread, but she wasn't interested in free food if it came from a stuffy interior room. Honestly, she wasn't that interested in the hot dogs at all so much as the opening they'd give her. She'd look like a real idiot if she messed this one up, but she hadn't gotten where she had in life by being afraid to make mistakes or worrying about other people's judgment. She generally followed her instincts first and examined them later. The practice seemed to work out for her…most of the time.

She waved to a vendor hawking hot dogs and held up four fingers. What did she have to lose? She'd already made an idiot of herself once. If she fell flat again, at least she'd have some hot dogs to help ease the embarrassment.

Taking the dogs, she handed him twenty dollars. She'd long since stopped complaining about the price of ballpark food. She could've made the same amount of food at home for three dollars, but it wouldn't come with this view.

She stopped once again to view the field and the battle raging there. Ben LeBaron threw another nasty curve for a strike, and the crowd cheered wildly as the umpire rung up a batter who didn't even try to argue. She made a mental note on LeBaron's strikeout count even as she scanned the jubilant crowd. She had to be in the right section, or pretty close by now, but the seats were packed with people all wearing the same colors. From behind, the boy and his mom would look like any of the other forty thousand spectators, and maybe they weren't even in their seats. The Cardinals had recorded their first out of the third inning. Maybe the family had already gone to a concession stand. She stood there holding four hot dogs and looked lost.

"Hot dogs," she heard a tiny voice yell.

"As soon as someone comes by."

She recognized the voice, even though it sounded infinitely more calm and patient than it had when directed at her.

A curly little head popped up above the crowd at the end of the last row of the section. "I see hot dog."

"Where?" The mother turned around and her eyes met Duke's. They were beautiful eyes, big, deep, and expressive. Duke froze under their scrutiny. She should say something witty, or charming, something disarming, or at the very least not creepy. Instead she held out her stack of hot dogs as an awkward peace offering.

The woman shook her head, but smiled, and Duke relaxed immensely. She couldn't recall the last time someone had bestowed such a stunning expression on her, and even if this one happened to be born out of pity, she'd take it.

"I got you guys some hot dogs to make up for earlier," she offered tentatively. "But then I worried buying food for kids without asking would kind of be like walking off with your son without asking, and I didn't want a repeat of earlier."

At the sound of her voice, Joseph turned around, his smile mirroring his mother's, but he didn't interrupt her continued grilling.

"So you intended to stand behind us all game holding a bouquet of hot dogs?"

"Uh, when you put it that way, it sounds much more appropriate."

"Much."

"I'm sorry, um…"

"Molly," she offered.

"Molly." Duke smiled as she said the name. "I'm sorry we started off on such bad terms. I'm sorry I scared you. I'm sorry I disappointed your son. I'm sorry I put a dark spot on the otherwise bright ray of hope that is Opening Day."

"You really are a sportswriter, aren't you?"

She grinned. "I am. I love this game, this place, this holiday, and it would bother me if I left here today knowing I lessened someone else's joy in this park."

"So you bought us all hot dogs?"

"Third inning," the little boy sang out loudly.

"Yes." Duke nodded in agreement. "And I waited until the third inning like you said the boys had to."

Molly pursed her lips like she wanted to remain stern but had to work hard to do so.

"If you can't accept them, I understand, stranger danger and all, but I wish you'd give me a chance to atone."

Duke and both boys looked at Molly expectantly, waiting for whatever verdict she handed down. She drew out the tension for a few seconds, pinching the bridge of her nose and scrunching up her expression before sighing exasperatedly. "Fine."

"Yes," Duke and Joseph cheered in unison as the younger boy grabbed for his hot dog.

"I got one extra," Duke said, holding up the fourth. "I didn't know if you had someone else with you."

"Someone else?" Molly asked.

"Yeah, I didn't know if it was just the three of you," she said as she scanned their row for an empty seat, but saw none.

Molly's expression sobered as she shot a look to her oldest son, who shared her stoicism. "It's just us, thanks."

She got the sense she'd stepped into something tense. Maybe Molly's husband was in the military or on a business trip. Then again, she snuck a peek at Molly's left hand as she unwrapped a hot dog. No ring. Not even the indent or pale white band that suggested she'd worn a ring recently. A rush of conflicting emotions surged through her. Was there any term in the American vernacular more loaded than "single mom"? She wanted to be respectful, tread carefully, but a part of her was also happy this fiery, young woman answered to no man.

"You do it," the little boy demanded, pointing once again to the hot dogs.

"No, Charlie," Molly said. "I'll do it."

"You do it," he repeated, pointing to Duke.

"I'm sure Ms. Duke has better things to do right now than fix your hot dog."

She winced at the formality. "I don't mind, but please, everyone calls me Duke."

Molly eyed her more closely, letting her gaze scan up her khakis and white polo. "Of course they do."

She didn't have time to wonder what that meant before Molly snatched one of the hot dogs and handed it to her oldest son, then accepted one for herself. "Did you get any ketchup?"

"I did, and mustard, too," she said, pleased to have finally done something right. Crouching down in the aisle next to the little boy, she asked, "Charlie, what do you want on your hot dog?"

"Ketchup."

Then looking around, Duke asked, "And you, Joseph? Ketchup? Mustard?"

The boy wrinkled his nose.

"What? You eat them plain?"

"He likes both ketchup and mustard, but he doesn't like to be called Joseph."

"Ah." Duke tucked the information away. "Let me guess, you're Joe unless you're in trouble. Then Mom gives you the full government name."

He laughed. "Yes ma'am."

"Wow." Duke rubbed her eyes. "Okay, let's make a deal. I'll call you Joe, if you promise to never call me ma'am again."

"Deal."

"And you, you can call me Duke too, Charlie."

"Duke," he said empathically.

She fished several packets of condiments out of her pocket, then paused to watch the Cardinals record another out. She passed the packets out before setting to work on Charlie's hot dog. "Do you want the ketchup on the bun or on the hot dog?"

"Bun and dog," Charlie said.

"You got it." Duke carefully zigzagged a red line from side to side, making sure to hit all points evenly. "Do you want me to break it into smaller pieces for you?"

"No, no, no."

"Okay, okay. Do you want me to unwrap it all the way or peel it off as you go?"

His little brow furrowed as he thought a moment. "I want to hold it."

"Great." She glanced at Molly one more time, confirming her permission to give food to her son. Molly smiled, sending a little jolt of energy through Duke's chest. Then she nodded, and Duke set the hot dog gently into Charlie's outstretched hands.

The boy looked inordinately pleased for all of two seconds, and then thrust the food into Molly's lap.

"What's wrong?" Duke asked.

"I don't want it," Charlie answered matter-of-factly.

"Why not?"

"I don't like hot dogs."

"What?"

"I don't like hot dogs," he repeated.

"That's un-American. You're at a baseball game."

"I don't want it."

"You told me exactly how to make it for you." Duke waited for a response that could possibly explain this, but got none. "But...but you've been asking for a hot dog for three innings."

Charlie stared at her, his eyes wide and his little face filled with exasperation before finally saying, "I don't like hot dogs."

Duke looked first to Molly, then to Joe for some sort of help, but they both seemed to be fighting back laughter. "Oh, I get it. You both saw this coming?"

They nodded, grinning.

"Let me guess? Charlie has done this before. From the looks on your faces I'd be willing to bet he does this a lot."

"Every night," Joe confirmed with a giggle.

"And still you let me do the song and dance."

"You never know," Molly said, her voice light with amusement. "He could've eaten the hot dog for you."

"Has he ever eaten one for anybody?"

She shook her head. "There's a first time for everything."

Duke turned to stare at the field, noticing she'd completely missed the last out of the inning. She burst out laughing. She might have been the butt of the joke, but it still felt good to get swept up in this family's humor, even for a moment. "I think I just got hazed, and you know what? I'm okay with that. Now we're even for earlier."

Molly's smile faded instantly. "We're not even close to even for earlier."

Duke sobered. "I'm sorry. You're right. I didn't mean to reopen old wounds. Is there any way I can make it up to you?"

Molly considered the request, frowning slightly as if the answer might be "Please leave us alone." But with a glance at Joe's expectant face, she softened. Pulling Charlie into her lap, she gestured to the now-empty chair. "Since it looks like you're going to be around for a while, I guess you could sit down and tell us a little bit about yourself."

Duke grinned so widely it stretched her cheeks all the way to her ears. She probably should be getting back to the press booth, but she could work from anywhere for at least a few innings. How could she pass up an invitation she'd had to work so hard to earn? As the Cardinals' lead-off hitter stepped to the plate, Duke sat down.

Joe flashed her a thumbs-up as she slid into the seat and immediately began bombarding her with questions. "Did you see Molina's hit? Isn't Ben LeBaron's curveball wicked? Do you think the Cardinals will make the playoffs?"

She laughed and tried to parse out her answers accordingly. "Yes, yes, and I sure hope so."

"Do you think this team could win a hundred games this year?"

"That's a pretty tall order. To love baseball you have to stick it out through a lot of ups and downs," she said seriously, then brightened. "But it's Opening Day, a time for hope and belief and trying to get off on the right foot. You can't win 'em all if you don't win the first one."

"You can't win 'em all if you don't win the first one." Joe repeated the old baseball cliché, his young voice matching the inflection and slow drawl Duke used. "Then do you think we're going to win this one?"

She scanned the field, the players, the scoreboard, then turned back to Molly and felt a familiar stirring of hope she'd come to associate with the start of a new season. "It's hasn't been the most impressive start, but I believe we might make something of this one after all."

BOTTOM OF THE FIRST

Play Ball

Molly rested her chin on Charlie's head. He was still and content, eating the peanut butter and jelly sandwich she'd packed for him. Joe was focused with his usual intensity on the game. For a moment, everything was calm and peaceful. These precious times of serenity were few and far between. She usually only felt this together at night, when the day's work was done and the boys were both safely tucked in bed. A crowded stadium, on the other hand, was full of dangers and distractions. Strangers, hot food, projectiles leaving the field, fights among spectators, bad language her three-year-old was bound to repeat at day care, and large crowds a child could simply disappear in. Everywhere a danger. And yet, here they all were, safe and content.

She glanced at the woman beside her. Was Duke responsible for this lull in her stress level? Had she somehow bewitched her children? Joe certainly seemed enamored with her, but the idea of bewitching felt discordant with a new mustard stain gracing the front of her shirt. Molly's earlier resolve to punish Duke waned. Despite the still-palpable fear and rage Duke had inspired by walking off with her son, she now seemed closer to a likeable muck than a child predator. What kind of woman left her job in the middle of what had to be an important time to make amends with a child and his combative mom? A sweet one, maybe. A thoughtful one, certainly. Then again, if she'd been a little more thoughtful in the first place, she wouldn't have needed to apologize. Still, she was pretty hard to stay mad at when she seemed so earnest.

"What?" Duke asked when she glanced away from the game and caught Molly studying her.

"You have mustard on your shirt," Molly said, simply because it was easier to explain than her other thoughts.

Duke looked down, then lifted the fabric to her mouth and tried to lick the yellow dab off.

"Good Lord, are you a five-year-old boy?"

"What?" She rubbed her thumb over the spot she'd just had in her mouth.

"Here." Molly reached into Charlie's diaper bag to grab a wet wipe.

"Thanks, these are handy." She started to wipe her shirt, but froze at the sound of the bat. Jerking her head up, she tracked the ball into the outfield, muttering, "Get down, get down, get down." When it hit the ground she gave a fist pump and grabbed her tablet. Her thumbs flew over the screen the way a boy's would a video game controller. Her focus was sharp and consuming for those few seconds, then with one emphatic tap, she put it back down.

Molly's curiosity piqued. "What happened?"

"Cayden Brooks got a hit."

"No, I meant with you. One minute you're licking your shirt, and the next it's like you can't see anything but your keyboard. You looked like a power shark sealing a business deal or something."

"Ah, I went into work mode." She held up the tablet. "I'm live-tweeting the game."

"So you typed that what's his name got a hit?"

"No, the team has people who do play-by-play. I stick to color commentary, fun facts, side notes, things that add to the bigger picture. So I tweeted that the first base coach tossed the ball to the dugout, and visitors to Cayden Brooks's home would likely see it on his mantel."

"Why?"

"It's his first hit since being called up to the major leagues."

"You know that off the top of your head?"

"Of course. It's my job. Shirt licking aside, I'm serious about my work and good at what I do."

She believed her. Her confidence wasn't cocky or boastful, but sincere. "What exactly do you do, other than tap a screen?"

"I interview players, I study the team, I report on trends and changing conditions. I write pre- and post-game reports for the biggest website in professional baseball. I live-post social media updates of my observations on the game. That's about it."

"Oh, is that all?" Molly teased. "How do you find time to buy hot dogs for all the mothers you offend along the way?"

Duke laughed, a good-natured laugh, hearty and unrestrained. "Well, it's not easy, but I have to pay those concession stand bills somehow."

"Are you here every night?" Joe cut into the conversation.

"Almost. I'll get a series off every now and then, like the players do, but if I want to stay at the top of my game, I have to show up ready to go every night, at home or on the road. What about you? How many games do you get to see each year?"

Molly hesitated, not sure she was ready to admit to Duke or herself how often their paths might cross. Joe shared none of her unease. "We've got season tickets."

"Really?" Duke sounded surprised, and Molly's defenses rose. Why did everyone assume a single mother of two couldn't afford season tickets? Probably because she couldn't, but she still hated the implication in Duke's raised eyebrows.

"You're the luckiest boy I know, Joe," Duke continued amicably. "You, too, Charlie. I would've given anything for season tickets when I was your age. I can't think of a better place to spend every night than at the ballpark."

Molly could think of several other places, a bubble bath for instance, but then she looked at her boys, and part of her agreed with Duke. They were happy here, and that made her happy. Still, her inner mom voice demanded she manage expectations. "Not every night. Not night games on school nights."

Joe and Duke both wore the same facial expression of disappointment, but thankfully Duke was mature enough to toe the party line. "Good call, Mom. School comes first."

"You go to fifth grade?" Charlie asked.

"Nope," Duke said. "I finished all my grades and then went to college and worked hard there, too. I studied more and worked harder than everyone else so I could watch baseball and get paid for it. Which reminds me, I better get back up to the press booth."

"You can't do your work from here?" Joe asked.

"Joe," Molly said in a gentle correction, "she's been more than generous with her time. We've probably already got her in trouble for keeping her away this long."

"It's okay. I like to get out from time to time, and I'm glad I got to know you all, but I really should check in."

"Thank you for hanging out," Joe said dutifully, and Molly felt a hint of pride he'd remembered his manners even through his disappointment.

"Yes," she added. "Thank you for your time, and the hot dogs."

Duke met Molly's eyes and held them with a focus akin to the attention she'd given the game moments earlier. The gaze warmed her in a way that felt disconcerting, but not necessarily unpleasant. "Thank you for giving me a second chance." Then with one last grin, Duke wove her way back into the crowd.

Second chance? Was that what Molly had given her? A second chance at what? Whatever it was seemed important to Duke. How had she conveyed so much in so few words?

Charlie shifted on her lap, squirming down to a standing position before facing her, raising one fist and saying, "I want a lion."

She and Joe looked at each other and laughed. The moment for deep thoughts had passed, once again leaving only her and her boys watching a baseball game.

❖

Molly set the final book on the floor and climbed out of Charlie's bed as she began to sing "You Are My Sunshine."

His big eyes remained open. His gaze followed her around the room as she turned on a night-light and pulled down his window shade. He watched her as though she were the center of the universe and if he were to blink she might disappear. He probably suspected she and Joe threw wild parties, jumped on the furniture, and ate ice cream as soon as he went to bed. Even at three, he had an imagination capable of creating such a scenario. Maybe he resisted sleep out of a simple desire never to miss something fun, but part of her, the guilty part, worried he followed her so closely because somewhere deep down, in a place before memory, he knew he'd been left before. She had to tamp down that fear, her own fear, lest it convince her to climb back into the bed and refuse to let him go.

"Good night, my sweet prince," she said, bending down to kiss his forehead and nuzzle his nose with hers. "I love you so much."

"I love you so much, Mommy," he whispered back, making all the hours she'd spent wrestling with him instantly worth it. She straightened up and walked away before the emotions could overwhelm her. Closing the door quietly, she whispered a prayer for his safekeeping and sound sleeping through the night.

Tiptoeing down the hall, she knocked softly on another door. "Joe, you about ready for bed?"

"I've got fifteen more minutes," he called back.

She pushed open the door and found him lying on his bed with a book in front of him. His wet hair indicated he'd already showered. "Did you brush your teeth?"

"Yes."

"Did you pack your backpack for tomorrow?"

"Yes."

"Did you wash behind your ears and in your belly button?"

He smiled. "Yes."

"Really? Do I need to check?"

"No." His cheeks flushed pink. "I'm too old, Mom."

He might be right, but that didn't mean she had to like his increasing independence. "Want to talk about the game?"

He finally set the book aside. "Really?"

"Of course, but you have to scoot over and let me in."

He acquiesced without much thought, which led her to wonder if he wasn't too grown up to cuddle with her after all. Then again, maybe the chance to talk baseball overruled all else.

"So, what did you like best about the game today?"

"I liked meeting Duke," he said without hesitation. "I can't believe a real sportswriter sat with us."

Molly stifled her defenses. She'd long been used to not being the coolest person in her son's life, but she still worried about his choice in role models. "Why was that important to you?"

He looked at her as if she might be a little slow. "She's a *real* sportswriter. She knows everything about the Cardinals. She's the person other people ask when they have questions about baseball. She can talk about baseball forever and not get tired of it."

"I bet you'd like a job where you get to talk about baseball all the time."

"Who wouldn't?"

"You know you can always talk to me, about anything, right?"

"I know."

"I mean it."

"Yeah, but you're a girl."

She made her most offended face. "And girls can't talk baseball?"

"No," he corrected quickly, "Duke's a girl, too…I guess."

Molly tried not to laugh at his "I guess." "Girl" was not a word she would've used to describe Duke. No girl she knew would've licked mustard off her shirt or wandered off with a child without thinking about his mother. She didn't walk like a woman or talk like one either. She occupied her space with a comfort and ease that usually accompanied entitlement. Still, she had a woman's softness to her eyes and her body, even under her gender-neutral attire. No pair of cargo khakis ever hung off a man's hips the way they had Duke's. She blushed.

"Duke likes baseball, though," Joe said. "She's…like a tomboy, but grown up."

A butch. Molly knew the term and recognized its fit for Duke, but she withheld it from her son for multiple reasons, some obvious, others she chose not to examine. "I like baseball. What's more, you like baseball, and I like to share the things you like."

He nodded thoughtfully. "So, what was your favorite part of the game?"

She pretended to think hard. "The Clydesdales."

He laughed and pushed her out of bed. "The horses aren't part of the game."

"Sure they are, for St. Louis anyway. But I also liked that the team won. That's a good omen for the season."

"You can't win 'em all if you don't win the first one."

Duke's echo was thick in his voice, not just her words, but her hopeful inflection, her slow, low tone, her slight Missouri accent. Molly's defenses rose. She wanted to be everything for him, not out of selfishness or inflated ego, but because she was the only person she could trust not to let him down or walk out on him or hurt him.

She wanted the world to be fair and honest and decent, but since she couldn't make that happen, she at least wanted to keep him innocent for as long as she could. Every outside influence reminded her she couldn't bubble-wrap him and lock him in his room.

She bent low and kissed his forehead. "You know I love you more than anything, right?"

"I love you, too." He eyed her suspiciously, as if sensing there was more to her non sequitur. He'd always been sensitive to her moods, probably more so than he should have had reason to be.

She brightened quickly. "Sleep tight. Don't let the bedbugs bite."

"'Night, Mom."

She closed the door and leaned up against it, praying once more for her sons, then with a deep breath, mentally segued into her nightly routine. With the boys bathed and safely in bed, she could now turn her attention to preparing for tomorrow. She'd already laid out clothes for the morning, but there were still backpacks and diaper bags to pack, lunches to make, dishes to do, and, for the love of all things holy, she could not forget to set the timer on the coffeemaker. There would be no time to think, to reflect, to wonder about the future, and she liked it that way.

A part of her might have enjoyed the luxury of letting her mind wander to Duke, to think of her simply as the most interesting person she'd met in a long time, to wonder what it would be like to have a conversation with a woman that didn't have anything to do with kids or work. To consider, for a second, their shared sexual orientation, or question whether or not Duke had picked up on it as well.

Probably not.

Duke seemed focused on the game, on her job, on the boys. She was such a guy, and Molly'd had enough guys in her life, in too many forms. She'd spent too much of her life trying to fight off men who wanted to rescue her. An ex-husband who saw her as a way to atone for his sins, an ex-father-in-law who saw her as a second chance at parenting, and a slew of men who wanted to save her by playing daddy to her kids. While Duke in no way reminded her of the first two, she could easily fall into the latter category, and Molly wouldn't have anyone, man or woman, use her as a ticket to a ready-made family. Duke and Joe might share baseball, but her family wasn't a game to be played.

Why was she fighting Duke in her head? She sighed. Duke had been absentminded, but sweet and good-natured. She hadn't tried to placate Molly when she blew up, handled Charlie with the sense of humor he required, and deferred to her on all parenting decisions. Why was she already listing the reasons they couldn't date when Duke had done nothing to suggest her interest, or even awareness of that possibility? Had she gotten so used to fighting she didn't know how to do anything else? Or was this another wall she'd thrown up to protect herself? She didn't want to be alone forever, but she'd settled before, and it never ended well. She swore this time around she'd listen to her instincts, and right now they told her to be careful. She'd had to fight hard for everything she had, and risking everything for a little fun didn't seem wise.

Maybe she wasn't ready to get back in the game after all.

"Mom, am I still ballpark grounded?" Joe asked.

"Yes, it's been only two games. It takes just a few minutes to break someone's trust, but a long time to earn it back."

"Yes ma'am," he said, looking properly apologetic.

"But if you don't mind your old mom coming with you, we could all go down and watch batting practice together.

He threw his arms around her. "Thank you."

Shifting Charlie on her hip, she slung the diaper bag over her shoulder and wove through the seats until they were on the edge of the field. Joe immediately pulled out his notepad and began to scribble while Charlie inspected the cup holders in front of them. She took the downtime to sit back in her chair. The seats this close to home plate were green, probably to remind people of all the money they cost. She preferred the red ones in their section. Red was cheerier. It felt more like part of the crowd, not that their seats were much cheaper. Her chest tightened with the sense of debt. She had to let go. The season tickets were a gift to her sons from someone who loved them, despite Molly's own misgivings about his motives in other areas of her life. She wished she could untangle his good deeds from her own resistance to giving up control.

Charlie said something that sounded like "Duke," but maybe she'd heard him wrong.

"What?"

"I want a hot dog."

"No, what did you say before?"

"I want a hot dog."

"In the third inning."

"Duke get it," Charlie sang to a melody only he knew. "Duke get a hot dog. Duke get a hot dog on the baseball game."

Joe and Molly looked at each other, then turned to the field. They needed only a second to pick out Duke striding toward them. By women's standards she was tall, probably five-nine, but every man on the field dwarfed her. She was also the only one out there looking back at them. She flashed a beautifully unrestrained smile. Molly raised her hand in a little wave of recognition, but Joe jumped up and blocked her view. "Hi, Duke."

"Hiya, kiddo." A security guard opened a gate and let her into the stands. "I thought you might be here, since it's not a school night."

"You remembered when we're allowed to come to the games?"

"Sure. I might be slow to learn your mom's rules, but once I do, I keep 'em all right up here." She tapped her temple with her index finger and winked at Molly.

Winked? Really?

"And with those rules in mind I promise I won't try to sneak you off to the bullpen today."

Joe frowned, but Duke grinned, tucking a tablet under her arm and shoving her hands into her pockets. "But if your mom wanted to go see the bullpen, I could show her, and since you're probably still ballpark grounded, I guess you'd have to come with us."

Molly rolled her eyes at the transparency of Duke's plan, but the hope animating Joe's features left little doubt as to how she'd ultimately answer.

"What do you say, Molly, have you ever wanted a sneak peek at a major league bullpen?"

She pursed her lips, trying to play hard to get. "I can't say that I have."

Duke shifted her weight and met her eyes, either seeing through her ploy or refusing to be deterred by it. "You don't know what you're missing. Big, strong, sweaty men, flexing muscles and, you know, stretching out." She wrinkled her nose, as if the act of describing the people she covered purely as pieces of meat rankled her senses.

Molly knew how she felt and threw her a line before she realized the implications of what she was about to say. "That doesn't do anything for me…not on any level."

This time Duke's smile grew more slowly, and more knowingly. "Yeah, me either."

"I sort of got that from you."

"Really? I sort of missed it from you."

"Most people do."

"Well, good for you, though," Duke said with fake resoluteness. "Two sons. And there's that, but also, no interest in anyone in the bullpen."

Molly waited, enjoying watching her stammer. She'd come out to only a few people in her life, and none of their responses had ever been quite so amusing. Duke had actually started to blush. She could almost see the wheels turning under her blond hair. How did Molly get the boys? Where was the partner? Were there signs she'd missed? Molly wouldn't answer unasked questions. She might not even if asked outright. She generally had a "none of your business" attitude with busybodies, but Duke hardly seemed nosy and certainly not judgmental. If anything, her confusion was endearing.

"Alrighty then," Duke continued awkwardly. "Some other time maybe, or not. About the bullpen visit, I mean. Not about anything else. Not that there's anything else. You know, I could just stop talking."

Joe looked from one adult to the other, clearly intuitive enough to realize the conversation had deeper meaning, but thankfully not old enough to realize what. "Are we still talking about watching the pitchers warm up?"

"We are now," Molly said, easily transitioning back into mom mode.

"Oh, thank God," Duke mumbled.

"It'll be a good learning experience for you boys to see some of the work that goes on behind the scenes of a game. We'll call it an educational field trip."

Joe gave a fist pump, and Molly scooped up Charlie before turning to Duke and uttering a phrase that didn't come easily to her. "Lead the way."

❖

They stood behind a fence, peering straight into the bullpen. Their position was below the stands and level with the field. High green walls on either side sheltered them from the noise of the crowd. The pop of the ball smacking against a leather catcher's mitt reverberated through the air around them. If pushed, she'd have to admit the vantage point did impress her. Aside from the chain-link barrier, they had the same view an umpire would see during the game. Sixty feet away, a lean pitcher in home whites reared back, then snapped forward with the violence of whiplash combined with the grace of a dancer to hurl a ball with lightning speed and pinpoint precision.

"A ninety-five-mile-an-hour fastball covers the distance to the plate in about four tenths of a second. The batter has about two tenths of a second to decide whether or not he wants to swing," Duke explained. She'd regained all of her confidence now that she'd found a more familiar topic. "Connecting a round bat to a round fastball is a feat of physics most people will never accomplish. The task is complicated enough to do even when the ball is headed straight down the pipe, but these pitchers make it move in wickedly deceptive ways."

"Like a curveball or a slider?"

"Yeah, here, watch this."

Duke crouched down to the side of the catcher, and Joe mimicked her stance. Molly felt a twinge of something she couldn't quite decipher. They looked so engrossed, so comfortable together. They shared a common language, an instant bond, a unifying passion. It all seemed so effortless for them. Was Joe even aware he'd started to mirror Duke's mannerisms, like the way she steadied herself with a few fingers on the ground, or rolled her shoulder forward with each pitch like she could somehow affect its direction as she talked about the various ways to direct a ball over the plate? Envy blended with affection at the sight of them huddled together.

Maybe he didn't have enough men in his life to connect with.

Then again, Duke wasn't a man, which made Molly feel a little safer and might have the same effect on Joe. Maybe he felt drawn to Duke because she was such a guy without actually being one. Still, women were every bit as capable of letting someone down. Her own family had taught her that, but she wouldn't let her mind wander there. Duke wasn't like her family in any way. She was fun and playful and good-natured. Her comical reaction to Molly's earlier revelation provided distraction enough to keep her from examining why she'd felt the need and the safety to reveal something so personal. Or at least it had until now.

Why had she come out? Was she simply trying to clear up a false assumption? She didn't like being put into boxes, especially ones whose labels didn't fit. Or was she looking for a little bit of the camaraderie like the kind Duke shared with Joe? Did she crave her own connection, some common ground, some unspoken bond? As much as she loved her boys, she did occasionally long for a conversation on something other than superheroes or peanut butter and jelly. There was no harm wishing for an adult conversation so long as it didn't cross into something more than casual, and Duke seemed safe enough on that front. She might be a lesbian, but she was far from the gracefully feminine form Molly envisioned when she examined her attraction to women.

"Hey, Colin," Duke called to a teenage boy sitting on a bench in the bullpen, "will you toss me a ball for a sec?"

The boy lobbed a ball over the fence. Duke snagged it out of the air with one hand before holding it out for Joe to see. "This is a standard fastball grip."

Molly glanced first at Charlie to see he was still fully absorbed in his inspection of the grounds crew's garden hose, then scooted closer to look over Joe's shoulder.

"That's probably how you throw a ball when you play pitch and catch. It's usually the first thing people learn to throw because it's the most accurate."

"And depending on where your fingers cross the seams, it can be a two-seam or a four-seam fastball," Joe said proudly, and Molly wondered where he'd learned that.

"You got it, and both pitchers tonight can throw both of those wherever they want in the mid-nineties. They can also both throw the curve." Duke slid her fingers deftly around the ball until her index and middle fingers pressed together and formed a smooth half-circle around the ball all the way down to her thumb.

She had long, graceful fingers, slender and completely unadorned. Her hands were feminine, smooth, and gentle, with a strength born out of skill rather than force. She didn't try to crush the ball in her grip, but rather cradled it artfully. Molly found it strange that in the midst of explaining a man's job to a boy, Duke revealed such a feminine trait. Right now she clutched a baseball, but Molly could easily imagine her using those hands to play a piano, or sew, or massage the nape of her neck.

She shuddered, and Duke looked up, her blue eyes still shining with the focus she'd directed at the baseball. They were clear eyes, open and filled with unfiltered interest and affection, now directed at her. Molly had to blink back unexpected emotions.

"Am I boring you to tears?" Duke asked softly as a shadow of self-consciousness flashed across her features.

"Not at all." She looked away, out to the wide open field, this space suddenly confining.

"It's okay. Not everyone wants to know the details. They can detract from the magic."

Magic? Was that what she'd felt when their eyes met? Absurd. She didn't believe in magic. "No, I just realized the game's about to start, and we're not ready yet."

Duke smiled brightly. "One of the great things about this game is it starts whether we're ready or not."

Molly's breath caught. She didn't find the idea of things happening without her approval or preparedness appealing. She didn't like the way Duke stated the fact so calmly, and she didn't enjoy the way the words lodged in her chest.

She wasn't ready.

She wasn't where she needed to be yet.

She wasn't with who she thought she'd be with.

She wasn't even sure she knew the rules of the game well enough to play, but none of those fears had stopped the players from taking the field. She stood rooted to her spot, staring disbelieving at the sparkle in the eyes of Sarah Duke, as somewhere from across the field she heard an umpire call "Play ball."

TOP OF THE SECOND

I'm Just Lucky to Be Here

The St. Louis Cardinals clubhouse was calm three hours before game time. Players lounged in their warm-up clothes or bare-chested, sprawled on leather sofas or perched near their lockers. One outfielder padded past her in nothing but socks pulled up to his knees. Duke had long ago grown inured to the sight of men in various stages of undress much the same way a doctor would. Some of the players, and even more of the old-time managers, didn't think a woman belonged there. She'd dealt with that attitude since middle school, when she'd first started writing for the school paper. The sexism started subtly, like her high school editor asking if she wouldn't rather cover field hockey, or her high school advisor suggesting her desire to cover baseball might be because she liked the view of the older boys in their tight pants. Thankfully her high school had been small, and most of the people writing for the paper wanted to be serious journalists and therefore looked down on sports writing, allowing the job to fall to her.

In college, things had been harder. There were lots of former athletes looking to retain their ties to the game via the sports pages. That was when the criticism about her place in the game really began to fly. How could she cover a sport she'd never played competitively? How could a woman relate to male players enough to get them to open up? How could she ever cover a locker room successfully with all those naked men around? She'd had to fight for every single story, sometimes even going to games being covered by one of her male counterparts and turning in a competing account of the game. That practice won her no friends, but her stories prevailed as better versions, more times than not. College was also where she found the anonymity of the Internet.

She submitted to sports blogs as S. Duke and began to earn recognition for covering both college and minor league teams. Soon the offers came rolling in, and by the time the editors found out she was a woman, it was usually too late for them to rescind those offers without breaking a contract.

Over time, she'd proved herself worthy of covering every aspect of the game, but a major league contract and lengthy résumé still hadn't stopped people from grumbling. Most of the younger ballplayers and managers left it at a smirk or a raised eyebrow, but a few of the older trainers had told her rather bluntly they didn't want her in the clubhouse unless the players were fully dressed. They continued to argue she'd be a distraction to the players or prevent them from relaxing fully, but between spring training and the start of the season, she'd seen most of these guys in nothing but their skivvies or a towel at least once, and if they hadn't distracted her from *her* job, she didn't see why her presence should prevent a multimillion-dollar-a-year player from doing his.

"Hey, Duke," Cayden Brooks said, glancing up from tying his shoes.

"How's it going?" she asked.

He spun his plush swivel chair. The high-backed leather with a cardinal red STL emblem across the back, the same kind as every other player had, was the type of chair one expected to find behind a desk in a swank office. They were likely meant to remind players of a business setting, but Cayden used his feet to roll the chair back like a child who wanted to spin around and around until he made himself dizzy. "Couldn't be better."

She smiled down at his expectant, eager-to-please face peeking out from beneath a mop of shaggy blond hair. He clearly wanted her to ask him a question, interview him, put his name in the paper. He was such a rookie that this part of the job still excited him in ways it didn't the veterans. She liked that about him, perhaps because she was a rookie, too.

She didn't need a quote from him. There were bigger names around, and his performance thus far on the field had been slightly below average, but she caved to his fresh-faced enthusiasm and opened her notebook. "How are you feeling about your time in the big leagues so far?"

He nodded, play-acting at solemnity. "It's a grind, but I'm learning a lot. I want to try to do whatever I can to help the team, ya know? I'm just lucky to be here."

She quirked one corner of her mouth at the string of baseball axioms. This kid couldn't have used more clichés if he'd tried, and actually he probably had tried pretty hard. He'd likely been waiting to feed someone those lines since the first time he saw *Bull Durham*, but who was she to deny him the moment? He was trying to do his job, and she'd do hers. Maybe he wasn't crushing the ball yet, and she wasn't writing Hall of Fame–style journalism, but they both had roles to play, and they were playing them well.

She thanked him for the quote and headed up to the press booth to work on her pre-game report, already thinking of ways to throw him a bone by working the quote in somehow. Maybe she'd do a short piece about pre-game routines. She'd leave out the parts about some players lying on leather couches in nothing but their underwear. The readers didn't need to know some of their favorite players thought of the clubhouse as their own personal nudie bar, though that was part of the routine, too. She could focus her story on the ways things build one after another, from the grounds crew rolling back the tarp, to the locker room staff hanging up the clean white uniforms, to the players pulling up one by one. Then the reporters always filtered in to ask the questions that would help dust off the cobwebs of yesterday's game before directing the dialogue toward a new day. They were all such little things, but they added up much the same way a few base hits and some sacrifice flies might lead to runs scored.

Her dad had taught her the art of small ball: the importance of doing all the little things right. He'd talked about the slap bunt, the secondary lead, and stepping off the mound to slow the running game. He'd taught her brothers how to time a pitcher, how to steal signs, and how to frame a pitch behind the plate. She watched as he spent hours dissecting infield footwork with his boys, and she'd listened carefully as he lectured them on the myriad of ways to manufacture runs. He'd said it was the Cardinal way. Everyone played a part. Now she couldn't wait to show him her part in it all when he visited the stadium with her mom in a few hours.

❖

"This is the press booth. I spend most of my time during the game up here." She pointed out her usual chair in the second row, behind a laptop and a stack of depth charts. The stadium style seating meant she didn't have to look around anyone's big head, and the long row desk gave her some distance from the person in front of her, at least a little bit more than the seats in the stands did.

"You have to be a member of the Baseball Writers of America, which I am," she said proudly, "to sit in the front row, but senior writers get first pick, so I'm still a row back."

"Do other sports journalists we would know sit around here?" her mother asked.

"Sure, Jenifer Langosch, Bernie Miklasz, even Rick Hummel."

Her mother smiled proudly and nodded the way she had when one of her children had babbled as a toddler, a nod of love, to say, "I'm happy because you're happy, but I have no idea what you're saying."

"The press booth is named for Rick Hummel. He's in the Baseball Hall of Fame," she explained.

"As a writer, not a player," her father clarified.

"Right," Duke said, trying not to grit her teeth as she added, "he's just a writer."

"What about Mike Shannon?" her mom asked quickly. "Where does he sit?"

"He's in broadcasting, so that's a different booth. He's a nice guy, though. I'll introduce you if we run into him."

Her mom beamed, clearly impressed her daughter knew someone famous. Duke turned to her father hoping to see the same expression, but found him studying a television hanging from the ceiling.

"Those are so we can see things like instant replays or get a close-up shot on the pitches. They are helpful on bang-bang plays, but I prefer the real deal to the TV screens."

He glanced out the wide window of the press box to the expansive panorama of Busch Stadium. They were three sections up from the field, which added some distance, but the position offered an unobstructed view of the field's grandeur and the St. Louis skyline all the way to the towering Gateway Arch glistening in the midday sun.

"I suppose if you have to work in an office, this is a pretty nice one," he replied.

"No doubt, but nothing beats sitting in the seats with the crowd. I usually head down there for an inning every game to get a feel for the atmosphere. Your seats are in one of my favorite spots, just to the third base side of home plate."

He rubbed the short brown stubble on his chin. "Never could afford seats like that."

"Well, now you don't have to." She heard the pride in her voice and tried to rein it in. She didn't want to seem boastful, but she loved giving him back a piece of the game he'd given to her.

"We're not keeping you from your work, are we?" her mom asked.

"No, I already checked in with batting practice and filed my pre-game report. I'm sorry I won't be able to go out with you after the game. I have to go to the clubhouse and get my post-game quotes, then file my story. I usually don't get out of here until at least two hours after the game."

"It's such a long day." Her mom squeezed her hand. "But it must be exciting to go out on the field with the players."

"It really is." She turned to her dad once more, not sure he was listening. "I waited so long and worked so hard to get on the field, I never take it for granted."

"You don't bother the men while they're trying to work, do you?" he asked, in the tone of voice he'd use when he came home from work and asked if she'd behaved for her mother.

"No sir," she replied, lowering her voice. "My work is part of the warm-up process for them, too. They're used to me being there. They recognize me. Every now and then one of them will seek me out. My pre-game interview is part of their routine."

He shrugged. "Maybe a small part of it."

"Yes, just a small part of it."

"Hey, did you hear Aidan started a traveling baseball team for him and the boys down at the Elks?"

She forced a smile even as her stomach dropped at his mention of her older brother. "No, he didn't tell me."

"Well, he did. And it's baseball, too, none of that softball stuff. He's still finding a way to play the game the right way."

She looked out onto the field where players stretched and jogged, athletes already at the top of their game still taking every chance to hone their skills. The sun shone on the grounds crew as they meticulously chalked white lines down the base paths, measuring down to the centimeter in search of perfection. Three umpires in all black huddled near the pitcher's mound reviewing the boundaries of play, the gleam of their freshly polished shoes visible even from this distance.

The crowd poured in beneath her, their hum growing with each passing minute as the sea of red spread like a rising tide. The energy built steadily, the heartbeat of the stadium pulsed rhythmically, but somehow, for the first time she didn't feel like a part of it. The expansive view seemed confined, the air dull and heavy. Her father's voice remained just an echo in her ears.

She had to get out of there, had to get away from the place she'd been so proud to occupy. "Hey, why don't we go find your seats?"

Her father quieted his chatter about her brother's glory on the beer league team, and her mother smiled weakly, making her suspect she'd been too abrupt with them, or too transparent. She tried to lighten her tone before saying, "You don't want to miss the first pitch."

Her father made a show of looking at his watch but said nothing about the official start time still being twenty minutes away as Duke led them down the stairs and out into the stands.

God, what had come over her? Had his talk of Aidan made her jealous? She loved her brothers, and they adored her. She didn't begrudge them their accomplishments, and they'd expressed envy at her position, too. Either one of them would've loved the tour she was currently giving their parents, but did she need any of their approval? Much less her father's full attention? She wasn't a child anymore, eager to garner a piece of the pride he lavished on her brothers. What did it matter if he didn't gush at her job or share her enthusiasm? She hadn't done all this for him, or at least not for him alone. Embarrassment burned her cheeks as they waited for the crowd to thin out around their section. She had to pull herself together. She was in her favorite place with people she loved most. She'd dreamed of this day for years. Why did she feel so hollow?

Someone touched her shoulder and left their hand there. The warmth and weight of the touch seeped through her oblivion, soothing her, calming her, easing the tension in her neck and shoulders. Slowly the haze of emotions evaporated, and she turned to meet Molly's deep brown eyes.

"Hi."

"Hi." Duke's voice sounded soft and raspy even to her own ears.

"You okay?"

"Yeah, why?"

"You looked, I don't know…lost."

She shook her head, trying to loosen the last cobwebs. "In work mode, I guess."

Molly's eye narrowed skeptically. "No, your work mode looks different, focused, intense. Like you're more here than anyone else around you. Just now you seemed far away."

Duke felt a surge of something new at the revelation, something hot and sweet, a more intimate connection than anything she'd shared with her family so far today. Molly was always so hard to read, but she'd clearly paid enough attention to her not only to recognize her moods, but to care when they altered significantly.

"I called your name three times. You were somewhere else entirely."

"Sorry." Had she really been so deep in her own head she'd missed Molly? Molly, with her deep eyes and lyrical voice? Molly, who didn't laugh but smiled often enough to keep her wanting more? Molly, who was gay and a single mother and a beautiful woman both so young and so old all at once? She wouldn't have thought it possible to miss someone like Molly.

"Hi, I'm Sarah's mother, Lorelei."

"Oh, it's so nice to meet you," Molly said, her eyes wandering from one person to another as if now tying the new additions to Duke's disconnect. She extended her hand. "I'm Molly."

"And how do you two know each other?"

Duke blushed at her mother's directness. There was nothing wrong with the question itself, but her tone of voice, or perhaps the unnecessarily dramatic rise in pitch, signaled she was digging for information.

Molly motioned to the seats behind her where Joe and Charlie sat. "My sons are enamored of your daughter."

"You have children?" Her eyes rounded like a kid who'd seen a lollipop as big as her head. "Dale, come meet Sarah's friend Molly and her two adorable little boys."

Her dad turned around and regarded the family, then turned to Duke. "Your friend, huh?"

She shrugged, not wanting to overcommit herself. She knew what her parents implied in their use of the term. They were dancing around the idea of Molly being a girlfriend, and while she certainly wasn't that, Duke wondered if she even fit the platonic sense of the word. They'd seen each other often over the first month of the season, and Molly's distrust of her had waned. They spoke amicably, even comfortably about neutral topics like the team, the boys, or their jobs. She looked forward to seeing her at every day or weekend game, and missed her and the boys while on the road. She supposed those things constituted a kind of friendship but still didn't know if Molly felt the same. As a writer, she understood more than most that words' meanings came only from a shared understanding. Did the definition of friendship demand a mutual regard?

Her mother had no such issue with semantics. "Are you all sitting here for the game?"

"That's Charlie's seat. Don't move it," Charlie said emphatically.

"My goodness, you are such a little man," Lorelei exclaimed gleefully, then turning to the people in the row in front of him, she orchestrated a seat swap so quickly that the terms of the trade had been agreed upon before Duke even realized what happened.

"Wait, those seats, I mean, you were supposed to be on the other end of that row, and um, Dad?"

"These are much better than I'm used to," he offered, knowing better than to contradict his wife when she went into grandma mode.

"Where do you usually sit, Mr. Duke?" Joe asked politely.

He regarded him seriously for the first time, glancing from his STL ball cap to the birds on the bat across his chest to the scorecard neatly balanced on his knees. The light in his eyes that signaled interest sparked blue against his tan skin. "Do you know what a Sherpa is?"

"Yes sir," Joe replied.

"Well, you need one to get to the places I can afford to sit in. I've only ever been this close for batting practice."

"You watch batting practice?"

"Always," he said, settling into the seat in front of Joe and leaning back to examine the scorecard. "That's good work you got going there. Keep solid records, and some day it will help you when you play against some of these guys."

Joe blushed. "I'll never play in the big leagues."

"Not if you think that way, you won't," he replied gruffly. "You gotta believe you are the baddest batter around every time you step up to the plate, even on your Little League team."

"I don't play Little League," Joe said softly.

"What?" Duke and her father asked in unison.

"I like to watch baseball, but I'm not any good at playing," Joe explained, sinking back into his chair.

"He's got a brilliant baseball mind," Molly cut in, the protective rumble in her throat belying her light tone. "He knows more about the game than most of the grown men in this stadium. Go ahead, ask him to explain the infield fly rule."

Her father looked at Molly, then back to Joe before saying, "It's important to know the rules. You should never underestimate the power of the playbook, but don't let people who've never played fool you: without the playing part, it's just a book."

Joe's shoulders slumped, but he answered with a polite "Yes sir."

Duke's stomach ached, and sweat pricked her palms. The little dig at people who don't play the game stung as much as it always had, but Joe's reaction hurt much worse. Didn't her dad see what a special kid Joe was? Couldn't he tell what his comment did to his enthusiasm level? Her dad was a master at breaking down little tics and triggers that made a ballplayer who he was. How could he miss something she saw so clearly in Joe? Was he not paying attention or did he not care?

Irritation burned the muscles in her jaw, but guilt followed quick on its heels like a cooling balm. Maybe she was too sensitive. Her dad was every bit as enthusiastic about the game as Joe, just in different ways. He valued different things than she did, she reasoned silently, then tried to end that train of thought before she reached the realization he didn't value her contributions at all. His gentle dismissal of Joe had nothing to do with her even if the look on Joe's face felt revealingly familiar.

"Hey," Molly said, touching Joe's shoulder and Duke's arm in much the same fashion, pulling both of their attentions back into their comfortable circle. "You two want to go over lineup cards?"

"Yeah," Joe said, brightening slightly. "Are the Reds going to have their left-handed batters in against Ben LeBaron today?"

"They sure are." She crouched down beside him and examined

his pre-game notes. They weren't as detailed as hers, but they were neat and thoughtful. He hit on a few of the key trends she'd listed in her report. The kid was a baseball savant.

"You must be so proud of your daughter," Molly said to her mom.

"I am," her mother answered quickly. "We both are, right, Dale?"

"Huh?"

"We're proud of Sarah."

He shifted in his seat to look at them. "Sure we are. Hey, any of you want a hot dog?"

"I want a hot dog," Charlie answered quickly.

"Not until the third inning," Molly and Duke answered in unison, then laughed together.

Her father stood up, oblivious to the connection passing between them. "You always were a superstitious kid, but I need something before the game. Any of you want to come with me?"

"No, thank you," Joe said. "I want to review the lineups before the game starts."

"And I need to do the same," Duke agreed. Knuckling Joe's shoulder, she proudly proclaimed, "It's time for us to get to work."

"Suit yourselves." He shrugged and tugged the bill of his hat.

They watched him go, the sting of his earlier comments subduing their normally jovial interactions.

"You're such a well-mannered young man," her mom finally said to Joe. "And you have your mother's beautiful eyes."

Joe blushed again, and this time pulled his cap so low it rested on the top of his glasses, but he still managed a mumbled "Thank you."

"And you," Molly said turning to Duke. "You clearly get your good nature from your mother."

Defensiveness pricked her skin and tightened her shoulders. "Both my parents are good-natured. Dad's got a one-track mind around ballplayers, but he's a good guy once you get to know him."

"I'm sure he is." Molly returned her hand to Duke's arm, instantly calming the heat rising in her chest. "But we all think you're a pretty great person, too."

Emotion sprang thick behind her eyes and in her throat. Normally she would've brushed off such a simple comment, but for some reason it tightened the connection that started with the brush of Molly's gentle touch on the bare skin of her arm. Just a little touch, but it left her feeling so vulnerable. "Thanks. I, uh, I gotta get back to work."

"I understand." Molly met her eyes with a seriousness that made Duke suspect she understood more than she wanted her to. Maybe even more than she understood herself.

"See you all later." She walked briskly away. She needed to get back into her game-day mode. She needed to get back to what she knew and understood. Perhaps she should have said more or hugged her mom, but she had a job to do, and whether that mattered to anyone else or not, she intended to do it well.

❖

Duke couldn't sit still. She checked her scorecard obsessively and tweeted twice as much as usual but couldn't shake the feeling she should be doing more. Restlessness jumped through her legs and twitched her hands. If she'd had more room, she would've paced. She could've gone out into the stands like usual, but even though her desk felt confining, the thought of what she'd find in the crowd seemed more daunting. Only questions remained there for her now.

Questions: her job was founded on them. But she did the asking, and her readers expected clear-cut answers, not murky, mixed emotions. She had to stick to what she could put into words, so she began jotting down post-game questions in her notebook. On the paper everything looked as standard as the game unfolding on the field. A few hits for each side, two walks, and the Cardinals down a run in the eighth. It wasn't a great game, but it wasn't terrible either. The players were settling into the season and bearing down for a long summer ahead. Why couldn't she do the same?

Turning over the page, she began to scratch descriptors along the margins. She'd developed the nervous habit in college when she used to practice listing all the words she could ever use to describe various aspects of the game. Sometimes, she'd focus on a specific play, like a home run, towering, arching, floating, stratospheric. Other times she'd work with an attribute ascribed to a player, like power, crushing, catastrophic, explosive. Words were tools, and she wanted to always have the right one handy. Tonight's list featured words like paradise, Eden, cathedral, heaven.

"When did you find Jesus?" Cooper asked.

"When I was eight," she answered blandly.

He stared at her, disbelieving. "Wow, you really are some sort of big gay choir boy, aren't you?"

"What?"

"I don't give a shit when you were baptized, I just wondered why you were writing down all the religious terms."

She glanced down at her list. "I didn't notice I was. I only meant to compile a list of terms to help me talk about the ballpark."

He snorted. "And those are the words you chose? Did you learn this game from a nun?"

"I learned this game from my father."

"He some kind of a saint or something?"

"You know what? He kind of is," she snapped. "He worked two jobs to feed his kids. He got nothing handed to him, no money, no family business, no education. He busted his ass day in and day out and still made time to coach his kids' baseball teams." She felt the rant get away from her as surprise registered in the deep creases along Coop's forehead, but she couldn't stop the words spilling out of her. "So he doesn't talk about the game the way you want. He's not the kind of guy who tells you what you want to hear, maybe he's not nice even, but—"

"Geez, Rook, what's gotten into you? I wouldn't have pegged you for a girl with daddy issues."

Her short fingernails dug into the palms of her clenched fists. "I don't have daddy issues."

"Whatever you gotta tell yourself, but it sounded to me like you were shadow boxing someone there. Let me guess. He never showed up to your softball games."

"I didn't play softball."

"I thought all your people played softball."

She should have been offended by the generalization, but she was already too upset about other things. "I love baseball. I couldn't settle for some approximation."

"Careful, you'll lose your women's-libber card."

"I've got nothing against softball. It's a great game, but it's not the same game. We're a baseball family. We play baseball."

"We? You mean you played on some team with your dad and brothers."

She opened her mouth and shut it. She didn't like this conversation.

She didn't like Cooper, either. The tightness was back in her neck, and now it tugged at her stomach, too.

"Let me guess, your old man didn't think softball was a real thing, but he didn't think baseball was a girls' game either. Classic. Damned if you do, damned if you don't."

"You don't know what you're talking about."

"Either way, you showed the old man, right? He's sitting at home in the armchair, and you're part of the grand game now." He raised his beer in a mock salute.

She stared at the field. It seemed so much farther away now. "Are we part of it?"

His studied disinterest returned as if he'd remembered he wasn't supposed to reveal how much the game mattered to him. "Who the hell cares? You're more a part of it than your old man is."

"My dad's a great man."

Coop rolled his eyes. "Sure he is. They all are. Doesn't mean they didn't screw us up. It's what parents do. They shatter their kids. His old man probably did it to him. Someday you'll do it to your kids. Whether you mean to or not."

An image of Joe's slumped shoulders and downcast eyes hiding under the bill of his cap shot through her memory so hard she grimaced.

"What's the matter, you don't want kids?"

"No. I mean yes." She scrubbed her hands roughly over her face. "I gotta go."

"They're down to the last two outs. If something important happens, you'll miss it."

She was already halfway out the door before she called back, "I might have missed something important already."

She jogged down the stadium stairs, weaving her way against the current of the crowd headed toward the exit. She hoped Molly and the boys hadn't already left. Her dad would still be there, but his presence no longer spurred or hindered her advance. As she broke through a group of raucous young men, she finally caught sight of Joe sitting just as she'd left him, eyes trained on the field, notebook across his knees.

"Duke," Charlie called, lifting his head from where it rested on Molly's shoulder. "Are you a lion?"

"No. I'm a Redbird." She turned to Joe. "And I was wondering if I could see your notebook?"

"Mine?" he asked as if Yadier Molina had requested his T-ball bat.

"Yeah, I got a little caught up in other things earlier. I missed something pretty big, but I knew I could count on you to keep me honest."

He smiled so broadly his little cheeks pushed his glasses up to the bill of his cap. "Sure."

She made a big show of studying his notes. They were actually better than hers in a couple places, which didn't surprise her. "I'm impressed. I didn't realize they moved Brooks over to right field on the double switch in the eighth inning."

"Yeah, he got the final out even though the batter was in the shadows and he faced the sun."

Duke glanced at her father long enough to note the grudging nod of approval. She would've killed for that little gesture as a child, but it was no longer enough. She got his understated nature, and she didn't fault him for his lack of expression. But now she also saw the damage his words, his tone, his disinterest had done. She understood the restlessness surging through her was the desire to do better, and for the first time in her life, it wasn't for herself or for him. She could and would do better for Joe.

Crouching down so her eyes were on level with Joe's, she said, "I'm going to ask him about that play in the locker room later. It'll help him know we see how he's growing. It's going to let a lot of people who didn't see the game tonight know he's capable of making plays he hasn't been trusted with yet. It's going to boost his confidence in himself and other people's confidence in him. It's a little thing, Joe, but little things make a big difference over the course of a lifetime. Remember that, okay?"

He nodded seriously. "I will."

She rose to face her parents. "I hope you enjoyed the game."

"I enjoyed the last part an awful lot," her mom said and patted her face.

"I did, too," her father added, then said, "We won't keep you, though. I know you've got work to do."

"Thanks, Dad." She hugged them both, then turned back to Molly. "Thank you, too."

"I'm the one who should be thanking you." She inclined her head to Joe, who was still reading over his notes with a big smile on his face. "What you did there wasn't just a little thing. You know that, right?"

"I want to try and do what I can to help the team. My team."

Molly looked from her to Joe and to Charlie, then back out over the field. Duke followed her gaze and was once again impressed by how close it all felt. The energy, the passion, the beauty, but now it wasn't past the fence. It spilled out over them. The feeling she'd struggled to find earlier now surrounded them all. She soaked it up, breathing deeply the scent of grass and popcorn tinged with the sweeter, more intimate smell of Molly's shampoo. Somehow it all fit, and she fit, too. It wasn't just a game anymore.

Molly rested her hand on her arm, connecting their comfort once again. "What are you thinking?"

She covered Molly's hand with her own. This time she felt no need to hide from the emotions expanding her chest. "I really am just lucky to be here."

Bottom of the Second

Never Let the Fear of Striking Out Keep You from Swinging the Bat

Molly carried another tray of salmon nestled atop risotto to a couple of men in expensive-looking business suits. The special of the day had been popular with the high-end lunch crowd, and it did look delicious even if she couldn't imagine spending thirty dollars a pop on a midday entrée, much less adding appetizers and drinks to the tab. This table alone would spend more on the bill for one meal than she needed to feed her family of three for a full week. It would've angered her to see such waste if she didn't look forward to the tip she'd likely get on the tab. That thought kept her smiling, even when one of the men insisted on referring to her as "sweetheart" and "honey."

Trying to walk the tightrope between being attentive and hovering, Molly retreated to the outer edge of the room and surveyed her other tables. Table four was cleared. Table nine had their orders in. Table twelve might be ready for the check soon. Table six had their bill paid but lingered. The group of three men and one woman had talked baseball for an hour, and she got the sense it wasn't a casual conversation. They must be affiliated with the team.

The restaurant was the nicest place within walking distance of the stadium, and owned by a former player, so anyone tied to the team got preferential treatment. In turn they rewarded him with their patronage and generous consumption of food and drink. She imagined many of the people she waited on were powerful and maybe even famous. She probably could have sold her fair share of gossip over the last eight years, but she'd never do anything to jeopardize a job of this caliber, and even if she did, who would she sell it to?

Immediately she thought of Duke and smiled at the absurdity of the idea. Duke wouldn't deal in gossip any more than Molly would. Honest, earnest, and almost maddeningly good-natured Duke. Despite the circumstances under which they'd met, Molly knew now she could trust her with anything, including her children. Her chest ached at the memory of Duke crouched down, her head close to Joe's as they reviewed his notes. She wasn't sure which one of them had needed the interaction more. Duke clearly carried more hurt and insecurity than her good nature and easy laugh ever showed. Molly hadn't enjoyed seeing the wounded side of her. It stirred a protective instinct that hinted at emotions stronger than a casual acquaintance should engender.

Of course she admired Duke for her dedication and her openness. She even felt drawn to her passion, but who wouldn't? She'd raised their whole family's baseball IQ several points and done so with an enthusiasm no one with a heart could resist. Molly could even admit she found a few of Duke's better qualities attractive. Her hands for one, strong, sure, and graceful. Duke's eyes were the clearest shade of blue imaginable. She would've compared them to ice except there was nothing cold in them. In fact, Molly had never felt so warm as when Duke had covered her hand with her own, caught her in that powder blue gaze, and said, "I'm just lucky to be here."

She shook off the chill that raised the hair on her arms.

"Where were you at?" Emma asked as she brushed past with a bussing tray full of dirty dishes.

"Nowhere," Molly said quickly.

"Looked like you had a happy thought that turned on you." Emma laughed. "Or turned you on."

Molly swatted at her. "Go clear table seven."

She hadn't been turned on. Duke stirred a lot of emotions, but arousal wasn't one of them. Finer points aside, she was such a guy. Molly had fought hard to own her sexual orientation, and she hadn't done so to date someone just like her ex-husband or father-in-law. When she finally got around to dating a woman, it would be a *woman*. Duke was a great person, a truly special person even, amazing friend material, but lacking fantasy potential. If her thoughts wandered anywhere near considering Duke romantically, it was only her mind and body in a desperate attempt to convince her she needed to get out more. Her last date had been the night Charlie was conceived, and he was the only good thing to come out of the experience. Well, him and the realization she couldn't live a lie any longer.

Four years later, she had a better understanding of herself and what she wanted, even if she wasn't any closer to finding it. At least now she understood Duke wasn't the answer. When she did start dating again, she'd find someone who wore skirts and perfume and talked softly about wine and romantic comedies. A woman like Lauren.

Molly stole another glance at table twelve. They looked like they'd finished eating enough to warrant another check-in. She caught Lauren's eye as she approached so she could speak directly to her. "How was everything?"

"Wonderful as usual." Lauren's smile was slow and appreciative. "The food is my second favorite reason for having lunch here."

"We aim to please."

"Come on," Lauren teased gently, tapping one manicured fingernail on the white tablecloth. "Aren't you going to ask what my first favorite reason is?"

"I assumed it was our wine list."

"Well, you know what they say about making assumptions."

"What do they say about it?"

The corners of Lauren's beautiful red lips curved up playfully. "Let's just say you shouldn't do it."

"Okay, then I won't assume you'd like to see the dessert menu."

"No, you can always assume that." She then turned to the other people at the table. "But these two have to get going, so why don't you have my crème brûlée sent to the bar along with two coffees and the check."

"Absolutely."

Molly retreated to the kitchen to deposit the order and pick up table nine's lobster roll and Greek salad. She made sure everything met with the patrons' approval and checked to confirm the group from table six had cleared out before ducking back into the kitchen to pick up Lauren's dessert and drinks. Setting them on the bar in front of Lauren, she said, "There you are, one crème brûlée and two coffees."

Lauren raised one delicately shaped eyebrow. "Aren't you going to ask why I ordered two coffees?"

"Fine." Molly played at exasperation but smiled anyway. "Why two coffees?"

"One for me and one for you."

Molly's heartbeat accelerated in a good way. "Then why didn't you order two spoons with the crème brûlée?"

Lauren laughed or at least chuckled softly. "I don't share dessert with anyone."

"I can't eat during work hours anyway."

"Then we'll wait until after you get off work."

"My shift isn't over until three o'clock, which is when I have to pick up my son from school."

If the revelation startled Lauren, it didn't show. Her perfectly fitted navy suit and long brunette locks suggested she wasn't the type to fall to pieces at a shift in the breeze or conversation. "What about this weekend? Will you get a break then?"

"No," she said sadly. "A single mom never gets a break."

"Everyone needs a break sometime, Molly."

She sighed, wishing that were true. She had a busy job, a tight budget, and two kids to raise. She simply didn't know how she'd fit something like a date into her life, much less a real relationship, and she had a feeling if she had one date with Lauren she'd leave wanting a relationship. Which was why she'd always played off Lauren's flirting, though it had been subtler until now. "Needing and getting don't always go together."

"Not always," Lauren agreed. Then pressing her lips together thoughtfully, she pulled a business card from her wallet and slid it across the bar to Molly. "But then again, sometimes they do. And whenever that happens for you, I hope you'll call me."

Molly picked up the card and promised the only thing she could. "I'll think about it."

❖

Joe hung his head as strike three buzzed past a hitter who didn't even bother to lift the bat off his shoulder. The game wasn't a pretty one, and even Molly could see it wouldn't end well. A loss seemed the only fitting end to the week she'd had. Work had been a mess, with two servers calling in sick on Friday night. She'd had to scramble to find a replacement for one and then call in favors to find play dates for Joe and Charlie so she could cover for the other. Then she'd had to go back on Saturday morning, dragging both boys with her to close out the accounts on receipts that refused to match up.

She appreciated the extra hours and responsibility management had given her by letting her learn the books. She hoped the added duties were signs she was being considered for a promotion, and she needed the money, but extra hours on the clock meant extra time away from her family. The boys resented missing their usual time with her and being stuck in a restaurant. Joe did what he could to help with Charlie, but it was ultimately unfair to ask a nine-year-old boy to control a toddler who often got the best of trained child-care professionals. Eventually frustration got the better of Joe. He signaled his surrender by withdrawing completely and burying his nose in a book. Charlie registered his discontent with their lack of attention by wrecking everything he touched. To count he'd dumped out two salt shakers, squashed four plastic cups of coffee creamer, and tried to catch fish from the aquarium with his bare hands.

She shouldn't have brought them to work. Empty restaurants offered nothing but trouble for two boys, but she'd already indebted herself to friends the night before. Besides, she was away from them all week, and she didn't want her kids to be raised by a sitter on the weekend, too. She almost let herself wish she had family around, but she refused to go there. She was capable of caring for her own family, but by the time they got to the stadium, she was a ball of nerves and running on nothing but coffee.

She caught Charlie by the straps of his overalls before he hurled himself over his seat back. "Please, sit still for five minutes and Mommy will buy you whatever you want, okay?"

"I want a hot dog," Charlie said.

"Of course you do."

"It *is* well past the third inning," Duke said, scooping Charlie into her arms and depositing him onto her lap as she took his open seat.

Molly snapped. "Do you think I don't know what inning it is in this painfully slow death march your beloved Cardinals are on?"

"Painfully slow death march?" Duke grinned. "Can I tweet that?"

"Go for it."

She whipped out her phone and tapped a rapid succession of keys. "Here, Charlie, push the blue button."

Charlie did as told, mesmerized by the technology before him.

"There, Charlie sent his first tweet. Joe is a baseball savant." She patted his cap-covered head. "And Charlie is a social media guru. You're raising a pair of geniuses."

How was she so damn chipper all the time? The Cardinal player at the plate looked at another called-strike-three on their way to an embarrassing defeat. Shouldn't that at least make her grumpy? "Your team is going to lose."

"Looks like it."

"Doesn't that make you angry?"

"It did, but I went to the bathroom to kick around some trash cans. Then I tripped an old lady."

"Really?" Joe asked, his eyes wide and horrified behind his glasses.

"No." Duke laughed before turning serious as she returned her focus to Molly. "I get frustrated, of course, but we're all human. Everyone has bad days, even heroes. I try to keep things in perspective."

"What's that supposed to mean?"

"It means everybody's allowed to have bad days from time to time."

Molly pursed her lips so hard she felt the tension through her whole face. Pinching the bridge of her nose to keep a headache from taking hold between her eyes, she tried to take a few deep breaths.

"How can I help, Molly?"

"I don't need any help." Her voice sounded harsher than she'd intended, but Duke didn't flinch.

"It's okay to need help."

"I'm just tired." She removed her hand from her face and met Duke's eyes. She made her best attempt at a confident smile, the one that fooled everyone from her boss to her customers to Joe. The look usually let people off the hook. They offered to listen out of politeness, she refused out of pride. They'd both done their parts and could now move on to more neutral topics. But Duke didn't blink, she didn't look away, the intensity of her gaze never wavered. She waited, quietly examining her expression, as if expecting it to crack open.

For the first time in years Molly thought she might actually fall apart. Sure, there'd been plenty of times she'd wanted to cave, to beg for help, to cry, but until now she'd never actually feared doing so. Her shoulders ached from the tension of the burdens she longed to loosen. What was it about Duke that made her wish for a breakdown?

"Hey, Duke," Joe interrupted. "Why hasn't Cayden Brooks gotten a hit all week?"

Duke's eyes twitched away, then quickly back, apology evident in her expression. She raised her eyebrows at Molly as if giving her one more chance to claim the attention she'd offered, but the spell had broken. Molly's walls remained firmly in place at the reminder of where her attention should be focused. With a flash of a frown Duke turned back to Joe.

"I think Cayden's afraid of striking out."

"But he strikes out anyway."

"That's the funny thing about being afraid to try. You usually end up getting exactly what you were afraid of anyway." Duke cast another quick glance at Molly. "You can't let fear of striking out keep you from swinging the bat."

"I don't get it." Joe shook his head. "When he doesn't swing, that's striking out, too."

Duke smiled kindly. "Did you know I didn't play baseball?"

"What? Why?"

Molly's interest piqued at the admission too. She'd assumed Duke had been a ballplayer. Sure, she'd never mentioned playing, in any of the many discussions they'd had about the sport, but she seemed like someone who wouldn't let anything stand between her and something she loved.

"It's a long story." Duke brushed off the question, but her brow furrowed with consternation or maybe regret. "But I didn't think I could do it well enough. Or maybe I didn't think anyone would let me do it right. The thing is, I was stubborn and I wouldn't settle for anything less than perfect control. If I couldn't be the best or play the best, I wouldn't play at all."

"But maybe you could have been the best."

"Maybe. More likely, though, I would've been average or below average. Maybe I would've been terrible. Maybe I would've enjoyed it anyway. At least I would've been out there. I would've known for sure."

"I don't play baseball either," Joe mumbled.

"Why?"

He wrung his hands, and Molly fought the urge to jump in and save him the way she had when his grandfather and then Duke's father started this same conversation. Only this wasn't the same conversation. Duke's tone held no judgment, merely curiosity. By making herself vulnerable, she'd made Joe safer. Molly suffered a twist of envy at both the vulnerability and the safety.

"I'm not very good."

"So you've played?"

"I played T-ball."

"Is it fun? It sure looks fun."

"Sometimes, but it's not fun to lose. It's not fun when people tease you."

Molly's chest ached. She understood how it felt to worry you were doomed before you began. She identified with the impulse to avoid situations with high rates of failure. She'd mastered the art of anticipating and preempting other people's judgment of her. Had she handed down those skills to him?

"You're afraid you can't play, so you don't play," Duke summarized. "I've been there. I don't blame you a bit." The sense of camaraderie in her voice softened the obvious lesson immensely.

"Thanks," he said, seeming relieved but not happy.

Then, focusing her attention on him in much the same way she had Molly, Duke added, "You're awesome at so many things. You don't have to prove yourself to me or anyone else. Ever. But if you want to give it another try sometime, just for the love of the game, I'd help. You know, like another chance for me, too."

Joe nodded solemnly and stared back at the field. Duke playfully turned his hat around backward. "Now, let's lighten up. I need a concession stand run before I get back to work. What do you guys want?"

"Popcorn, please?" Joe asked.

"I could actually use another coffee," Molly admitted.

"I want a hot dog," Charlie said.

"You got it." Duke bounded up the stairs and out of sight.

❖

"Mom," Joe said, as the game wound down.

"What, honey?" She absentmindedly bounced Charlie on her knee.

"I've been thinking about what Duke said."

"What about it?"

"About how you can't let the fear of striking out keep you from swinging the bat."

Damn Duke and her catchy phrases. She'd done plenty of thinking, too. It was bad enough having to use every win as a learning experience, but now she couldn't even check out emotionally during an obvious loss. "What have you been thinking?"

"Could I play baseball this summer?"

"Do you want to?"

"I think so."

She eyed him suspiciously. She didn't need him putting himself at risk to please Duke. "Why?"

"I like baseball," he said simply.

She pulled him into a one-armed hug. "Good enough for me."

Her heart swelled with pride. For most people a little boy wanting to play baseball would've been pretty standard fare, but he wasn't any little boy. He was her little boy, smart, thoughtful, and sensitive, with impossibly high standards. He came by all those traits honestly, but he must have gotten his bravery somewhere else, though certainly not from his father. Either way, he'd taken a big step to look past his fears and focus on the heart of what he wanted.

"Hey, guys," Duke said from behind them. "I don't want to interrupt family cuddle time, but I was hoping to talk to Molly real quick before the game ends and I descend into the unhappy place that will be the clubhouse tonight."

"Sounds serious," Molly said, untangling her arms from each of her boys. "Joe, don't let Charlie get up," she warned, but Charlie was clearly fading fast, and she stepped only far enough into the aisle to allow Duke space enough to whisper without being overheard.

"Thank you for what you did for Joe earlier."

"What do you mean?"

She searched Duke's eyes looking for any hint of false modesty but found none. "You really don't know, do you?"

"We just talked about baseball like we do every night."

Maybe that was how Joe learned courage. He'd seen it so fully displayed in Duke's willingness to be completely open about what she loved. She didn't see her actions as unusual because for her they weren't. Molly had the urge to touch her face, to run her fingers across the smooth skin of her cheek, to place a soft kiss against her temple.

She stepped back. Where had that come from? Had Duke's vulnerability inspired hers?

"Are you okay?"

"Yes," Molly said, as if a resolute tone could make it so. "What did you need?"

"Well, I have an off-day next week, I mean the team does. They don't play on Thursday. And I thought maybe I could have a play date with the boys."

"A play date?"

"Yeah, I mean that's what you call it when I come over and play with them, right?"

"You want to come play with my children at our house?"

"Yeah." Duke blushed. "That sounds kind of creepy doesn't it?"

"A little bit."

"Would it sound creepier if I said you didn't have to be there?"

"Yes, much creepier."

Duke hung her head. "I'm not good at subterfuge."

"It's not your strong point. How about you try the straight shooter thing you're so fond of."

"I thought you might like a break. A night off to go out to dinner, or dancing, or a movie. You could call a friend or go someplace quiet. I'll feed the boys and get them to bed."

"That's very sweet of you, but I don't need—"

"I know you don't need the help. You're a great mom. The best. Which is why you deserve a night off. And I'm being selfish, too."

She shook her head, skeptical of even the notion that Duke had a selfish bone in her body.

"Really. All the games next week are at night, then we head out on a weeklong road trip. I don't want to go two full weeks without seeing the boys."

Molly noticed Duke only mentioned the kids. Did that mean she didn't mind going two weeks without seeing her? What a silly thought.

Duke had made an amazing offer to babysit on the only night off she'd have for weeks. Why wouldn't she accept gratefully?

Perhaps because she didn't know what she'd do with the time. She hadn't had a night to herself in years. What if she didn't know how to be anything other than a mom anymore? Could she even handle a purely social situation? Who would she call? She knew people from work, or parents of Joe and Charlie's friends, but they never hung out. She couldn't think of any one person in either of those circles she wanted to get to know on a deeper level.

There was someone she did want to spend some time with, though, someone who sparked a set of conflicting emotions, someone whose persistence more than piqued her interest. She met Duke's eyes, a subtle stirring of hope and fear swirling through her chest. It would be a risk. She'd have to be the one to make the move, to make herself vulnerable.

"Come on," Duke urged. "I can see the wheels spinning in your head. You're thinking about it. What are you afraid of? I'll take care of everything."

Molly nodded. She'd be fine, more than fine, she'd be wonderful. Molly's reservations now rested solely on her own ability to seize something she'd claimed to want for a long time.

"There is something I've been wanting to do for a while now. I've been too wrapped up in all the reasons I couldn't, or shouldn't."

"Sounds interesting. How can I help?"

"You've already done so much," she said, gratitude tightening her throat. "You gave me the opportunity and inspiration to take a chance."

Duke straightened her shoulders proudly. "Well, good for me. Does that mean I'm babysitting on Thursday?"

"Maybe. Would you mind if I asked one more favor of you?"

"Shoot."

"Would you watch the boys for a minute now?"

"Sure."

Molly ducked into a quieter pocket of the concourse, grateful the lackluster performance of the team had significantly quieted the crowd. Pulling a card from her purse, she dialed the unfamiliar number.

"Hello?"

"Hi, Lauren, it's Molly, Molly Grettano, from, um, the restaurant."

"Molly, I know who you are," Lauren said in a tone as soft and warm as a caress.

"Good, well, the thing is, my Thursday night opened up rather unexpectedly." Her mind flashed to Duke with her broad smile and her passionate blue eyes, but she shook the image away. "It looks like I might get the break I needed after all, and I hope your offer still stands."

"Of course. May I buy you dinner? Let someone serve you for once?"

Molly's stomach fluttered. "I'd like that a lot."

"Good, I would, too. Pick you up at seven on Thursday?"

"Yes, I'll text you my address."

"Great. But before you go, can I ask what changed your mind?"

"What do you mean?"

"I don't know. Maybe it's just your schedule, but I got the sense something else held you back before."

Duke's soft, sincere voice echoed through her ears, and she had to shake off the accompanying chill. "Let's just say I decided not to let the fear of striking out keep me from swinging the bat."

TOP OF THE THIRD

If You Want to Be the Best, You Have to Beat the Best

The midday sun shone brightly on the expanse of grass and clay as if God herself were smiling down on Busch Stadium. Today was a new and glorious day. Early June in St. Louis brought enough warmth to help lift the balls over the outfield wall without the oppressive heat that zapped stamina and shortened fuses. During pre-game warm-ups, most of the players seemed eager to put last night's loss in the review mirror, and Duke had no immunity to their energy. She wanted to face the new day with excitement and anticipation. Certainly the game itself offered promise, like always, but despite the buzz on the field she found herself looking to the stands.

A one o'clock start time on Sunday should be perfect for Molly and the boys, but if they were coming, it wouldn't be in time for batting practice. She checked her watch again as the grounds crew signaled for the press to exit. With her pre-game report already filed, this was her downtime. She could review game notes or statistics on the visiting team. She could talk trends with the other sportswriters. She could check scores from the games starting on the East Coast, but still she lingered. The time before the game was her best chance to see Molly and the boys, and sometime over the last six weeks she'd come to anticipate the moment when her eyes met Molly's as much as she did the first pitch.

She strolled a lap around the stadium relishing the sights and sounds of the crowd, the hum of energy, the smell of hot dogs and fresh-cut grass. Her eagerness to see Molly didn't lessen her enjoyment of the ballpark. It added to it. She was truly blessed to share her favorite place in the world with her new favorite people.

As she rounded the backstop, her heart rate sped in anticipation, and a smile stretched her cheeks when she caught a peek of Molly's glossy black hair above two little red ball caps. They still had their backs to her as they worked toward their seats. They moved so well together, such a tight little unit, a family. Even in the crowd of similarly dressed people, anyone could see these three belonged with one another. Longing pushed at a spot beneath her rib cage, an inborn desire to share in their connection.

Then Charlie turned, looking over his shoulder as if he could sense her affection, and maybe he could, since it always seemed to be Charlie who noticed her first.

"Duke," he called as she walked toward them. "Do you know God?"

"Well, in a way, I suppose I do."

"Is he a lion?" Charlie asked.

"Hmm, have you been reading some C.S. Lewis?"

"Yes," he said seriously.

"No," Molly explained patiently. "They talked about Daniel and the lion's den in church this morning."

"Oh, you went to church this morning?"

"Does that surprise you?" Molly asked, the defensive edge back in her voice.

Duke wasn't sure what she'd stepped into, but she wasn't surprised she had. Molly, she'd learned, was a complicated woman who didn't like being told she couldn't do something. She would've said she found the trait endearing if she didn't fear Molly would find the term patronizing. "Not surprised, impressed."

Molly eyed her suspiciously, but Duke met her gaze and held it to show she had nothing to hide. Finally Molly sighed. "Well, you shouldn't be. I mostly did it so I could have a few minutes of quiet while they were in Sunday school."

"So you're not a true believer?"

Molly shrugged. "I've seen it all go so horribly wrong, seen religion hurt so much more than it helps, and cried out for answers only to find none. Then every night I look in on two sleeping angels, and it's hard to believe they could be some sort of accident."

"Wow." Tears stung her eyes.

"Sorry." Molly brushed off the emotion. "I didn't mean to bring you down on game day."

"No, you didn't. I get it. What you just said. I know what you mean." She was babbling, but she ached to cement their connection, to make Molly feel what she felt for this place, this game, the way it tied them to each other or to something larger than any of them. "I don't get to go to church much anymore. My schedule doesn't allow it. But sometimes I look out on all of this, the field, the stadium, all the people coming together in hope and anticipation to believe in something bigger than them. I know it's not the same thing, but I feel a spirit moving here. It's something you can't see and no amount of science can quantify. It's something we're all a part of and yet so much bigger than any one of us."

Molly's lips parted slightly and her cheeks colored a delicate pink as she rested her hand on Duke's arm. "Exactly. I want that for my boys. I want them to be able to believe in something bigger than themselves. I don't want them to be limited to their immediate concerns or the things they can explain. I want them to have the capacity to love something they have no control over."

The words and the sentiment behind them were beautiful, and so was the woman who'd given them voice. Molly's eyes shone brightly against her tan skin, and her dark hair cascaded over her shoulders. Duke's stomach tightened at the surge of attraction pulsing through her, but what sent her over the edge was the gentleness of Molly's fingers on her bare skin, as if she'd somehow perfected the blend of sweet and sexy, intimate and elusive. God, she wanted this woman.

"Boo!" Joe called, jarring Duke out of her haze and reminding her why she needed to be more careful with how she directed her attention.

"What's wrong?"

"They announced Jacob Burell."

"And you booed him? What are you, a Yankees fan?"

"No, but I hate that guy."

Duke's eyes widened and she clamped her jaw tightly to keep from snapping at him. She turned to Molly, who looked as surprised as she felt.

Charlie ultimately broke the stalemate. "Hate's a bad word."

"It's not a bad word," Joe replied, too casually.

"Maybe not a cuss word, but it sure is an awful thing to feel toward another human being." She sat down on the step next to Joe's chair. "What did he ever do to you? Did he kick your puppy? Punch your grandma? Spit on a baby?"

"No. He threw a shutout in the playoffs last year to keep us out of the World Series though."

"Ah, yeah that one hurt." She scrubbed her face with her hands. "I was here. I saw Yadi make the last out in the ninth. You know what he did before he went back to the dugout?"

"Did he cuss?"

"Nope. He tipped the bill of his batting helmet."

"What's that mean?"

"It means he respected Burell. He beat him fair and square. It means he recognized Burell as a worthy opponent." She sat for a moment to let that sink in. "Do you know what a worthy opponent is?"

"Yes," Joe muttered. "They're good. They play the game right."

"You got it. They're among the best in their field. They can break your heart, but ultimately they are the guys you want to face in big games."

"I don't want to face him ever."

She laughed. "Don't get me wrong. I love those weekends when we play the Cubs because they're fun and easy, but they don't make us better. They don't tell us a whole lot about ourselves other than we're not the worst. But I don't want to judge myself against the worst. I want to be the best, and to be the best you have to beat the best."

Joe nodded, looking like he wanted to disappear under the bill of his cap. "Okay."

"Hey," Duke said, grazing a knuckle under his chin, "buck up, slugger. The great thing about baseball is, every day is a new chance to prove yourself."

"Do you think the Cardinals really are the best? We got beat pretty bad last night."

"On any given day, anyone can be the best or the worst. The best teams in the league will still lose a third of the time, and the worst teams will still find a way to win a third of the time. The best hitters get out, seven out of ten at bats, and even the best pitchers to ever live give up home runs. It's the long run that makes a real champion."

Joe smiled brightly. "I like the way you talk."

"I do, too," Molly said, her chin resting on Charlie's head and her eyes resting on Duke. "You ever consider a career in sports writing?"

"Hmm." She tapped her chin as if thinking it over. "Now that you mention it, I might give it a try sometime."

"I hear the Cardinals have a hot new writer following them, Sarah something or other."

"Yeah, I heard she's pretty amazing, also kind of cute." Okay maybe she'd pushed too far there, but she enjoyed this playful side of Molly.

"I think so, cute would be a good word for her."

A rush of butterflies floated through her stomach. "I hear she's single, too."

"What a shame." Molly shook her head in mock seriousness, then brightened as if something shiny caught her attention. "That reminds me, we're still on for Thursday, right?"

We? Did Molly really segue from Duke's relationship status to their Thursday night plans? If her heart rate had accelerated before, now it tap-danced. "Yes, I'll pick up some Imo's Pizza on the way over, whatever kind you like."

"The boys eat cheese and only cheese, and for once I won't even try to talk them into mushrooms and olives since I'll be dining at Charlie Gitto's."

"What? How? That's..." Her mind fought to catch up to her mouth.

"I've got a date, thanks to you." Molly tapped her on the shoulder, but the touch didn't carry the same power surge the others had. "Lauren's taking me to The Hill."

"Wow. Lauren? Huh. Well, good for you. And her. Good for both of you."

"Good for you, too. She's asked me out a few times, but I would've never taken the chance if not for your offer to watch the boys."

"Me?" She lifted her ball cap and settled it back onto her head. "I'm, well...apparently awesome."

"You are," Molly said sincerely. "Awesome and wonderful and inspiring. I'll have the boys all ready for the night. You'll just have to feed them and put them to bed. Don't be nervous. I'm sure you can handle them."

"Of course I can." She didn't worry at all about her ability to handle two kids for a few hours. She hadn't been nervous at all until Molly mentioned this Lauren woman. Now her palms felt clammy and her heartbeat no longer danced so much as thudded dully through her ears. Someone else was taking Molly out, pampering her, sweeping her off her feet. She'd thought that would be her job, or at least she'd hoped so anyway. Had she missed her chance, or had it never been hers to claim in the first place? "The game is about to start. I better get to work."

"Sure, we'll see you on Thursday, right?"

"Absolutely. You can count on me."

Molly smiled sweetly. "I know I can. Thank you for being such a good friend."

Duke couldn't speak around the knot in her throat, so she waved before she jogged off. Once in the stairway she waited for the heavy metal door to slam satisfyingly behind her before leaning against the gray concrete wall. She sucked in a few deep gulps of air, but they did little to ease the suffocating thought of Molly in another woman's arms. She was overreacting. She didn't have any claim on Molly. She'd never even seen her outside of work. They'd only just become friends, so why did it feel like a needle under her fingernails when Molly had used the term?

She had to pull herself out of this mental fit. So what if she'd looked forward to seeing Molly outside of the stadium? So what if she'd hoped Thursday would be a gateway to something more for them? So what if Molly had a date with someone else? She could still have a great night with the boys, and maybe this Lauren woman wouldn't even like Molly.

She exhaled heavily because, really, who wouldn't fall for Molly?

❖

She stood on the welcome mat outside the door to Molly's apartment, listening to the deadened noise of footsteps and roughhousing. Something crashed, and Joe shouted an apology while Charlie let loose a deep, resounding belly laugh. She lifted her hand, but hesitated. No one would blame her for not wanting to knock. Her instinct to run, however, had nothing to do with the hectic vibe behind the door. She actually looked forward to some carefree time with the boys and liked the idea of being able to get rowdy with them. They all had to use their best behavior at the ballpark, but living rooms were made for pillow fights and wrestling matches. Getting wound up was the fun part. She would've gladly faced a horde of wild banshees a hundred times over if only she didn't have to see Molly leave for a date with another woman.

She had no right to think that way. She'd offered Molly a night off to do as she pleased, and if that meant dinner at a swank restaurant with this Lauren character, then she should have that. She took a deep breath, inhaling the rich scent of the large Imo's pizza she held in her arms, and leaned forward to press the doorbell with the corner of the box.

Molly opened so quickly she must have been waiting for her. A rush of energy hit Duke and flooded the surrounding hallway as both boys rushed to meet her.

"Duke, you want to see my baseball cards?" Joe asked.

"Sure, buddy, let me—"

"I'm going to eat you!" Charlie shouted, then punctuated the threat with his best roar.

"Don't eat me. I brought pizza as a substitute sacrifice."

"I don't like pizza," Charlie said, then ran down an adjacent hallway.

"Come on in," Molly said, then added nervously, "I'm running late. Do you mind feeding them while I get changed?"

"Not at all." She finally stepped all the way into the apartment, carrying the pizza before her like some peace offering for whatever havoc was being wreaked ahead.

A small living room stood just beyond the entryway with an open kitchen and dining area to the right. The hallway both Molly and Charlie had disappeared down extended off to the left. She set the pizza on the table and wandered into the kitchen. "Hey, Joe, where do you keep the plates?"

"The cabinet next to the fridge." He came in behind her carrying a three-ring binder open wide to a plastic photo sleeve holding several baseball cards. "I have Molina's rookie season here."

She pulled down a few plastic plates with superheroes on them, then glanced at the card. "Nice. Way to hold on to that. I bet a lot of people threw it out because he didn't hit well those first few seasons."

"It'll be worth a lot more if he wins the MVP," Joe said, with a seriousness of a bond trader.

"It'll be a neat keepsake either way." She pulled a few squares of pizza from the box and put them on the plates. "Where did your brother go?"

"He's probably in the bathtub," Joe replied casually as he flipped through some more cards.

"Does he take baths by himself?" She hadn't been around a ton of kids outside her brother's baby girl, but something about a three-year-old running his own bath didn't sound right.

"He doesn't put any water in. He just gets in the tub and closes the curtain."

"Why?"

Joe shrugged. "He's Charlie."

"Right, well, why don't you go tell him dinner's ready?"

"He'll just say he doesn't like pizza."

"Try anyway, will ya?"

He shook his head at the futility of the exercise but dutifully strolled off down the hall.

Alone in the dining room, she began to blow on the slice of pizza Charlie probably wouldn't eat. She wanted it to be ready on the off chance he felt adventurous. Her attempt to prepare for an improbability was interrupted by a knock at the door.

"Can you get that?" Molly called.

"Sure." She didn't know what she was thinking. She didn't think really. She just swung open the door to greet a truly beautiful woman. She wore a soft cream-colored scoop-neck sweater, charcoal slacks, and low sling-back heels that made her almost Duke's height. She extended her hand amicably.

"Hello, I'm Lauren. I'm here to pick up Molly."

Of course you are. Her stomach clenched, but she tried to smile in a way that didn't appear as though she were experiencing physical pain. "Come on in. I'm Duke. I'm watching the boys tonight. Molly's still getting ready, but you can wait for her in here." What a mess. She had to stop babbling.

"Thank you," she replied as she stepped gracefully past Duke into the entryway of the apartment.

Charlie came tearing around the corner at full tilt and nearly slammed into Lauren before Duke instinctively caught him with one outstretched arm.

"Well, hello there," Lauren said in a voice an octave higher than the one she'd used to greet Duke. "And who might you be?"

"I might be Batman," he responded dryly.

She raised her exotic hazel eyes to meet Duke's.

"This is Charlie." She swung him around until he faced Lauren. "Say hello to Miss Lauren."

"Hello to Miss Lauren," he repeated without a hint of irony.

She smiled, a small, sweetly polite smile. "You're adorable. Look at your eyes."

He crossed them as if trying to follow her directions, and Duke laughed, grateful for the distraction.

"He's got Molly's eyes," Lauren said, sounding almost awestruck.

Both the words and the tone caused Duke's heart to twist in her chest. Apparently, Lauren wasn't only beautiful. She was also attentive and clearly already a little enamored with Molly.

"Yeah, both the boys look like her, but Joe has more of her personality than this guy."

"Joe?" Lauren said the name with a subtle rise in inflection.

"Yeah, he was around here somewhere." Duke took the opportunity to step away from Lauren enough to peek down the hallway. "Hey, Joe, come say hi."

One of the doors opened, and she expected him to emerge. Instead, she got her first peek of strappy black heels and a tan calf before the rest of Molly came into view. Her breath stalled as her eyes worked their way up to the knee-length hem of Molly's little black dress and over her perfectly curved waist to the V-cut of her neckline. She wore her dark hair down over her shoulders, and her lips shone an even deeper shade of red than usual.

Molly froze when she saw Duke staring, nervousness evident in her hesitation. Duke wanted to rush to her, to pick her up and twirl her around, to tell her how beautiful she looked, but her legs wouldn't move, and the words didn't come. All she managed to do was mouth a soundless "wow."

Molly blushed a beautiful shade of rose as she walked forward.

She gave Duke's hand a little squeeze on her way past. Just a small touch, a brief connection that didn't last nearly long enough to make what happened next bearable.

"You look stunning," Lauren said, kissing her on the cheek.

"Thank you," Molly replied. "No one's told me that in a long time."

"Then you must be surrounded by blind fools," Lauren countered.

Fools, yes. Blind, no. Duke tried to shake off the hollow feeling in her limbs, but it seemed impossible not to compare herself to Lauren and realize she came up depressingly lacking. Lauren was graceful, smooth, beautiful, classy, and feminine. In short, she was Duke's opposite. If Molly went for women like Lauren, she was screwed.

"Duke," Molly called, "we won't be late. We're only having dinner."

"It's fine." She almost choked on the next words. "Take all the time you want."

"I left some notes on the counter for you about Charlie's bedtime routine, and Joe will help, too. You have my cell phone number, right?"

"I've got it all under control."

"I know, but Charlie might not eat pizza. There's peanut butter and jelly if he'd rather have that, but you have to—"

"Cut the crust off, I know."

"We're going to be at—"

"Charlie Gitto's on The Hill. Now go."

Molly released a shaky breath. "You're right. I trust you."

Well, at least she had that going for her. She told herself being trustworthy with the boys had to count for something in Molly's world, but somehow it didn't seem quite so impressive compared to Lauren's graceful manners and easy compliments.

Molly bent down and kissed Charlie on his head. "Be good for Duke. I love you, my boy."

He put one tiny hand on either side of her face. "Love you, my mama."

She looked like she might have blinked back a tear before she straightened and called to Joe.

A door slammed somewhere down the hall. Joe came into view, his head down and his feet shuffling against the carpet.

"Joe, I'm heading out now. Will you be a big helper for Duke?"

"Yeah," he said abruptly.

"I'm counting on you."

He shrugged.

"We'll be great. We're best buds." Duke cut in.

Joe lifted his head and grinned at the characterization. Whatever was bothering him didn't extend to her.

"Hi, Joe, we didn't get to meet yet. I'm Lauren," she said hopefully.

He looked at her long and hard, his jaw set and his mouth a tight line. As a writer, Duke would've described him more as a gunslinger in a showdown rather than a kid ready for a play date.

"Where are your manners?" Molly prodded.

"Hello, Miss Lauren," he said in his best impression of a sullen teenager.

Molly looked wide-eyed from him to Duke.

"Don't worry. I've got this, too. You two get going."

Molly hesitated, her eager glow from moments before fading into worry. She pinched the bridge of her nose for a second, then smiled a smile that didn't crinkle the corners of her eyes. "Okay, you're right. We'll talk when I get home."

She dropped a kiss on Joe's head, then whispered, "I love you, always."

Duke waved good-bye and closed the door behind them. "All right, you two, we've got a lot to do tonight, but first things first. It's time for pizza."

Joe sat quietly while Charlie proceeded to speed-walk around the table.

"Come on, Char, into your booster seat."

"I don't like it," he answered matter-of-factly.

"What? The pizza or the booster seat?"

"I don't like it."

"Both of them?"

Charlie nodded and kept lapping them.

"Okay, but there's a tollbooth here now," she explained, kicking one foot onto another chair. "Every five laps you have to pay the toll."

He regarded her suspiciously and slowed his gait without stopping.

"No worries. The first five are free," she said, taking a bite of pizza. "We'll eat without you in the meantime."

"It is good pizza," Joe said softly, resting his elbow on the table and his chin on his fist.

"Good. I was worried earlier because you seemed kind of upset. Glad to hear the pizza isn't the problem."

"No, I'm happy about the pizza."

"You don't look happy. You look like I'm making you eat creamed spinach."

He sighed. "My mom said Lauren is a friend, but I think they are having a date."

"Yeah, I got that sense, too." Her heart ached, but she tried to focus on his needs. "Do you have any questions?"

"I think it's the kind of date boys and girls go on together."

Uh-oh. Had Molly not come out to Joe? That could complicate this discussion considerably. "Which part bothers you, the date part or the boy/girl part?"

"I don't know," he said, clearly wrestling with concepts he'd never voiced before. "It's all mixed up right now."

"Fair enough. You don't have to have all the answers. Sometimes it's okay to mull things over." She kicked her foot up on the chair, abruptly stopping Charlie. "Toll booth time."

He laughed and tried to back up, but she raised her other leg, trapping him between them. "You have to pay the toll. Five dollars, please."

He stared at her before lifting his empty hands.

"You don't have five dollars? Oh, well, that's an issue. I can't let you through if you don't pay the toll." She pretended to think hard, buying herself some time to calm her nerves and Charlie's energy level at the same time. "Hmm. I've got an idea. How about instead of giving me the money, you could have one bite of pizza?"

He seemed to consider the offer. "One bite?"

"Just the one." She held the small square slice out for his inspection. "Gotta be a big bite, though, like a monster lion Batman bite."

Charlie roared and chomped on a nice chunk of the pizza.

Duke and Joe's surprised grins mirrored one another. Duke dropped her legs so Charlie could resume his loops around the table.

"How did you get him to do that?" Joe asked.

"I don't know."

"Yes, you do. You know everything," Joe exclaimed excitedly. "Why can't my mom go on a date with you?"

"Yeah," she sighed, then caught herself. "Wait. What?"

He blushed and looked away.

"I thought you didn't want your mom to go on a date with a girl?"

"I don't know. I never thought about my mom going on a date with a girl. I never thought about her going on a date at all. But if she's going on a date with a girl, why can't it be you?"

Duke's eyes widened at the stream of thoughts he'd worked through. "Well, it's not that simple, I suppose."

"Why? Don't you like her?"

"I do." She wasn't sure she should admit that, but she'd never lied to Joe before, and she couldn't bring herself to do so now. "But sometimes liking someone isn't enough."

"It's enough for me. I like you. You like her."

"What I want or what you want isn't as important as what your mom wants in this situation. She has to like me back for things to work."

"She likes to talk to you. And you're a girl, kind of."

Duke grinned in spite of the fact he might have hit the target. She ran her hand through her short blond spikes of a haircut, trying not to compare it to Lauren's silken locks. "I think it might be the 'kind of' part that's causing the problem. Your mom likes Lauren, and Lauren and I don't seem to have a lot in common."

"Yeah, like nothing."

"Is that why you were rude to her?"

"I guess." He shrugged. "I didn't know what to do. I didn't want to talk to her, so I tried to hide, but then Mom made me talk. I didn't want you to think I liked her more than I like you, even if Mom does."

Sadness, pride, love, and appreciation all rolled together to form a hard lump in her throat. Joe had wrestled the best he could with so many emotions she herself couldn't even put into order. "I don't even know what to say, buddy."

He looked at her, eyes filled with hurt and confusion. "But you always know the right thing to say."

She kicked up her leg to stop Charlie again. "Toll time."

"I did four laps," he argued. "Toll booth times five."

"Really?" She hadn't been counting. She didn't even care about the pizza anymore, and she was clearly out of answers. "I guess tonight is going to follow the rule of diminishing returns."

Charlie eyed her indignantly. "Baby lion bite?"

"At this point I'll take whatever I can get." She held out the slice of pizza, and he nibbled a bit before she released him. Then she turned back to Joe. "I'm good at baseball conversations, Joe. The rest of it, not so much."

"But isn't baseball, like, everything?"

"It's a lot of things, but not always everything. I adore you and Charlie. I like your mom a lot, too. I like her so much I want her to be happy, but we have to trust she knows what will make her happy. Right now, tonight, she thinks that's Lauren."

Joe scrunched up his nose, as if Lauren's name carried a funky smell.

"Come on," she prodded. "Lauren seems nice. She's polite, and she made your mom smile. She's treating her to a fancy dinner and giving her some of the attention she deserves. I respect her."

"So she's like a worthy opponent?"

His ability to tie their current situation to their common ground should have made this conversation more comfortable, but instead it only drove home her earlier point that she was probably outmatched.

"Maybe, but I don't want you to view her as my competition. I don't want you rooting for team Duke or against team Lauren. We're all on team Molly."

"But what if Lauren isn't the best? Shouldn't the best person win?"

Duke sighed at the conflicting mix of feelings the prospect inspired, hope for herself, fear for Molly, and protectiveness for their little family. "That's for your mom to decide. I won't step in there, and you shouldn't either."

"But that's not what you said. You said you can't let the fear of striking out stop you from swinging the bat. You said you should do the right thing because it's what you love, not because of what anyone else thinks."

"This isn't a game, Joe."

"No." The anguish rose in his voice. "This is more important than even baseball, and you aren't even trying."

"I am trying. I'm trying to do what's best for your mom."

"You could be the best for my mom. You could take her to dinner and make her smile and give her attention, too, but you're not." His voice cracked with emotion. "You said if you want to be the best, you have to beat the best. Don't you want to at least try to be the best?"

The words hit her like a curveball to the ribs. Had she tipped her hat to the competition without ever taking the field? She'd grown used to hard work and being underestimated in every other area of her life, but she'd never backed down. She had to fight her father's ideas about a woman's place in baseball, the other sportswriters' criticism about her capacity to cover a sport she'd never played, the baseball establishment's prejudices against women in the locker room. No one in her life had thought she'd been the right person or had what it took to chase any of her dreams. Why was this any different? She'd never had anything so wonderful as Molly at stake. Then again, she'd never had anyone put their faith in her the way Joe had either.

"I want…" Exasperated, she blew out a heavy breath. She wanted too many things. She wanted to do right by the boys and herself and most of all Molly, but for once she let herself consider the idea that she could be what was best for Molly. She let the idea rattle around her head and spread into her chest, invigorating her as it went. "I do want a chance."

Joe hopped out of his seat and pumped his fist.

"Hey now, calm down." She immediately regretted getting his hopes up. "You and I both have to remember, at any given time any team has a chance to be the best. You don't win championships in one day. You win them by doing the little things right, through the long days and late nights, and sometimes even when you do everything right someone else does them better. If that's the case, you and I have to respect that."

Joe nodded, but this time with none of his earlier solemnity. "I promise, but it makes me happy you're at least going to get in the game."

His enthusiasm inspired her, even though she understood this was no game. She'd known since the day they met that Molly deserved the best in everything, but for the first time she relished the challenge of being that for her.

Bottom of the Third

The Games Aren't Played on Paper

Molly stopped outside the door to her apartment. For the first time in longer than she could remember, she didn't want to go inside. It felt surreal to stay out past eleven o'clock and not long for sleep. Normally she stayed up this late only with a sick kid or housework or trying to figure out how to make ends meet financially. Those times, eleven o'clock seemed as late as the hours leading up to it were long. With Lauren the evening had flown by. Dinner had ended in a flash, and dessert didn't last nearly long enough. Even the hour they'd spent lingering over coffee felt more like minutes. Lauren proved every bit as socially adept as she was beautiful.

Any time the conversation faltered, Lauren picked it up and carried them through. Molly, too, had found it easy to mask her initial nervousness as they successfully dodged many of the topics she'd feared, like why she was raising two boys alone without any family in the picture, or the fact that this was her first date with a woman, ever. Lauren kept the conversation moving by providing the right mix of lightness without being superficial, and personal without prying. The blend made for an all-around perfect evening, and Molly hated to see it end.

"I had a wonderful time tonight," Lauren whispered as though she feared being heard by the children or the neighbors.

"I did, too. The best time I've had in…ages."

Lauren smiled sweetly as though waiting.

Panic pricked at Molly's skin. Did she expect to be invited in? Molly glanced back at the door separating them from her boys and the carefully protected life she'd built for their family. She wasn't eager to say good night, but she wasn't ready for Lauren, and all the emotions she inspired, to invade her sanctuary. A few hours ago, she wasn't even sure she was ready to date. Now she was contemplating…nothing. She wasn't contemplating anything. She'd taken a huge step tonight, a wonderful one, but still monumental. She wasn't ready for anything more, and even if she had been, the boys weren't. As amazing as her grown-up time with Lauren had been, she had to put the boys' needs ahead of her own. Of course they should be in bed by now, but she didn't have high hopes, given Duke's inexperience at babysitting. She wouldn't be surprised to find the place looking like a war zone and Duke hogtied under Charlie's bed. Lauren couldn't come in for a whole myriad of reasons.

"So…" Lauren said, "I guess I should go."

Molly felt her pulling away, and her chest tightened. She'd avoided reminders of the constraints on her life all night, but this one wouldn't disappear.

"I guess so." She watched the disappointment register in the slight frown tugging at Lauren's beautiful red lips, and her own walls began to go up. She should have known this couldn't work.

"I don't want to pressure you too much," Lauren continued. "I know it's not easy for you to find time off, and I'm honored you chose to spend some of that time with me. If dinner and drinks are all you can offer I understand, but I don't want this to be good-bye."

Molly's breath caught in her throat. She didn't want to have to tell Lauren no, but clearly she was going to have to. Surely when she told Lauren she couldn't come in that would be the end of the hope and excitement she'd experienced over the last few hours.

"I'd like see you again sometime. If you'd like that, too."

"Lauren, I'm—what?"

"I know you're busy, and you've got the boys. I promised myself I wouldn't pressure you for anything more than dinner tonight, and I am willing to go as slow as you need to, but I'd love a second date."

Her smile stretched her face until her cheeks felt tight. "Yes. I'm not sure when, but I definitely want to do this again."

"Really?" Lauren's smile was more subdued, but her relief seemed sincere. "Wonderful. And thank you, for tonight and for the hope of something more to come."

"No, thank you. For so much more than you even know."

Lauren leaned close, and Molly's cheeks grew warm with anticipation. She closed her eyes and tilted her chin, her body seemingly remembering its role now that her mind had cleared. She'd been kissed before, but the gentle brush of Lauren's lips held nothing familiar. The touch was light and hopeful, soft and gentle. The kiss, like their evening, was sweet and over too soon but ended with a flutter of promise.

Molly stood still for a long time after Lauren left, simply enjoying the lingering tingle of soft lips on hers.

When she finally opened the door, still feeling a little dreamy, it took her a few seconds to adjust to the sight of Duke sitting on her couch watching ESPN. She stood up as soon as she heard the door. "Hey, welcome home. How did it go?"

"Lovely." Molly felt a smile tugging at her lips again, but she tried to hold it in check. She didn't want to act like a silly little schoolgirl, even if she felt a little like one.

"Good," Duke said, then rubbed her hands together, almost nervously. "She treated you well?"

"Yes, better than I've been treated on a date maybe ever."

"Ever? Wow. That's saying a lot."

"Not really," Molly admitted. "I only ever dated the boys' father."

"And he wasn't a real Romeo?"

"No. Not Tony." She almost snorted as she sank onto the couch. "But he was only a boy at the time. You can hardly blame him."

A muscle flexed in Duke's jaw as she sat down beside her. "I can blame him for not treating you right, Molly."

"I blame him for plenty of things, just not his lack of romanticism. We were only in high school, nervous and bumbling, both of us doing what we thought we were supposed to want. It was all so clichéd. I got pregnant with Joe on prom night."

She hadn't told anyone that since she was a teenager, largely because she'd quickly grown tired of their reactions. She couldn't handle any of them. Not the judgment of the people she'd grown up with, or the pity of the more sympathetic souls she'd met in St. Louis. They offered condolences she didn't need. She'd never considered that night a mistake. Her defenses stirred at even the prospect of having to explain that, but when she met Duke's eyes, she saw only rapt attention.

"Anyway, Tony did the best he could for a long time. We both did, but I didn't give him much to work with. I'd only slept with him to see what everyone else found so exciting. I never got the appeal."

"That's how you knew you were gay?"

"Not right away. When we got married, I blamed the stress of the pregnancy. Then came the sleepless nights of new motherhood. I diverted all my attention to Joe. With him I felt all the love and warmth and devotion I didn't for Tony. I wanted my son to have all the best parts of me."

Duke reached for her hand, and surprisingly Molly let her take it. There was no pity there, only affirmation. "You're an amazing mom."

"I don't know about that, but I do know I wasn't a good wife. Even when we settled into our life, I never settled into marriage. Tony didn't either. We both did the right things for the wrong reasons."

"What were those?"

"He tried to please everyone else. I tried to prove them wrong. I was so stubborn for so long."

"What, you? Stubborn?" Duke grinned. "I can't imagine."

Molly rolled her eyes, but she appreciated the way Duke's gentle humor softened the edges of bitter topics. "His father never liked me. He wanted to mold Tony into something he wasn't. Instead of seeing that his son wasn't a chip off the old block, every time Tony'd fail, Anthony blamed me. He thought I held him back. I didn't support him enough or challenge him enough. I even believed him for a while. I didn't love Tony the way he deserved, and no matter how hard I tried to convince both of us otherwise, I think he knew all along."

"What did he do?"

"He did his best. He went to work for his dad's furniture wholesale company. He wore a tie and brought home a paycheck and took Joe to the park on Saturdays. We both went through the motions while his father found fault in everything but Joe. That's the only thing I ever had in common with the man."

"He liked Joe?"

"Loved him and Charlie, too. Believe me, that's the only nice thing I can say about Anthony Grettano Senior. He loved his grandsons more than anything. Maybe that's why he pushed Tony so hard to be a family man. I always thought he saw my sons as his second chance to do better than he'd done with Tony, but maybe he feared losing the boys more than he feared breaking his own son."

"What a horrible trade to have to make, for all of you."

"We spent years trying to push or please or survive the others, each of us sandbagging our rising discontent, fearing no matter how high we built the walls, they'd never hold out the flood."

Duke squeezed her hand and waited quietly, never pushing, never asking for more but never backing away either. She remained steady and open for whatever Molly chose to share. Maybe her openness, her willingness to give all the power away kept Molly going into parts of the story she'd never told anyone.

"Tony grew more withdrawn. He began to mess up at work, and when he came home, he never touched me. I was relieved, and I'm sure he could tell."

Molly shuddered but kept going. "His father came over one night and offered to babysit Joe so we could go out, but I didn't want to go. A free babysitter for a night out at his expense, and I would've rather spent the night with Joe than my husband. Then I realized Anthony was right, I was an awful wife."

"Molly, you were young and in a terrible position."

"So was Tony, but at least he tried. I felt like I should, too, like I owed it to him, and more importantly to Joe, to make us a family. I put on a dress and went to dinner and smiled at him even when he spilled his wine. I held his hand even when it grew sweaty. I kissed him even though he smelled like garlic. I slept with him even while thinking of our waitress."

Duke's eyebrows shot up. "Your waitress?"

"Yes, our waitress at dinner was young and blond and beautiful. She had the softest looking hands with long, elegant fingers." She blushed. "I'd always found women so much more compelling than men, but for the first time I fantasized about her hands on me instead of his. I told him the next morning."

"Wow. How did he handle it?"

"He was relieved. He tried to act sad, but I watched all the weight fall off his shoulders. He wasn't the problem. I was. Neither one of us had to keep pretending anymore. We made plans to divorce amicably. He didn't want the apartment or the furniture, nothing. And he promised not to ask for custody of Joe as long as I promised his father visitation. Then he cried. He sobbed like a baby, he was so grateful for his freedom."

"What about you?"

"I didn't cry for a month. That's when I found out I was pregnant with Charlie."

"Oh, Molly," she sighed, then smiled. "The boy does know how to make an entrance. At least it's fun to know he's been wrecking well-laid plans from the beginning."

Molly laughed, actually laughed about one of the more terrifying times of her life. No one else had ever seen Charlie's personality so clearly in the events surrounding his birth. "Anthony Senior didn't see it that way. He'd barely tolerated plans of the divorce before he knew there was another grandson at stake. He spent days screaming at Tony and threatening me with a custody battle. He offered to buy us off, then he cut us off."

"But you didn't fold? Even with a baby on the way?"

"Tony caved. He begged for another chance. I couldn't summon even the slightest bit of sympathy for him. His remorse wasn't about me or our children. He'd merely let his father badger him into submission once again. I felt nothing for him anymore, not respect, not pity, certainly not love. I released him again, and he ran."

"Ran to where?"

Molly shrugged. "I hear from him a couple times a year. Last Christmas he was in Amsterdam, before that, Cabo. I swing wildly from hating him for not wanting anything to do with his boys to feeling overwhelmingly grateful to him for the same reason."

"You're a strong woman. Most people would've taken the security, at least until they were in a more stable position."

"I didn't see it as strength then. I wanted my life and my boys all to myself. My resilience was selfish, which is ultimately why I let Anthony back into their lives when Charlie was a few months old. They deserved a chance to have a family even if I feared being hurt again."

"That's generous after everything he'd done to make you miserable."

"I kept a tight handle on the terms of their relationship. I wouldn't accept a penny from him. Not for the house or the child support Tony

should've paid but didn't, not for myself at all. I refused to be indebted."
The muscles in her neck tightened at the thought of her final unresolved
conflict with her ex-father-in-law. "But over time I softened on what I'd
let him do for the boys."

"How so?"

"He paid Joe's private school tuition. He set up a college fund for
each of them. He was smart and always couched his gifts as educational
opportunities so I couldn't find a way to say no."

She hung her head for a second, rolling it from side to side to
ease some of the tension before meeting Duke's blue eyes once more.
"He bought the season tickets to the Cardinals games because he knew
how much Joe would love them, and he said sports would teach him
important life lessons."

Duke nodded. "That's the first ounce of connection I've managed
to feel for the man. Why doesn't he go to the games with him?"

"He died last fall. This is the first season he hasn't been there."

Duke folded like a rag doll on the couch. "How do the hits keep
coming in this story? Where's your happy ending?"

Molly ran her hand through Duke's short shock of blond hair. The
touch was natural, soothing, and Molly chose not to examine her need
to comfort this woman or think deeply about Duke's ability to feel pain
over a loss that should've only been Molly's or Joe's alone.

"Well, it's not exactly a happy ending, but on Opening Day when
I was overwhelmed and struggling to fill the void he left, wondering
how I could possibly prevent Joe's heart from breaking at every game
without his grandfather, you showed up. You sat in Anthony's seat and
talked about baseball with my son, and you bought hot dogs in the third
inning like he used to. You made Joe smile again."

"Yeah?" She lifted her head, her eyes hopeful. "What about you?
Did I make you smile?"

"Not at first. I tried to be mad at you," she admitted. "I'd just
finished being indebted to Anthony. I wanted so much to prove I could
do everything on my own."

"You do more than any person I've ever met. I think you're
amazing and strong and capable."

"I think that's why I've been comfortable sharing my son with
you. You've made me feel safe and in control. That's probably why I

told you all this tonight." She stopped, for the first time realizing how much information, how much of herself she'd shown Duke. "I've never told anyone the things I just told you."

"Ever?"

Molly shook her head, worried she'd given Duke too much power. She'd certainly exposed herself to all sorts of rejection and opened old insecurities. Why now, when she was finally back on her feet, should she relive those traumas? And why choose Duke? She'd spent her whole night with Lauren grateful to avoid the topics she'd just spoken about so freely with Duke. She hadn't even made a conscious decision to let her guard down. The walls she'd built and maintained for years simply evaporated to let Duke in. And now Duke had seen past the façade. What must she think of her?

She searched Duke's wide eyes for any hint of a change but found only compassion laced with a hint of wonder.

"I don't even know what to say. I'm honored. I promise I'll never betray your trust."

The tension eased from her chest. For all the questions she couldn't answer, she did know without a doubt she could trust Duke with anything.

❖

Molly slathered another coat of sunscreen across Charlie's nose while he tried to squirm away. A six o'clock start time lessened the length of exposure to the summer sun, but not enough to ease her worries completely.

"Honey, you have to wear it. It's keeps you safe."

Charlie waved his arms in a wide cross swath like an umpire and shouted, "Safe!"

"Exactly. Like the baseball players."

"Like Duke."

"What?"

"Duke is safe," he said again, making the same hand motions. Molly's heart beat a little faster.

"Thanks, buddy. I didn't even have to slide."

Molly didn't turn around right away but continued to apply the sunscreen while she waited for the subtle buzz of anticipation to fade from her nerve endings. She hadn't seen Duke in over a week, and given the way she'd opened up to her that night, she worried something might've changed between them.

She listened while Duke greeted Joe, and they chatted a bit about the Cardinals' road trip. Then even without looking up, she felt Duke's attention shift to her. There was a certain energy she couldn't put into words, but she recognized the sensation of being caught in her soft blue gaze.

"Hi, Molly."

"Hi, Duke."

"I'm glad you guys are here today. I missed you all while we were on the road."

Molly didn't want to admit she'd missed her as well, but Joe had no such problems.

"We missed you, too, but we read your stories online every morning."

"Really?"

"Yeah, Mom has me read them to her while we eat breakfast."

Duke grinned at Molly. "I never considered you among my readership."

"Well, you know, now that school's out, I want to make sure he keeps reading."

"School's out for the summer?" Duke turned back to Joe. "That's fantastic. Now you can come to more games, right?"

"Yes, and we can stay up later because the babysitter comes to our house in the morning, so we can sleep in."

"You're a lucky guy, Joe." Duke tapped the bill of his cap for emphasis. Then to Molly she added, "I bet those later bed times are a blast for you."

"Pure joy, let me tell you."

"Is that why you weren't here last night?" Duke asked casually, but the way she turned to look at the field instead of meeting her eyes made Molly suspect there was some emotion under the question. Had Duke expected to see them? Was she disappointed when they weren't there? The thought made Molly's chest tighten.

"We went out to dinner with a friend last night," Molly explained.

"It was Lauren," Joe deadpanned, leaving her to wonder both why she'd withheld the information and why he always used that tone when talking about Lauren. He'd been polite and respectful at dinner, much better behaved than when they'd first met, but the extra time together hadn't raised his enthusiasm level for her.

"Really? You guys all went out to dinner with Lauren? Together. Well. Great." Duke nudged Joe. "That's great, Joe. It must make your mom pretty happy to have her kids and her friends all together."

Joe nodded. "Lauren's coming to the game today."

Duke ran her hand through her hair and looked back out at the field. "That's just great. And fast. Things must have gone well while I was out of town."

Even though Molly wanted to be careful and not rush the relationship, she had to admit things with Lauren were going well. It hadn't even been two weeks since their first date, but she'd seen Lauren several times since then. They had coffee together almost every morning before starting work and occasionally again at three.

Lauren had also come over for dinner at their apartment last weekend after Charlie went to bed, and Joe had spent the night with a friend. She'd been engaging and understanding, and while each date ended with a slightly longer kiss, she hadn't pushed for anything more. When she'd invited the boys out to dinner with them last night, it seemed like the natural next step, and everything went as well as could be expected with Charlie in a restaurant. So maybe the kids hadn't fallen instantly in love with her, and Lauren might have looked overwhelmed a time or two, but she hadn't run away. That had to count for something.

"Molly?" Duke asked gently.

"Yes?"

"I said, I take it things are going well?"

"Yes, sorry. Things are wonderful."

"Good." She looked back at Joe. "If you're happy, that's all that matters, right?"

"Right," Joe and Molly answered in unison.

"Right," Charlie echoed.

"Seeing a game together should be fun," Duke added cheerfully.

"The game should be fun," Joe said, then after a glance at Duke added, "I mean because we should win this one easy. The Cubs are terrible."

"Don't get too cocky there, little man," Duke warned. "Remember what I said. Even the worst team in the league still wins games."

"Yeah, but the Cubs are in last place. Their team batting average is .250, and their on-base percentage is .300. Their pitchers give up more home runs than any other team in the league."

Duke shrugged, and Molly wondered if she realized Joe committed her articles to memory.

"I don't doubt we're a better team on paper. If you're a sabermetrician you'd call us a sure thing. I like statistics. They're a big part of my job, but they aren't everything. If they were, why would we even care about playing the games?"

"I guess because playing the games is the fun part."

"Exactly. The games are the fun part, and they aren't played on paper. I've seen perfect rosters crumble on the field, and I've seen terrible squads come to life at the right time. You can read all the signs, know all the stats, and set up the most favorable pairings weeks in advance, but no one can know anything for sure until you see the matchup unfold for real."

"Did I miss our private pre-game scouting report?" Lauren asked, coming to a stop in the aisle next to Duke. Seeing the two of them side by side provided such a contrast for Molly. Even dressed down, Lauren's appearance screamed of elegance. While Duke's short blond wisps were lightly gelled and tousled, Lauren had threaded her long brown hair through the back of a red ball cap. Her white jersey was a baby-doll cut that accentuated her hips and curves, while the only thing feminine about Duke's red polo shirt was the hint of slender collarbone she'd revealed by leaving the second button open. Lauren's jeans were designer and slim-fitting, leaving no doubt about her gender. While Duke's cargo khakis did hang beautifully off her hips, their sides dropped straight to her loafers, hiding any physical features farther down.

She scanned back up their bodies and found both women staring at her expectantly. Had she been caught comparing them? And why bother? They had nothing in common, certainly not in ways that had anything to do with her.

"Hi, Lauren," Duke finally said, taking care of the awkwardness by extending her hand and sparking the conversation. "It's good to see you again."

"Likewise. Joe explained last night that you often stop by and talk about the important parts of the game."

"Joe gives me too much credit," Duke said, her smile turning a little sad, and Molly's chest tightened once again.

"Not at all," she cut in. "Duke's taught us more about baseball in three months than we've learned in the rest of our lives combined. She was just talking to Joe about not taking an opponent for granted. Apparently it doesn't matter how good a team looks on paper if they don't execute on the field."

"Sounds like a good lesson for life in general."

Duke shrugged. "Life is just a metaphor for baseball."

"Don't you mean that the other way around?"

Duke grinned. "Not really."

"Duke buy hot dog," Charlie cut in.

"Sorry, buddy. I have to stay in the press booth today."

"Why?" Joe and Molly asked in unison.

Duke shifted from one foot to the other and looked back across the field. "It's my job."

"But you always—"

Joe's protest was interrupted by the chirp of Molly's cell phone. She fumbled for it in the diaper bag, then glancing at the screen noticed a text message from the boys' babysitter. It simply read, *Last minute trip. Cancun. Can't babysit Mon. Back Tues.* She stared at the screen, blinked a few times, and reread the message. The familiar tension in her shoulders tightened another notch.

"What is it, Mol?" Duke asked softly.

She sighed. "The babysitter ran off to Cancun for a long weekend. She won't be back to watch the boys on Monday."

"Are you kidding?" Lauren snapped. "How unprofessional. Are you going to fire her?"

"No. She's a college student. When she gets back we'll have a talk about job skills and leaving other people in a lurch and I'm not sure what else, really. I'll deal with the teachable moment stuff later. Right now I need to find another sitter or find a replacement for me at work on Monday."

"Can't you call a service or something?" Lauren asked.

"No, I don't use sitters I don't know. And my current girl works for cheap because she's just a teenager herself."

"But she's unreliable. Wouldn't you rather pay more for a professional?"

Her frustration bubbled up. Like she didn't have enough on her plate already, now she had to defend her parenting decisions to someone who didn't have kids? "Sure, in a perfect world I'd have an au pair who was fluent in three languages, held a degree in early childhood education, and doubled as a gourmet chef."

"If money is the problem," Lauren said slowly, quietly, "I'd love to help."

Molly's jaw tightened as she fought the rising tide of anger at Lauren's insinuation that she needed saving, financially or otherwise. How was she even supposed to respond?

"Hey," Duke said, leaning into Molly's line of sight and pulling her attention gently away from her frustration. "I was going to ask for a play date with the boys later in the week anyway. I haven't gotten to see them much lately. Why don't I watch them Monday?"

"Yes," Joe cheered. Charlie clapped.

Molly eyed her suspiciously. The play date excuse sounded awfully convenient. She didn't need two women trying to save her, but she had a harder time seeing Duke in that role.

"Come on. I'm an awesome babysitter, and you know I'll have more fun than the boys will."

She felt a smile trying to break through her jaded exterior as she realized Duke was probably telling the truth on both counts. "What about work? That's a game night for you."

"The game isn't until seven o'clock." Duke rubbed her face as if trying to make the math work. "If you can get home by three, I can still get here two hours before the clubhouse closes. Please let me come over and play. I'd really appreciate it. I'd even owe you one."

Now she was being silly and transparent. Clearly Molly'd be the one indebted to Duke, but for some reason it didn't feel that way, which made it virtually impossible to say no.

"Fine." Molly relented. "But I will owe you."

"Nah." Duke waved her off. "It'll be the highlight of my whole week. I'm so excited, you can even send me an absurdly long email with detailed instructions and I won't mind. But now I do have to get to work."

"Right. Go."

"Okay. And, Molly, thank you." Duke grinned, then jogged off.

Molly watched her go until she faded into the crowd completely, then turned back to see Lauren watching her. "Sorry for the interruption there."

"It's no problem. I'm glad it all worked out so we can enjoy some baseball together."

"Me too." Molly pulled Charlie onto her lap and motioned for Lauren to sit, but Charlie squirmed away.

"That's Duke's seat."

"No, honey. Lauren's going to sit there today."

"No, my seat. Duke's seat."

"I'm so sorry." The burn of her earlier frustration segued to embarrassment. Nothing was going right for her today. She wouldn't have blamed Lauren if she wanted to run away, but her polite smile never faltered. "Go ahead and sit. He'll be fine in two minutes. He's funny about his routines, and he's used to Duke sitting there."

Lauren seemed to choose her words carefully. "There's no need to apologize. Duke is…well, she must be a very special friend."

Molly wasn't sure if there was something more underlying the sentiment, but for once she didn't feel an ounce of defensiveness or even the need to explain. Settling back into her seat, she only said, "Yes, she is."

❖

"What on earth is that smell?" Molly asked as soon as she walked in the door. It was a strong smell, a unique smell, but not unpleasant. Certainly not the type of scent she expected to come home to after leaving the boys with Duke all day.

"Hey, Mom." Joe came tearing around the corner. "We made lasagna."

"Lasagna?"

"Yeah, Duke called her mom, and she told us how. It's already cooked and everything. You have to…" He paused, his little face scrunched in concentration. "Oh yeah, you just have to put it back in the oven at 375 until it heats through again."

"And Duke's mom taught you that?"

"She taught Duke, and Duke taught us, but me and Charlie helped put it all together in the pan."

"Impressive. Where's Duke now?"

"She's getting Charlie out of the bathtub."

"Isn't it a little early for a bath?"

"Didn't you hear what I said? Charlie helped put the lasagna together."

"Ah, now I get it. Tomato sauce everywhere? I'm surprised Duke doesn't need a shower, too."

Joe grinned sheepishly, causing Molly to laugh. "Okay, let's see what's going on back here."

"We're in Charlie's room," Duke called.

Molly pushed open the door to see Duke on her knees on the floor holding up a set of dry clothes while Charlie ran circles around her in wet swim trunks.

"Sorry." Duke looked chagrined. Her gray shirt was soaked in the front and clung to her chest, revealing subtle curves Molly found more than a little surprising. "Bath time may have been a bridge too far for me today."

"It's okay. You seem to have fared better than most." Honestly, Duke had fared better than Molly did some days. Charlie was clean, the house was clean, dinner smelled delicious. "Can I ask, though, why the bathing suit?"

"Well, I'm not his mom, and I didn't know the rules about unrelated adults and naked kids. You see such awful stuff on the news. I wanted to respect his privacy."

Molly bit her lip to keep from laughing. Duke was so silly and yet so sincerely good. "I'm sure he appreciated that very much, along with the idea of treating the bath like his own personal swimming pool."

"Yeah, he had so much fun he doesn't want to get out of the trunks now, and I really do have to get going."

"Of course." Molly felt a little twist of disappointment in her stomach that she quickly shook off. "Joe, will you help Charlie get dressed while I walk Duke out?"

"Sure," he said. "Thanks for today, Duke. I had fun."

"Me too, bud." She extended her fist, and Joe tapped it with his own several times in a choreographed routine ending with explosion noises.

"We have a secret handshake now," Joe explained to Molly.

"I see."

"I bet you're jealous," Duke teased.

"Totally."

"See you later, Batman." Duke kissed Charlie on the head, but he turned and threw his arms around her neck. He had to be soaking her clothes all over again, but Duke never pulled away. "You give the best hugs, cuddle monster."

Molly's chest expanded with emotion. Charlie did give the best hugs. He threw his whole self into them, but she doubted anyone else would have ever called him a cuddle monster, because outside of Molly or Joe he'd never slowed down enough to show that side of himself.

Duke set him down and headed for the door. "I'll see you tomorrow night."

"Wait." Molly caught up with her in the living room. "I know you have to get going, but I just wanted to say thank you. You went overboard today."

"It's nothing."

"It is something. You not only took great care of the kids, you cooked, and you cleaned up after yourself."

"Joe said Lauren was coming over tonight." Duke looked at the floor, then the kitchen, anywhere but Molly's eyes. "I didn't want you to come home from a long day at work to find a messy house, then have to juggle two kids and dinner."

"I do those things every day. That's my life. I can handle my own responsibilities. I've been doing it for years." Her familiar argument flowed easily from memory but failed to gather steam in the face of Duke's easy smile and sparking blue eyes. She would've found the expression maddening if she weren't so endearing. "What? Why are you so happy?"

"Because you're right. You're perfect. You amaze me even more after spending a full day with the kids. I see how hard you work, how much skill and energy it requires to do what you do, but you do it all so beautifully and without complaint. You had to deal with so much so young, and you've excelled. I know you didn't need any of the things I did today. I know you don't need me at all, so I did everything to say thank you for letting me hang around anyway."

"Duke…" No more words would come. She thought she'd experienced everything another person could make her feel. She'd fought every fight and countered every judgment, but she had no response to Duke's version of her.

"I'm in awe of you, Molly," Duke whispered. "I wish I were more like you."

"No." She blinked back tears and reached up to cup Duke's cheek in her hand. "Don't ever say that again. Don't ever wish to be anyone but you."

Duke's lips parted and Molly's did the same as a sharp breath escaped. Painfully aware of their proximity, the intimacy of their bodies brushing together, the feel of Duke's impossibly soft skin under her fingertips, a rush of heat flooded her chest and she stepped quickly back. "You, um, had some tomato sauce on your cheek."

Duke lifted her hand lightly to the spot Molly had touched, but made no attempt to brush anything away.

"I just"—Molly sighed—"thank you."

Duke continued to stare at her, eyes wide with confusion, or maybe something more. "Molly—"

"It's okay. You better get to work."

"Yeah." She nodded slowly. "Right. Work." Duke shook out her arms as though trying to make sure all her limbs still functioned, then, with one more smile, turned and left.

Molly closed the door behind her and rested her forehead on the cool wooden surface, grateful for something steady to hold on to while she wondered what'd just happened.

❖

Molly had come to no more conclusions about her moment of connection with Duke several hours later. If she closed her eyes and cleared her mind, she could still feel Duke's skin under her fingers, so she didn't close her eyes or breathe too deeply or do anything to center herself for fear the spark of heat would spread through her once again. Instead she stayed busy with the boys. They built a fort out of sheets and couch cushions, then climbed inside to talk about their days and read books until Charlie decided he was a monster. Joe and Molly were still fighting valiantly to defend the castle when Lauren knocked on the door.

Glancing around quickly Molly realized, too late, the house was no longer in the pristine shape Duke had left it in, and she'd forgotten to reheat the lasagna.

"Damn, I mean darn." She jumped up and gathered the sheets in her arms. "Run these back to my room please, Joe."

He scrambled to obey her, but she noticed the look of disappointment on his face. She couldn't help but wonder if he resented Lauren for interrupting their family time or if he just resented her, period.

Lauren knocked again.

"I'll be right there," she called, running to the kitchen and sliding the pan of lasagna into the oven. Then straightening her shirt and hair as much as she could without a mirror, she opened the door. "Hi."

"Good evening," Lauren said, holding out a bottle of wine. "I thought you might need this tonight."

The comment tweaked Molly's natural defenses, but Lauren's sweet smile helped soothe them. "Thank you, but it's actually been a pretty nice day."

"Really?"

"Yes, why?"

"Nothing. You're looking a little, um…windblown." Lauren pressed her lips together, but they curled upward anyway as she lifted her eyes to Molly's hair.

Lauren reached up as if to touch her hair, but Molly stepped back. "Sorry, I was sort of wrestling with the boys."

"It's okay. Windblown looks adorable on you."

The compliment was nice, but it did little to stem Molly's self-consciousness. "Thanks. Come on in and make yourself at home. I'll be right back."

Ducking into the hallway bathroom, she looked in the mirror to see her dark curls piled in a haphazard mop atop her head. Clearly the fort wasn't the only thing to suffer surface damage in the great battle of Charlie. She finger-combed the mess of tangles back into something resembling presentable, then added some lip gloss before mumbling, "That's as good as it gets."

Stepping into the hall, she heard Lauren talking to Joe and paused out of sight to listen.

"Right, but don't you want to do anything other than baseball?"

"Not really," Joe said, a slight hint of exasperation in his voice. "Baseball kind of has everything important already wrapped up in it."

"It's just a game."

"It's not," Joe protested. "Baseball has math and physics. It can teach history and storytelling. It's about playing fair and how to overcome challenges and how to work as a team or push for a personal best. Oh, and it can teach people how to learn from mistakes and make adjustments."

Molly's chest swelled with pride that her nine-year-old son had such a firm grasp on so many intersecting concepts most adults never fully connected. Sometimes she wondered if she should encourage his one-track mind about baseball, but when he talked like that, he made it clear it wasn't really a singular focus, but rather high-level critical thinking. Of course, when he talked like that, he also sounded exactly like Duke. Some of Joe's comments there were direct quotes from his hero.

"But don't you ever think about what you want to be when you grow up? Baseball isn't a way to make a living."

"I want to be a sportswriter, like Duke."

"And he doesn't have to worry about making a living yet," Molly cut in, not at all liking the conversation. "I like that he's passionate about something. If he turns his passion into a career, that will be wonderful, but even if he doesn't, the ability to believe in something bigger than himself is a good capacity for a young man to possess."

Lauren regarded her with an unreadable expression before her features softened. "I would've pegged you for more of a pragmatist."

"Does that disappoint you?"

"Not at all. You're full of wonderful surprises. It's one of the many things I love about you."

Love? The word hit Molly like a blast of cold air, and she excused herself quickly. "I'd better check the lasagna."

Did Lauren say something about love? No, not quite, she reasoned. Surprises, Lauren loved surprises, and Molly surprised her. A coincidence. Surely every person had some characteristic any other person could love about them without loving the actual person. For instance, Lauren had so many good qualities about her. Molly certainly liked her gentle manners and her soft demeanor. She liked that she didn't push her. Liked, not loved. Were those the kinds of things a person could like enough to love, or were they simply pleasant? Lauren was beautiful, without a doubt. She looked the part of someone Molly would want to love. But could physical attraction build the basis of love? Or only lust?

What did she even know about love anyway? Of course she loved her children, but she hadn't loved their father, not in any all-consuming way. She'd never been in love with a woman, either. Would she even recognize it if she felt it? Lauren was exactly the type of person she should fall in love with, the type of woman she wanted to fall in love with. Wouldn't that happen as they got know each other better?

"Hey, are you okay?" Lauren asked quietly.

"Yes, of course. Why?"

"You seem a little distracted tonight."

"I'm sorry. I got frazzled. The house is a mess, and dinner wasn't ready on time."

"I didn't expect to be waited on. Honestly, I sort of expected this place to be a wreck since Duke had the kids all day."

"Why?"

"Don't get me wrong. She seems like a great person and good with the boys, but she's more like a big playmate than a responsible adult."

"That's not true." Defensiveness roared to the surface so quickly she didn't have time to consider the fact that it wasn't stirred for herself or her boys, but for Duke. "She did an amazing job today. I came home to a clean house, clean kids, and dinner. She made the lasagna, not me. Duke was perfect. I lost track of time."

"Okay." Lauren looked like she didn't know what to say. "Everybody makes mistakes. I would've bought you all dinner if you didn't have enough time or resources to get things done."

Now the defensiveness was hers alone. "We didn't need someone to rescue us."

"No, of course not, but no one can do everything."

"I can do everything where my family is concerned. I've done everything for years."

"Why won't you let me help?"

"I don't need help."

"Then why accept it from Duke?"

Molly opened her mouth to retort, only to find she didn't have one. She hung her head.

"I'm sorry," Lauren said. "I didn't mean to push you."

"No, it's a fair question. I just don't know the answer."

Lauren shifted from one two-inch heel to the other, seemingly weighing whether or not she wanted to continue down this path. "You don't know the answer, or you don't like the answer?"

Molly's chest tightened. "I'm sorry, Lauren."

"You don't have to apologize."

"Maybe not, but I *am* sorry. I wanted things to work out between us."

"But they aren't, are they?"

"No, and that makes me sad." Her limbs felt heavy. "You made me feel hopeful for the first time in years."

"But?"

"But the hope of something more never turned into something more." She covered her eyes. "That sounds so stupid."

"Not stupid." Lauren summoned one of her polite smiles. "Vague, maybe."

"I know. I wish I could figure it out. You're smart and polite and beautiful. You've been patient and understanding, and you've let me set the pace. I like talking to you. I like you as a person."

"But you don't feel a spark?"

"I want to, I really do. But I don't. It doesn't make sense. On paper you're everything I want in a woman. But, much like baseball games, relationships don't unfold on paper."

TOP OF THE FOURTH

Keep Your Eye on the Ball

"Hey, Coop," Duke called. He was leaving the locker room as she headed in.

"Hey, Rook. Better hurry or I'll scoop you."

"Yeah yeah. You might have beaten me to the quote this time, but my blog will still be up eight hours before your column goes to print."

"Blogs, tweets, Internets." He rolled his eyes. "It's not real journalism unless it leaves newsprint on your fingers in the morning."

"And lines litter boxes by afternoon?"

"Ouch, kid. You're getting cocky here in the big leagues. You better be careful or someone will give you a little chin music."

She shook her head and laughed. No one was likely to hurl a fastball under her nose. What would that even look like in the blogosphere?

The players were in their usual state of disarray, or at least that was how the locker room always appeared at first, guys half-dressed, some eating, some playing cards, others sprawled on everything from leather couches to trainers' tables. Duke opened the electronic notepad feature on her tablet and scanned the list of players she hoped to talk to. The pitchers were already taking batting practice, so she'd have to approach them later, but the first round of position players should be killing time before their turn in the cage.

Spying Cayden Brooks in the corner, already fully dressed in his warms-ups, she decided to start there.

"Hey, Cayden. How you feeling tonight?"

He regarded her more suspiciously than he had a month ago, his dark eyes narrow. "Fine."

"Fine?"

"Yeah." He chewed a little harder on his pink wad of bubble gum.

Something seemed off. She'd given him no reason to clam up on her, and he'd done nothing to warrant defensiveness as far as she'd seen. He might not have performed up to the club's hype for his rookie season, but he hadn't been terrible either, with a .270 batting average and solid defense in center field. "You got anything specific you're working on in batting practice?"

"Quick hands."

"Opposing pitchers do seem to be busting you inside lately."

"They think they've got the book on me."

"What do you think?"

"They got nothing."

She raised her eyebrows.

"Go ahead." He lifted his chin defiantly. "Print that."

"Cayden..." She tried not to seem motherly, but even to her own ears the tone sounded similar to the one Molly used when Charlie was about to do something he knew he shouldn't. Cayden, much like Charlie, clearly wouldn't heed the warning.

"I told the same thing to every other reporter in here. If you don't print it, someone else will."

"Okay." If he wanted to piss off the guys hurling ninety-mile-an-hour heaters his way, that wasn't her fault. If she got her blog posted early enough, he might even see one of those fireballs up close tonight.

She made a note to publicize the comments in her headline or first paragraph because they'd be sure to pique the interest of readers and opposing pitchers alike.

Her phone began to vibrate along with the opening strains of "Take Me Out to the Ball Game."

She accepted the call quickly, but not before a few of the players smirked in her direction. "Duke here."

"Hey, Duke. It's Simon Beach."

She grimaced. Her editor didn't call her often. They mostly communicated via email or text message. "Hi, Beach. Gimme a sec. I'm in the locker room."

She pushed open the large metal door and then walked quickly down the tunnel toward the field where she'd have more privacy and better reception. "What's up?"

"Not too much. I just wanted to check in with you."

"Uh-huh." She didn't buy that. Editors never called to chat.

"How're you doing?"

"Fine."

"Yeah?"

"Yup," she said, then remembered how suspicious these one word answers sounded when Cayden had given them a few minutes earlier and added, "I'm great, trying to do the pre-game round-up so I can post my report in time."

"About that." Simon cleared his throat. "You ran kind of late yesterday. By the time we got the blog edited and up on the website, the national anthem was almost over. Not so much pre-game as an in-game report."

She hadn't actually cut it that close, but she didn't bother arguing since she had in fact been late. "I apologize for putting you under the gun. I got hung up before getting to the park, but it's no excuse. Won't happen again."

"No, I'm sure it won't," he said amicably. "I wouldn't have even mentioned it this time, but one of the interns pointed out you also made some weird tweets yesterday afternoon, and the two things combined made me wonder if something happened."

Weird tweets? She flipped open the cover to her tablet and tapped the Twitter app. She scanned through her post-game tweets from last night, all the way up through the pre-game before she found anything out of the ordinary, but sure enough at around one o'clock yesterday afternoon there had been three back-to-back tweets of pure gibberish. They would've been utterly baffling if not for a fourth and final one that simply had 140 letter *C*'s. Her memory flashed to an image of her finding Charlie under the dining room table holding her phone in his tiny fists. She asked if he'd hit any buttons, but he'd only whispered, "C says Charlie."

There weren't any apps open at the time, so she'd thought his remark was just Charlie being Charlie, but now she suspected he'd been tagging his cyber graffiti. She stifled a groan, not wanting to explain her professional account had been hijacked by a three-year-old hacktivist. "I'm sorry. I must have forgotten to turn my phone off and sat on it in the car."

"You butt-tweeted to thirty thousand followers?"

"Um, well, when you put it that way…yes."

He snickered. "You haven't had a series off yet this season, have you?"

"No, but really, I'm fine."

"I know. You've been stellar so far."

She heard the implied *up until now* on the end of the comment and frowned. "Okay then, no need to bench me."

"I'm not benching you. We're almost to the All-Star break, and you haven't used a single day of vacation."

"What would I do with a vacation? Sit around and watch baseball games on TV?"

Simon laughed. "You know there are other things in life than baseball. Surely there's something else you enjoy."

Her mind immediately flashed to Molly and the boys. She liked them. It would be fun to babysit the boys for a few days in a row. Maybe go to the zoo, or the City Museum, but she could do so without taking a day off. Although if she didn't have a game to run off to, maybe she could stick around and have dinner with them, too, or perhaps see a movie. Dinner and a movie with Molly sounded nice and exactly like the sort of thing that might move them closer.

They'd actually felt pretty close yesterday, though. She could still feel the feather-light brush of Molly's fingers against her skin, see the emotions in her deep brown eyes, and hear the slight gasp of her breath. Had she felt the spark between them, too? If so, she hadn't liked it much because she'd pulled back so quickly she'd left Duke's head spinning. Even by the time she got to the game, she still couldn't shake the haze Molly had left her in. She'd almost gone back over after work to try to reconnect but reasoned Molly had probably gone to bed, and if she hadn't she was likely with Lauren.

Lauren.

She sighed. Duke kept waiting for her chance. She did want to be the best for Molly, but she wouldn't foul the competition to get her way. She respected Lauren, maybe even liked her a little, not so much as a person but for what she gave Molly. She wouldn't take any cheap shots. She'd have to wait for her own opening, but how could she find time alone with Molly if Lauren came to every dinner and every baseball game? What if she took a series off only to find Molly already had plans? Dinner and a movie with Molly and the kids *and* Lauren would be a nightmare. She didn't want to sit around and watch someone else in the role she wanted to play.

No, the evenings seemed to be Lauren's time at the plate, which left her only the days with the boys while Molly went to work. Not that she didn't want to spend more quality time with them, but she worried about getting Joe's hopes up too much. She might never get a real shot with Molly, and even if she did, Lauren might still win. What would it do to Joe to lose her? Hell, what would it do to her if she lost him? She couldn't think of herself here. She couldn't even focus fully on Molly. Anytime anyone chased a relationship, they had to acknowledge the risk of getting hurt, but dating a single mom came with a lot of added responsibility.

The situation and the possible pitfalls would likely be too much to navigate. She'd probably sit around watching baseball games, so she might as well stay at work. She loved her job. She'd reached the pinnacle of her field, and until yesterday she'd functioned at a high level. There was no reason to abandon that now, especially without a clearly superior alternative.

"Duke, you still there?"

"Yeah, sorry. I was thinking over your offer, but I'm going to pass. I love baseball, Beach. I know its ins and outs. I like the routine, the certainty of it. I like how everybody gets their turn at the plate, and I like that there's always another game. This is all I have for sure right now, so I'd just as soon hold on to it, if you don't mind."

"Not at all. I'll let you get back to work, then," he said, then added, "but I need you to keep your eye on the ball."

"You got it." Keeping her eye on the ball had been her strategy for years, and it had gotten her everything she'd wanted in life up until now. She needed to get back to what she knew.

❖

Duke made it a point to get her blog posted early and tweet a few of the more juicy tidbits, like Cayden's comments, to make up for her mistakes the day before. Then she headed down to Molly's section during batting practice in the hopes of spending a few minutes with her and the boys before the game started, but they weren't there yet. The

Cardinals had long since left the field, and the Giants were wrapping up their turn in the cage, too. Glancing at her watch, she noticed they were about half an hour from game time. She wanted to make the most of the pre-game lull because she intended to head back up to the booth before first pitch and stay there for the entire game. No more sneaking off to see Molly and the kids during live play.

She watched the grounds crew prepare the field as a few of the outfielders ran. She tried to quit worrying she wouldn't get any time with Molly or the boys today. The thought made her stomach tighten more than it should have, but she told herself she needed to focus on her job as any professional would. She also suspected Lauren's presence during the games might have put an added emphasis on her desire for professional distance.

"Hi," Molly said very close behind her.

Duke jumped out of her seat and turned around quickly. "Hey."

"Were you lost in work mode there?" Molly asked.

"Something like that." She tapped Joe on the bill of his ball cap. "You guys ready for the game?"

"Yeah, are you going to stay with us for a while?"

"Actually, I need to get back up to the press booth pretty soon."

Joe frowned slightly, but Molly cut in. "Duke's at work, honey. We're lucky she can even spare some time now."

"I know," he said in a tone that implied he might have understood the situation, but he didn't have to love it. "I thought since Lauren wasn't coming tonight we'd have an extra spot for Duke."

"Lauren's not coming?"

"No," Joe answered, but Duke looked to Molly, who in turn looked back to the boys before seeming to ponder her response carefully.

"No, she's not. Something came up." She hesitated like maybe she wanted to say more but decided against it. "You're welcome to sit with us, but I know you're working, so please don't feel obligated."

"I've never considered you an obligation, Molly. You and the boys are always one of the best parts of my day."

Molly's expression softened. "Wow, that's saying a lot given what you do for a living and how much you love it."

Maybe she'd said too much, revealed too much, but she'd told the truth, and she wouldn't backtrack now. The bigger problem, though, was what she intended to do with the information that Lauren wouldn't be joining them. It shouldn't have made a difference. She had work to do, and she'd sworn she wouldn't cut any corners today. Still, she'd also been looking for a chance to spend quality time with Molly for weeks now. Why did the two most important things in her life have to require her attention at exactly the same time?

Baseball was the safe bet. Baseball also didn't have a girlfriend. Then again, baseball didn't have big brown eyes or show a little hint of cleavage under its uniforms. Decisions, decisions.

"I guess I might be able to stay for the first inning." Duke couldn't help herself, and she reasoned the game would last nine innings, so working from the stands for one of them couldn't hurt much. "I'll have to tweet, though...by myself, Charlie."

He laughed, giving every indication he knew he'd been caught and didn't care. Then he patted his chair. "You sit here."

The game got off to an inauspicious start, an easy ground ball to shortstop, then a foul out along the first base line. Joe and Duke both noted each play on their scorecards, his on paper, hers on the tablet, while Molly chatted about her day at work. It was so easy to sit with them, to chat with Joe about each play or smile over his head at Molly whenever one of the kids said something cute or funny. She could almost imagine there was no Lauren or no job to worry about and she was just enjoying an evening at the ballpark with her family, but the ease and appeal of thinking that way also made it dangerous. Molly's family wasn't hers, and she did have an important job to do.

As if highlighting the work ahead, the batter at the plate connected with a fastball, arching it toward the outfield wall. She couldn't track the ball into the late-day sun, so she instead tracked Cayden Brooks as he rushed to intercept it. He broke hard backward toward the outfield wall. Sprinting across the grass, his eyes focused over his head, his glove rose to partially shield his eyes from the sun. He seemed to have a perfect bead on the ball until his first foot hit the red clay warning track. The minute his cleats touched the dirt, he looked back, just a little glance, then a stutter step before he put his free hand back to brace himself. A fraction of a second later, he casually reached up with his glove as if to snatch an apple off a high branch, only to come up completely empty-handed.

The ball thudded to the ground on the opposite side of him. He peeked into his glove, appearing surprised the ball wasn't there, then looked frantically to the ground before scrambling to pick it up and make an off-balance throw to second base. The batter already stood securely on the bag without even having slid.

The crowd released a collective groan with Joe and Duke joining in.

"What just happened?" Molly asked.

"He made an error, dropped the ball."

She rolled her eyes and elbowed Duke. "I saw that, but why? He made it to the right spot in plenty of time."

"He glanced back when he hit the warning track to see how far he was from the wall, and when he looked back up, he'd lost track of the ball."

"I thought he had it," Joe said.

"He did, too. Did you see the way he lifted his hand expecting a sure thing?" Duke sighed and tweeted the error. "I'm willing to bet he tried to catch a shadow, literally."

"What does that mean?" Molly asked.

"When he took his eye off the ball, he lost sight of the real deal, and the only thing in the sun was the ball's shadow." Duke shifted in her seat, worried she should be taking more than a tweet away from the play. "He mistook the shadow for what he really wanted and tried to grab it."

"You can't catch a shadow," Joe said sounding confused. "They aren't real."

Duke's chest constricted. "But sometimes they look that way, and it's easy to get confused."

"Then why did he do it?"

"He shouldn't have. He should know his job well enough to measure the depth of the warning track by feel, but if he doesn't, if he misjudges it by even half a step, he's going to hit the wall hard."

"I would've kept my eye on the ball anyway," Joe said.

He was right. Playing the game right meant more to him than the prospect of getting banged up. She felt the same way, or at least she had until recently.

"I don't doubt it, buddy. And I agree with you. If you can't play the game right you don't deserve to play at this level. Which means I need to get back to work."

"What?" he asked, disappointment flashing across his features in the form of a furrowed brow, but Molly put her hand lightly on his leg and he said, "Okay, I hope we can see you tomorrow."

"I look forward to it." Every minute she wasn't with them, part of her would wish she were. She wanted to spend time chatting with Joe or wrestling with Charlie. Mostly, though, she wanted more time with Molly, time to sit close and listen to her talk like they had after her first date with Lauren. They'd been so close there. She'd held Duke spellbound. If she'd suspected Molly was special before, that night had confirmed it.

Molly was strong, smart, resourceful, noble, and inspiring. She was exactly the type of person Duke would want to build a life with, but was that a real possibility? She also dreamed of a life spent around the game of baseball. She'd worked for years, and through steadfast dedication and single-minded focus she'd achieved her goal. She loved her life. She loved her work. Maybe she could fall in love with Molly, too, but what would she have to give up to find out?

❖

"Hey, Duke, Simon Beach here."

"Two calls from my editor in one day," Duke sighed. She'd almost made it out the door without any more problems. The locker room had been quiet after the Cardinals' loss. Players not eager to talk generally meant she had less to write about, and she'd turned in a short, comprehensive game report with plenty of time to spare. At least she thought she had. "It's not that I don't love to chat with you, but I get the feeling something's up."

"Yeah, I wish I could deny it, but I actually do have to address a problem here."

Her palms instantly began to sweat. She'd been writing about baseball since her freshman year in high school, and she'd never had an editor rate her performance as anything but stellar. She didn't even know what to say now, so she leaned against the concrete wall outside the press booth to brace herself. "Okay, um. Lay it on me."

"I'm not trying to bust your chops. I'm trying to understand how one of my best reporters missed the hottest items on the stove tonight."

"Um. I'm sorry?"

"Yeah, that's what I'm talking about. You've got nothing.

SportsCenter keeps showing the Cayden Brooks play, and I've seen several other pieces on the ruling online already, but you didn't even mention the changed ruling."

"I tweeted the play."

"You tweeted it as an error."

Her stomach dropped. "Hey, hold on for a sec, please."

She put her hand over the phone and stepped around the corner back into the press booth. The only writer left in the box glanced up from his papers. "Hey, Coop, what did they rule the Brooks play in the first inning?"

He regarded her over the rim of his reading glasses much the same way a teacher looks at student who's asked a stupid question. "If you'd been in here in the first inning, maybe you would've heard the ruling."

"Seriously?" She didn't feel much like bantering right now.

"Hey, you could always read about it in the paper tomorrow morning. You know, use the print media to save your skin before you use it to line your litter box."

She stared at him for a long, heavy moment, disbelief turning to frustration and adding to the fire under her skin. Whether he was legitimately pissed or hoping to use this as some sort of sadistic teaching moment, he wouldn't tell her what'd happened.

Uncovering the phone, she returned her attention to Simon. "Hey, I'm sorry. About everything. I'm going to do a separate piece on the whole Brooks thing tonight. You'll have it for morning roll call. Something's going on with him."

"Fine, but he's not the only one dropping the ball right now, Duke. These mistakes are highly irregular for you. I want to know what's going on."

"I won't make excuses. I messed up. I wasn't where I needed to be on this play. It won't happen again."

"I hope not. You're a good writer, and personally, I like you. I'm not one of the many people hoping to see you fail at this job, but if this trend continues, the vacation days I mentioned won't be optional. Got it?"

Her heart rate accelerated, and her cheeks burned with embarrassment. She hadn't been reprimanded since she was a child, and never for anything even remotely related to baseball. The little dig about people wanting her to fail hit home too. "I got it."

Simon hung up, and Duke stood staring at her phone for several more minutes. What was happening to her life? She couldn't do anything right these days. Her disorientation and uncertainty had been hard enough when they centered on Molly. Women were supposed to be confusing, but baseball had always offered a refuge.

She shook her head and lifted her messenger bag off the concourse floor. Now wasn't the time for introspection. She'd have to face those larger questions eventually, but before that, she had to go back to work. She'd already dropped the ball once tonight. She couldn't afford to do so again.

❖

The sunlight streaked through Molly's hair, revealing natural highlights of auburn and chocolate. Duke fought the desire to run her fingers through the long, graceful strands. She had to remain impersonal and impartial tonight, but it wasn't easy to keep her distance when Molly spotted her and gave her a smile so radiant, it could have made a statue's knees buckle. No, she couldn't think that way. If her knees felt weak, she had only her late night to blame.

She'd stayed at the ballpark until almost two o'clock in the morning trying to drum up anything that might help her offer the readers some insight on Cayden Brooks and the play in question, but Cayden had only himself to blame, and in one post-game interview on ESPN, he'd practically said as much before retreating to the showers. Everything about the play screamed error. And errors happened. No matter how much fans and writers tried to paint ballplayers as demigods, they were human. Nothing struck her as out of the ordinary about the error except for the fact that the official scorer hadn't ruled it an error.

Official scorers were supposed to be neutral and employed by the league instead of individual teams to prevent the appearance of impropriety, but like the players, they were human and tended to have a slight home-field bias. Every judgment call had a winner and loser, but there was no statistical neon sign to explain the ruling.

Ultimately Duke had published a short blog on the play and concluded both Cayden Brooks and the Cardinal's official scorer had committed errors, but something still didn't feel right about the situation. Perhaps she'd missed some connection between the ruling and Cayden's inflammatory comments before the game. Or maybe she merely wished for a bigger story to help cover up her own errors in reporting the event. The latter worried her most of all.

"You're clearly in work mode today." Molly interrupted her musing.

"Sorry," Duke said, flopping into an open chair, quickly checking to be sure she didn't bump Charlie, who was sitting cross-legged on the ground with a single-serve box of Cheerios.

Molly put her hand lightly on Duke's arm. "It's okay. You're allowed to focus on work, especially while you're at work."

"I know. I feel bad because I wish I could spend more time with you and the kids without having to give up my work time."

"That's sweet of you, and we appreciate your time. The boys love being around you, and I..." She moved her hand, a hint of pink tinting her complexion. "I do, too."

"Really?" Hope pushed professional concerns to the side once more, but the seesawing from personal to professional drained her energy.

"Of course. Don't you realize that? I've told you things I haven't told anyone in years. I've trusted you with my children. I wouldn't have done so if you weren't special to me."

The heat under her skin made Duke suspect her blush mirrored Molly's now.

"We all look forward to seeing you at the games, but it's not a game for you. It's a job and a passion. I envy that. Passion isn't something I've had much of in my life." She frowned slightly, sadly.

"You have the boys. You're passionate about them. And there's Lauren—"

"No." Molly shook her head slowly. "There's no more Lauren. We broke it off. Well, I did."

Duke's chest felt impossibly small compared to her heart. "I don't know what to say. I'm sorry. I don't understand what happened. I thought you two were close to something."

"We were close, but not quite right. We lacked spark, passion. In a way, you helped me see that."

Guilt kept her from soaring at the admission. "I didn't mean to come between you two."

"I didn't mean to imply you did." Molly rushed to correct her. "I didn't mean to implicate you romantically at all. It's not like that."

"Oh?" The little noise was all she could manage around her disappointment.

"I only meant the passion you bring to everything you do, whether it's helping me with the kids or talking about baseball, helped me see what I've been missing."

"Passion?"

"Yes, passion. I haven't inspired it in myself or in others."

"Molly, how can you even think…" Duke's thoughts swirled around her head, the logical battling the emotional for supremacy, but both sides lost when Joe came racing up the stairs from where he'd been studying the field.

"Hey, Duke," he said tossing his arms around her shoulder. "I read your article on the Cayden Brooks play. You were totally right. He made an error. I think he didn't want to run into the wall. He should've kept his eye on the ball."

The greater message clearly went over his head but lodged firmly in Duke's chest. "He's still learning a lot about himself and how to play the game. We all are."

"Are you going to sit with us today?"

"Actually, I'm not." She stood, at the reminder she wasn't on her personal time, no matter how personal the conversation had gotten. "I have to focus on work."

He nodded stoically. "I understand. You have the coolest job in the world."

"I sure do," she said, but for the first time the sentiment seemed forced. "I gotta get going. I need to make a call before the game starts."

"Are you okay?" Molly asked.

"I think so, but in case I have a few questions, will you be around this weekend?"

Molly's lips quirked up with a hint of amusement or curiosity. "I'm off Saturday and Sunday."

"Good," Duke said, then sprinted up the stairs, pulling out her phone as she went and redialing the last number on her caller ID.

"Simon Beach here."

"Hey, Beach, it's Sarah Duke."

"What's up? I already signed off on your pre-game notes. They looked great, as was the Brooks piece. You're back on track so far."

"Yeah, about that." Part of her didn't believe she was about to ask the question on her lips. "What if I wanted a few days off the track?"

"What?"

"You mentioned I have unused vacation days."

"Really? You want today off?"

"No, not today. This weekend. The series in Milwaukee, but I'll be back for the All-Star Game next week."

He chuckled. "No desire to see the Brew City or their consistently underperforming team?"

"It's not so much a desire to avoid something so much as a desire to explore something else."

"Uh-huh. Sounds personal and perfectly suited to a personal day."

"It's not that I don't love the job, it's just—"

"No need to explain."

"Oh, okay. I've never done this before."

"Taken a vacation day?"

"I've never taken my eye off the ball."

"Ah, well, you know, in life sometimes there's more than one ball in the air at any given time."

"Multiple walls to run into, too."

He laughed. "You really aren't someone who ever stops thinking about the game, are you?"

"I'm not sure I know how."

"I'll tell you how. File your report after tomorrow afternoon's game, then cancel your hotel in Milwaukee. I'll get some local coverage for you. I don't want to hear from you until Monday unless something major hits. Sound easy enough?"

"I got it, thanks." She hung up. Checking out of work might be as easy as he said, but this vacation wasn't about getting away from something so much as getting closer to something new, and the thought of taking her eye off the ball didn't scare her nearly as much as the prospect of chasing a shadow right into a wall.

BOTTOM OF THE FOURTH

Better Than the Box Score

"The penguins are my favorites." Duke looked up at Charlie the best she could with him sitting on her shoulders. "Do you mind if we go see them before we get some cotton candy?"

"Do penguins swim?" Charlie asked.

"They do, and sometimes when they dive they make bubbles. Want to see?"

"Yes." He grabbed two fistfuls of her hair like reins and steered her toward the penguin house.

Molly couldn't believe she was at the zoo on a Friday night in July. The whole excursion seemed too idyllic to be part of her real life. She would've normally been hesitant to bring Charlie to a place with real lions by herself for fear he'd try to move in with them. And Joe had no interest in staring at animals when baseball could be seen on TV or in person. If she'd suggested this trip, he would've argued he was too old for the zoo and wanted to stay home to watch the game, but the excursion had been Duke's idea, which carried a lot of weight with him. Though, to be honest, he might have argued with Duke, too, if he weren't so shocked to hear she'd taken the weekend off of her own free will.

In fairness, the news had thrown Molly a little off balance, too. She got the sense Duke didn't miss work often, if ever, and she'd said nothing about the upcoming vacation until she'd called after yesterday's game to invite them all to the zoo.

Twenty-four hours later, she still had no answers as to what prompted the vacation or the desire to spend her first night off with the boys. Duke seemed more carefree and open than she'd ever seen her, laughing easily and chasing Charlie so Molly didn't have to. Still, something seemed different about her. Maybe she was always more relaxed away from work, or maybe it was the way her eyes seemed to linger on Molly longer and more often without a ball game to turn toward. Perhaps the echo of their conversation about passion still hung in the air between them, but whatever the reason, there seemed to be something deeper below Duke's good-natured façade.

"You want pink or blue cotton candy?" Duke asked the boys as they stood in line at a food cart a little later.

"Blue," they answered in unison.

"And you?" she asked Molly.

"None for me. I'm more of a popcorn kind of gal."

"Salty instead of sweet, why doesn't that surprise me?"

She raised her eyebrows, and Duke blushed instantly. She'd never had the power to make anyone bashful before, and while she suspected Duke to be easier than most, she enjoyed it nonetheless.

"Two blue cotton candies, one pink, and a large popcorn, please," she ordered, then passed out the treats, keeping the pink cotton candy for herself.

Joe eyed her suspiciously.

"What, you got a problem with my pink cotton candy?"

"No, I just…you don't usually seem like someone who likes…" His voice trailed off as he looked from Duke to Molly and clearly realized the odds of getting a gender stereotype lecture, then switched gears quickly. "Anyway, I didn't get to see the Cardinals game yesterday. I went to the science center with a friend."

"The science center sounds fun," Duke said enthusiastically, causing Molly to smile. She hadn't bitten on the baseball bait as Joe clearly intended.

"Yeah, it's okay, but I missed the game."

"It was a good game," Duke admitted, "but I've never been to the science center."

This time Joe refused the redirect. "How could it be a good game? The Cardinals lost. They dropped the whole series *to the Royals*. And now they aren't even in first place anymore. They're tied with the Pirates. Aren't you worried?"

"I'm not. Not yet anyway. We've had a rough patch, but I think they've been playing pretty well."

"How can they play well and lose to a team in last place?"

"This is one of the odd occasions where we're better than the box score."

"What does that mean?"

"It means at the end of the game, all the scoreboard tells you is the important stats. The hits, the runs, the errors, the final score, but it actually tells you very little about what happened over the nine innings that led to those final results."

"Like what?" Joe asked, his eyes wide with attention. Molly couldn't blame him. Even she couldn't resist the pull of Duke's magnetism when she talked about the broader lessons of baseball.

"Well, for instance, yesterday's score column didn't tell you we had five or six players smash the ball, just right, at opposing players. It may tell you our starting pitcher gave up three runs in the first inning, but it doesn't indicate he fanned seven of the next nine hitters. It tells you the Cards recorded all the requisite outs, but it doesn't say Cayden Brooks made a leaping catch near the outfield wall to rob the Royals of a home run in the ninth. The box score also doesn't mention that our bullpen hasn't given up a hit in three games."

"Wow," Molly said.

"Impressive, no?" Duke grinned.

The stats were impressive. Molly was even more awestruck that Duke not only remembered all of them, but also strung them together to paint a picture so different than what ordinary people would see.

"Hits, runs, and errors certainly tell you who won, and if that's all you care about, it's all you need. The stat sheets give you a snapshot of the game, but it's a black-and-white one. There's no stat to quantify the hustle from first to third on a single, or the fortitude a batter needs to go deep into the count to make the pitcher reveal his best stuff earlier than he wants to."

"So the papers show the big picture, but not the full picture?"

"Exactly. We love a game of inches, of split seconds, the sum of many moving parts. Normally doing everything right leads to the W, but sometimes a team's performance can add up to something better than the score can reveal."

"I get it now."

"Good." She tugged the bill of his ball cap over his eyes, which pushed his glasses askew. "'Cause I'm done talking baseball for tonight. It's my day off and yours, too. Go be a kid and chase your brother for a while."

Molly watched him run off, then she and Duke flopped onto the nearest seat. Their bodies molded exhaustedly to the park bench overlooking the children's playground while Joe chased Charlie underneath a spiderweb-inspired jungle gym. After visually scanning their surroundings to make sure they were safely corralled in the play area, she turned her attention to Duke. Her blond hair stood straight up where Charlie had braced himself, and Molly couldn't resist the urge to smooth it out, or maybe she simply didn't want to resist. She ran her fingers through the short, fair strands, finding them softer than she'd imagined. She shouldn't have been surprised. Everything about Duke, from her hands to her heart, seemed softer than she'd first suspected.

Well, maybe not everything. Tonight she'd traded her khakis for a pair of frayed gray shorts that showed off muscled calves and tanned thighs, neither of which appeared soft. The thin, worn T-shirt she wore in place of her usual polo offered enough outline of her torso to suggest she hadn't gone soft there, either. The look was more than relaxed, cool, confident, and undeniably sexy.

Duke turned to look at her, causing Molly to realize she'd been playing with her hair more than fixing it. She removed her hand slowly. "Sorry, it was just sticking up a little bit."

"Thanks." Her smile caused a little flutter in Molly's stomach. "And hi."

"Hi."

"We haven't gotten to talk much tonight with the boys on the go."

"Such is life with boys who are *always* on the go. There's rarely a minute to think, much less chat."

"There's now," Duke offered. "What are you thinking right now?"

"I'm thinking…" *I'm thinking your eyes are so blue. I'm thinking I don't know what to think when you look at me that way. I'm thinking I can't tell you any of this.* "I'm thinking I like you at the baseball park, but I may like you even better away from it."

Her smile widened to encompass her cheeks and the corners of her eyes. "Thank you. I wasn't sure I could do this, take a night off when the Cardinals didn't have one, but with you, it's easier than I expected."

They sat quietly for a few minutes, letting the revelation settle over them, before Molly decided to push for more.

"All right, Sarah Duke, your turn to spill. What prompted this vacation you're on?"

She shifted on the bench, crossing one leg over the other, then straightening them out in front of herself once more. "I guess it's like I said to Joe. I love baseball. I love my job. I wouldn't trade it for anything, but sometimes when I'm around you and the boys, I wonder if maybe there could be more to me than my job."

"So you took some time off to explore?"

"Yes."

"And what have you learned so far?"

"Well, it's been only one night, so I don't want to overstate anything, but I'm more relaxed than I expected. I'm capable of having fun doing something other than baseball. I haven't thought about the game nearly as much as I expected. All good things." She ran her hand through the patch of hair Molly had recently touched. "The best news of the whole night is that you like me outside the ballpark. That's a big part of what I hoped to accomplish."

Where was she going? "You hoped to make me like you?"

She blushed. "Among other things, but yeah, pretty much."

"You didn't know I already liked you?"

"Well, the other night you said you loved being around me, but we haven't been around each other much outside of my work, so I sort of hoped we could test that theory a little bit more this weekend."

Her heart rate accelerated. Was Duke asking her out?

"You see, I'm going to my niece's first birthday party on Saturday. It's at my parents' house. They have a pool. The boys could swim and play, and I'd drive, so you know it wouldn't cost anything…"

"Are you asking us to come with you to a family gathering?"

"Well, I mean, not like that. Not like come meet my family, but yeah. It wouldn't have to be a big deal, except it would mean a lot to me, and fun. Did I mention there would be cake?" Duke exhaled. "I'd like for you all to join me."

Duke's first date offer, if a family pool party could be considered a date, certainly wasn't as smooth or as polished as Lauren's had been. For someone who made her living with words, Duke didn't seem nearly as well versed in the romantic category. Then again, maybe simpler was better, or maybe the sincerity of the request stuck in her chest so fully it displaced her usual misgivings, because for some reason Molly didn't feel nearly as conflicted about her answer as she had the last time someone had asked her out.

"That sounds like a lot of fun."

"Really?"

She laughed. "Don't sound so surprised."

"I am surprised, happily surprised. That was easier than I expected."

"Maybe there's more to me than you are able to read in the box score."

Duke's smile returned with less playfulness than before. "Now, that would not surprise me at all."

❖

What had she been thinking agreeing to come to a family event with Duke? The request had seemed so simple, free of pressure, and easy to accept when it had been only the two of them the night before. Now with Charlie and Joe tucked neatly into the back of Duke's RAV4 as they exited Interstate 44 toward Union, Missouri, the excursion felt like a much bigger deal. She was going to spend an entire afternoon with Duke's family, and what's more, she'd brought her children. She'd always known her kids would be part of her dating life someday, and she'd never let herself get close to someone who didn't mesh with them, but she'd also thought she'd protect them from getting too attached to anyone she dated until she felt certain the relationship would last. She'd never considered the possibility that they might already be attached before she even seriously considered going on a date.

A date? Most of the time it didn't feel like she and Duke were on a date. Dates didn't involve children. Dates didn't involve parents. Dates didn't usually involve midday drives to middle-of-nowhere Missouri. She could generally convince herself they weren't on a date at all until Duke would glance away from the windshield long enough to make eye contact. When their eyes met, Duke communicated a hope she couldn't deny feeling, too.

"Can we at least watch the game at your parents' house?" Joe asked, obviously still trying to work through his conflicting emotions about the schedule for the day. His excitement about being invited to Duke's family's home warred with his discomfort about the two of them missing yet another game, and this time to attend a birthday party for a baby.

"Absolutely." Duke pulled the car onto a residential street at the edge of town. "You're headed into friendly territory, Joe. Almost everyone there today will be as excited about the game as you. It'll be on in the living room and the kitchen, and they'll listen to it on the radio out by the pool."

The news seemed to relax him a little. "And we'll get there before first pitch?"

"We're here now." Duke pulled into the driveway of a tidy little ranch home with beautiful landscaping.

"Good." He unbuckled his seat belt and reached for the door, but Molly stopped him in mid-grab.

"Freeze. No one goes anywhere until we lay down the ground rules." She turned in her seat until she could see both boys. "I want best behavior. That means your table manners, yes ma'ams, pleases, and no thank yous. Got it?"

Both boys nodded.

"I want you to be polite to Duke's family and careful around the pool. Sunscreen for both of you, and floaties for Charlie anytime we're outside."

"Yes ma'am," Joe replied.

Charlie added a "Yes, Mama."

"And you." She turned to face Duke. "No running off with your brothers as soon as we walk in the door."

"Yes, ma'am," she answered with only a hint of irony.

"I'm serious. You need to make proper introductions and stay by our sides until we get acclimated. I haven't been to an event like this since before Joe was born."

"Really?"

"Yes, really. Tony's family was entirely too formal for pool parties or cookouts."

"But what about your family's—"

Her stern glare did its job of cutting off the line of questioning, and Duke recovered quickly. "Right, stay by your side. No argument there."

"Thank you." She nodded and unbuckled. "Then let's go."

They got out of the car, but before Molly could turn to undo Charlie's car seat, Duke gave her hand a little squeeze.

The move was sweet and reassuring, but the intensity in her eyes carried something deeper, more intimate. "My family's close. I can't promise we won't get rowdy or goofy or socially awkward, but I promise you won't feel alone today."

And she hadn't. An hour later they sat together in folding chairs between the main pool and the kiddie version Duke's parents had set up nearby for the little ones. Charlie splashed happily in the children's pool while Joe dangled his feet in the deeper water and talked baseball with Duke's younger brother, Nate, as they listened to the start of the game on the radio. Duke's mother and sister-in-law were inside with the napping birthday girl. Her father and older brother drank beer on the patio. Everyone seemed happy and accounted for.

The Duke gene pool was nothing if not persistent. Duke's siblings all had their father's coloring: sandy hair with complexions that seemed almost golden in the sun. The only major indicator of Duke's mother's involvement was her daughter's bright blue eyes, though those were currently covered by a pair of aviator sunglasses.

"Those two hit it off," Duke said, nodding in Joe and Nate's direction.

"Yes, I heard them talking about on-base percentages versus batting averages earlier."

"That's not surprising. We all love sports, but Nate's the intellectual of the family, while Aidan's more of the natural athlete."

"And which one are you?"

"The middle child. Not the oldest, not the youngest, and not happy about being the only girl."

"Your parents noticed you only for the wrong reasons?"

Duke shifted in her seat, reminding Molly she was almost absurdly protective of her parents. "I wouldn't say that exactly, but…"

"It's okay. Me too."

"You're a middle child?"

"One of them, anyway. Two older and two younger. Three boys and two girls total."

"Wow, that's a lot of kids. How did you ever get noticed at all?"

"I didn't usually, unless I got in trouble." She kept her voice steady and light despite all the memories that could've overwhelmed her. She'd had plenty of practice keeping them at bay. "Usually for sassing my parents or refusing to fit their expectations of how young ladies should behave."

"What—you? Speaking your mind?" Duke feigned disbelief. "I can't picture you bucking up against authority at all."

Molly smiled despite the fact that those encounters hadn't seemed funny at the time. "I guess I've always been independent. Maybe that's why I'm not tougher on Charlie. I should probably make him eat better or rein in his wild streak, but I remember what it felt like to chafe against their ideas of who I should be. I want my boys to be themselves with me without having to fear…" She trailed off, not wanting to even think about the end of that sentence.

"You're an amazing mom, Molly." Duke turned to face her, but Molly couldn't see her eyes under the dark glasses. Still, her voice held only sincerity. "And you're raising two wonderful sons. I'm not a parent, but if I were you I wouldn't change a thing."

"Thank you. I'm not sure about the amazing part. I make plenty of mistakes, but I know I won't make the same ones my parents did."

"Earlier, I got the sense you didn't want to talk about your family."

"I don't usually." Maybe the family-centered setting or the relaxed atmosphere opened the door to subjects she normally avoided. Talking about her family reminded her of a time when she'd felt terrified, isolated, judged, and worst of all, vulnerable. Duke made her feel safe and secure and admired in a way that balanced out or even overruled the emotions tied to her past. "They're conservative, my parents. Ultra-religious—not the loving, faithful kind, the fire-and-brimstone variety."

"How did they handle your coming out?" Duke asked cautiously.

"They didn't. They never got that far. They threw me out when I got pregnant with Joe."

"What?" Duke sat up, planting both of her sandal-clad feet on the ground between them and snatching off her sunglasses.

"Sex before marriage is a sin." She tried to shrug off the comment, but she couldn't help steal a glance at Joe. "They saw him as my punishment and couldn't stand the living reminder of my shame."

Duke's face flamed an angry shade of red, the bright blue of her eyes fading to ice. "Sin? Punishment? Shame? How can anyone look at that boy and not see what a miracle he is?"

Molly's eyes filled with tears she'd held back for a decade, and Duke's hardened features melted as quickly as they'd frozen. "I'm sorry. I didn't mean to upset you. I wanted to keep things light today. I'm not good at small talk, though."

"No." Molly pressed one of Duke's hands between her own, feeling the strength shrouded in softness, a combination that carried through all the way to Duke's heart. "You're very good, actually. You expressed my feelings on the subject perfectly. That's why I got choked up. I was happy you saw the situation so clearly. People usually react with pity. That's why I quit telling them."

"Pity for who? I hate that you had to go through such a major life event without a supportive family, but you got the better parts of everything. You got your freedom, you cleared your life of people who didn't love you like you deserved, and you got Joe." Duke's smile once again encompassed her whole face at the mention of his name. "The only person I might pity is your family for not getting the chance to know him, but honestly, I can't find any sadness in myself for people who choose judgment over something as beautiful as the life you created."

Duke had reached inside her heart and given voice to her most deeply held beliefs. The feeling of connection, of belonging, of relief pushed out from her center, expanding her chest, washing out through her limbs. Riding the wave of emotion, she impulsively kissed Duke on the cheek. "Thank you."

Her eyes widened, and she lifted her finger to the spot Molly's lips had touched as the area blushed crimson. "For what?"

"For being so…so you."

"Sarah's got a girlfriend. Sarah's got a girlfriend," Aidan called from across the pool. Molly looked up to find everyone looking in their direction. How long had they been watching?

"Shut up," Duke called.

"Shut up's a bad word, Duke," Charlie called in a singsong voice loud enough for everyone to hear.

The whole family laughed, breaking the tension. Molly quickly looked to Joe, who was laughing along. If the girlfriend comment bothered him, it didn't show.

Duke's blush deepened, and her eyes narrowed like a cat ready to pounce, but she turned back to Molly. "I didn't tell him you were my...I mean, he's just...he teases me."

"And what do you usually do when he teases you?"

She grinned slightly. "I usually dunk him."

"But?"

"You asked me to stay with you."

Molly squeezed her hand tightly once more, then let go. "You have my permission to go throw your brother in the pool."

That was all the encouragement Duke needed. She already wore a pair of red swim trunks, but she stood and stripped off her baggy Cardinals T-shirt, revealing a sleek black swim shirt that hugged her skin tightly enough to showcase the indent of her oblique muscles. Molly hadn't given any previous thought to what kind of swimsuit Duke would wear, but now she couldn't imagine her in anything else. The combo was tomboyish and playful on the surface but showcased a powerful female form underneath. Molly couldn't do anything but stare as Duke strode confidently around the pool.

"Hello there, little sister." Aidan smirked. "Nice to see you."

"Yeah, it's been a while. How about a hug?"

Aidan rose slowly until he stood several inches taller than Duke. He also carried at least an extra forty pounds.

"You might want to get your wallet out of your pocket," Duke warned. She had everyone's attention now as they all stopped what they were doing to watch the exchange. Even her mother stepped into the doorway from the kitchen.

"Getting a little cocky up in the big leagues, are we?" He chuckled, looking her up and down as if sizing her up. She wasn't a small woman, but compared to his build, she didn't look like much of a challenge. Still, he must have seen something there or maybe he'd learned from past experience because he reached in his pocket and tossed his wallet onto the patio table.

Duke lunged. She struck fast with a ferocious bear hug, pinning Aidan's arms to his side and lifting him off the ground. Caught off guard, he stumbled a few steps toward the pool, but she couldn't carry him the whole way. He regained his footing a few feet from the edge and crouched low in a wide stance. They scuffled and twisted, both of them scraping for more leverage. Aidan could have probably overpowered her if Duke hadn't gotten the better position early on. She slid lower and worked her shoulder into his chest, then with one last thrust sent him over the edge. The splash of his body sent a wave crashing over the wall, and Duke did a little rain dance in the puddle.

Everyone cheered and laughed, even Aidan as he bobbed up and down in the deep end. "Good to know you haven't gone doughy sitting in the press box all day."

Molly shook her head. Nothing about Duke could ever be described as doughy, and she'd be damned if that didn't turn her on a little bit.

"No hard feelings?" Duke asked.

"Not at all," he answered overenthusiastically and reached out to her. "Give me a hand up?"

Duke shook her head. "Not a chance."

"Sarah," her mother warned in a tone only a mother can use. "Don't be a poor sport. Go help your brother up."

She sighed heavily but didn't dare argue with her mom. "Yes ma'am."

Seeming resigned to her fate, she neared the edge of the pool and extended her hand to Aidan. He wasted no time in taking the peace offering and using it to pull her in beside him. She curled into the water with much more grace than he had, then surfaced a few feet away and shook the water out of her hair. If Molly had found her sexy before she dove into the pool, the wet and disheveled look pushed her over an edge of her own.

God, what had come over her today? Duke wasn't her type at all. She didn't tick any of the boxes on Molly's must-have list. She wasn't feminine, or even pretty really. She wasn't quiet or refined. She didn't lead a normal, steady life. Sure, she had a good job, a cool job, but she didn't work normal hours or bring any sort of consistency to their lives. She liked boys' games and roughhousing instead of bubble baths and romantic comedies. She liked hot dogs and soda instead of wine and fine dining. Duke had nothing in common with the woman Molly'd dreamed of meeting.

Duke splashed Joe, teasing him away from the radio and into the water. Molly had to concede one point to Duke: she was amazing with the boys. The one item she did satisfy on Molly's wish list in a partner happened to be a pretty big one. And while she was being honest, Duke wasn't as feminine as the type of women she generally found attractive, but she did have more than a few appealing physical features. Her eyes, for one, were enthralling; her hands, too, soft and strong, with long, graceful fingers. Today's swimwear also revealed a few of the curves her work clothes often kept hidden, though even her usual khakis flattered her hips and backside.

"May I join you?" Lorelei Duke interrupted Molly's thoughts.

"Of course." She hadn't had much time to talk to the matriarch of the Duke family yet, but she liked her, and Lorelei had doted on the boys all afternoon, stuffing them with treats and spoiling them with compliments. "Thank you so much for having us. It's been such a wonderful day."

"I'm glad you're enjoying yourself."

"I am, very much so. And the pool is such a nice way to keep the kids cool on a hot day." She smiled as Charlie jumped from the edge into Duke's arms. She made motorboat noises and spun him around.

Lorelei laughed lightly. "Then again, some of the kids are bigger than others."

"Sometimes she does seem like one of the boys."

"She always has," Lorelei said wistfully. "When I had a girl I envisioned pink dresses and pigtails, baking and baby dolls. Instead she wanted grass-stained jeans, muddy boots, and baseball. Always baseball. When she told me she favored women, I thought, thank God she's got an interest in something that doesn't involve a bat and a ball."

Molly marveled at the admission of how Duke's upbringing differed from her own. "So you're saying nothing much has changed."

"She's been pretty much the same person from the time she turned eight until a couple months ago."

"Oh, what happened then?"

"I'm not certain, but the day we met you at the stadium, Sarah seemed different. She paid attention to you and your sons, even with the expanse of her home field in front of her. She turned to you and Joe for affirmation instead of to her father. I've never seen her seek anyone's approval but his."

"Not even yours?"

Lorelei waved her off. "She never had to work for mine. Dale always presented more of a challenge for her, and her for him. They've danced around each other their whole lives. His interests always became her interests until she saw him next to your family. Now when she calls, she's as likely to tell us stories about Joe or Charlie as she is about baseball."

"I didn't know." Molly remembered that day, but she'd been in mom mode, eager to protect Joe. She hadn't considered Lorelei might have also been seeing her child in a new way. "I'm surprised she thinks of us outside of the ballpark."

"Are you? She brought you here, and on a game day no less."

All true. She'd known instinctively this weekend was important for Duke, for all of them maybe. She'd admitted last night she was learning to see herself differently. Maybe Molly was seeing her differently, too, or maybe not new so much as a more complete version of the woman she'd already known was special. Watching her wrestle with her brother showed a physicality Molly'd never seen before. Talking with her about her own family showcased first ferocity, then tenderness and understanding of someone she could confide in. Seeing her brother's teasing, her mother's adoration, her father's challenge made Molly marvel even more at Lorelei's comments about Duke choosing to share that kind of attention and affection with her.

Molly could practically feel her heart opening, expanding, as Duke took hold of an ever bigger piece. She tried to remember her earlier internal arguments about why Duke wasn't her type. She attempted once more to list all the reasons she didn't fit the list in her head, but every time she looked at her, bright-eyed, playful, attentive, and even sexy, she had a harder time summoning the image of some abstract dream date she'd so recently held in her mind. Duke might not have been anything like the woman she'd wanted to fall for, and yet she was falling for her anyway. Maybe there was no logical explanation, or maybe Sarah Duke had simply revealed herself as better than her box score, too.

TOP OF THE FIFTH

Don't Mess with a Winning Streak

"Hey, Pop, need any help with the grill?" Duke asked as her dad loaded a platter with ground beef patties.

He eyed her seriously for a moment as if trying to decide if she was up to the task. His serious gaze served as a mirror to her own. She was used to these moments of scrutiny. He usually decided she was fit for whatever duty she'd volunteered for, especially since she'd grown into adulthood, but part of her still held her breath until he handed down his verdict.

He finally nodded. "Yeah, actually, grab the tongs and the grill spatula. And get me a beer while you're at it."

She tried not to let him see her grin as she collected his tools and a cold can from the fridge before following him out.

He'd set the grill up in the backyard far enough away from the pool that he wouldn't have to worry about the kids running into it or splashing water on any of the food, but he still had a clear sight line to the rest of the party. This was his domain, and she was happy to share it with him.

They hadn't had a chance to talk much throughout the afternoon. She'd spent the first part of the day engrossed in Molly, then got lost in the fun of playing with the kids and her brothers. Now she caught a glimpse of Molly and her sister-in-law chatting comfortably by the baby pool while Charlie and her niece poured water over each other's toes. Her mom had enlisted Joe in setting up the table, and she could hear her fussing over what a helpful young man he was. Now with the sizzle of the first burgers hitting the grill and the charcoal scent of flames licking the fat, all was right with the world. She sat down on a lounge chair and folded her hands behind her head. She couldn't remember the last time she felt so at peace.

"What are you doing, Sarah?" her dad asked, quietly.

She looked up. "Excuse me?"

"I asked what you're doing."

She looked from him to the chair she was sitting on. Was he disappointed she was lazing around? "I didn't want to get in your way. Did you need something? Or was this your chair?"

He shook his head. "It's a game day. The Cardinals are in Milwaukee only one game out of first place. Why are you here?"

"I had a few days off."

"You had a few days off, or you asked for a few days off?"

She looked down, noting the contrast between the pale skin of her bare feet and the green of the grass. The yard seemed dull and flat compared to the shade of green at the ballpark. Funny she hadn't realized that until now. "I took a few days off."

"Why?"

"I haven't missed a game all season. I had the vacation time coming. My editor suggested it." Somehow all the logical reasons sounded like little more than the excuses she'd employed for not doing her homework as a teenager, and they met with the same disappointed stare.

"I've never known you to need a day off. Not in college when you had a full load of classes. Not in the minor leagues when you had to drive your own way to all the games. Why now?"

He was right, of course. She'd worked longer days under rougher conditions without ever wanting even a few hours of sleep. She couldn't blame him for finding her actions surprising. What didn't make sense, though, was why he suddenly cared. "Where is this coming from?"

"That's what I'm asking you," he said. "This isn't like you. You worked too hard to get to where you are. You're at the top of your game. Why risk everything now?"

"Dad, I don't know where this is coming from. You've never seemed the least bit interested in *my game* before. Why does it matter whether I'm in the big leagues or on the bench?"

He rolled his eyes. "You see what I mean? When did you get so lippy? That's not like you. I've never questioned your dedication before because I've never had to. You were always a worker. I never worried about whether or not you'd make it to the show."

He'd never said anything like that to her. Ever. She hadn't seen her arrival in the big leagues as a foregone conclusion, and she wouldn't have thought he had either. He certainly hadn't acted as though he expected anything from her. He hardly ever asked her about work. He never mentioned reading her columns. They talked baseball constantly, but he hardly ever acted like she had any more to say on the subject than she had when she was ten. She'd always thought she hadn't proved herself to him yet. Could it really be he'd not shown an interest in her career because he didn't have anything of value to add to it? "Okay."

"Okay what?"

"So you never worried about me making it. You thought I could make it all along." She shrugged and tried to shake off the foreign sensations accompanying the sentiment. "What's changed? My taking my first day off since I was twenty?"

"Is that all you're doing? 'Cause it looks to me like you're playing house with some woman and her children."

She rose to her feet quickly. "That's not fair. Not to me and not to her."

He raised his eyebrows, making it clear she'd blown any casual cover she'd tried to project. "That's something we agree on. It's not fair to either of you. You're one of the youngest writers in the major leagues and the only woman working for your website. Why would you risk all that? For some woman?"

"I'm not risking anything, and she's not some random woman," she said with all the adamancy she could muster, while trying not to think about her recent conversations with her editor, the missed plays, or all the time she spent outside of the press box during games. "Molly is not a risk to my career."

"If you both believe that, you're lying either to yourself or to her. You work one hundred and sixty-two games a year, plus pre- and post-season. If you count spring training, you're on the road for more than half of the time. You work late nights and weekends. Your job is more than full-time, as is being a partner and a parent. I know you, Sarah. You don't do anything halfway. You can't give a hundred percent to two different things."

"You did. You have a full-time job and a successful marriage, and you raised three kids."

"I'm a roofer. I go to work in the morning, and I clock out at dusk." He sighed and flipped a couple burgers before continuing. "And still I missed out on things with you and your brothers. I missed school plays and parent-teacher conferences. I didn't drop you off at college or stay home when you were sick."

She heard the regret clearly in his voice and immediately rushed to defend him. "You're a good dad. You provided for us and taught us about hard work. You did your best."

"It doesn't matter now. You can make excuses for me, but if you let yourself get tied down to a wife and kids, will you be able to make the same excuses for yourself?"

Her stomach clenched. She wanted to tell him he'd read the situation wrong, but he'd made some legitimate points. She didn't have a normal job, and she couldn't do it halfway. Would Molly and the boys get the lesser parts of her? She couldn't refute his assertion that she couldn't commit just a part of herself to something she cared about, but she also didn't like his conclusion that she had to give up on part of herself, either. She had no real answers to offer either of them, so instead she dodged the question. "I'm not tied down to Molly. We're not even dating. We're just hanging out."

"You're better than that, Sarah." He lifted a few burgers off the grill. "A woman with kids isn't someone you play around with. Either you're in this thing with her all the way, or you shouldn't string her along. Don't let her come to depend on you. It'll trap you both."

"Molly's a strong woman. She won't be strung along. She doesn't need me or anyone else."

He smiled faintly. "I think you may be right, but it's beside the point. A relationship is a silly risk for both of you right now."

She sighed. This wasn't going anywhere, at least not anywhere she wanted to go. "I don't know what to say."

"You don't have to say anything, but you do need to think about the future you worked so hard to secure." He pointed at her with his grill tongs for emphasis. "You're a baseballer, a gamer, a true believer. You're on the biggest win streak of your life. You know better than anyone that you never mess with a winning streak."

❖

Day had long since faded into night by the time they'd left the party, and both boys fell asleep before they were even back on the interstate. They were still in the long stretch of farmland before reaching the suburbs when Duke felt Molly's fingers brush against hers.

"You're quiet," Molly said. "Did the boys exhaust you today?"

"Maybe a little, but it's a good kind of tired. The sun, the pool, the food, you and the boys by my side. I guess you could say I'm sated."

"Are you sure that's all it is?" Molly asked the question softly as she ran her hand up Duke's arm and twirled her fingers lightly through the hair at the base of her neck. "I saw you talking to your dad before dinner. Looked pretty serious."

Normally any question about her relationship with her father would've made her defensive, but whether it was her tiredness or the soothing effect of Molly's touch, the urge to make excuses wasn't as strong. "My dad is a complicated guy."

"He's tough on you?"

"Not really. Not in the traditional sense. He rode the boys a lot harder. I always thought he wasn't as interested in me, or maybe I hadn't given him enough reason to engage me."

"And now?"

"I don't know. Turns out he might've left me alone because he thought I was doing okay."

"Doing okay at what?"

"Life, apparently." She smiled. "Or baseball, which is pretty much the same thing."

"Did he say that?"

"Actually, he kind of did. He sort of implied he was proud of my accomplishments as a female sportswriter at the big league level."

"That's a big deal."

"I've been waiting my whole life to hear him say that."

"Maybe I'm missing something here. Is there more to this winning streak analogy, because you don't seem very happy."

Her chest constricted. Molly was right. She should've been happier. Her father had given her more praise today than he ever had.

Maybe she shouldn't have cared so much about his approval. She was a grown woman who'd made so many of her own dreams come true without his praise, not some child eager for her dad's attention. Their connection went deeper. He'd given her the game she loved, the game she'd built her life on, and even though she made her living surrounded by the brightest minds in the business, he was still smarter than them all when it came to analyzing a player's makeup. He simply had a brilliant baseball mind. She'd always believed she inherited those traits from him. His passion had become hers, as much as his bloodline or his name.

"It's complicated," Duke admitted.

"How so?" Molly asked, still playing with her hair. The casual touch was new and welcome, but the intimacy of it disarmed Duke's natural defenses. She wasn't sure she liked it, but she didn't want Molly to stop, either.

"I've always thought he was the smartest guy I knew, at least when it came to the things that really mattered. I also thought I had good instincts." She glanced away from the road long enough to meet Molly's deep brown eyes, so full of compassion. "But now I know one of us is wrong."

"Why?" Molly said. "I think you're on a winning streak, too."

"Really?"

"Of course. But not because you write for the major leagues."

"What else is there?"

Molly gave her hair a little tug. "So much more. Having a job you love is great, but you also have a larger passion driving you and people who adore you. You're winning at life in ways much bigger than baseball."

"It never really occurred to me there was anything bigger than baseball, or that I could win at it."

"I believe you can, though I have no idea what sort of baseball cliché you or your father would attach to any of those things that don't happen on the field."

"Actually, I think the lesson is the same, whether he realizes it or not," Duke said, this time focusing not on his doubts but on Molly's belief. Could there really be something more out there for her? Could she have that something more without becoming something less in other areas of her life? Maybe she already did have it all and only needed to learn to recognize it. Despite her fears, or her father's concerns, she'd kept her job and built a good relationship with Charlie and Joe. Even more importantly, she'd managed to endear herself to Molly enough that this amazing woman trusted her, wanted to spend time with her, believed in her. Maybe she could win at more than baseball.

"So?" Molly asked. "What's the great bit of baseball wisdom to come out of all of this?"

"You never mess with a winning streak."

Bottom of the Fifth

Home Run

"I'll get Charlie. You get the bags," Duke whispered as they stood in the parking lot of Molly's apartment complex. Joe, at least, had woken up when they got home and kept himself upright long enough to shuffle his feet ahead of them down the hallway. He rested his head on the wall while Molly fished the keys out of her pocket and got them inside, then he practically sleepwalked to his room. She followed him long enough to make sure he kicked off his shoes before falling into bed.

She hadn't seen him so tired in a long time. She sent up a silent thanks to the Duke family for exhausting both her sons into deep sleeps. She kissed him on the forehead, then closed the door softly behind her.

Duke came down the hall with Charlie asleep on her shoulder. The child did everything full force, even crashing. His cheek pressed against Duke's shoulder and his limbs dangled limply at her sides. Duke had to scoot sideways through the door to angle him toward the bed. Charlie wasn't a petite three-year-old. He was built more like a miniature linebacker or a sandbag, but Duke cradled his head gently all the way down to the pillow. Before she straightened up, she tucked the blanket under his chin and kissed him lightly on top of his head. "Sleep tight, little lion."

Molly's heart tightened once again at her tenderness, and she stepped back into the hallway to gather herself.

"Where did Joe go?" Duke asked after she'd shut the door to Charlie's room.

"Straight to bed. He's beat."

"Yeah, we had a big day."

Molly put her palm on Duke's shoulder and then slid her fingers down along her collarbone. "It was a great day. Thank you."

Duke's pupils dilated, darkening her eyes. They didn't seem as playful now as they had throughout the day. Something had changed on the ride home, as though her resolve had shifted. There was a need in those eyes, a desire Molly felt radiate through her. Duke covered her hand with her own. For a second their fingers intertwined, and Molly's pulse picked up speed. The touch was soft and sensual, the slide of skin against skin making her crave more of the same, but Duke lifted Molly's hand from her chest and stepped slowly away.

"I had a wonderful time today, Molly," she whispered. "I'd like to see you again, outside the ballpark."

"I'd like that, too."

"I don't want to pressure you or go too fast."

Affection mingled with the heat spreading through her body raised the temperature in the hallway to sauna level.

"Mmm-hmm." Duke was being honorable, trying to do the right thing, which made her even harder to resist. They should slow down. The dynamics of their relationship were changing too fast, and they both stood to lose a lot if they made a misstep this early in their relationship, but somehow it seemed harder to focus on those facts in the small hallway with little more than a breath between them. She could literally feel the heat emanating from Duke's body, or maybe her own.

"I want to respect your wishes, your boundaries. You have all the control in this situation," Duke whispered, her voice low and raspy. "But I need you to know I'm all in. I want to be here for you, with you. I want you to be part of my life, and I'd like a chance to be part of yours on whatever terms you set for me…for us."

Molly couldn't summon any restraint when Duke gave her all the power. So many people had tried to push and threaten her into breaking, and she'd never so much as bent for any of them. Yet, for some reason, being told she had all the control only made her ache to surrender to the uncontrollable.

"You're too special to—"

"Kiss me." Molly lifted her fingers to Duke's lips.

Duke arched her eyebrows.

"You said I could set the pace." Molly slid her hands back up Duke's chest. "Now kiss me."

Duke needed no more instruction. She didn't blush or bumble, and if she had even a hint of nervousness, it didn't show. She clasped her hands on Molly's hips, pulling their bodies flush against each other. Then, sliding one hand up the side of her body, Duke burned a trail lightly across the ribs, her shoulder, her neck, and eventually her jaw before she cupped Molly's cheek in her hand. Guiding her in, holding her a willing captive in a haze of anticipation, Duke kept her on the edge of their combined longing. The spark passing between their bodies connected them like the crackle of electricity before their lips even touched.

Her body cried out for more, and mercifully Duke answered the unspoken plea by sealing their lips, fusing them together, all tentativeness vanished. Her mouth was exactly what Molly expected, only amplified. Soft and sweet, giving and commanding all at once, the kiss became the sensual embodiment of her personality. Duke threw all her focus, all her passion, and her insatiable energy into kissing Molly. The effect was dizzying. Molly tilted her head back, lips parted in obvious surrender, but instead of taking, Duke met her, eager to share, opening her own mouth, offering herself in kind. Molly had never experienced anything like this all-consuming openness. The boys she'd been with had only taken, where Lauren had only given. With Duke, the give and take existed in one fluid action.

The kiss deepened slowly, a passionate dance, a mutual exploration of lips and tongues. Duke wrapped her arm around her waist and across the small of her back while the other twisted delicately in the hair at the base of her neck. A world of contradictions spun through her mind. How was it possible to fall while being held so securely? Reaching out, inspired purely by desire, she sought the curve of Duke's hips and anchored herself to the feminine arch she'd admired for so long. Her hands slipped beneath the hem of Duke's thin T-shirt, and her fingers clutched smooth skin while her thumbs traced the grooves of solid abs. Her breath grew ragged with want. She stole air in tiny gasps from the corner of her mouth rather than pull away.

Duke groaned as Molly worked her hands farther under her shirt, strumming her thumbs over the ridge of her rib cage and into the swell of softness near the side of her breast. Duke's muscles contracted beneath

Molly's fingers. A heady sense of power shot through Molly at the way this beautiful body reacted to her touch. She brushed her fingers over the same spot again, and Duke arched into her, pressing their chests together. Another surge of heat crested inside her. Her hands had pulled need from this amazing woman. She wanted more, had to see what else they could inspire in each other.

She didn't break the kiss so much as shifted it, moving to suck lightly on the corner of Duke's mouth before pulling her lips along her firm jaw to the delicate skin of her neck.

"God, Molly, you're making me crazy." Her voice sounded even lower now, breathier too, causing Molly to smile through the kiss she placed on the curve where shoulder met neck.

Duke worked her hands between them, running quickly over Molly's chest, her fingers twitching as if they ached to linger there. Instead she clutched at the fabric separating them. She twisted the barrier, coiled strength threatening to shred it, but Duke exhaled forcefully and pushed away as if trying to wrestle her body back into submission.

Molly stared at her, taking in her dark eyes, her bruised lips, and the way her chest rose and fell dramatically with each breath. What were they doing? A few hours ago she'd been reminding herself of all the reasons Duke wasn't right for her, but all she could process now was how wrong the minute amount of space between them felt. She stepped forward again, desperate to fuse their bodies together once more, but Duke stepped away, her back colliding with the hallway wall. Looking nearly frantic, her voice cracked. "Please, Molly. I'm not strong enough to go slow when you look at me that way."

"What way?"

"Like, you…like you want me."

"I do want you. Very much." Saying the words only cemented what her mind and body had been screaming at her.

"If I don't stop now," she rasped, "I won't be able to stop at all."

She smiled at Duke for trying to do right by her. She smiled at her ability to wreck such a strong, centered woman. Mostly, though, she smiled because the battle for self-restraint, while noble, was totally unwarranted. "Don't stop, Sarah."

"Don't stop?" Her knees seemed to waver as the weight of the command settled on her. "What? Wait—did you call me 'Sarah'?"

"Yes, I did." Molly stepped closer once more, allowing their bodies to brush chest to chest, hips to hips, as she ran her fingers lightly up Duke's neck and into her short, fine hair. "The people closest to you call you Sarah, and I like it. It's softer, sexier. It suits this version of you away from the ballpark. And besides, if I'm going to sleep with a woman for the first time, I want to be able to call out a woman's name in bed. If it's okay with you?"

Duke's lips parted on a silent breath, and she nodded. "It's fine. Yeah—bed?"

"Bed," Molly confirmed.

The look on Duke's face spoke the words she couldn't seem to find. Eyes first wide with surprise transitioned quickly under lids made heavy with lust. Clutching her tightly once more, she unleashed the hunger she'd previously fought to hold at bay. Molly relished the wave of passion and allowed herself to be swept away in the tide.

The renewed kiss left her gasping in a matter of seconds, but Duke remained relentless, her mouth pressing, her tongue searching, pulling every ounce of desire from her. Her hands moved over her hips, kneading, working into her, driving Molly wild. She wrapped her arms around Duke's back, pinning them together tightly.

Duke arched off the wall, pushing Molly back as they went. Unwilling to break the kiss, they performed a lip-locked tango down the hall, stumbling and bumping off walls as they went. Grabbing and scratching at each other's clothes, almost frantic for bare skin, Molly's back pressed against the wall once more. They weren't getting very far very fast until Duke cupped her ass with both hands. She lifted her easily. Molly wrapped her legs around her waist and allowed herself to be carried to bed. The move was sexy and raw, and she thrilled at the ripple of muscle in Duke's biceps against her sides.

Molly leaned back as Duke laid her on the mattress, then scooted backward up toward the pillows. The separation of bodies was enough to bear—she refused to break eye contact as well. Duke grabbed the thin collar of her own shirt and pulled it quickly over her head, revealing tight abs and muscled shoulders meeting in a swell of soft breasts. Molly couldn't wait a second longer to touch the breathtaking display of strength and femininity. Sitting up, she caught Duke by the waistband of her shorts and pulled her toward the bed.

Duke lowered her head, capturing Molly's mouth once more, but this time she didn't get lost in the kiss. She slid her hands under the hem of her tight shirt, pushing up as she worked her way along Molly's side. She paused only momentarily to toy with the cups of her bra before breaking the kiss to remove the shirt completely. Dropping it to the floor, she returned to worship Molly with her lips, this time kissing down her neck, sending a trail of heat through her core and to places lower. Molly arched up to meet her, so lost in the luxury of her lips on sensitive skin she didn't even notice Duke had unsnapped the clasp on her bra until she pulled it gently away. She'd expected her to be an attentive lover, a passionate one, but she'd never expected her to be so smooth or skilled.

Duke's eyes raked over her body as she eased herself over Molly and guided them both back down to the bed. No one had seen her naked in more than three years, and she would've been nervous about such a blatant appraisal now if not for the awe in Duke's expressive eyes.

"You're amazing, Molly," she whispered before kissing her again. Molly swept her tongue through Duke's mouth one more time, gathering in the taste of her. Duke pulled away slowly to start a sensual descent along her neck and chest. To her credit, she didn't go straight for Molly's nipples, instead kissing and sucking a slow path around them until Molly couldn't stand the suspense anymore and arched up to meet her. Duke complied with the unspoken request instantly, and Molly moaned in relief. She ran her fingers through Duke's hair, soaking up the softness there while encouraging her to continue the work her mouth excelled at.

She took her time tracing the curves of Molly's body and thoroughly explored every area Molly granted access to. Only when she began to squirm for more did Duke move her trail south, placing hot, wet kisses along the way. Her lips skimmed over the plane below Molly's breast to the rise of her stomach until she reached the thin, pale line just above the waistband of her shorts.

Duke ran her fingers lightly over the scar, then looked up, the question quietly in her eyes, as always, leaving the decision to Molly.

"Charlie was a C-section."

"Of course he was." She smiled. "What a beautiful reminder of your resilience."

"Beautiful?" She'd always worried that the marks the boys had left on her body, the scars, the stretch marks, the stubborn belt of extra weight that had protected them in the womb, would be a turn-off to women who'd never experienced the miracle of giving birth.

Duke kissed the scar. "This body created life and sustained life, and healed and adapted. So amazingly strong, and yes, beautiful."

No one had ever seen her body in such a powerful way. Now on top of inspiring a desire that ignited her every nerve ending, she'd also opened a window to her heart and released emotions she'd never associated with sex before. She'd never felt beautiful or wanted. She'd never felt sexy or in control. Most importantly, she'd never let herself feel vulnerable.

She didn't have time to reflect on any of those emotions now, though, not with Duke unzipping her shorts and pulling them slowly down her legs. The heat of Duke's breath on her thigh returned Molly's focus entirely back to the physical. She kicked off the shorts, allowing Duke to move up once more, this time peeling away Molly's bikini briefs. The wait was excruciating as Duke slowly pushed them all the way down before running her hands back up, massaging her calves and kissing along her inner thighs.

Molly parted her legs and reached for her. She wanted to pull her in, craving her in ways she couldn't have believed possible even a few hours ago. It felt as if a dam had broken inside her to release a flood of want and need she'd denied for years.

"Sarah, please, touch me."

She brushed the backs of her fingers along Molly's clit, causing Molly to lift her hips off the bed in search of greater pressure, but Duke had more exploring to do before she'd give in. Parting Molly open gently, she paused, poised to enter her, and looked up, silently asking permission.

"Please," Molly couldn't say anything more through the desire clogging her throat. She nodded, almost frantically. She needed more of those skillful fingers on her, in her.

She pushed forward deliberately, their eyes locked as Duke became part of her. Molly held that deep blue gaze so full of wonder and lust for as long as she could. She wanted to remember the way she looked right now. This captivating and skillful woman, so gentle and so strong, had surprised her at every turn of their relationship. Now with the hands Molly had long admired, she'd unlocked a new world, both physical and emotional.

As Duke withdrew and then pushed forward once more, Molly's body arched up to meet her. Her hips rocked and her head fell back on the pillow. The rhythm of their rise and fall accelerated in time with their increasing need. The next time Duke thrust into her she followed her fingers with her mouth. She wanted to luxuriate and incinerate simultaneously. The impulse to wait and the one to rush warred within her, but the press of Duke's tongue ultimately proved too much to bear. Molly clutched at the back of her head, sinking her fingers into her short blond hair, and held her in place while waves of pleasure coursed through her. Bursts of red and white flashed behind her eyelids as her muscles tightened and then collapsed, leaving her spent and gasping for breath.

Duke kissed her way back up over her stomach, abs, and breasts before snuggling in beside her and kissing her temple. Then she whispered, "Thank you."

"Thank me?" she laughed. "Thank *you*. Wow."

"Wow?"

"Yes, wow. I did not expect that. I mean, I hoped someday I'd experience something like that, but…did I mention, wow?"

Duke grinned. "You might have."

"Well good, because you…I underestimated you."

"I merely followed your lead."

"No." Molly shook her head but didn't have the energy to actually lift it off the pillow. "I only opened the door. You did the rest. And honestly, if I'd known what we had, this thing between us, could be like that, I might have opened the door a lot sooner."

Duke propped herself up on her elbow, looking more serious and introspective. "Do you regret it now? I mean, if it was a heat-of-the-moment sort of decision, I understand. You could have your pick of women, Molly. Why me?"

The honest question deserved an honest answer. "I didn't see it right away, but it turns out I'd been looking for the wrong things, surface things. I guess the more time I spent around you, the more I began to suspect you were better than your box score."

"It's sexy when you speak baseball."

"Yeah?" Molly liked the idea of Duke finding her sexy. "Then here's another little bit of baseball terminology for you. You knocked this one out of the park."

TOP OF THE SIXTH

Swing for the Fences

Duke fell exhausted to the bed once more. She lay on her back, one arm behind her head, the other wrapped around the amazing woman next to her. Molly ran her hand up Duke's chest between her breasts, and Duke watched hypnotized as it rose and fell with each breath. Even after hours of relishing each other's bodies, the mere sight of her fingers, soft and slender, against bare skin could turn her on again. Molly might have been a novice when it came to making love with women, but over the last few hours she'd proved herself a quick learner.

"What are you thinking?"

"When you do something, you really do it."

"The same could be said for you, you know? You're nothing if not dedicated."

"I'm glad you think so. I do believe anything worth doing is worth doing well, but I'd set much lower expectations for tonight."

"What did you expect?"

"I don't know if I had specifics in mind. I wanted to get closer to you. A kiss would've made my whole weekend, but, you? You swung for the fences."

Molly rolled onto her back, giving them the first separation their bodies had experienced in hours. "I didn't really intend to either, but when you kissed me, I got swept up in you. I've never lost control like that, not in my whole life. I didn't know what had come over me. All I knew for sure was I didn't want you to stop."

"And now?" Duke's chest tightened as the silence stretched between them while Molly considered the question. She stole a glance at her across the pillow, Molly's dark hair splayed out across crisp white sheets, her body ample and alluring in all its glory beside her. She ached to touch Molly to rekindle the fire that burned between them, but doubt began to creep in.

"I don't know what comes next," she admitted, and Duke felt her slipping away.

"Well," Duke rolled over to stare into those deep dark eyes, "it's up to you, of course. You've been in the driver's seat with me since day one, but usually when someone hits a home run, they take a victory lap."

Molly kissed her tentatively on the mouth before pulling back far enough to say, "Tell me more."

Duke kissed her again quickly but deeply. "Well, you see, that there is first base. You're already on it."

Molly pressed her lips together playfully. "Nice, I like first base."

"Yes, it's a good base. Mind if I enjoy it with you for a moment?"

"Please do," Molly answered, then connected their lips once more, her tongue brushing against Duke's in a delicious dance.

Duke took the increase in momentum and pushed for another, running her hand up the curve of Molly's hips until her fingers brushed against the soft swell of Molly's breast. She gently caressed the smooth skin, working slowly toward the center until she palmed her completely. Then she broke the kiss long enough to whisper, "There's second base."

"Hmm." Molly hummed a little noise of contentment. "I like that one, too."

"Yes, as you can see, baseball is a most wonderful game."

"I don't know if I can decide for sure until I've touched all the bases. Why don't you show me the way to third?"

"It'd be my pleasure…and hopefully yours, too."

Duke splayed her fingers and slid her hand smoothly downward, across the rise of Molly's stomach, over the thin white scar toward dark curls, but her path toward a triple halted abruptly when Charlie shouted, "Mama!"

Charlie's shrill cry was instant frostbite. Both she and Molly jumped out of bed and grabbed whatever clothes were closest. Molly obviously had more practice responding to these types of interruptions, because she rushed out the door and across the hall while Duke was still trying to retie the drawstring on her swim shorts. By the time she made it to the door of the bedroom, she could hear Molly talking to him. She stepped out into the hallway but froze with her hand on the door to his room.

"It's okay, Mommy's here," Molly cooed. "Everything's fine."

Her initial impulse had been to help, but would her presence be more disruptive than soothing? Surely he was too young to assume she'd stayed until the middle of the night for any sort of ulterior motive involving his mother, but her showing up in his room in the middle of the night could confuse him. Molly clearly had the situation under control, and Duke had learned her lesson about the need to defer parenting decisions to the actual parent. Maybe she should go back to bed and ask Molly about the best way to handle similar situations in the future.

Just then the door to Joe's room opened, and he padded into the hallway. She froze in place, hoping he was sleepwalking, or maybe he really needed his glasses, which he wasn't wearing, but Joe apparently only needed to rub his eyes, then widen them.

"Hey, Duke," he exclaimed happily, but his initial excitement faded into suspicion. "What are you still doing here?"

"I just…I'm…Charlie had a bad dream, but everything's okay now." Her attempted redirect might not have been her most subtle work of persuasion, but it was all she could think of on the spot. "Why don't you head on back to bed?"

He narrowed his eyes. "Your shirt is on backward…and inside out."

Embarrassment burned her face. "Buddy, it's three o'clock in the morning. Why don't we hold off on this conversation until tomorrow?"

He nodded thoughtfully and started to shuffle away, then stopped and turned to look at her. His eyes focused and his cheeks flushed as though he'd put the pieces together all on his own. "Are you having a sleepover with my mom?"

She didn't know what he knew about adult relationships, but he was a smart kid and more attuned to people's emotions than most. He clearly understood enough to realize this wasn't the type of sleepover where they stayed up late watching scary movies or doing each other's hair. She didn't want to overstep her bounds, but he'd asked her a direct question, and she'd never lied to him.

"Joe, you're the man of the house here, and I respect that. I respect your mom, too. You know I like her a lot, right?"

"Joseph Landon Grettano, it is way too late for you to be up," Molly snapped, her gaze jumping back and forth between them pointedly. "Go back to sleep, and if anyone needs to discuss anything, *I* will do so in the morning."

"What about Duke?" Joe asked. "Will she be here, too?"

"Yeah," Duke answered automatically. Now that Molly was here, they could get through this together.

"No," Molly corrected. "Duke is leaving."

She stared at Molly but knew better than to contradict her in front of the boys. Apparently Joe did, too. He headed back toward his room and closed the door behind him.

"What were you thinking?" Molly snapped as soon as the door clicked. Her cheeks were flushed and her eyes wide and wounded.

"Excuse me?"

"I went in to check on Charlie and came out to find you telling Joe we're sleeping together."

"That's a little unfair."

"Maybe"—she rubbed her eyes and took a deep breath, then continued more quietly—"but when it comes to my kids, I don't care. You have no right to talk to my son about my sex life."

"Come on. You know I wasn't going to tell him we'd had sex." She reached out only meaning to touch her hand, but Molly stepped back. Her eyes had gone cold in the minutes they'd spent apart, without the warmth and affection that had stirred Duke earlier.

"I have no idea what you intended to tell him, but you shouldn't be telling him anything. You're not his parent. You're not anything to him."

She stepped back, feeling every bit like Molly had hit her. "Do you really believe that?"

Molly flinched and frowned. "No, I don't mean it like that, but—" Pinching the bridge of her nose, she released a heavy breath. "We shouldn't have done this. I'm not ready to have my family swept up in whatever's happening between us. I'm not even sure I'm ready."

"It's too late, Molly. I tried to go slow. I gave you all the power, but you can't undo what's been done. And even if you could, would you take back tonight?"

"You're right," she said, covering her face with her hands. "I'm sorry. We can't take anything back now, so it doesn't make any difference what I would or wouldn't do if I could."

The non-answer compounded the ache in her chest. Why was Molly pushing her away? Having Joe catch them together was awkward and unexpected, but Molly wasn't making any sense. Duke had tried to do right by her at every step. "You're the one who pulled me into bed."

Molly flushed. "Fine, you're right. I made a mistake. For once in my life I acted on my own desire without thinking about the consequences."

"I didn't mean that, Molly." She reached for her again, the ache spreading from her chest and into her limbs, but Molly wouldn't stand to be touched.

"I can't do this. I can't. I'm sorry, so sorry. You have to believe me. I wanted this, I wanted you, but it's not just about us." There was a pleading in her whisper, one for understanding, for forgiveness, but she left no room for compromise. "God, Duke, I can't even think with you standing there. You have to go."

"Please don't say that. We weren't ready for what happened, but just because we didn't think about the future earlier doesn't mean we can't think about it now. We can work through this as a team. You and me and the boys, we're a great team."

Molly shook her head sadly. "We're not a team, no matter how much you or I may want that. Me and the boys. We're a family. They're *my* family. I have to put them first. I have to protect them no matter what, even from you."

Duke nodded and stepped backward, the ache growing into a sharp pain. "Fine. They're your family, and I'm some mistake you made. If that's what you need to tell yourself right now, go ahead, but I've never pressured you, and I'd rather die than hurt those boys."

She edged her way down the hall, refusing to break eye contact with Molly, silently praying, begging God to make her see what she'd seen in them earlier, but Molly refused to give voice to all the emotions swirling in her dark eyes. "I said all along, the decision is yours, but the mistake you referred to, it's not what happened between us tonight. It's what you're doing right now."

Molly pursed her lips and clenched her fists as if fighting not to call out, but her feet stayed rooted to her spot in the hall. She was a single woman fortress now as each brick of her impenetrable defenses slid slowly back into place. There was nothing left for Duke to do but live up to her word and walk away, even if doing so felt a little bit like dying.

※

Two weeks later, the overwhelming sense of loss still permeated Duke's every sense. She'd waited all the next day to hear from Molly. She'd even rescheduled her flight to the All-Star Game hoping she'd call after she put the boys to bed, but ten o'clock came and went without a word, so Duke had traveled to Minneapolis in a haze.

She must've made it through the All-Star Game. Her columns appeared on the website, though she didn't remember writing them. The only recollection she had of her time in the Twin Cities was staring at her cell phone, waiting for it to ring. It hadn't. She'd gone three days without hearing from Molly. The only bright side was, she hadn't heard from her editor either, which meant even if she couldn't eat or sleep, she'd managed to at least get her work done.

She flew back to St. Louis on the Cardinals' off-days, hoping her proximity to Molly would somehow reconnect them, but she wasn't telepathic, and that was the only way she could have gotten through to her. She'd tried texting, then left a message, before finally trying an email, all of them simply asking how Molly and the boys were doing. She'd mentioned she had two off-days before heading out again, but didn't ask to be invited over. She wouldn't pressure her. She wasn't that person, and even if she were, Molly clearly didn't respond well to being pushed.

Duke understood so little about what had happened, or how an innocent question about their relationship could rip them apart. One minute she'd been rounding the corner from second to third, and the next it'd felt like she'd taken a fastball to her chest. She constantly replayed everything she'd said and done, trying to find the error egregious enough to get her banished, but part of her had begun to suspect she had never been in the game to begin with. Maybe Molly had never intended for Duke to be part of her life. What if she truly saw the love they'd made as a lapse in judgment?

Her memory flashed back to the moment her lips had first brushed Molly's. She could see her now so clearly, their bodies pressed together, Molly's chin tilted up to meet her, the depth of emotion in her dark eyes deep enough to drown in. She'd paused, then decided to imprint the image into her mind forever, convinced she could be experiencing her last first kiss. The thought seemed silly now, so over-the-top, but at the time she'd known without a doubt she'd never again want another woman the way she ached for Molly. Perhaps the saddest part was she still felt that way.

"God, what's the matter with this kid?" Coop interrupted her thoughts, and she wondered briefly if he'd read her mind or was just sick of her moping about. She'd thrown herself into work, arriving early and staying late in an attempt to avoid thinking about her personal life, but she hadn't been great company. Still, they were in the final innings of a nine-game West Coast road trip, and everyone on and off the field looked tired.

"He's a mess," Cooper added.

"Who?" Duke asked, realizing she'd missed something.

"Brooks." He snorted, punctuating the sentence with a parenthetical "dumbass." "He used to be a gamer. Now he's dogging fly balls on the warning track and bailing on pitches inside."

She refocused her attention on Petco Park in time to see Coop's point illustrated perfectly. A heater from the Padres' fireball closer hurtled down the inside track and crossed the plate on the corner closest to the batter. The borderline pitch could've been called a ball or a strike depending on the umpire's zone, but the call didn't matter nearly as much as the way Cayden flinched as it passed him by. The ball might have been a close call but hadn't come close to actually hitting him. Major leaguers hit pitches in that area all the time, or at least swung at them.

She remembered his comments before the All-Star break about working on fast hands. Clearly he'd yet to perfect the skill, and advance scouts had picked up on the weakness.

"Three months ago he would've tried to go deep with that pitch."

Duke searched her memory of his at bats. He'd never established himself as a high average hitter, but his numbers had fallen off even more over the last six weeks. Was there more behind the frustration he'd vented to her in the locker room? Was the shot of bravado meant to challenge pitchers or cover an insecurity?

"He's never had stellar plate coverage there," she remarked more to herself than anyone in the San Diego press box. "I'm not sure he's ever gone yard on the inside pitch."

"Maybe not," Coop conceded, scratching at the salt-and-pepper stubble on his chin. "He might've missed, but earlier in the season he would've swung for the fences."

The phrase echoed her words to Molly in bed. The players, the field, the San Diego skyline all vanished again. In her mind they were together in a tangle of sheets. She pictured Molly's eyes, felt her arms around her neck once more, registered the press of her lips so soft as they yielded to her.

"Definitely a home run," Duke mumbled.

"What?"

She shook her head. "I was thinking about something someone said to me about home runs. Doesn't matter now, though."

How could something that had felt so perfect, so right in the moment, hurt so badly now? Molly had said herself they'd hit a home run, and then moments later she'd bailed on them. The complete turnaround hurt, even weeks after the fact.

Hurt, home runs, bailing out, swinging for the fences…How had her conversation about Cayden become about Molly? Was she stretching a connection that shouldn't be there, or did the two fit somehow? Could anything tie her to Molly, or to Cayden, or Molly to Cayden? They had nothing in common but her pain.

Pain.

She hopped up and threw her tablet, phone, and notepads into her messenger bag.

"What's going on?"

"I've got a lead."

"How about running it by your old mentor here?" Coop asked.

"Mentor?" Now it was her turn to snort. "Maybe if it pans out, you can read about it in my blog tonight. Don't worry. It'll be posted hours before your column goes to print."

She didn't wait for his response. The game was nearly over, and she wanted to be the first one Cayden Brooks talked to in the locker room. All the other press filtering in headed for the area the pitchers used, since the Cardinals staff had thrown a combined shutout. Brooks's strikeout in the top of the ninth didn't even rank on most reporters' radar, and he seemed surprised to see her waiting against his locker when he finally arrived.

His uniform shirt was unbuttoned and untucked, while the side of his away gray pants had a grass stain from his knee to his hip. His forehead shone red where the band of his cap had crossed it earlier, but his short brown hair stood out sweaty and disheveled.

"Hey, Cayden. I've got a question if you've got a minute."

"Don't you want to talk to someone who actually had something to do with our win today?"

"I will, but I've just been meaning to ask how you're feeling."

He frowned. "I'm fine."

"Yeah, I remember you took a bit of a…" She wasn't sure what word she wanted to use, something vague enough to encompass a variety of issues without making it clear she was fishing. "A, um, bruising."

"I'm back to one hundred percent, if that's what you're hinting at."

He hadn't given her much, but he'd at least confirmed he'd been hurt at one point though he'd never appeared on the injury report. Had the organization hidden something from the press, or had he hidden it from the training staff?

"There's nothing there, Duke," he warned her off again as he lifted off his sweat-soaked undershirt and pulled on a clean one. She scanned his body quickly but found no bruising, no outward signs of injury, only the flush of recent athletic activities. Why was he so invested in convincing her he'd healed from a trauma she didn't remember him sustaining? She reviewed her recent memories of him…there was the flinching today, the comments about not busting him inside, the dropped ball at the wall, and the strange ruling on the play. Then there was the hit by pitch—*bingo*.

"But it hurt for a long time after Pistas drilled you with the fastball in May?"

His eyes widened then narrowed. "It doesn't hurt anymore."

"But it hurt to swing for a while, didn't it?"

He turned away.

"It hurt so bad you hesitated before you hit the wall in center field last month."

"We're done here."

"Look, a few months ago you told me to run a quote because you were going to get it out there one way or another and you'd rather give it to me. Now I'm telling you the same thing." She lowered her voice so only he could hear. "Someone's going to put the pieces together or run something purely speculative. Give me the info. Let me make sure it gets out there the right way."

He didn't respond, but his body language softened, and the defiance drained from his eyes.

"I'm going to run this story either way, so you've got nothing to lose by listening. Let me tell you how it looks to me. If I'm right, you don't have to give me a quote, but if I've got anything wrong, you get a chance to correct me. Deal?"

He shrugged noncommittally.

"In May you got hit in the ribs hard enough to drop you, but you got up because that's what professionals do. Only, the pain continued in ways you didn't expect. Things hurt a long time after they should've healed, more than you cared to admit. You didn't want to seem incapable, so you didn't tell anyone how bad you hurt. Not the press, not the trainers, no one." She paused waiting for him to contradict her, but he continued to stare at her, stone faced.

"Okay. You shortened your swing because it hurt to hit, and it probably hurt even worse to miss. No more swinging for the fences for fear of making things worse. You also got cautious around the outfield wall, which made you drop the ball on a big play."

He looked down at his cleats, clearly embarrassed.

"Still, you'd rather look like a screwup than admit you needed help. But why did someone cook the books?"

"You'd have to check with them. I didn't ask for any favors."

She pondered the question again. Maybe the scorer had taken pity on him, maybe they'd made a mistake, or maybe the organization knew he was hurt and put pressure on someone to cover for him. "Are you on the trading block?"

He clenched his jaw and shrugged again.

"Do you want to be traded?"

"I grew up in Southern Illinois. I'm a fifth-generation Cardinals fan."

"Drafted out of high school as a hometown hero." She finished the line of his bio. "I'll take that as a no, but the organization might be trying to make you look like a hot prospect."

"I'm just a ballplayer," he said. "I can't control the suits in the front office. I have to play my game."

"But the mistakes you've had pinned on you lately can be tied directly back to an injury. You're still fending off pitches inside rather than swinging for the fences."

His eyes widened, and he sucked in a breath of air. "I'm not. I'm fine now. No pain. None at all."

The reaction was the most animated and vehement she'd seen out of him in a long time. Something didn't feel right, but he seemed entirely sincere.

As if to further illustrate his point, he lifted up his shirt and patted his side firmly. "Nothing hurts."

She wanted to believe him, but why the defensiveness? Then again, he had gotten better in the field over the last few weeks and he certainly didn't look hurt. If anything, he seemed scared.

Scared.

She flashed to the image of him flinching at the inside pitch. The physical pain might've ended, but the fear, the stress, the memory he'd associated with getting hit still shook him. He was afraid of getting hit again.

She sighed heavily, realizing what plagued him now wouldn't be as easy to overcome as a bruised rib. She chose her words carefully, quietly. "Once you've felt pain like that, and for the first time understand what an injury of that nature could do to your career, to all the people who look up to you, it must be pretty hard to open up on those close pitches again."

"Please don't print that," he whispered. "Pitchers are already testing me on the corners. If you tell them I'm scared it'll be open season for cheap shots."

The information would certainly hurt him and the team, but

she wasn't a Cardinals employee. She was a journalist. She had a responsibility to keep readers informed. Still, she wasn't the paparazzi or an ambulance chaser. She wasn't out to drag anyone down.

"Duke, it's getting better. I'm back up to speed on defense. I'm only overprotective of the inside."

Something stirred in Duke, a memory, an emotion, a connection pulled at her chest. Protective of the inside. She closed her eyes, trying to focus, and remembered the look on Molly's face when she'd seen her in the hallway with Joe.

Fear.

Duke had initially thought she'd hurt her and spent the last two weeks wondering what she'd done to cause that kind of pain, but what if she hadn't caused the pain at all? What if she'd only triggered the memory of it?

"Are you going to run the story?"

"I have to run something. I have to call out the injury. You'll have to deal with it, so you might want to talk to your coach about what happened. You can't hold the whole team back because you're scared of getting hurt again."

He nodded solemnly, but she softened the blow by adding, "I don't want to hurt you any further, though. I'll tell my readers you're back to one hundred percent. I'll point to your strength in the field. I'm going to tell them to be patient with you while you get your timing back at the plate."

His expression shifted from one of embarrassment to surprise. "Why would you do that for me?"

"Because I hope you're with this team for a long time, and I hope I am, too. You've got a lot of big interviews left in you. I want you to learn to trust me now so that when that time comes you'll come to me first."

"I will. Thank you." A flash of his boyishness returned before he regained his business face.

"I'm going to file my game report right away, but I'm going to try to catch an earlier flight back to St. Louis, so I'll write the piece about your injury on the plane. You've got at least six hours before it hits the web, enough time to talk to whoever you need to."

"Thank you," he said. "It won't be an easy conversation, but it's probably time to have it anyway."

She smiled the best she could with the ache in her chest throbbing once again. "I know exactly what you mean."

❖

West Coast routes back to the Midwest were brutal, but she'd been unwilling to wait another day and caught a red-eye from San Diego to St. Louis. Now at quarter till six she was sitting in the hallway outside Molly's apartment. It was too early for the boys to be awake, but she'd got the sense from the amount of caffeine Molly consumed that she had to be an early riser. She was taking a gamble, but this whole ordeal had been a huge gamble for both of them. She only hoped she could renew some of that renegade spirit in Molly, or at least not get thrown out again.

Taking a deep inhale for courage, she hit send on a text message simply saying, *I'm out front. I brought coffee.*

Less than a minute later, Molly opened the door—well, not opened as much as cracked enough to peek out.

"What're you doing here?" her voice was low with more exhaustion than anger.

"I miss you. I'm sorry for how things ended. I want to talk."

"There's nothing to talk about. We made a mistake."

"I respectfully disagree. I thought we did pretty well together, and you did, too, for a while."

She could see only about half of Molly's face, but the corner of her mouth in view curled up slowly.

The little hint of a smile served as confirmation enough to raise Duke's heartbeat. Whatever had gone wrong between them hadn't occurred in the bedroom. "Swinging for the fences with you wasn't a mistake, Molly. My only regret was letting you throw me out before we made it home, but I think I finally understand why you did."

Molly arched her one visible eyebrow but didn't budge.

She couldn't say what she needed to say in the hallway. "I understand you're scared, but am I really so threatening we need to have this conversation with a door between us?"

She sighed. "You said you had coffee?"

Duke held up the matching carry-out cups. "I do. And if you open the door a little wider, you can have some, too."

The door opened slowly, revealing Molly in a threadbare T-shirt and well-worn pajama bottoms. She looked so casual, so comfortable, so cozy, Duke wanted nothing more than to hold her. Instead, she held out one of the coffee cups.

"Thank you," Molly said, taking it in a way that didn't allow their fingers to touch. "It's been a long two weeks."

"Indeed. A lot of long, busy days spent trying to stay focused, followed by even longer and more restless nights."

She nodded, taking a sip of her coffee, then closing her eyes to savor it, or maybe to avoid eye contact. "Do you see now why what we did was such a bad idea?"

"No. What we shared was amazing, life-altering even. We were perfect together. You already agreed with me, so don't even try to say you didn't feel it, too."

"Of course I felt it in the heat of the moment. God, Duke, I lost all control." She looked around as if embarrassed to even admit that, then nodded for Duke to come in and shut the door behind her.

Bolstered by both Molly's words and her invitation into the apartment, Duke pressed on. "That's a good thing, a great thing. We have something powerful between us if it shook you up."

"There's no us. There's not even a me right now. You understand, right?"

"I didn't at first. I replayed that night a thousand times trying to figure out what I said or did to hurt you."

"You didn't hurt me."

"But you have been hurt. You've been disappointed and abandoned, first by your family, then by the boys' dad. You've been strong and kept going because you're amazing, but the reminders of the pain will never go away."

"I'm doing fine without them, so please don't make this some sort of sob story about my past."

"I'm not, Molly. I don't pity you. I'm not pacifying you. You're strong and steady, and I don't flatter myself enough to think you wouldn't be fine without me." She steeled herself for what she had to say next. She'd made all the right jumps in the locker room. Could she make the same connections here? "I think you could survive being let down again, but you're afraid the boys couldn't. That's why you didn't freak out until you saw me with Joe. You know what it feels like to have the people who should love you and protect you unconditionally turn their backs on you. You panicked because you want to protect your kids from that kind of pain."

She finally looked up, her deep eyes dark and wounded. "I'm the only one they have left."

"That's not true. I don't have the relationship with them that you do, but I love them, Molly. It hurt me every bit as much as it hurt you to think something I'd done, some sort of carelessness on my part, no matter how unintentional, might upset Joe. It hurt me for all the same reasons it hurt you, but I had no intention of running away. I'm not Tony. I won't leave because things aren't ideal."

"Please stop bringing him up. He didn't leave me. I left him."

Duke eyed her carefully, from her rigid shoulders to the tint of embarrassment or frustration coloring her cheeks. Duke was on the right track, but she hadn't gotten there yet. She waited, silently asking for the rest of the story.

Molly pinched the bridge of her nose. "I asked for too much. I pushed him out. I've already gotten my children hurt once."

"Oh, Molly." Duke reached for her, no longer able to resist the crushing need to hold her. Molly resisted only a second before folding into her embrace. "You aren't responsible for him. You may've ended the marriage, but you didn't end his chance to be a father."

"I did."

"You didn't. He's a coward, a self-centered, immature coward, but more importantly, I'm not him. I want to be part of your team, even when we're down in the count, even if you and I don't make things work as a couple. I'll never abandon you or those boys." Duke held Molly at arm's length. "Look me in the eyes and tell me you don't believe me."

Molly didn't shy away from the eye contact, but she didn't cave either. "It's not you I don't trust. It's me. What if I don't know how to do this anymore? What if I never really knew how? I've never had a successful relationship in my life."

Duke shook her head. "You said it yourself. It's not just about you. We're all in this together."

"I've been doing everything on my own for so long it's all I know."

"We'll learn together. That's what being a part of a team is all about. Me, you, Joe, and Charlie, we'll take the field together." Duke pulled her near once more, this time cupping her face in her hands. "What do you say?"

Molly smiled, slowly at first. "How do you manage to make sports talk sound so damn romantic?"

"You must inspire those sentiments in me."

Molly finally brushed her lips to Duke's, melting weeks of tension and sadness as heat and relief raced through her in equal parts. Duke soaked up the feel of soft skin and the taste of coffee as they pressed into each other. She wrapped her arms around Molly's back, holding her close as their mouths got reacquainted. She felt so amazing her mind needed a minute to reassert itself. She pulled back far enough to murmur, "I'm going to take that as a yes."

BOTTOM OF THE SIXTH

Take One Game at a Time

Molly hurried through the door to her apartment at quarter till three. Joe was lying sprawled out across the living room floor, surrounded by sports magazines and the cushions to the couch. Charlie stood on the now-bare sofa wearing nothing but his red hooded bath towel and Iron Man underwear. A plastic spoon protruded from the waistband of the undies.

"Watch me, Joe," Charlie yelled as he leapt from the couch and did a full extension into Superman pose before falling face-first into the cushions on the floor. His curls shook as his hearty laughter muffled against his crash-landing pad.

Joe didn't even look up from his magazine, but Duke came half running, half hopping down the hallway, trying to pull on her shoes as she went.

"What's going on, guys?" Molly asked.

They all looked up at her, then back at each other before the boys scrambled to their feet and Duke straightened up as if trying to pass inspection.

Charlie charged first. "Mama!"

She scooped him up, hugging him close. There was no feeling in the world better than a hug from a child who was truly happy to see her.

"Hi, Mol." Duke leaned over Charlie's head to give her a quick kiss.

Molly lingered on her lips just a moment, soaking up their softness and the scent of Duke's cologne. She got a little light-headed at the surge of attraction, which was a pretty amazing feeling, too.

"Hi," she said, pulling back and letting Charlie wriggle free.

"Hi, Mom," Joe called.

"Hi, honey. How was your day?"

"Awesome," he said with a grin.

Molly glanced around the room, from the couch cushions to the magazines to the dining room table covered in baseball charts and coloring books. "It looks like it."

Duke grinned sheepishly. "Yeah, about that—"

"No need to explain. I'm glad you were here. Did you have any fun?"

"Of course. We watched cartoons. We tossed a baseball around. We ate mac and cheese for lunch."

"Did you jump on the couch cushions, too?"

Duke shrugged. "Maybe, but it's part of my hazing. Charlie got me to rush his fraternity."

Molly laughed. "Did you just call my three-year-old son a frat boy?"

"Come on, you know he's going to rock the keg parties in college. I want to be invited to them."

"What about Joe? Is he in the frat?"

"No, he's going to be one of those kids who actually studies at college."

"I certainly hope so," Molly said, enjoying the banter. She hadn't had another adult around to unwind with at the end of the day for a long time.

Duke glanced at her watch. "I'm sorry to run out on you so fast, but I have to get to work."

Work. Molly didn't mind the messy house or the rowdy kids, and she loved coming home to all three of the people she enjoyed most. Everything would've been perfect if not for work.

She'd left the restaurant a mess and chose not to think about how that might reflect on her come promotion time, but she was cutting it close. Duke had been great with the boys while their babysitter was out with strep throat, and Molly didn't know what she would've done without her. No, that wasn't true. She'd dealt with child-care emergencies plenty of times. She would've had to miss work, then rearrange the budget to prioritize things like food over the cable bill that might or might not get paid due to the loss of income. She would've been stressed out and worried for weeks afterward. Duke's willingness to watch the boys until she had to get to the ballpark solved ninety percent of the problem and meant Molly had to worry only about getting home half an hour early. She couldn't repay Duke's good faith by making her late to work.

"You understand, right?" Duke asked.

"Of course, go. We'll talk tonight." She hated the thought of going back out tonight. "Thanks for watching the kids."

"My pleasure," Duke said in a way that made Molly believe her.

"Have a good game tonight."

"Thanks." Duke headed for the door, then turned back and kissed her once more, slow and sweet, but not nearly long enough. Then she was gone, leaving Molly to catch her breath both literally and figuratively.

❖

Molly's vibrating phone startled her awake. She rubbed her eyes and squinted at the screen. *U still awake?*

"I am now," she muttered, then texted back, *Yes, come on by.*

She stood and stretched her arms over her head, trying to decompress her spine. She hadn't meant to fall asleep on the sofa, but the boys had worn her out. Charlie had dumped his entire cup of red juice down the front of himself two minutes before they were supposed to leave for the game. She had to wash him off, change his clothes, and sop up the mess on the floor, making them late. There'd been nowhere to park, and they'd had to walk an extra-long way through the busy downtown streets of St. Louis, then run down the stadium concourse to get there in time for the national anthem. Then after all the hassle, Duke hadn't even been able to sit with them.

Molly had been too frazzled to pay attention to Duke's full explanation—something about the trade deadline passing and the Cardinals still being out of first place. She got the sense the clubhouse wasn't the happiest place to be right now, and Duke wasn't the kind of woman who detached herself emotionally. While Molly loved her dedication, she also wondered what kind of toll it took.

She focused her eyes on the digital clock on the DVD player. 12:32 in the morning. If she'd realized it was so late, she wouldn't have told Duke to come over.

She smiled at her attempt to intellectualize her decision, but she'd made that call with her heart, not her head. She liked being around Duke. She liked to talk to her, to hold her, to kiss her and to—

A soft knock on the door interrupted that train of thought. She rose and answered it, trying to restrain herself from jumping Duke the minute her blond hair and blue eyes came into view.

"Hi," Duke said with a grin. "I worried I might be too late."

Molly closed the door behind her, then reached for Duke's hand and led her to the couch. "I worried you might not call since the game was so bad."

She blew out an exasperated breath and hung her head. "Yeah, another long game. And the Reds won, too. We're four games back now."

Molly noticed, not for the first time, Duke said "we" when referring to the Cardinals. "I guess the clubhouse was a bit somber tonight?"

"That's one way to put it. The more they lose, the tighter they get. Everyone's on the defensive. No one wants to talk. I can only rehash the play-by-play so many times before readers get bored."

"No one could ever get bored with you," Molly said as she ran her hand through Duke's hair. In their short time together, she'd found the move soothed them both.

"Honestly, I'm bored with me right now, or at least with the stories I'm filing. They're glorified closed-captioning of the games. They're hitting, but they can't string hits together. They're making good pitches, but the other teams are still connecting. They're playing well and still losing. I've got no real insights on why, though. They're simply underperforming, and it's frustrating to watch, much less rehash in print."

"What are they going to do about it?"

"I don't know. That's what I spent the last few hours trying to get out of them. I must've asked the question of thirty different people from players to coaches to front office guys."

"And what did they say?"

"They have to take one game at a time."

"Really?"

"Yeah." Duke rubbed her face and stifled a laugh.

"What?"

"It's true. That's the most maddening part. They're right. They have a good team. They have good fundamentals."

"But they're four games out of first place."

"Yes, they are." She sighed. "And they can't get tonight back. They can't make up four games in one day, either. They have to keep going out there and playing the game right every night until something breaks in their favor. In the meantime, they can't press too hard."

"And what about you?" Molly asked. Despite all Duke's talk about not pressing or trying to do too much, she was clearly tired. The circles under her eyes were a dark contrast to the pale blues. "Are you trying too hard to make something out of nothing? You're out until the wee hours of the morning trying to drum up explanations that don't exist and then poring over depth charts all day."

"Maybe. I probably should've gone home and let us both get some sleep."

"Why didn't you?" Molly asked, silently hoping Duke's explanation for this late-night meeting would be the same as hers.

"Because I needed to see you, Molly." She shook her head. "I needed you more than sleep, more than food, more than anything. Even with everything in my mind and body clamoring for my attention, all I crave is you."

Molly didn't even try to respond to the perfection Duke had given voice to—at least not verbally, anyway. Instead, she captured Duke's mouth with her own. Duke's body responded immediately. Her lips softened as the muscles along the plane of her abs contracted. Molly loved the way she could turn her on. She still had moments of panic when she let herself examine how out of control Duke made her feel, but all she had to do was watch desire transform her body to realize she was not without power in the flood of need between them.

The kiss escalated quickly. They had too little time together, and given their combined exhaustion, stamina was not something she could count on. She worked her hand under Duke's red polo, raking her fingernails across soft skin. Crawling forward down the couch and over Duke, Molly pushed the shirt up as she went until she slipped it over Duke's head. She then kissed her way back down from her lips to her neck to her chest. Duke smelled of cologne and ballpark, heat and dirt and fresh air mingled together. Molly's heart rate accelerated like a car stuck in second gear, steadily revving as she closed her lips around one hard nipple.

Duke threaded her fingers into the thick hair at the base of Molly's head, massaging her scalp while gently holding her in place.

"Mol," she mumbled, "we should go to the bedroom."

She was right, but Molly couldn't imagine leaving this spot until she finished what she'd started. Still, time was not their ally, so she slid her palm down to the button of Duke's khakis and nimbly flicked it open. Pushing the zipper down, she slid under the waistband of Duke's boxer briefs. Duke's hips lifted off the couch, asking for more even as her consciousness made one last attempt to regain control.

"Molly, the bedroom. We have to move."

"Shhh." Molly silenced her with another kiss, then grazed her fingers through soft curls to the pool of wetness beneath. Her breath caught as her own hips rocked forward in some primal response. "You'll never last that long."

Duke's eyes glazed over with arousal, and her head rolled back in acquiescence.

Molly stroked her in small, light circles, relishing the swell and fall of the beautiful body beneath her. Duke's stomach dipped with each jagged exhale, and the muscles in her legs twitched and tightened with each pass of Molly's fingers. She was as fine a model as any of the athletes she covered. Her body moved with a fluidity and grace that belied her power, and Molly marveled she shared those gifts with her. She knew instinctively that despite her openness, Duke didn't make herself vulnerable to many people. The fact that she'd put that kind of need and trust into her hands only magnified Molly's desire.

She increased the pressure and speed of her touch, feeling Duke's body respond beneath her. Duke clutched at her now, holding tightly to her hips, her sides, her ass, anything she could use to pull her closer.

"So close," Duke muttered. "So close."

"Quietly," Molly warned as she upped her pace once more, using the weight of their bodies to increase her pressure on the one point Duke needed the most.

Duke nodded frantically. "Yes, there. God, Molly, kiss me."

She complied readily, greedily taking Duke's mouth and absorbing the groans accompanying her release. Duke's body arched as much as it could beneath her, but Molly refused to relent until she'd pulled every last shudder from her. Even then she lingered in the warmth she'd helped create.

Duke lay beneath her, arms still wrapped around her back, holding her loosely as the rise and fall of her chest slowed and deepened. She placed a kiss on Molly's forehead. "Amazing. You're amazing."

Molly snuggled into her embrace. "You're pretty special yourself."

"You know I didn't come over here for that, though, right?"

She did know. "And you know I didn't tell you to come over just for that, right?"

Duke nodded. "So we've got a lot going on between us, huh?"

"Mmm-hmm," Molly hummed, sensing the magnitude of what Duke was hinting at. "More than we should try to talk about at two o'clock in the morning."

Duke lifted her chin to check the clock. "Oh, Molly, it's so late. What time do you have to get up in the morning?"

"Charlie will be up by six thirty. I try to be fully caffeinated by then. I'm sure you understand why."

Duke's chest shook with a little tremor of laughter. "I can only imagine."

"He's a wild man, but he's my wild man."

Duke sighed and tried to give her a little squeeze, but didn't seem to have the energy. "I should go, I guess."

Molly lifted herself up from the place she'd been resting on Duke's shoulder. She regarded her there on the couch, eyes heavy, hair a mess, muscles limp, looking completely spent and deliciously sexy. Even if the idea of letting her drive in that condition wasn't a terrible idea, Molly didn't think she could let her walk out the door right now. "Why don't you stay here tonight?"

Duke raised her eyebrows without fully opening her eyes. "Really?"

"Yes," Molly said, extracting herself from Duke's embrace and rising on shaky legs. Her mind wasn't processing everything clearly, but her body knew what it wanted, and given the absence of a coherent objection, she surrendered to the more basic need. "I want you in my bed tonight. All night."

Duke sat up and made a valiant attempt to focus, her blues still foggy but full of questions. "What about the morning? And the boys? And…and…other stuff?"

Molly smiled at her concern, at her confusion, at her ability to make adorable mixed with sleepy seem sexy. She pulled Duke up to her. "Let's go to bed now, slugger. We'll take the rest one day at a time."

❖

Molly had slept only for five minutes, or at least that was what it felt like. There was no possible way Charlie should be awake, and yet there he stood completely silent and wide-eyed two inches from her face. How had he gotten in without her hearing? Had she slept that soundly, or had he revealed some stealthy ninja skills he'd always possessed without her knowing? Either way, the experience of opening your eyes to see another pair mirroring them had a high creepiness factor. She didn't have the energy to jump or shout, though. Instead, they looked at each other as if in a staring contest, each one waiting for the other to blink, as though winning the showdown might set the tone for the rest of the day.

Molly lost.

The minute her heavy eyelids slid shut, Charlie pounced. "Mama, it's get up morning."

Duke startled awake at the sound of his voice. She jumped, and Molly felt her muscles tense, then go completely still, like an animal trying to play dead, but nothing got past her little lion. Charlie grabbed a fistful of covers and part of Molly's arm to hoist himself onto the bed. Then scrambling over her, he threw all his weight right onto Duke's stomach.

"Duke," he shouted happily.

"Hey, buddy," Duke said, her voice hoarse and tentative.

"You make pancakes." It was not a request.

"Um, well, that's an option," Duke said slowly. "Also there's sleeping."

Molly snorted.

"Or not. 'Cause we're all up now. And I'm still here. In the morning, the very early morning." Duke yawned. "You're here, too, and you know I'm here, and your mom knows you know I'm here."

"Pancakes." Charlie tried to pull the rambling monologue back to the point.

"Right. Pancakes. Completely normal. No one's freaking out."

Molly's shoulders shook from silent laughter. She should probably help Duke, offer her an out, but she liked waking up with her, and clearly Charlie had no problems with her being there either. While the impulse to roll with the changes wasn't something she had much experience with, she wanted to see how Duke would handle a morning at the Grettano house. She decided a little test drive couldn't hurt.

She rolled over to face Duke. "Morning."

"Good morning."

"So this is new."

"It is."

Duke deferred to Molly as she usually did when it came to the kids, but for once Molly didn't need it. Instead of handing her the answers, she scooted close enough to give her a little kiss. Duke started to return it, her tense muscles sinking back into the mattress, but Charlie put a little hand on each of their foreheads and pushed them apart.

"Pancakes."

Duke looked from Molly back to him before laughing and scooping him into her arms. "Pancakes it is."

She groaned only a little as she rose, then whisked him out of the room, leaving Molly to wonder if she might have actually hit the relationship jackpot. Duke was smart and sensitive and so sexy. She'd driven her crazy with lust last night and opened parts of her heart and body she hadn't even been sure existed anymore. Now she was letting her sleep late while she made breakfast for her children. Could any of this be real? Her experiences told her no. The cynical voice in the back of her head warned her to be suspicious, but for the first time in almost ten years she sank deeper into the comfort of her covers and told that voice to shut up.

She must've dozed for a bit because when she woke again, sunlight streamed through the blinds in her window. She smelled bacon cooking and coffee brewing. Her stomach rumbled at the scent. She stumbled out of bed and down the hall. She let her eyes adjust to the brighter lights of the living room, but when they did, a smile stretched her face and her heart expanded her chest.

Charlie sat at the table holding a plain pancake in each hand. Next to him Joe had her laptop open and was reading aloud from what had to be Duke's post-game report. Duke came out of the kitchen with a platter full of pancakes and another piled high with bacon. She spotted her and grinned that trademark grin of hers, the one that showed joy and sweetness and playfulness with a hint of cocky swagger underneath. "Good morning, again."

"It's a much better morning now than the first time around."

"Bacon makes everything better."

"Not until after coffee."

"Sit down. Let me pour you a mug."

Molly was so used to waiting on other people she almost didn't know what to do with the offer, other than accept it, of course. She sat down next to Joe and kissed him on top of his head.

"Good morning," he said without looking up from the computer screen.

"In baseball, as in life, you can do everything right and still not get ahead, but in both situations panic isn't nearly as helpful as continued productivity," Joe read. "The Cardinals don't need a fire sale on young talent. They don't need to fire their manager or hitting coach or front office staff. They don't need to shave their heads or offer burnt sacrifices to the baseball gods. They need to keep playing solid baseball, one game at a time."

"Very nicely written," Molly said as Duke returned with her coffee.

"Do you believe that?" Joe asked.

"Of course. I wouldn't have written it if I didn't." Duke sat down and snagged a piece of bacon. "Why?"

"I don't know." He frowned and kept staring at the screen.

"This team works hard. They play the game right and leave everything they have on the field. It's all we can ask of them."

Joe didn't respond. His eyes continued to scan the page as his cheeks grew redder and redder.

"Hey, what's wrong?" Molly asked.

"Nothing," he mumbled.

Molly looked from him to Duke, who eyed him carefully, her blue eyes narrowing before shooting open.

"Get out of the comment section, Joe." Her voice was low and commanding. She hadn't raised it, but the tone left no room for discussion. It was a mom voice pure and simple, one Molly recognized carried both authority and fear. What she didn't understand was, why.

"What's in the comment section?"

"Nothing good. Ever. The comment section is where America keeps its crazy."

Molly still didn't get it. "You mean people leave comments about how terrible the Cardinals are? They disagree with you about the story?"

"Sometimes." Duke pulled out her phone, and after a few taps, her jaw clenched. All the blood drained from her face.

"What is it?" Molly asked. All the hope and joy surrounding her earlier gave way to her more dominant nature. "What did my son just read on your webpage?"

"Mom, it's nothing," Joe defended her quickly. "It's not Duke's fault."

Duke wasn't so quick to respond. She took a deep breath and let it out slowly. "Joe, we don't keep secrets from your mom. You're growing up. You're going to be exposed to a lot of stuff in the coming years." She addressed him, but she was looking at Molly. "You have to be able to talk to her about anything. To me, too. When you see things or hear things that upset you, you don't have to hide it. We're here to listen, to work through things as a team."

Joe nodded, but he wasn't the only one who'd gotten the message. Molly was being told to calm down and focus on Joe. She wasn't sure if she was grateful for the reminder or pissed Duke implied she was too irrational to effectively parent her child.

"Do you have any questions for me?" Duke asked softly.

Joe shook his head.

"Are you sure?" she prodded gently. "'Cause you're a smart kid. A curious kid. Me and your mom won't get mad at you for asking questions, even hard questions."

He seemed to think for a second, his lips pressing together tightly. Then lowering his eyes, he asked, "What's a dyke?"

Molly gasped, a shot of pain shooting through her chest, but she clenched her fist to hold back any further outbursts.

"It's not a nice word," Duke said, carefully measuring in her response. "It's not a word nice people use, at least not in the way it's used in comment sections. It's a mean way mean people talk about women who are in love with other women."

"But why would someone say it about you?"

"Well, for one I am a woman, and I date other women. A nicer term would be 'lesbian' or 'gay.' Have you heard those words before?"

He nodded, his brown eyes still troubled.

"Well, some people don't like people like me."

"And my mom?" he asked, looking toward Molly.

Her chest constricted, and she reached across the table for his hand, but Duke kept talking.

"Usually people who have those sorts of blind prejudices against people don't point them at individuals so much as groups, and they rarely limit themselves to one group. They are usually racist and sexist and all-around bigoted, too."

"But why would they say that stuff on your blog?"

"Because they are sad and angry and usually dumb." She forced a grin. "They are too dumb to argue with the points I make and too angry at the world to value a different opinion from their own. And they don't like that a woman, especially a gay woman, knows more about baseball than they do."

"But you do. You know more about baseball than anyone," he said, lifting his chin. "You're smarter than them."

"And a better person, too." Molly finally managed to cut in.

"Which is why I don't sink to their level. I never have, Joe, and I don't want you to either. Just know when people resort to name calling and temper tantrums, it doesn't reflect poorly on you. It reflects poorly on them."

"It makes me want to yell at them and tell them they are wrong."

"That would make you like them, and we're not. We're better, and the best way to prove it is to keep doing whatever got them so riled up in the first place."

"Then I hope you write ten blogs today," Joe said, finally cracking a genuine smile. "Long ones."

Duke laughed. "Oh great, more work for me."

With the two of them happy and the immediate threat avoided, Molly gave Joe's hand a little squeeze and quietly left the table. She walked as calmly as she could to the bedroom, shut the door gently, then proceeded to punch the stuffing out of her pillow. The rapid movement of her fists burned some of the energy pounding through her, but the easy crush of cotton didn't have the satisfying impact she craved. She wanted to break something or hurt someone, but what or who could she blame? Some faceless Internet troll? An anonymous username on a webpage? Some vague concept of inequality? If someone had knocked her son down or stolen his lunch money, she would've wrung the culprit's neck, but she couldn't get her hands on any of the things that had stolen his innocence about his hero or Molly's own relationship to her.

"Hey," Duke whispered as if on cue, "you okay?"

Molly jumped, grabbing the pillow and hurling it back onto the bed. "Do I look okay?"

She shrugged. "If it makes you feel any better, the pillow looks worse."

"Don't."

"Don't what?"

"Be all casual and even-keeled." Molly blew out an exasperated breath. "Don't be understanding either, or reasonable."

"Okay." Duke grabbed a pillow and drop-kicked it across the room. It hit the dresser, rattling a bottle of perfume and some jewelry.

"Don't break my furniture either."

"I'm sorry, Mol. I don't know how to handle this."

"Really?" she snapped. "'Cause you seemed to do a damn good job out there."

"Um, thank you?"

Molly dropped onto the bed and pulled her knees to her chest. "I froze."

"It's okay. You were caught off guard."

"I was, and totally unprepared to deal with any of that. I wasn't ready to talk to him about homophobia or Internet trolls or you being a public figure. I didn't think this through."

"Think what through?" Duke asked, sitting down next to her.

"You or your job or what it means to date someone in the public eye, to expose my sons to comments on message boards. God, what if someone sees us together at a game? What if they take pictures of you out with the boys? What if someone makes a comment to them directly? I could barely handle it in the safety of my own home."

Duke wrapped her arm around her shoulder and pulled her close. "I wish I had some magic answer, but I don't, Molly. I can't plan for everything that could ever go wrong. I can only promise I'll be here with you all, no matter what life or the Internet throws at us."

"What if it's not enough?"

"It was enough today. We made it through, together, as a team."

She felt her resistance crack. She found it harder to focus on some shadowy future with Duke so close and reassuring in the present. "But this is just one day, one example of all the things we can't prepare ourselves for. I worry about what else might pop up."

"Things will come up. You cannot anticipate everything, and you cannot overcome a challenge that hasn't presented itself yet."

"So what am I supposed to do? Sit around and wait for the next attack?"

"No, it's just what I told Joe, and what I said in the article to begin with. We have to keep going. We have to keep doing things the right way. Other than that, we take one game at a time."

"My family isn't a game."

"Of course not, but the same concepts hold. We can't freak out or hide ourselves away or let a stranger steal all the good things we have between us. We can't let them terrify us into changing who we are, or they win."

Molly shook her head. She wanted to argue. She wanted to take some drastic measure, to rearrange the world into a more loving place, or at least bubble-wrap her sons and lock them in the apartment, but Duke was so maddeningly right. She couldn't let some asshole keep her from being who she was, and she couldn't keep her boys in a bubble. All she could do was take each battle as it came. "One at a time," she repeated slowly.

Duke kissed her head then, and as if to punctuate the point added, "Together."

Top of the Seventh

It's a Long Season

"Damn, it's hot," Cooper grumbled as he wiped sweat from his forehead and dropped with a loud thud into his seat.

Duke set aside the spreadsheets she'd downloaded on the Phillies offense and checked to see if the armpits of her polo were soaked through as badly as Coop's. They weren't, but after another hour in the stands they might be. Molly had texted; they were almost to the stadium. She wished she could bring her and the boys up to the booth, but kids in computer central this close to game time was a non-starter.

"Did you hear me, Rook?" Cooper asked. "It's hot as balls on the field. Not that you'd know anything about that."

"About how hot your balls are? No, thank God. I'm blissfully ignorant."

"You know enough about busting them. Geez, are you on your woman time or something?"

She gave him her best you-did-not-just-say-that stare.

"Kidding," he lied.

She stood and collected her tablet and phone.

"Where ya going?"

"Taking a walk."

"Outside? I wasn't kidding about the heat, just the woman parts. One of the grounds crew guys said the temp reading at home plate registered a hundred and fourteen degrees."

Her shoulders sagged. Welcome to St. Louis in late August, the only time of the year she wished she'd been born a Twins fan, or a Blue Jays fan, or any other team from a temperate climate or a dome. No, not a dome. Things weren't that bad, but maybe she'd consider a retractable roof. It was also one of the only times she felt sorry for the players. It didn't matter how much money a person made. No one could train his body to enjoy three hours of maximum exertion at one hundred and fourteen degrees.

"The players are out in this heat, the fans, too. I wouldn't be doing my job if I didn't at least check in with them."

It was Cooper's turn to roll his eyes. "Fine, if you want to risk heatstroke to bust out your twitters, go ahead."

She laughed as she headed for the door. She suspected he knew what a tweet was and chose to keep saying it wrong to annoy her, but her mind was already on the little family sitting in the sun.

"Hey," she said, laying a hand on Molly's shoulder. She wanted to lean down and kiss her cheek, but given their conversation last week about exposing the kids publicly, she refrained from too much physical contact.

Molly looked up, her tan skin seeming even darker against the white of her T-shirt. "Hey, how are you holding up?"

"I'm fine. The press box is cooler."

"Lucky you."

"How about you, Joe? Staying hydrated?"

He held up a bottle of Gatorade. "I'm fine. Will the players be okay?"

She marveled again that a nine-year-old had the capacity to worry about the players more than his own discomfort, but she wasn't surprised. "Some of them may be moving a little slow by the end of the game, but they're professionals and they have amazing trainers to help them stay hydrated. They've been getting tons of fluids and eating bananas like a bunch of monkeys."

"I'm a monkey." Charlie finally acknowledged her. When he looked up his cheeks were as red as the bill of his cap.

"Oh, buddy, you're already sweltering."

"No, I'm not," he pouted. "I'm too hot."

"That's what 'sweltering' means. Too hot."

Duke and Molly exchanged a look of concern.

"Are you coming over tonight?" Joe asked.

"I leave for Colorado tomorrow morning."

"Then Chicago, then Washington D.C.," Joe recited.

"It's the longest road trip left on the schedule." Duke tried to lessen the communal sadness settling over them, every bit as stifling as the ungodly heat.

"Nine games," Molly said. "And we won't get to say good-bye tomorrow morning."

She got the hint. She didn't look forward to the road trip any more than they did. She didn't relish the thought of saying good-bye in a ballpark either. She wanted to pull Molly into her arms and kiss her soundly to give them both something to go on until they saw each other again. She'd have to leave for the airport at six to make her flight, though. If she went to Molly's, neither one of them would be able to keep their hands off each other. Starting a nine-day road trip on a sleep deficit was a terrible idea. Then again, leaving without a proper send-off sounded pretty horrible, too.

"All right, I'll come over. We can say good-bye in the morning if you get up early and promise to get some more sleep after I go."

"I promise," Joe said.

"Promise," Charlie echoed.

She looked at Molly, who said, "I promise to do my best."

"And when I get back it'll be September, and maybe the weather will turn for us." The players took the field. She needed to get to work soon, and she wanted to end on an optimistic note.

"Remember, school starts that week," Molly warned.

Her heavy sigh must've sounded like Joe's. Even when the Cardinals had home games in nice weather, the kids wouldn't attend night games. That also meant they'd have to get moving a lot earlier in the mornings. And she'd be gone to work when they got home.

"It's the longest season in all of professional sports," she said with a shrug. For the first time in her life she didn't find the fact comforting.

"I wish we could go with you," Joe said.

Duke caught Molly's eyes over his head and raised her eyebrows. Molly shook her head slowly. Duke frowned, then lifted her hands, palms up, hoping to convey "Why not?"

Molly shook her head again.

Duke pulled out her phone and typed, *Just to Chicago. I can fly back here after Kansas City, then we can drive up together.*

She hit send, and a second later Molly's phone buzzed. She picked it up and smiled faintly, then began to type until Duke's phone vibrated in her hand.

She opened the text message to a simple and definitive *I have to work. I'm trying to get promoted.*

She thought for a moment, then typed, *You'd only have to miss Friday. We could be back Sunday night. Let's go away together before the boys go back to school. It'll be good for them.*

Molly rolled her eyes when she got the text, but she smiled, too. Was she considering it? Why wasn't she typing? Duke didn't want to push, but she also worried the longer Molly waited, the more reasons she'd think of not to go. She was such a pragmatist.

Duke typed more. *I'll see if the hotel has an adjoining room available, and I'll throw in a trip to Navy Pier after the game on Saturday.*

Molly looked at the text but didn't respond in kind. Instead she pursed her lips and said, "Don't you have work to do?"

"All right," Duke said, "but think about it. Please?"

Molly nodded.

"Think about what?" Joe asked.

"Getting you kids out of this heat and to bed early so you can say good-bye to me properly tomorrow morning."

"Oh," Joe sounded disappointed. "Okay."

"See you tomorrow," she said, but as she was walking away, Molly caught her hand.

"Thank you."

"For what?"

"For looking out for us."

Duke grinned. How could she not? "Of course."

She'd just entered the press booth when her phone buzzed again. Molly's message read, *Okay, I thought about it.*

Already? *And?*

I can find a way to make Chicago work if you can.

Duke let out a whoop and pumped her fist in the air. Several other sportswriters turned to stare, and she slid a little lower in her chair.

"What are you so freaking chipper about?" Coop asked.

"We're going to Chicago."

A couple people around her nodded slightly. Chicago meant cooler temperatures, more day games and easy wins, but for Duke, now it also meant three away games were going to feel a lot more like a home stand.

❖

"How much longer do we have to go?" Joe asked in a voice loud enough to be heard over Charlie's wailing.

"I don't know." Duke gripped the steering wheel so tightly her knuckles turned white. "Only ten more miles to the hotel, but that could be another hour in this traffic."

"I thought this drive lasted only four and a half hours."

"Apparently I was wrong." A fact that should've been evident to all of them hours ago. They'd started on the road late since the frustrating task of jamming everything they'd need for four people for three days into the car took longer than expected. She also hadn't planned on the hourly potty breaks or the stop-and-go traffic they'd crawled through for more than an hour now. Charlie's screaming along the way hadn't actually added any time to the trip, but it sure felt that way.

"Duke, please," Charlie begged at the top of his lungs. "Help me. Help me."

"You're all right, Charlie," Duke called, glancing at him in the rearview mirror. "Relax."

"No relax, no help me," he cried and tugged the straps of his car seat. "Let me out."

"I promise you can get out as soon as we get there."

"Out now," he sobbed.

"Let's sing a song," Molly tried for the fiftieth time. It didn't go over any better than the coloring books or movies had. Charlie had simply hit his limit for how long he could stand being confined. Duke couldn't blame him. Six hours in the car under these conditions felt like torture.

She rolled down all the windows, causing Molly and Joe to both shout, "No."

"Just for a minute, guys. I can't stand to hear him cry."

Molly reached for Duke's hand. "I love that you're a softy for him."

She looked in the rearview mirror one more time to see Charlie with one hand in his mouth and the other out the window. Removing the barriers was the only way she'd found to ease his claustrophobia. Of course, without the window up, the air conditioner was worthless, and the stale, hot exhaust fumes clouding the Stevenson Expressway flooded the car.

They were late. She'd given up on the family tour of Wrigley two hours ago. Half an hour ago, she'd made peace with the fact that she wouldn't have time to change at the hotel before going to the field. Now she did the math in her head to see how long she'd have in the clubhouse before it closed. That window was shrinking with every minute.

She pulled out her phone and put on her Bluetooth earpiece. "Guys, I have to make an important phone call. Can you promise me to be super quiet?"

"Yeah," Joe said.

"Charlie?"

"No."

"No, you won't be quiet?"

"No talking."

Did that mean he wouldn't talk or she couldn't? It didn't matter. She had to risk it.

She hit the voice command button and said, "Call Beach."

The phone rang twice before she heard Beach's voice in her ear.

"What's up, Duke?"

"I'm going to be late filing my pre-game. I got stuck in traffic coming into Chicago."

"This is a big series."

"I know. And I'm sorry. I thought I left in plenty of time."

"Why didn't you fly from Kansas City?"

"Something came up, family stuff."

"You need to let me know sooner if you need time off."

"I didn't think I needed time off," she said tersely.

"Well, it's too late to do anything now."

"No talking," Charlie yelled.

"What was that?" Beach asked.

"Nothing, I mean, I don't know. I'm pulling onto ninety now. It's moving faster."

"I don't need a traffic report. I need a pre-game report. Get it to me as soon as you possibly can."

The wind picked up as they gained speed, up to a whopping twenty-five miles an hour. She raised her voice to be heard, but she didn't dare roll up the window. "I will. I promise."

"And, Duke, this is your team's chance to make up ground against their number one rival…"

"Yeah." She tried not to snap. Did he really think she didn't understand the implications? "I'm on it. Day and night. Double the output for the rest of the weekend."

Out of the corner of her eye she saw Molly's head snap over, but she could deal with only one person's disappointment at a time.

"You don't have to tell me," Beach said with a sigh. "Show me."

"You know I'm a pro—"

"No talking," Charlie shouted again.

"Charlie," Molly snapped, "Shh."

"I gotta go." Duke pushed the disconnect button and mumbled, "That went well."

They rode in silence until Duke turned onto North Sheffield.

"There's the hotel." She pointed to the the Inn at Wrigley Field sign. She'd paid a small fortune to get a room there on a Cardinals/Cubs game day, but now she was glad she had. It was only a block from the stadium, and she needed to get there fast. "I put your name on the reservation, so you can get checked in."

"Aren't *you* going to get us checked in?" Molly asked.

"I'm sorry. I don't have time. The tickets are in my bag. Call me when you get to the game, and I'll try to come find you." Duke pulled up in the front of the hotel. "Boys, please be good for your mom. I'll see you at the park."

"I thought you were going to show me around Wrigley," Joe said.

"I will, tomorrow, okay?"

Joe frowned but nodded. She didn't have time to try to appease him any more. Leaning over, she kissed Molly quickly on the lips. Molly didn't really kiss her back though, something she added to the growing list of things to worry about later. Tossing the keys to the valet, she called "I'm sorry" one more time and ran down the block.

She was sweat-soaked by the time she got up to the press booth. The dugout had already closed by the time she got there, and she'd caught only the last few batters to warm up. None of them gave her any quotes, so she'd raced upstairs to try to piece together something about the lineup and the importance of the weekend series.

Cooper stared at her in amusement. "Getting a little out of shape, Rook?"

She wasn't in the mood for backhanded banter today. She dropped into her seat and began typing, but he didn't get the hint.

"What? The schedule getting to you?"

She snorted. That was part of the problem. Late nights, weeks away from home, they'd all pushed her into thinking this family weekend was a good idea. No, it was a good idea. She needed tonight to go well, and she'd get back on track. They could still tour the ballpark tomorrow morning and Navy Pier after the game. This was an important series, both on and off the field, but she could manage everything.

Her dad's voice echoed through her head, asking if she could do everything one hundred percent. Sure, she could sneak some time with Molly, but enough to justify dragging her family up to Chicago for the weekend? And she could get her stories filed, but would all of them be two hours late and patched together? Was that fair to anyone? Especially herself?

No, she needed to add those insecurities to a pile of problems she didn't have time to deal with right now and get back to work.

❖

Duke incessantly tapped her pencil on the green table in front of her. She had an amazing seat with an expansive view of one of the most beautiful, historic fields in all of baseball. Despite the Cubs' lackluster record for the past one hundred years, they still boasted an envy-inspiring home field. Wrigley was a true cathedral of the game. From the sun-soaked bleachers beyond the outfield to the outer surrounding of rooftop terraces, fans had their pick of glorious views. The old-fashioned chalkboard green scoreboard was nothing short of iconic, and the ivy along the outfield wall held more history than most other major league ballparks combined. Duke fully understood why so many of the Cubbies faithful wanted their ashes scattered here. It would be a beautiful place to rest eternally. And yet, here she sat, grinding her teeth, desperate for her chance to get away.

She should've been wrapping up her post-game interviews at this point. A one o'clock game could've reasonably ended by four, giving her an hour in the clubhouse and another hour to file her story. They could've headed downtown no later than six for a nice dinner and some family fun on Navy Pier. None of that could happen until the game ended, though, and the game couldn't end until someone scored another run, which both teams had failed to do since the sixth inning, when Yadier Molina was hit by a pitch and came around to tie the game on a double from Cayden Brooks.

Now, in the bottom of the twelfth inning with the bottom of the order up to bat, the Cubs looked to go down easy, meaning they'd have to play a thirteenth frame. Even if someone ended things in the next twenty minutes, she wouldn't get out of here until almost eight, too late for dinner, too late to go downtown with a three-year-old, too late to salvage the weekend.

She stood, grabbed her tablet, and headed for the door.

"Piss break?" Cooper asked. "Are the women's rooms here any nicer than the men's rooms?"

"From what I hear, they couldn't possibly be worse."

He let out a snort of a laugh that shook his beer gut.

"I'm going to stretch my legs and get some quotes from the crowd."

"Take your time. It doesn't look like anything's happening here for a while."

Duke prayed that wasn't the case, but either way she owed Molly an apology.

She wandered through concrete corridors and under exposed beams until she stepped into the late-day sun. The field was captivating in this light, but she didn't have time to marvel at the view.

"Molly," she called, coming up behind them.

She turned the best she could with Charlie on her lap, the frustration and exhaustion in her deep brown eyes visible even from a distance.

"I'm so sorry," Duke said as soon as she got close enough to be heard in a regular voice.

Molly sighed. "I know it's not your fault, but this isn't the family trip you promised."

"I know, and I mean it. I'm sorry the game has gone on so long."

"It's not just the game. It's you being out until midnight last night and all of us spending all day here today."

"Come on, the Wrigley tour this morning was good family time. Joe loved it."

"I did," Joe said enthusiastically. "This place is amazing."

"See? He's having a great time."

"What about Charlie? He's been confined in a car, then in a hotel room, now in a stadium seat for hours, and he got nothing out of the tour."

"I know, and I also know it's been hard on you."

"I'm sorry if you want me to say it hasn't, but it's hot and I'm tired, and I don't know how much longer I can keep Charlie from climbing the outfield ivy." Molly shook her head. "I know you think I'm supermom, but there's only so much I can do."

She could clearly hear the warring emotions in Molly's voice, anger, exhaustion, the attempt to be understanding butting up against the realities of her situation. Duke didn't blame her for wanting out. "Why don't you guys go to Navy Pier without me?"

"Really?" Molly snapped. "You want me to load Charlie onto public transportation after he's been cooped up all day and haul him downtown only to let him loose on a crowded pier that juts out onto Lake Michigan all by myself?"

She rubbed her forehead. "When you put it that way, it sounds like a disaster waiting to happen."

"Because it is." Molly fanned herself with a program.

Duke's shoulders sagged. Navy Pier was out. Tomorrow was another early game, and they needed to get on the road as soon as possible afterward. They were out of options. Guilt weighed heavily on her chest.

"And it's so hot."

"How about some snow cones?"

"Yes, because sugar ice is always a good idea when trying to keep a child in his seat."

"Okay, I get it. You're in hell right now."

"Hell's a bad word," Charlie shouted, causing several people around them to laugh.

"I'm sorry, Charlie, you're right. Molly, why don't you go back to the hotel?"

"And do what? Watch the game on TV? Order a pizza? We could've done that at home. I took off work, dragged my kids all the way to Chicago, and all we've seen is Wrigleyville. I've eaten nothing but hot dogs for two days. Great hot dogs, but still, you promised more than a hotel and a baseball game."

"I don't know what else you want me to say. This is what I do for a living, and more than that, it's what I love."

"I love it, too," Joe said, causing Molly and Duke to exchange a look that clearly said they shouldn't be having this conversation in front of him, but he went on. "I don't care about Navy Pier. This is the best vacation I've ever been on. I got to spend all day at one of the coolest ballparks ever. My favorite team played their biggest rival, and it's so close I get to watch extra innings."

"I'm glad you're enjoying it," Duke said with a little grin.

"Me too, honey," Molly said softly.

"No, you're not," Joe continued. "You two are arguing about being hot and having to work. You don't understand. It's like heaven, and you're not even enjoying it with me."

Emotion clogged Duke's throat. She used to be able to enjoy a game without worrying about the start time, or the weather, or what extra innings would mean for a bedtime schedule. She always took her job seriously, but she'd never considered it work. Writing about baseball was a labor of love. When had it become an inconvenience? Of course she felt terrible for the ways in which the Cardinals schedule wrecked Molly's, but the game wasn't just her career. It lived in her heart. Joe could see that so clearly. Why couldn't Molly?

"You're right, Joe," Duke said solemnly, then turned back to Molly, meeting her eyes, searching for some deeper level of understanding. "This isn't the trip I planned, and I *am* sorry, but it's not hell-er-Hades either. This game is a big part of who I am and what I love."

"I know." Molly held her gaze, a pleading of her own evident in her eyes. "But I'm asking you now, if this game has your heart and your mind, where does that leave room for us?"

The question that had hovered over them for days, if not weeks, had finally been asked. Her chest ached as her father's voice sounded in her ears. *"You can't give a hundred percent to two different things."*

The clouds of tension between them were near suffocating as she struggled through the haze of heat and sadness tinged with anger. It was the perfect storm, and she didn't know why she didn't anticipate the lightning. She was so engrossed in Molly she didn't even see it.

She heard the thunder, though, a loud crack of taut leather against plastic reverberating through the park, followed by a dull thud and a collective gasp.

She wheeled around to see Cayden Brooks lying in a cloud of red dust.

A flood of players spilled onto the field. Instinctively Duke grabbed her tablet and began to film. She zoomed in on the melee of players pushing and shoving. Umpires shouted and tried to get between them. Both benches had cleared into the middle of the infield. At the plate, trainers from both teams helped Cayden Brooks to his feet and led him out of the way. Duke turned the camera to him and saw for the first time the crack in his helmet, just above the ear.

"Shit," she swore under her breath. The ball had hit him in the head, an inexcusable mistake to make. Rage boiled up under her skin as she noted the glassy sheen of disorientation and the unfocused gaze, clear warning signs of a concussion. A hit like that could end a young career, and if she could've thrown a punch just then, she might have ended her own.

Shutting off the video, she flipped over to social media and tried to block out the sounds of the crowd cheering, jeering, and booing, like they couldn't make sense of everything happening at once. The brawl continued as she attempted to type her view of what was happening. Molina swung at a Cubs player, who had him by the jersey. Ben LeBaron elbowed the Cubs first baseman with his non-pitching arm. A Cub player chest-bumped an umpire, all offenses that carried automatic suspensions if the league ever sorted this out. The fight wouldn't just change the course of the game. It could change the entire rest of the season.

Duke finally turned back to Molly, who cradled Charlie's head on her shoulder, covering his ears from the noise. She turned to Duke, whose face had gone as red as his jersey. *Shit.* Their jerseys. They clearly marked them as Cardinals fans in an increasingly hostile crowd.

"You have to get out of here," Duke shouted. "Get the kids back to the hotel and stay there."

All the blood drained from Molly's face. "Are we safe?"

"No one will purposely hurt a mother and two young kids, but fights will break out in the stands and maybe in the streets. Language, beer bottles, pushing—I…I don't know." God, how could she have put them in this situation? She should escort them back to the hotel, but she couldn't leave now. She had to get back to the booth.

"Are you coming with us?" Molly asked as she swung Charlie's diaper bag onto her shoulder and caught hold of Joe's arm.

"I'll get you out of the stadium."

They wove as quickly as they could through the crowds on the outer concourse. Once they were inside, the path got easier as most of the rowdy spectators were still fixated on the fight.

They reached the front gate as someone shouted, "The Cardinals fucking suck!"

Molly turned around to look, but Duke nudged her forward. "Go."

"What about you?"

"I'm going back to the booth. I'll be fine. Text me when you're in the room."

Molly nodded grimly. "When will you be home?"

"Late. Very late."

The anger returned to burn her cheeks and force her pretty lips into a hard pale line.

"I'm so sorry, Mol. I'll make everything up to you."

"You keep saying that, but when?"

"Now isn't the time for that discussion." And even if it were, she wouldn't have the answer. "Please, be patient and have a little bit of faith in me."

Molly shook her head, then squeezed Duke's hand. "Just get home safe tonight. We'll talk about how much longer this can go on later."

❖

Duke opened the hotel room door as quietly as possible and tried to squeeze through a tiny opening to minimize the cone of light from the hallway. They'd given the boys the double bed closest to the door in the hopes of distancing them from the noise of the street outside, but she imagined the hotel hadn't exactly been quiet tonight either. If she woke the kids up at one a.m., after everything they'd been through today, Molly would kill her—and she'd deserve it. Honestly, she feared Molly might want to strangle her anyway, so she didn't really want to wake her up either.

Hopefully they'd all stay asleep and never know how late she'd had to work. She shut the door, easing the handle back in to place in super slow motion, then inched her way into the bathroom and repeated the same painstakingly quiet motions there. Only when the door was fully sealed did she turn on the light.

She closed her eyes against the blaze of light, but when she opened them Molly was sitting directly in front of her.

"Holy shit." Duke jumped back and Molly sprang to her feet to cover her mouth.

"Shh," she whispered. "Don't wake the boys."

Duke's heart raced for about the fifth time that day and she worried her arteries couldn't handle this sustained barrage of adrenaline. "God, you scared me."

"Good. You deserve it for what you put me through today."

"Really? You hid in the bathroom for hours so you could give me a punishment heart attack?"

Molly snorted. "No, that was just an added bonus."

Duke rubbed her face and glanced in the mirror. God, she felt as tired as Molly looked. They had a lovely set of hers-and-hers red-ringed eyes, and the fluorescent hotel light did nothing for the pallor of either of their skins. This horrible day had gone on so long, it had now become a horrible tomorrow. She ached to go to bed and wake up in a different time and place, but Molly waiting in the bathroom half the night didn't bode well for a swift or easy surrender to darkness. "I guess we need to talk about what happened."

"We really do," Molly said quietly.

"I'm sorry."

"I know you are."

"I had planned for this whole trip to go so much better."

"I know you did."

"I wanted to come home sooner, Mol."

"But you didn't, and maybe it's better that way," Molly admitted, sitting down on the edge of the bathtub. "I was so mad at you when we left the game I don't even remember walking home. I could hardly see through the red tingeing my vision."

"I sure hope there is a 'but' coming in this story."

Molly's mouth quirked up for just a second. "Not yet. You were the one who pushed for this vacation. You sold me on this great cultural outing filled with family time and nice dinners."

"I know, Molly, and I tried—"

Molly held up a hand. "Let me finish, I've had four hours to lie here and think about this. Let me get it out."

Duke nodded and leaned against the sink to steady herself. Her legs wanted to give way and her head throbbed, but Molly deserved to be heard.

"My fuse had already burned down to a nub when you came down to see us, and instead of getting a sincere apology or some helpful advice, you wrote me off as not understanding your love of the game. That felt really unfair given everything I'd gone through in the last forty-eight hours. Then the fight broke out, and it felt like you just pushed us out of the way."

Duke hung her head. She wished she could have the moment back. Molly's first instinct had been to protect the boys, and what had she reached for? Her camera. "I didn't mean to just push you out of the stadium, Molly. I know it might have looked like I was in a hurry to get back to work, but really I just wanted—needed—for you and the boys to be safe."

"I understand that now."

"Really?" Duke waited for the "but" on that statement, too.

"Yeah, as much as I hate to admit it, once the boys fell asleep, and I had a chance to breathe again, I started thinking about you back in the stadium with all those angry drunk fans. And when I saw the Cardinals won the game, I started to think about how hard it would be to get out of there, how resentful the fans in the street would be. I worried about all the things you said I had to get the boys away from."

"You don't have to worry about me."

"Why not? Maybe I don't worry about you hearing bad language, but you could get in the middle of someone else's fight. You could get hit with a beer bottle. You could get attacked, probably easier than we could. You didn't have any little kids with you, and you don't always come across as a woman even. What if some drunk thug thought you were a guy, or worse, recognized you as that gay sportswriter he says awful things about online?" Molly shuddered and Duke went to her, pulling her into her arms.

"I'm right here, nothing happened to me." She inhaled the scent of her shampoo and kissed the top of her head. "I'm sorry you worried. I wish my job wasn't so hard on you."

"It doesn't have to be like this all the time, does it?"

"No, it's usually not." She said what she hoped was the truth. "Today was crazy. This whole weekend was crazy."

"Extraordinary circumstances," Molly murmured. "I'm trying to be understanding of that."

"And I appreciate it, Molly. I really do. You're the best, I can't tell you how much it means to hear you understand."

"I'm trying to. It's hard to stay mad when all I could think about was how much I wanted to see you come home safely."

"I'm here now, and I'm sorry."

"You don't have to apologize for doing your job."

Duke's chest expanded, filled with gratitude and relief and so much adoration for this woman. She'd put her through so much this weekend, tested her patience and her resolve, and she'd still forgiven her. No—more than forgiven: she'd understood. It had not been their finest hour, or forty-eight hours, but Molly had given her the green light to keep doing what she loved. She didn't have to choose between her and the game.

"Thank you, Molly." She kissed down to her ear and along her jaw. "I know it's a long, hard season, but I really am going to make it worth the grind, for you. I promise."

"Good, and you can start fulfilling that promise tomorrow. Right now, I want to be in bed with you. Sleeping."

She grinned. "For the first time all weekend, you'll get no argument from me."

BOTTOM OF THE SEVENTH

You Win Some, You Lose Some

"Charlie, where are your socks?"

"In my shoes," he said without looking up from his bowl full of dry Cheerios.

"Logical, I suppose," Molly admitted, "but your shoes aren't on your feet. So where are those?"

"In my backpack."

"Fair enough." Molly sighed. She did tell him the new shoes were for preschool, though she hadn't specified how they were to get there.

"Joe, will you get your brother's shoes out of his backpack and on his feet?"

Molly listened for confirmation as she grabbed a juice box and a bottle of water from the fridge. She put the water in the lion lunch box and the juice in the Cardinals lunch box before closing them both, then realized she'd done that backward and opened them again. Why hadn't Joe answered yet? "Joe?"

"What?" he called.

"Did you hear me ask you to put Charlie's shoes on him?"

"Uh-huh."

"Did you do it?"

Silence.

Molly grabbed the lunch boxes and deposited them by the backpacks near the front door, then turned back to the living room. "Joseph Landon Grettano, what on earth could be so engaging you'd ignore me completely?"

Joe looked up from the family computer. "I'm reading."

Molly fished a pair of tiny sneakers out of a miniature backpack. "Do I even need to ask what you're reading about?"

"Mom, the Cardinals are only two games out of first place."

"And you, son, are only three days into a new school year. Let's not build a reputation for being late so early in the game."

He didn't answer again. She stared at the back of his head for a few seconds longer before sighing and going to put on Charlie's shoes herself. "I guess I should be happy you're reading at all, but why don't you at least share what you're learning with the rest of us."

That got his attention. "I think the fight in Chicago sparked new life in the team, like it got them excited or made them work together better."

The team had gone on a tear over the last few days, and Molly wondered about the connection to the fight as well, but she didn't want Joe to think bench-clearing brawls were something to admire. "Fights don't generally help teams."

"They've gone three and one since then with no errors."

She couldn't refute the statistics since they no doubt came directly from Duke's columns, which Joe followed religiously. She actually wondered if maybe this entire conversation stemmed from something Duke had written. Surely she didn't condone violence on the baseball field, though. Then again, she'd gotten awfully caught up in the fight at the time, and the video she'd shot from the stands had gotten her a lot of attention in wider media circles.

Molly had waited up for her long after the game had finally ended. She'd lain awake for hours, seething, but the longer Duke stayed out, the more she worried something had happened. At the time with tensions high and the streets filled with threats, the danger had seemed so real. She's never heard of anyone targeting a sportswriter, but stranger things had happened because of sport rivalries. By the time Duke had finally snuck quietly in the door, Molly felt mostly relief and chose to let the rest of her mixed emotions wait for another time, but now, with time and space between them, she wished they'd gotten another chance to talk about what had happened before the fight. It felt like, in the rush to forgive, a few major questions might have gone unanswered, but after the week she'd had, the memories jumbled together in her mind. Their original argument seemed all tangled up with the brawl on the field. The fear and loneliness from the hotel room had blended into missing

Duke on her road trip. All the stress simply fed into the hectic first week of school. She couldn't even remember what had sparked this most recent round of rehashing everything.

"Duke says last weekend could've been a real turning point for the team," Joe said, bringing Molly back to the previous conversation.

"What about the suspensions for the players in the fight? Won't those hurt the team?"

Joe seemed to think for a moment, then shrugged. The move was pure Duke. He even mirrored her Missouri cadence when he said, "You can't win 'em all."

"Did Duke say that?"

"Not about the suspensions, but she's said it before. It's a baseball thing."

Molly found the baseball clichés less endearing every day. She couldn't just put her life on hold for six months every year when the Cardinals took the field. She had a job to do, a home to maintain, and most importantly two boys to raise, which reminded her: they were going to be late for school.

"Joe, where's your math homework?"

"Um, it's in my backpack."

Something about the hesitancy in his voice set off her internal mom alarms.

"Did you finish it?"

"Mostly," he mumbled.

Molly picked up the Cardinals backpack. This early in the school year there wasn't much homework, so she found the page of multiplication review problems easily. He'd completed the front of the worksheet but left the back completely blank. "It is only half done. That's a failing grade."

Joe didn't even have the sense to look properly embarrassed. "It's still early in the year. You win some, you lose some."

"No sir, this is not baseball," she snapped. "Your education isn't a game. Your grandfather paid to send you to one of the best schools in the city, and by God, I let him. We did not all go through that for you to shrug and say 'you win some, you lose some.' What on earth has gotten into you?"

"It's boring, Mom. I already know multiplication, and I don't need it anyway. Stats sheets already have batting averages and on-base percentages calculated. If I'm going to be a sportswriter, I need to watch the games and—"

"You didn't finish your homework because you were watching baseball?" Molly interrupted.

"Yes," Joe said defiantly.

"Uh-oh," Charlie said. Apparently even he could see Joe's misstep.

"You're grounded."

"What?"

"No baseball game tonight, and from now on you don't watch baseball at all until I've checked every stitch of your homework."

"What about day games? I can't finish my homework by three."

"You should've thought of that sooner," Molly said, struggling not to yell. "You'll get it done and done right before you so much as check a score."

Joe balled his fists and expelled a heavy breath of air. "You don't understand anything. Duke's the only one who gets me. I can't wait for her to get home tomorrow."

"Well, at least we agree on the last part," Molly said. She might not like everything Duke had said or done lately, but she missed her. She missed having someone to talk to. She missed her calming presence. She missed the easygoing way she helped with the boys. Mostly, though, she missed having her arms around her at the end of a long day. As much as she'd started to resent the grip Major League Baseball had on their lives, she sent up a silent prayer of thanks to whoever scheduled those games for giving them an off-day when she needed it most.

❖

"Duke!" the boys both shouted as soon as Molly opened the door. They dropped their bags and ran to her. Molly couldn't blame them. Seeing Duke standing in her kitchen with a cookbook in one hand and a spatula in the other was almost enough to make her cry happy tears. Molly had to curb the impulse to push the boys out of the way and jump into her arms. Instead they made eye contact over the kids' heads and smiled.

"I'm so glad you're home," Joe said dramatically.

"Me too," Duke gave him a big squeeze, then set down the cookbook and lifted Charlie into her arms. "You've actually gotten bigger since Sunday."

"I did. I'm all grown up now."

Duke laughed and kissed his cheek. "I missed you guys."

"They missed you, too," Molly said, setting down all the bags she'd been carrying.

"What about you?" Duke asked with a shy grin. "Did you miss me, or were you too happy to have a few days away from the madness of baseball season?"

"Actually, I did enjoy some time away from the game," she said, but at the first hint of Duke's frown she added, "but I missed you more."

She closed the distance between them and kissed her as best she could with Charlie still clinging to Duke. She'd only intended a little peck on the lips, but as was so often the case with Duke, a little wasn't enough. Soon Duke's arm was around the small of her back, holding her close while their lips parted, begging for more.

"Eww," Joe said.

"Squished," Charlie added from between them.

They laughed and stepped back. Molly wasn't sure she'd laughed at all for the past three days, maybe a polite chuckle at work or the boys, but not the simple, easy kind of laughter Duke always inspired.

"What's for dinner?" Joe called from the living room.

"Chicken with bacon, mushrooms, and cheese," Duke said.

"Yum."

"I don't like it," Charlie said in his usual singsong protest.

"Peanut butter and jelly for you, mister," Duke said, then turning to Molly, added, "if that's okay, I mean. I started the bacon. I can save it if you had something else planned."

"I'll never complain about your having dinner started by the time I get home."

"Long day?"

"Long week."

"Why don't you go change into more comfortable clothes? I'll handle things here."

"You're a Godsend."

"Just a sportswriter, but I can see how you'd get confused."

Molly laughed again and shook her head. How could she stay mad at this woman? Though that did remind her. "Joe has to do his homework right away."

"Mo-om." Joe drew out the word to make it sound like it had multiple syllables.

"Don't worry. I've got it." Duke punctuated the assurance with a kiss, and Molly believed her.

Duke helped with Joe's homework and dinner and the dishes. They talked about the boys' experiences at school and Duke's trip to Washington DC. Molly told her about a possible interview for the promotion to daytime manager of the restaurant. Duke wrestled with Charlie and read with Joe before helping to get them both into bed by 8:30. They worked so well together Molly almost felt like they'd been a family all along. If only every day could be an off-day.

"Hi," Duke said as they met in the hallway after tucking the boys in.

"Hi," Molly replied. "Did I mention how happy I am to have you back?"

"Maybe once or twice. Did I mention how happy I am to be back?"

"You might have, but I missed it in the whirlwind of little boys clamoring for your attention."

"It's nice to come home to people who missed me instead of a quiet apartment."

"Quiet is not something we're known for around here."

"It's quiet now." Duke wrapped her arms around Molly's waist.

"Right, but only because we're all exhausted."

"How about we go straight to bed?"

Molly rested her head on Duke's shoulder, breathing in her unique scent mixed with the lingering traces of bacon grease. "I wish I could, but there are lunches to pack and laundry to do."

"I'll help with the boys in the morning so you can make lunches then, and I'll do the laundry later. I've got ten days' worth of my own to add to the pile."

Molly popped open the final button of Duke's polo shirt, revealing that delicious spot just above her sports bra. "It seems like there's something else we should be doing right now, but for some reason I can only think of one thing."

Duke hooked a finger under her chin and lifted it gently until their lips met. They kissed slowly, passionately, as they edged down the hallway to the bedroom. Shutting the door quietly behind them, Molly flipped the lock. She didn't want to risk any interruptions for what her body was begging to do and have done.

Duke caught the hem of Molly's shirt and separated from the kiss long enough to lift it off. Then clutching her own shirt by the collar, she yanked it over her own head. The sports bra followed the shirt quickly to the floor. At the first sight of bare skin, both of them raced to remove the rest of their clothes. Molly wasn't sure who removed each pair of pants, and she didn't care. A week's worth of pent-up sexual tension coursed through her now unabated.

"Molly," Duke breathed her name against her neck, "I need you."

"Take me." She lay back on the bed, catching Duke's hips and pulling her down on top of her.

The firm weight of her body contrasted with the softness of her skin, and Molly wanted all of her. The flat plane of her stomach, the hard muscles of her arms, the soft curves of her breasts, she wanted all of them. She wanted Duke's amazing hands all over her. The need burned so hot she didn't have time to think. Duke slid down her body, blazing a trail of heat with her mouth across her breasts toward her stomach. Molly sank her hands into Duke's blond hair again, grasping for a way to hold her close while pushing her lower.

"Please, Sarah, don't make me wait."

She felt her smile against her skin. "Why not? I'm enjoying myself."

Her hips tried to lurch up, but the press of Duke's torso held them in place. "I need it. I need you."

"I like the sound of that," Duke mumbled against her stomach as she continued to kiss. "Tell me what you need, and I'll give it to you."

She groaned.

Duke brushed her hand over Molly's legs, gently urging them apart so she could settle in. "Come on, Molly. Tell me what you want."

"Your mouth," Molly panted. "Take me with your mouth."

Duke complied immediately. With one broad stroke of her tongue, Molly's hips lurched forward and a dizzying rush of relief spread through her. She sank more deeply into the bed, but the next pass of

Duke's tongue, more purposeful and direct, caused Molly's muscles to tense once more. Her stomach contracted, and Duke found a rhythm, relentlessly urging her higher, faster, stronger.

"God, yes, don't stop," she begged, surrendering to incoherency. "Sarah, yes. Harder. Yes."

Lights flashed, red and white, behind her eyelids, then went black as her shaking muscles faded to tremors, then went limp. Still, the fire didn't fade. She clutched the side of Duke's shoulder and pulled her back up her body. "Come here."

Duke's grin was anything but shy or sweet now. Cocky, rakish, confident, she slowly crawled back over her. Molly grabbed a fistful of Duke's hair and pulled her down to kiss her again. Refusing to let the momentum fade, she swept her tongue through Duke's mouth, searching, taking, possessing. She grabbed her ass with both hands, kneading as she pulled her up higher. Breaking the kiss, she dragged her teeth across Duke's lower lip, giving it a little nip before slipping down the bed. She ran her hand up Duke's chest, pushing her up as she positioned herself between spread knees. They held eye contact until she was directly beneath her body. Molly grabbed Duke's hips, and Duke grabbed the headboard. Then at her urging, Molly took Duke in her mouth.

There was no time for exploring or teasing now. She went right for the evidence of Duke's need, stroking her with broad, flat passes of her tongue. She drank in the taste of her as the scent of sex overwhelmed all her other senses. She wanted to drown in her. It could've lasted minutes or hours and still wouldn't have been long enough before Duke's thighs tensed and tightened on either side of her. She cried out in a hoarse breath, then doubled over as Molly extracted herself slowly, and they both collapsed in a heap of tangled body parts.

"Oh my God," Duke panted flopping on to her back. "Where did you learn to do that?"

"I don't know," Molly said honestly. "I've never wanted anything so badly. Maybe it's like this between women, but—"

"No," Duke cut in. She closed her eyes and tried to steady her ragged intake of breath before rolling onto her side to face Molly. "It's never been like that for me before, Molly. No one's ever made me feel the things I feel for you."

"Really?" Molly's chest tightened at the emotions stirring there.

Duke took her hand and lifted it to her lips. She kissed the tip of each one of Molly's fingers. "I mean it. It's only you. It's only us."

Molly closed her eyes to hide the tears forming there. She pulled Duke back to her chest and hugged her tightly. They lay holding each other as their breathing returned to normal, then grew shallow.

"I'm sorry, Mol," Duke mumbled. "I meant to go slower. I wanted to talk about your week, but I'm fading fast."

"It's okay." Molly kissed her forehead. "We can talk later."

"Really? Are you sure?"

She wasn't sure, not really. They did need to talk about what had happened in Chicago and the problems with Joe's attitude and their schedules and their priorities, but even if she did have the energy left, she wouldn't have had the heart to let anything shatter the perfection of this moment.

❖

"We could take over second place this weekend," Joe said excitedly as he and Duke sat down next to each other.

"Don't get ahead of yourself. All we can focus on is beating the Reds, and even that won't be easy," Duke said seriously, then cracked a smile. "But with the way we're hitting right now, we do have a great chance to put the Reds behind us."

"Then we get the Pirates next week," Joe added hopefully.

Duke laughed and shook her head, but instead of managing his expectations, she threw her arm around his shoulders and squeezed tightly. "Is anything more fun than a pennant race?"

Molly's heart swelled at the sight of them having so much fun together, but she didn't have enough energy to laugh. The last week had been exhausting, full of early mornings, busy days, and late nights. Duke's being home helped somewhat with the busy days but had the opposite effect on the amount of sleep she got. That thought actually did spark a smile.

"You read a story," Charlie said, pointing to Duke.

"I don't have a book," Duke said. "Do you want me to tell you a story? I know a great one about the 1982 World Series."

"No. Books in bed."

"He wants you to read his bedtime story," Molly explained.

"I'm sorry, buddy. I have to work tonight," Duke explained. "You'll all be asleep long before I get home."

Molly's shoulders tightened. "How late are we talking?"

"After midnight for sure," Duke said, her eyes trained on the field. "I have a good feeling about some leads I got today."

"Is that why you didn't come by the restaurant this afternoon?"

"Yeah. I got lost in the job. By the time I looked up, it was after four."

Molly tried to not let the comment or its cavalier delivery sting too much. They hadn't made firm plans, so Duke hadn't stood her up exactly, but she'd said she'd try to come by for a few minutes so they could talk without the kids around. It didn't sound like she'd tried very hard.

"What if nothing exciting happens during the game?" she asked, "or the Cardinals lose?"

"Mom, don't jinx 'em," Joe said.

"I'm actually working on a supplemental column. There's more at stake here than tonight's game," Duke added. "I can't be worried about sleep."

Molly ran her fingers lightly up Duke's neck and tugged on her earlobe before leaning closer to whisper, "There's more at stake at home than sleep."

Duke finally turned to face Molly. "Oh yeah? Instant replay of last night's highlight reel?"

"And then some," Molly confirmed.

A subtle blush spread across Duke's cheeks, and Molly suspected it had little to do with the heat of the sinking September sun. "You sure do know how to make me question my priorities."

"Does that mean you'll make it home a little earlier than originally planned?"

"Sorry, no can do. For the first time in weeks I have something worth writing about. I have to seize the momentum," Duke said, then nudging Molly, added, "but I promise not to exert all my energy on the ole keyboard. You and I can go a few extra innings when I get home."

Molly shook her head. She'd already overlooked a lot in order to feed her libido. She still hadn't brought up Chicago. She let Duke's forgetting to come see her today slide. She'd said nothing about Joe's attitude problems, and she'd been more than understanding about

Duke's crazy schedule, but she refused to become a post-game booty call. "I plan to be asleep before midnight."

"Will you be able to come to my baseball game tomorrow morning?" Joe asked.

"Of course, buddy. I even got someone to cover my pre-game report so I can stay the whole time."

Molly stared at her, wide-eyed. Did she really say she'd rather work on supplemental stories than spare even a few minutes of time for Molly, but she could casually get someone to cover one of her primary job responsibilities in order to go to a child's baseball game?

"I better get back up to the booth," Duke said, oblivious to Molly's rising frustration.

"Already?" Joe asked.

"Yeah. I need to stay focused. We're on a winning steak."

"And you never mess with a streak," Joe finished for her.

"That's my boy," Duke said with a tap on his cap. Then she turned to Molly and gave her hand a little squeeze. "And you're my girl."

The old defenses she'd let go of tried to rise again. She was not some little lady sitting in the stands to support her man or her butch or whatever Duke was to her.

"I'll see what I can do about getting home, but if the Cardinals win, you shouldn't wait up past midnight for me," Duke said as she turned to go.

"I won't be waiting up either way."

Duke froze in mid-step. Either the words or their cold delivery was enough to make her turn around. "What's that supposed to mean?"

"It means I'm not a groupie, or the baseball equivalent." She lowered her voice. "My love life will not be dictated by the Cardinals' win/loss record."

Duke's face flamed red. "Where is this coming from?"

"From you being gone for two weeks, then buzzing in like you never left. It's about you being nonchalant about everything that doesn't involve a bat and a ball. It's about my son refusing to do his homework because you told him 'you win some, you lose some,' and he believed you."

"And you thought a crowded stadium with..." Duke nodded to the back of the boy's heads, "sitting right there while I'm at work, in the middle of a pennant race, would be the time to discuss this?"

"Of course not, but when else do we have? You leave before I get home, you won't come by the restaurant, you can't even tell me when you'll get in after work."

She rubbed her face. "You don't get it at all, do you?"

"What don't I get?"

"You sound like I'm carousing in the bars or chasing skirts till all hours. I'm working my tail off. This is what I do for a living, and I'm proud of doing my job well. I studied and worked and put in horrendous hours for over a decade to get where I am right now. I'm proving every sexist, bigoted, good ole boy who ever doubted me wrong, and I love it."

"Maybe I don't get your single-minded focus. I've never had the luxury of doing one thing to the exclusion of everything else, so maybe there are some things I don't get." She sighed and pinched the bridge of her nose in an attempt to stem the headache starting to throb there. "But apparently I'm not the only one, because there are some things you don't get, either."

"What's that?"

"When you focus so much on trying to keep up your winning streak in one area of your life, you tend to lose them in others."

"Molly…" Duke said, then bit her lip.

"No, don't bother. That's how it goes for you. Right now the Cardinals are winning more than they lose, but the same can't be said for you and me." Molly shook her head as sadness settled across her slumping shoulders. "That's a trade you're willing to make, so get back to work, but you should know I can't brush those losses off as easily as you do."

Molly heard Duke, first in the hallway, then in the bathroom brushing her teeth. Then her footsteps got closer, and the door made a soft swoosh across the bedroom carpet. When the rustle of her shirt hit the floor, Molly tried to stifle the desire to feel Duke's bare skin against hers. Still, she listened for the soft jangle of her belt buckle unclasp and wondered if she'd left her boxers on or removed them with her khakis. She wished she really were asleep.

The mattress gave slightly as Duke slid in next to her, but she stayed facing the other way. It didn't matter how good it felt to have her body, warm and soft, behind her. She hadn't let go of her anger yet. It didn't help that, once again, she found herself listening to Duke slipping quietly into bed at one in the morning. Duke knew Molly was upset, that she wanted to talk, but she still hadn't made it home until more than three hours after the game ended.

"Hey," Duke whispered.

Molly rolled her eyes in the dark. *Great opening line.*

"Come on, Mol, I know you're awake."

Keep trying, sportswriter.

"Look, I'm not going to apologize for doing my job, but I am sorry for the strain my hours are putting on our relationship."

She rolled onto her back. "Well, that was a classic non-apology."

"Oh good, you're speaking to me."

It was dark enough that she could only make out the outline of Duke's face, but she was clearly smiling. She could hear it in her voice, the lighthearted tone that so casually brushed off every concern Molly tried to raise. The good-natured approach became less and less effective every time she used it. They had some very real problems, and joking about them only went so far to ease the tension.

"Please don't do that."

"Do what?" Duke asked, snuggling closer and throwing an arm around Molly's stomach.

"Make light of this."

"I'm not really sure what *this* is. I thought things were going well. I'm happy, the boys seem happy."

"And the Cardinals are winning again."

"Yeah," Duke admitted. "That matters to me."

"What about the fact that you and I haven't had a legitimate conversation in the light of day without little ears around in more than two weeks? Does that matter to you?"

"Things have been a little busy."

"A little?"

"My job requires a lot of travel. I have never lied to you about my hours either."

"No, but you also said you were all in on this relationship. You said we were a team, and it doesn't feel that way."

Duke pulled her away and her voice softened. "I'm sorry if you doubt my commitment to you and the boys. I'm trying to be good for them, and you, but I've never done this before."

"I know." Molly had never done this successfully either. Did she have unrealistic expectations? God, was she being unreasonable? "And you are good with the kids, it just feels like we're in a joint custody agreement instead of a new relationship. You have them while I work, I have them while you work, and you and I never have any time alone together."

"Our schedules aren't ideal."

"That's a pretty big understatement, but I'm not sure it's just the schedules causing the problem." She sat up and pulled her knee to her chest. "I'm worried it's the values behind them."

"What's that supposed to mean?"

"It means, everything I do, everything in my life is centered around my family. Work is something I do to make a better life for them. Yes, I want to do my job well and I'm trying to move up, but I'm only really putting in the extra hours for the promotion because of what it will allow me to do for the boys."

Duke frowned, her brow furrowing before she shook her head. "I wish you loved your job, but I can't feel guilty about loving mine because you don't feel the same way."

The frustration bubbled up again, tightening her chest and pushing at her temples. Why didn't Duke get it? Why was she the only one trying to understand here? She worked so hard to respect the things that mattered to her, but she wasn't getting the same effort in return. She didn't want to be the only one in this relationship; she didn't want to be the only one trying. What if Duke didn't really feel the same way? Was she just setting herself up for another fall?

No, she fought the urge to disengage. They had to learn to work through things together. They had to communicate. "I am not asking you to feel guilty about loving baseball. I am asking you to create a little more space in your life for us, though."

"I'm here now."

"At one o'clock in the morning?" She sounded harsher than she'd meant to, but damn it, they were going around in circles with diminishing returns. "Where were you at three o'clock when you said you'd come by the restaurant? Where were you when I put the kids to bed? Where were you at midnight, long after the game ended?"

"Work, work, and work." Duke snapped back. "I was at work. I don't ask you where you were at eleven, twelve, and one today. I don't fault you for working when I'm home."

"And I am not faulting you for doing your job. During game time, you belong to the Cardinals. I get that. Batting practice and press conferences, too. Road trips and travel days have first dibs as well, as hard as they are on all of us. I understand that your job takes a lot of time and energy. I'm talking about the extra hours, the going in early and staying late. The supplemental stories."

"We're in a pennant race. It's my first year on the job, and I am the only woman at this level in my entire field. Don't you get what kind of pressure I'm under?"

"It's always something, Duke. You had to work extra hard when they were losing. You called it extraordinary circumstances in Chicago, now you have to put in overtime when they win, too. There's always something more important than us, and I'm afraid there always will be." There, she'd said it—the thought she'd been dancing around for weeks.

"Mol," Duke whispered. "That's not true. Nothing is more important to me than you and the boys."

"It doesn't feel that way. It feels like you give your attention to everyone and everything else ahead of me. Everything else comes first, and I get the parts of you that are left over at the end of the day." Her chest trembled, and it came out in her voice. "And I'm not going to beg, Duke. I spent too much of my life depending on other people's approval, and I worked hard to break free. I shouldn't have to plead with you to want to be with me."

"It's not like that between us."

"It is, that's what I'm telling you right now. I have worked so hard to be patient and understanding, but nothing is changing and I'm done waiting for you to throw me some scraps of your attention. I lived alone for years, yet I never felt as lonely as I have the past two weeks."

"I'm sorry, Molly," Duke said, her voice so soft and close. "I don't ever want you to feel lonely because of me. I don't ever want to let you down." Duke wrapped her arm around her shoulder and eased her closer, until her chest rested against the bare skin of Duke's chest.

"I'm not sure you can help it," Molly said weakly, her resolve fading as the distance between their bodies disappeared.

"I can. I can do better for you. I will do better."

Even as she said it, Molly could hear the doubt in her voice. "You say that now, but what about tomorrow when a new story breaks? Will we have the same argument again? Because I'm tired of going around and around."

"No," Duke whispered and kissed her forehead. "I can't promise to be perfect, but I do promise to be better. Please don't be mad at me anymore. I can't stand disappointing you."

Molly inhaled a deep breath filled with Duke's scent and pressed her lips to the skin above her heart. The fear and the doubt still pulsed below the surface, but they no longer drove her—at least not as much as the desire to revel in the closeness she'd craved all day. "I'm not mad at you. I can never stay mad at you."

"Good, that means you have to give me another chance."

"I guess so." Though she wasn't as happy about that as Duke sounded.

"I'm going to get it right this time."

The day's worth of frustration and anger faded, leaving a void for exhaustion to numb her mind and weigh on her muscles. She snuggled closer, giving into the need to touch, and feel, and believe. "I hope so, because I'm not sure how many more losses we can take."

Top of the Eighth

There Is No "I" in "Team"

"I thought the Mets were going to blow it open in the sixth inning when they had two on and nobody out," Joe said between bites of his cereal.

"They should have," Duke said. "If Benton Rollins would've laid down a bunt, they could've advanced both runners. Then they would've needed only a long fly ball to tie the game. I'm almost certain the bunt sign was on."

"How do you know?"

"The coaches flashed a bunch of signs, and when he swung, they all looked confused, then angry. He also got pulled into the tunnel after the at bat. It could've been nothing, but I think he got a talking-to."

"Maybe he missed the sign," Joe said.

"Possibly. I try to never judge someone without knowing the facts, but I think Rollins was thinking about himself and only himself right there."

"Like his own stats?"

"Yes, and his own wallet. He has all sorts of bonuses in his contract that only kick in if he gets one hundred hits or keeps his batting average above three hundred."

"But his team can still get a wildcard spot if they win."

"That matters only if you actually care about the team more than you care about your personal stats, and he'd rather pad his résumé than help his team win. Sadly it's a common attitude, but it disrespects the game and everyone around him. He thinks he's more important than the game itself."

"No one can be bigger than the game," Joe said, "not even a superstar."

"And there's no 'I' in 'team,'" Duke added. "The whole only works if each member is dedicated to the others. Which reminds me, I'm taking you and Charlie to school this morning."

"You are?" Molly asked, finally looking up from the accounting books she studied at the other end of the table.

Duke rose and collected all the breakfast dishes. "You have a big interview this morning, and your whole team is going to help you get the W, which means we'll get out of your hair and help you focus on whatever you need to do to get ready."

Molly smiled as broadly as if Duke had said she was taking her to Paris. She must be more stressed out about the morning than she let on. Molly had kept quiet about the prospect of the promotion in front of the boys, but it would be a big deal for her. As the daytime manager, she'd have more job security and greater control over her schedule than she did as a waitress. Better pay, too. Molly had already done the books for a few months, and she'd been at the restaurant for years, so she should be a clear favorite for the job, but she didn't take anything for granted. She'd studied everything from restaurant trends to accounting practices for two weeks. Still, whenever Duke asked questions, she tried to play it off.

Maybe Molly didn't want to jinx the promotion by acting overconfident, but Duke worried Molly's history of being disappointed made her leery of admitting how much she wanted something for fear of being let down again. Things had gone wrong so often in her life. She hadn't learned to trust in things she couldn't control, and as much as Duke wanted to change that, she couldn't do it overnight. Still, she could lift a couple little things off Molly's plate occasionally, and today those little things happened to be named Joe and Charlie.

"Guys," she said, pulling both boys into a huddle. "Today Mom's our starting pitcher, and she's walking up to the mound for a big game. We need to back her up like a team of all-stars."

"Okay," Joe said.

"'Kay," Charlie echoed.

"Joe, I need you to get Charlie's shoes on, then both of you get your backpacks. Got it, team?"

"Got it," they said in unison.

"I'm going to get your lunch boxes, then we're going to line up, shortest to tallest, to kiss your mom good-bye before we march out the door." She looked them both in the eyes. Joe looked intense. The kid was a gamer no matter what the game. Charlie, on the other hand, was, well, Charlie. His eyes were glazed over and unfocused. She wondered briefly if he'd gotten enough sleep, but then shook off the thought because there wasn't any amount of sleep in the world to provide the energy Charlie needed to be himself on a daily basis. "Hands in, boys."

She put her hand out in front of them. Charlie put his little warm palm on top, then Joe covered it with his own. "Team on three."

They all counted together. "One, two, three, team!" Then they broke off in separate directions. Within five minutes, Duke kissed Molly good-bye.

"Thank you," Molly said. "This means a lot to me."

"Then it means a lot to me, too."

"Thanks, Coach." Molly kissed her again, then, before she had the chance to lose her focus, nudged Duke out the door.

Duke was still grinning after she dropped Joe off and turned the RAV4 toward Charlie's preschool. "You ready for school, buddy?"

He didn't respond. He often got lost in his own world, but he'd been subdued all morning. She glanced in the rearview mirror. His eyes were heavy, like he was seconds away from nodding off.

"Char, Char, Charlie," she sang. "Are you falling asleep on me?"

He gave a little pitiful whimper. She'd heard him scream and shout and cry. She'd seen temper tantrums and excitement. She'd even had him fall asleep in her arms, but she'd never heard him whine. The hair on her arms stood up in some sort of premonition or instinct. Something was wrong. She pulled over in the first parking lot she found and hopped out.

"Charlie, what's wrong?"

His bottom lip quivered, and her heart ached. She didn't care about being late or standing exposed in a bank parking lot as traffic buzzed by. She wanted to hold him, to soothe him. She unstrapped his car seat and pulled him into her arms. "Come here, sweet boy."

He rested his head on her shoulder, and she rubbed his back gently. Even through his shirt, heat radiated off his skin. "You're burning up."

She held him back to put her hand on his forehead in time for him to cough, choke, and then vomit down the entire length of her arm. She was so shocked she froze, and the second wave hit her, too, before she could react. She angled his body away from her, then ran toward the small strip of grass between the parking lot and the street. Charlie continued to throw up the eggs he'd eaten for breakfast along with several things Duke didn't recognize, not that she was trying to examine it too closely. Still, the sight wasn't nearly as troubling as the smell. She fought to breathe through her mouth and focus on Charlie instead of thinking about what she was covered in.

"Okay, okay, okay, you're okay," she muttered to both herself and to Charlie. "Everything's okay. I can handle this."

As Charlie's vomiting subsided, he began to cry, and the instincts that had emerged earlier returned. The desire to comfort him overshadowed her own gag reflex. She kissed his head and rubbed his back, then carried him carefully back to the car. She found a bottle of water and used it to douse her arm the best she could, then gave it to Charlie. "Just a little sip, okay?"

He nodded and tipped the bottle up in his tiny trembling hands. He sipped, then grimaced. "Tastes bad."

"I know. Put some in your mouth then spit it out, like toothpaste."

He tried it, then almost smiled when the water splattered against the pavement.

"Better?"

"My tummy hurts."

"I bet. Mine's churning a little bit, too." She stared at him for a second. What was she supposed to do now? She'd never dealt with a sick kid before. Did he need to go to the doctor? Back to bed? Should she make soup? What about medicine? It seemed like he had a fever, but she didn't have a thermometer. Oh Lord, was she going to have to use a rectal thermometer? She hadn't even considered what that would entail.

Of course she'd spent plenty of time dreaming of being a permanent part of the kids' lives, but when she thought about parenting the boys, she always imagined birthday parties and story times, family vacations and baseball games. Never once had she considered the possibility of being puked on. "What are we going to do now?"

"I want to go home," Charlie said.

"Right," she sighed. Home made the most sense. Then she could call Molly.

❖

"Hello?" Molly whispered loud enough to be heard over the clanging of pots and pans in the background.

"Hey, I'm sorry to bother you at work, but—"

"You just had to hear how my interview went?" Molly laughed. "You're wonderful."

Shit. The interview. How had she forgotten? Oh yeah, a three-year-old had coated her in vomit and everything else had sort of slipped her mind.

"I don't want to jinx anything, but I think the partners were impressed. A lot of nodding, a lot of smiling."

"That's great, Mol. I knew you'd do great but—"

"They said they should know by the end of the week if I got the job, so we can either celebrate or commiserate this weekend."

Duke rubbed her face with her free hand. She didn't want to trample on Molly's accomplishment. She deserved this moment, but a sick kid trumped everything. "Charlie threw up."

"What?" Everything about Molly's voice changed, the volume, the tone, and the pitch. She went from an excited up-and-coming manager to mama lion instantly.

"He didn't seem to feel good on the way to school, so I pulled over and he threw up. I'm pretty sure he has a fever, too."

"Where is he?"

"We're back at the apartment. I got him cleaned up and changed, and he fell asleep on my shoulder."

"Oh, Duke, I'm so glad he's with you."

"Thanks?"

"No, I didn't mean I'm glad you have to deal with this, but if he couldn't be with me, I'm glad he's with someone who loves him."

"But I don't know what to do." Her heartbeat still raced.

"Sounds like you did great."

"Doesn't he need a doctor or something?"

"If he's sleeping now and doesn't seem to be in pain, it's probably a stomach bug."

"What about the fever? Shouldn't I give him something?"

"If it's a low-grade fever, I try to let it run its course. It's nature's way of fighting back. There's an ear thermometer in his bathroom medicine cabinet along with some Tylenol. If you're worried, you can give him the dosage on the bottle, but if he's resting peacefully, I wouldn't worry."

Why wasn't Molly freaking out? "I don't know anything about taking care of sick kids. He was sad and scared, Mol. He whimpered. Charlie whimpered."

"I know it's hard. It breaks my heart every time, but this is part of parenthood. Kids get sick. This isn't the first time, and it won't be the last, especially since he's in preschool."

Her chest constricted at the idea of her being a parent. She wanted that, and she certainly loved Charlie, but that didn't mean she was qualified for the job. "I think I should call the babysitter."

"You can't have a babysitter watch a sick kid, Duke." Molly's voice held a blend of amusement and disbelief. "Relax and trust your instincts."

Her instincts told her two different things. Part of her knew Molly was right. Charlie needed a parent right now, but the other part of her said she needed to get to work. Work was safe, work was what she knew, work was where she felt in control. "How soon can you get home?"

"I can't get off early today." Molly's voice fell back to a whisper. "The owners are here. My promotion's on the line."

"But the Pirates are in town," Duke countered, "with second place on the line."

Molly fell silent. If not for the restaurant noise in the background, Duke would've thought the call dropped. "Are you still there?"

Molly sighed. "I'm waiting for you to realize you put the National League standings above caring for a sick kid."

"That's not fair. I got puked on, for crying out loud. Maybe you're used to that, but you can't expect me to jump into this with no warning, no training, during the biggest series of the year so far."

"No, you know what's not fair? All your talk about being a team, all of your corny lines about taking care of each other, because you don't mean any of them. What you mean is you want to be part of our family when it's convenient for you and drop us when it's not."

"You're being completely unreasonable. I'm not running out on you or Charlie. I have to work."

"I have to work, too. I used vacation days to come to Chicago with you. I left early twice last week so you could spend time with the kids before your games. I did that because I wanted you to be a part of our lives, because I'm trying to be supportive of you, but now I'm up for a big promotion, and I'm not seeing the same kind of commitment from you."

Duke's head throbbed. She saw Molly's point, but she'd given up a lot lately, too. She'd had people cover for her more than she should have lately, and they were in the middle of a pennant race. "Tonight's game is important. I can't use my vacation time right now."

"Is that some rule from your editor?"

"No, I mean not a written rule, but—"

"So what you're saying isn't that you can't miss the game, it's that you won't."

She sighed. "Yeah, I guess. I'm giving you every waking minute I'm not working, but I can't risk losing my job."

"What about my job? Why is your work more important than mine?"

"I'm a professional sportswriter. You're just a waitress." As soon as the words left her mouth, she wanted to reel them back in. She would've gladly choked on them, but she couldn't have them back.

"So much for being part of a team." Molly's words were clipped, her voice cold. Duke remembered the hollow sound, the one that came with the walls she'd worked so hard to get past. "I'll be home in half an hour."

"No, Molly, I'm sorry. I didn't mean that. You don't have to come right away. I meant…can't we compromise…Molly?" The line went dead. Molly was on her way home, and for the first time Duke wasn't looking forward to seeing her walk through the door.

❖

Duke jumped to her feet as soon as she heard Molly's key in the door, and she was apologizing even before she came fully into view. "I'm so sorry. I was an ass. I was scared. I messed up."

Molly didn't even look her in the eye as she walked right past. Duke followed her down the hall.

"Molly, I know your job's important to you. I know you worked hard for this promotion," she whispered as they neared Charlie's door, then fell silent as Molly opened it.

She watched Molly bend over her sleeping son. She gently pushed aside his sand-colored curls and rested her hand lightly on his forehead for a few seconds. He didn't stir. He looked almost cherubic there, sleeping peacefully; the hint of rose in his chubby cheeks the only evidence of his illness. Molly kissed his head lightly, then tucked his security blanket under his arm.

She moved with such grace and tenderness, a natural mother and such a strong contrast to Duke's fear and bumbling. Molly rose and left the room, brushing by Duke like a cloud of ice.

Back in the living room, she tried again. "Molly I'm sorry. I freaked out. I didn't know what to do."

"So you ran. There was a crisis here, a conflict that made you uncomfortable, so you did what you always do: you tried to bolt back to baseball," Molly said calmly. "That's where you want to be. That's where you feel safe and in control. My family doesn't make you feel any of those things."

My family.

Not our family.

Molly had once again put the walls around her world, around the things she needed to protect, and Duke was on the outside. Little more than a stranger. No, that wasn't true. Even when they'd first met, Molly'd had a fire in her eyes, but it wasn't there anymore. When Molly finally looked at her now, that deep brown gaze was empty, and Duke felt herself falling into the void.

"Molly, please. Can't we just talk about this? I think it was a misunderstanding. Let me tell you what happened."

Nothing.

No response at all.

She might as well have been talking to the walls.

"Molly," she said, exasperated at being shut out.

"What are you still doing here?"

"I'm trying to explain."

"I didn't come home for an explanation. I came because you said you had to go to work. So go."

She'd been dismissed. Coolly, calmly, and completely detached, Molly had not made a request. She'd ended their non-conversation and all but showed her the door. She'd been so prepared for Molly's anger, but this nothingness was new. Sadly, Duke's confusion and uncertainty was not. She'd grown so accustomed to apologizing, to feeling guilty, to always trying to make up for something, that it almost felt natural now. So she did what had come to be her default over the past few months: she gave in to what Molly wanted and walked out the door.

❖

Duke stared at the expanse of Busch Stadium from the large open windows of the press booth. Six months ago, she didn't think she'd ever grow tired of this view, and even now it stirred too many emotions to name. Not sadness or regret, though she did feel those things. The view inspired something deeper, something soothing, something comforting but empty. She didn't know she could ever feel so alone in the midst of forty thousand fans, and she never knew the middle of September in St. Louis could feel so cold. Then again, it wasn't the stadium or the weather making her feel those things. The empty chill clearly emanated from her own heart.

"Are you going down to the stands?" Coop's voice startled her. She hadn't even seen him sit down.

"What?"

"It's a home game. You always leave the press box about now."

"I'm surprised you notice. I wouldn't think you cared about my habits."

"I'm a reporter. I notice things. Doesn't mean I care."

She nodded at the subtle truth of their lives, or maybe their differences. Duke cared about all of it. She cared so much she couldn't juggle everything. Well, tonight she didn't have to. Molly and the boys weren't in the stands. She had nothing to focus on but her job. So why couldn't she? She'd finally separated her love life from her professional life. She should've been more clearheaded than she'd been in weeks.

"So are you going or not? It kind of gives me time to spread out," Cooper said, elbowing into her space.

"Not."

"Why? This crowd isn't interesting enough for you?"

"No, actually, it's not. It's just the people…I don't have any reason—ugh, do you have kids?"

"Sure. Two of 'em, one from each ex-wife."

"I didn't know. How old are they?"

"Sylvie is eight. Will is eleven. No, wait. Sylvie's eleven, Will is thirteen, maybe." He paused and tapped several fingers as though silently counting. "One of 'em just had a birthday. Sylvie. She was born during a stretch run. Will, during spring training."

"You can't remember how old your kids are?"

"Things start to slip your mind when you're my age."

He couldn't have been more than forty-five. "What's Cayden Brooks's batting average?"

"He's up to .292," Coop answered effortlessly.

She waited for him to show some sort of chagrin, but none came.

"If you're hoping to guilt me into admitting I'm not the world's most attentive parent, I'll gladly do so, but don't get all judgy until you've been there. There are only so many hours in a day, and our job eats up most of them. If you ever have kids, you'll be the same way."

Duke opened her mouth to protest, but nothing came out. What had she wanted to disagree with? That she had been in his position? That she wasn't like him?

He turned away to stare out across the field. "I could be a part-time parent. I could spend the whole off-season with them, go to the park or the movie or whatever they like to do, but when spring training rolls around again, I'm going to hop on the caravan. It's what I do, who I am. I'd only end up resenting them if I tried to be someone else."

"Don't you wish you had some time with them? Isn't a little bit better than nothing?"

"Maybe for some people, but I don't like to do things halfway, and I can't give up the game. Parenting's a full-time, two-person job. If I'm not up for the task, why not step out of the way and let someone who's able and willing get the job done right?"

She would've argued with him. She would've told him he couldn't talk about people's lives like he talked about laying down a bunt, but she couldn't have made herself heard over the echoes ricocheting through her brain. She heard Cooper say, "I can't give up the game."

She heard Molly say, "So much for being part of a team." Her father's voice filtered through the clutter, too. "That's not fair to either of you... you can't give one hundred percent to two different things."

She shook her head, trying to silence the rumblings of her conscience. Could they all be right? Was she being unfair to Molly and the kids by not being there enough, or was she being unfair by even being there at all? She didn't want to let them go. She didn't want to let them down. But was being part of a team or a family really about what she wanted? What about the good of the team?

BOTTOM OF THE EIGHTH

There's No Crying in Baseball

"Hey." Duke slipped in the front door and closed it behind her quietly. "I'm glad you're still up."

Molly didn't know what time it was. She hadn't looked at the clock or done any of the post-game mental countdown she'd grown accustomed to. She hadn't tried to calculate when Duke would get home or figure out how much sleep they'd be able to get before the boys woke up. So much of her time with Duke had been spent either counting time away or trying to keep from counting the time they had left. She couldn't tell which was harder, but now she'd have her answer.

"I left as soon as the post-game press conference ended," Duke continued as she set her messenger bag on the table, then flopped onto the couch next to Molly. "I know I made a mistake today, Mol. I'm sorry. I should have…" Her voice trailed off, and Molly followed Duke's gaze to the suitcase on the floor in front of them, then back to her. She didn't say anything else. She didn't have to. Her expressive eyes widened, then shimmered in the dim light as the questions, the understanding, the hurt ran their course.

"Please don't do this. I know I made an error. I should've stayed here today, for you, for Charlie, for our team." Her voice cracked, and it took all of Molly's strength not to crack along with it.

"But you didn't. I asked you to, and you didn't. You chose your job over me and my family, once again."

"But I know now I was wrong. I wasn't a team player, but I'm telling you I learned my lesson. I want to be the kind of teammate you and the boys deserve."

Molly rubbed her face. *Again with the damn sports clichés.* "You keep talking like that. You keep calling us a team, but I don't want to be your teammate."

Duke winced. "What do you mean?"

"Don't you see? I don't want to live my life in some grand sports analogy."

Duke stared at her, tears filling her eyes. "So it's just over? You're giving up on me? On us?"

"There is no us, Duke. There's been you and me and the boys and the game, always the game. It's like you've got a mistress, only worse because I can't even compete with a game."

"You don't have to compete. This isn't a competition."

"Everything is about the competition with you. The winning gracefully and losing with honor, you embody everything that's good and noble about baseball, but even with your no-'I'-in-'team' mentality, you're missing the point."

"What's the point?"

"You should've asked yourself if there was an 'I' in 'parent,' because that's what Charlie needed today." Molly sighed. "And there's no 'I' in 'partner,' and there's no 'I' in 'forever,' either."

Duke opened her mouth, but Molly cut her off. "I want to be with someone who puts me and the boys first. I don't think you're capable of that. You might learn to say the right things or do the right things, and you're great about apologizing when you don't, but we're never going to have your whole heart, and we deserve better."

Duke hung her head, and her shoulders started to shake. Molly's resolve began to crumble. She exhaled as evenly as she could, but her chest trembled at the sight of Duke's grief. She'd said good-bye enough times in her life to know what the end felt like. She knew how to shut down her emotions, to stay logical and stoic, to dissociate herself from what had to be done. She'd spent years perfecting the art of burying fear and sadness beneath a stony façade, and she'd never doubted her ability to protect herself until now. She'd stood up to threats and tears, begging and yelling, isolation and total bombardment. None of them had touched her the way Duke's quiet tears twisted her heart.

Duke balled the cuff of her shirtsleeve in her fist and used it to wipe her eyes. The move struck Molly as so innocent, so vulnerable, and no matter how she tried to raise those old familiar walls, she suspected they'd fall again if only Duke would mount one more attack, one more impassioned speech, or so much as caress her cheek.

Instead she nodded and said, "You're right."

"What?"

"You and the boys deserve better. You're amazing. This family you've built is so beautiful, and I wanted so much to be a part of it." Duke sniffed back another bout of tears. "But you should have someone who makes you feel like the center of the universe. I wanted to be that person, but I failed you. I don't know what to do now. I'm so sorry."

Molly bit her lip to keep from crying, too. Why wasn't Duke fighting her? Where were her catchy replies and heartfelt life lessons now? She should've been countering Molly's every point, not agreeing with them. She wasn't prepared for this. She'd expected to have to defend herself against Duke's best. Instead, she was fighting her urge to defend Duke against her own brokenness. "You didn't fail."

"I did," Duke said. "I should've been better, at everything. I shouldn't have put you through this in the first place."

Molly reached to touch her, then pulled back. If they were in agreement, and if Duke wasn't capable of being what Molly needed, there was nowhere left for them to go. She stood and collected the suitcase.

Duke followed her to the door and opened it, but before stepping through she turned and met Molly's eyes one more time. "I'm sorry I didn't have enough heart when it counted."

"Don't say that. You have the biggest heart of anyone I've ever met. It's just full. You've got an amazing ability to love. Everyone who meets you can see it and feel it like the light or warmth from the sun, but it's only a reflection like the moon giving light that isn't its own." She wiped her eyes before going on. "What we had was wonderful, but it was always going to be eclipsed. You're never going to love anything the way you love baseball."

Duke hung her head as the tears began to fall once more, but she didn't disagree. Apparently she couldn't fight the truth any more than Molly could, and maybe that was what hurt most of all. There was no anger, no blame, no more options.

Molly kissed her tear-streaked cheek. "Come on, slugger, there's no crying in baseball."

The corner of Duke's mouth curled up slightly, and she nodded.

Swallowing her emotions once more she managed to say, "Good-bye, Molly."

Molly closed the door before whispering, "Good-bye, Duke."

She stumbled over to the couch and curled into a ball before the sobs came. There might not have been any crying in baseball, but she was done with that game and the hold it had over her life.

❖

"Yes, sir, I'm still interested in the job," Molly said, then immediately covered the phone with her hand so her boss's boss couldn't hear Charlie singing loudly in the bathtub. She stuck her head into the hallway and snapped her fingers to get Joe's attention. He looked up from the television long enough for her motion for him to come into the bathroom.

"We'll have the paperwork all sorted out in the next week or so." He continued, oblivious to the parenting juggling act she was performing. "But the job is yours."

"Thank you, thank you." Molly pointed from her eyes to Joe's to Charlie, who was still splashing happily. Joe nodded, and she left the bathroom. "I promise I won't let you down."

"I know you won't. We're just glad no one stole you away from us. When you took off a few weeks ago, we thought you might've had another interview."

Molly didn't know what to say. She didn't want to tell him she hadn't even considered other jobs, much less had the time to search. "I'm dedicated to being the best daytime manager you've ever had."

"In that case, go celebrate. We'll talk details about salary and benefits on Monday."

Salary? Benefits? She felt so light-headed she had to sit down on the edge of the bed. "Thank you. Again, thank you."

She hung up and flopped back onto the mattress. Relief flooded through her. She was moving up. No more waiting tables. No more coffee stains. No more kissing butts of picky clients. Well, maybe there'd still be plenty of that, as the manager always got called into those situations. But still, from now on she'd be giving as many orders as she followed. And regular hours, or more regular at least, no more wondering if she'd have enough hours to feed her family or too many to cover with child care. And insurance, guaranteed. Tears filled her eyes again.

Crying had become a more frequent occurrence since Duke had left five days ago. She'd rarely let herself dwell on her absence or wallow in heartbreak, but those emotions seeped through every crack in her façade. She'd never been sentimental, but now she found herself fighting tears over little things, Charlie's bedtime stories, Joe's evening prayers, commercials for animal shelters, and at least with this announcement, she could identify the overarching emotion as relief and not sadness.

She wiped away a tear that spilled over and pushed herself back to a sitting position. No matter what the reason, she shouldn't be crying right now. *Celebrate.* That's what her boss had said, and he was the boss, after all.

"Hey, boys," she called out, "who wants some ice cream?"

"Yay!" Charlie called.

"Really?" Joe stuck his head into the hallway. "Why?"

"Because I got a promotion."

His smile spread so wide his cheeks pushed up his glasses. He threw his arms around her. "I knew you would get it."

"Thanks, honey, you might have been the only one."

"No, Duke knew, too," he said. "She told me you were a no-doubter. We should call her."

Her chest constricted, not because she didn't want to call Duke, but because she did. Joe was right. She'd been such a big part of this process it didn't seem right for her to not be a part of the celebration, but nothing about Duke felt right anymore. Maybe that was why she hadn't told the boys about the breakup, or maybe she didn't know how. As far as they knew, Duke was on another road trip. Which she was, with her real team, the team she'd consistently chosen over them.

She sighed. "Duke's working right now. We can't interrupt."

Joe's big brown eyes narrowed skeptically. She'd have to have a serious conversation with him soon, but tonight she wanted to enjoy her accomplishment. She grabbed a towel and swooped Charlie out of the bath. "Here. You get this little fish dried off and into his pj's. I'll dish up some ice cream."

She headed to the kitchen and filled three bowls with mint chocolate chip, then rummaged around the fridge for some chocolate syrup. She knew it would likely turn Charlie into a sugar tornado, but she was in no hurry to put the boys to bed. A little chaos seemed so much better than a quiet house.

She listened to the sounds of them laughing. That was her family, everything that mattered. Then she heard Duke's voice and froze.

She sounded far-off and filtered, but there was no mistaking her good-natured laugh or her easy cadence as she said, "I'm so glad to hear that, and to hear your voice, Joe."

Molly's chest ached as the longing to hear that voice say her name again rose to overwhelm her.

"Is she there?" Duke asked as Joe walked around the corner into the kitchen.

"Yeah," Joe said, extending the phone to Molly.

She tried to give him a stern look. "I told you not to bother her at work."

"I didn't. Charlie did," he said seriously. "He knows which button is her number in your phone."

"I told you he was a social media guru," Duke said through the speaker.

Molly made a mental note to add a password to her phone. She took the call off speaker and lifted the phone to her ear. "Hi."

"Hi," Duke said softly. "Congratulations."

"Thank you. I'm sorry the boys interrupted you at work."

"Don't be. My heart about leapt out of my chest when I saw your number. I've wanted to talk to you so much these past few days."

She refrained from mentioning she'd actually picked up the phone to call her more than a few times. "The boys miss you."

"Just the boys?"

"Duke…"

"I'm sorry. You're right. That's why I haven't called. I'm not what you need right now. We both agreed on that."

Had they? They must have, but now with Duke's voice soft and low in her ear, all those memories seemed hazy.

"I know we can't be together, and I'm not going to try to win you back, but I don't want to lose you all from my life completely."

The statement about Duke not wanting her back stung so badly she almost missed the second part. "What do you mean?"

"We were friends first, Mol, and I know it won't be easy for you and me to go back, but I promised both you and the boys I wouldn't ever abandon you. I meant it then, and I mean it now."

"I don't know, being around you right now…" Her chest ached so sharply she couldn't finish her sentence.

"I know. It won't be easy for me either, but this isn't about us. We have the boys to think about, too, and my disappearing isn't fair to them." Duke sighed and Molly heard a loud cheer go up behind her. The Pirates must have gotten a hit. Molly wondered if Duke's attention was divided as she continued. "What if I didn't come over there but planned to spend some time with them at the ballpark?"

"I don't know. I hadn't planned on going to the games this weekend."

"What? It's the last home stand of the season."

"I know, but it'll be too hard for us all to be there together but not together."

"It doesn't have to be. We can all still have a relationship to each other through the game. I know you don't want to hear about baseball right now, but this is an important time for Joe. He's learning that people come and go, relationships shift and change, and few things last forever. He needs something constant, something steady. Baseball can be all those things, especially now as the season comes to a close. He deserves closure." Duke's voice had risen steadily, then dropped to almost a whisper. "Please, Molly, it's almost killing me to know I ruined our chance at a relationship. Please don't make me the reason those kids lose their relationship to baseball, too."

She wanted to snap back that once again Duke had her priorities out of line. As usual, she'd put baseball above everything else. She couldn't find it in her endless amounts of love and devotion to fight for them as a couple, but she had no trouble crafting an eloquent defense of the relationship between a fan and the sport. She should've hung up on her, and if Duke had made any of that about them, she might have, but Duke's only concern had been the boys' well-being. She hadn't asked for a single thing for herself. If anything, taking more time off to see her ex right before the biggest games of the season should've been more torturous for Duke than for Molly, and yet she was the one putting the family before her own convenience. Molly had a hard time questioning the roots of her devotion when it so clearly benefitted her sons.

"Molly, please. You don't ever have to see me again outside of the ballpark."

"Fine." Why did she even argue with her? Duke never pushed or overpowered her. She never yelled or browbeat or bullied. Molly could've withstood those tactics without struggle, but Duke always appealed to her better angels, usually the boys, and she won. "The ballpark is neutral territory. We'll see you before the game on Friday."

"Thank you," Duke said quietly, "and I'm sorry we got off track earlier. I'm happy you got the promotion. I'm glad my distractions didn't get in the way of at least one thing you truly deserved."

Molly's eyes filled with tears again as her emotions ran full circle. She considered telling her that their godforsaken trip to Chicago might have actually helped her in the long run, but she refrained, either because she wasn't ready to admit that to either of them, or maybe because she simply didn't have the fortitude to dive back into their unraveling one more time. Instead she said, "Thank you," once again before hanging up.

She wiped her eyes and turned around to see Joe standing in the doorway.

"Is everything okay?" he asked softly.

"Yeah," she said with a smile she knew he saw through. "Everything except our ice cream. It's melting."

He stared at her for a second before finally wrapping his arms around her waist and squeezing her tightly. "It'll be okay, Mom."

She hugged him back tightly, fearing he'd stolen her line, but if only one of them could believe those words, she was glad it was him.

❖

"We're going to be late if you two don't get dressed." Molly nudged the boys toward their rooms. "I already laid out your clothes. Long sleeves under your jerseys tonight. It'll be cool once the sun goes down."

Charlie went eagerly, but Joe lingered. "It's only four thirty. The game doesn't start until seven."

Molly stopped packing a bag with Charlie-friendly foods she'd spread out on the table. Had Joe actually complained about going to the stadium early? She reached out and laid her palm across his forehead.

"What was that for?"

She cupped his cheeks in her hands and looked into his eyes, so similar to her own. "Checking to see if you have a fever, but you don't seem sick."

"I'm not sick."

"Has your body been snatched by aliens?"

He rolled his eyes. "No."

"Then why aren't you more excited about your first Cardinals game in a week?"

He shrugged. The move looked so much like Duke she winced. She'd left an impression on their lives beyond what she'd shared with Molly, and pretending like that wasn't the case simply wasn't an option.

She motioned for Joe to sit next to her at the dining room table. She'd put off this conversation long enough. He might not know what happened, but he clearly understood their relationship with Duke had changed, and she needed to give him a chance to talk about those things even if it hurt her to do so.

"You know sometimes in relationships, things change. People change, or don't, but relationships are complicated." Too abstract, but she didn't know how else to start. She didn't want to drag him into the details of what had gone wrong. She wasn't even completely sure of those things herself.

"Did you change, or did Duke?" Joe asked.

"Well, maybe we both did, or maybe we only thought we had." They'd both compromised to try to sustain the relationship. She'd given up on her dream of a steady partner for someone who lived on the road, and Duke had spent time away from the job she loved in order to please her. And yet, neither of those concessions had truly been enough. They couldn't overcome their natures. Joe didn't see any of that, though. He stared at her blankly. "I guess I'm saying no matter how hard we both tried, we ultimately wanted different things."

"What did you want?"

"It's hard to explain, honey, but I need someone who's dedicated, someone who's one hundred percent with us, someone who will put me and you and Charlie ahead of everything else in her life."

He nodded. "You wanted her to love you more than baseball."

Her eyes watered at his insight. How had her sweet, intuitive little boy been able to grasp what Duke couldn't? Or maybe she understood but simply couldn't deliver. "It's not Duke's fault. Love isn't something you can make yourself feel. It's something that either develops naturally or doesn't."

"Did it develop for you?"

Molly sighed. She didn't want to answer the question. The truth would only hurt them both more. "I don't want you to worry about us right now. What's most important for you to remember is we're both still here for you."

His mouth quirked into a little smile of amusement.

"What?"

He shrugged again. "I don't know. That sounded kind of funny."

"Why?"

"Of course you're both still here for me."

"Good, I'm glad you know that, but it's okay to feel sad or worried, and you can talk to me about your feelings." Seeing his confidence gave her the strength to voice her own fears. "This isn't going to be like when your dad left."

"Mom," he drew out the word, "I know."

"Do you?" How could he when she didn't know herself? Until two days ago, she let herself believe she could never see Duke again.

"Duke loves us. She promised no matter what she'd always be on our team."

"I know, honey, but sometimes people say things they don't mean or make promises they can't keep."

"Not Duke."

"She's not perfect, you know. She makes mistakes." The words came out in a flash of hurt, and she regretted them immediately.

Joe frowned, then continued more slowly. "She didn't promise to be perfect. She promised to do her best."

Something twisted inside her chest. Duke had done her best. Molly knew that with everything in her. She saw it clearly. Joe did, too. Why had they come to such completely different opinions about what would come next? Was it his childish faith in other people? He might have been wise beyond his years, but he was still a kid. He didn't know what it meant to be disappointed, left, let down the way she did.

"I remember Dad, too, you know," he said softly as if he'd read her mind.

"What do you remember?"

He looked away. Why couldn't he look at her? Did he miss him? Of course he did. Did he know she'd failed them all? Did he blame her for Tony's abandonment? He deserved a chance to say so. "We've always been able to talk, even when you were Charlie's age. You're my number one man. You can tell me anything, Joe, even about your dad."

"I was happy when he left," he blurted out.

She gasped.

"What? I didn't like it when he came home from work. He didn't talk to me or you. You didn't smile at him. He didn't smile at all."

"I'm so sorry you remember that." All those years of trying to protect him were for naught. And now she'd put him in the same position with Duke. "I tried to make things good for you, but you've always been sensitive. I'm sorry for that, too. I think you were too aware of my unhappiness. I should've been stronger for you."

"We weren't unhappy when he left. I liked it." His cheeks grew pink with either embarrassment or guilt, but he forged on. "It was just me and you, then Charlie, too. I liked that. I didn't want you to date anyone until Duke. Duke was the opposite."

"How was she the opposite?" The situation felt very similar to her.

"We were happy with her here, and when she left, you were sad."

"What about you? Aren't you sad she's left us?"

He looked at her like she'd lost her mind. "Duke didn't leave us. Duke will always be there for us."

Molly swallowed the lump of emotions clogging her throat. "Then why do you seem so sad?"

"I'm afraid I'm not supposed to love Duke anymore because you don't. Maybe I shouldn't even love baseball, but I don't know how to stop loving them."

"Oh, honey, why would you think I wanted you to do that?"

"Because I love you, and I'm not sure I should be happy when you're so sad."

She grabbed his shoulders and pulled him to her chest. Her breaths came in ragged bursts as if the love filling her heart might crush her lungs. How had she ever made something as perfect as the little boy in her arms? All this time she'd tried to put him first, and he'd been trying to do the same for her. She'd spent years making up for a trauma he'd never suffered and the last few months guarding him from an abandonment that would never come.

How much time had she wasted looking through a distorted lens, and what kind of damage had she done to them all along the way? She couldn't even begin to make sense of everything right now, but she did know one thing she could fix immediately. She held him back at arm's length and crouched down until her eyes were level with his. "Joseph Landon Grettano, you're too good for your own good, but if you ever sacrifice your own happiness for my sadness, then I haven't taught you what love is."

He looked down at the floor, and she gave him a gentle shake. "I mean it. I always, always, always want you to love whoever and whatever makes you happy, no matter what."

"But isn't that what Duke did?"

Molly could no longer hide her tears. They spilled down her cheeks in a steady stream. What had she done? To her son, to Duke, to herself? She'd been so caught up in trying to protect them all she'd taken away everything worth protecting.

Love.

Her chest ached. She'd had a real chance at love. She'd been surrounded by it, and she'd rejected it. More than that, she'd taught the people she loved most that love was something to fear, to be ashamed of, to hide.

"I'm sorry, Mom, I didn't mean it. I didn't mean to make you cry."

"You didn't, honey." She sniffed and wiped the tears away. "I did this, not you."

"We don't have to go to the baseball game."

She shook her head and hugged him tightly again. "No, the baseball game is exactly what I need right now."

"Why?" he asked skeptically.

She forced a smile and said, "Because there's no crying in baseball."

TOP OF THE NINTH

The Heart of the Game

"Duke!" both Joe and Charlie shouted as they hurled themselves at her.

She caught them in her arms and hugged them so tightly she lifted them off the ground. She inhaled their scent, sweet and warm, like fresh air on a summer's day. "I missed you."

"We missed you, too." Joe stood back and straightened his ball cap, then glanced behind him, causing Duke to turn her attention toward Molly. The sight of her sent a shot of pain through her chest. The distance between them hurt even more. Molly stood back a few feet, her smile encouraging but reserved and pointed at Joe, not her. Duke wanted to step back, too. She'd barely been able to focus on her work when she'd been in Pittsburgh, far from Molly and the void she'd left in her heart, but now, within sight of her, she couldn't escape the emptiness. If not for the little boy looking back and forth between them, she might have given in to the urge to flee.

Molly gave Joe a little nod, and he turned back toward Duke, his expression hopeful. "Do you think we'll clinch the pennant this weekend?"

Duke shook her head, but Molly's frown stopped the jaded laugh bubbling up in her. She stared back into Joe's big brown eyes and felt another piece of her heart crumble. She'd almost done exactly what she'd warned Molly against. He deserved the comfort baseball afforded right now even if she didn't think the Cardinals would clinch the pennant this weekend.

They were two games back of the first-place team with three games left to go against them. To take sole possession of first place, they'd have to win them all, and if any team was more likely to walk away from this series with a sweep, it was the Reds. The Cardinals had rebounded from their slump earlier in the month, but not fast enough and not soon enough. One of the hard lessons she'd learned this season was sometimes heart and grit and will weren't enough to win an unevenly matched contest. Still, she couldn't and wouldn't dash Joe's hope.

She started to sit down, to brace herself and gather her thoughts, but the stadium was filling quickly, and it occurred to her the seat she'd grown accustomed to occupying wasn't hers. The Grettanos had three seats, one for each of them, and she wasn't one of them. Not anymore. Maybe she never really had been. Molly and her boys formed a unit, a family. What was she? A friend? Maybe the boys saw her that way, but what about Molly?

She couldn't even look at her now. She couldn't give into the questions still pounding through her head or the emotions that came with them. Maybe that was why she didn't share Joe's excitement. Excitement was an emotion, along with joy and hope. Opening the door to any one of those feelings would be like trying to let a single grain of sand slip through an hourglass. She'd be cutting it close to even acknowledge those attributes in Joe, but she had to try.

"You're a true believer, kiddo," she said, bending her knees to reach his eye level. "If the Cardinals are going to win three out of three from the Reds, they'll need to have a heart like yours."

"Oh, they have it," he said confidently. "They've also got Molina's big bat, and that's the heart of the game."

"Some people say a strong defense is the heart of this game," Duke said. "They argue pitchers who don't let anyone get a hit tend to win the most ball games."

"What do you say?"

Duke mulled the question over in her head, trying to grab a hold of something, anything familiar. She knew the arguments to both sides of the clichéd debate that raged constantly, even among the most novice fans. What was the heart of a winning team? The crack of the bat? The sizzle of a fastball? The pop of a glove? These questions made up so much of her job, and yet she felt completely unable to give even the most conventional of answers, much less an articulate one.

"I think a good catcher's every bit as important as a good pitcher or a good batter," Molly finally said. "He's the one who calls the game, isn't he?"

"Absolutely." Duke looked up quickly, registering the compassion in Molly's eyes and realizing she'd lobbed her a softball. A swirling mix of gratitude and embarrassment stirred in her chest, overwhelming her. She turned back to Joe quickly. "A catcher's got to have the highest baseball IQ on the team, and he's got to be able to withstand a beating, too."

"Brains and brawn," Molly said, her voice higher than usual as though laced with forced cheerfulness. "Our catcher has both to go with the big bat you mentioned, Joe."

Duke nodded thoughtfully. What change of heart allowed Molly to make baseball small talk easier than she did? Nothing about this conversation felt right.

"And we've got Ben LeBaron on the mound," Joe said. "It's a powerful battery."

"I heard someone say once Molina would have an MVP year. Has he lived up to the prediction?" Molly asked.

"I think so," Joe said quickly, then looked to Duke. They both watched her now, hopeful, waiting for her to confirm something they believed in could still be real. Should she lead them on? Hadn't she done enough of that already? They'd only be let down eventually. Maybe it would be better to ease them into the disappointment and perhaps help guard their hearts from the inevitable crash.

"He's had a career year. He's done a lot to be proud of, the whole team has, but there's more to the game than stats and trophies. No one can win all the time."

"You don't think he can do it?" Joe asked, his voice low with suspicion. "You don't think we're going to win the division either."

"I didn't say that." Duke's defense was halfhearted. "We're up against hard odds. Life's like that sometimes. So is the game, and we don't have a lot of time left."

"We have some time," Joe said.

He was right, of course. They weren't mathematically eliminated yet, but for some reason, the series didn't strike her as a final push toward glory so much as a swan song, or a long good-bye, and for the first time in her life that didn't bother her. She'd been a fan through good and bad, seen World Series wins and losing records, but for the first time she didn't mourn the end of a season. She couldn't say that to Joe, though. She'd promised Molly this game would bring him more than just heartache. "I suppose anything is still possible."

"Yeah, because we're Cardinals fans," he said emphatically. "We don't play games on paper. We win World Series we only backed into. We make mad dashes toward home plate. We never give up even when we're down to our last strike…twice."

Duke smiled in spite of her malaise. He knew more about the game, the team, the history than most people ever would. Why had she tried to rein him in? Perhaps his optimism served as such a stark reminder of how lacking her own faith had become that she couldn't process the disparity. Or did misery love company? Maybe seeing the team she loved come up short would make her feel better about her own failures.

"What did I say wrong?" he asked.

"Nothing. You're right." She grabbed the bill of his red cap and spun it around backward. "You should believe in the team, in rally caps, rally towels, and rally squirrels. You've got the right idea, and you give a great pep talk. Maybe you should write my column tonight."

He shook his head. "Never. You're the best sportswriter ever."

She gave him a half smile. "All right then, I better get back to work."

She glanced one more time at Molly, who opened her mouth like she wanted to say something, then closed it again before offering a fake smile of her own. Duke wondered briefly about the unspoken sentence, but her heart and her mind were too emotionally spent to dwell on any more unknowns. Molly had already made it clear Duke had disappointed her, and she had no argument to the contrary. None of the shadowy reasons to keep fighting mattered now. Molly needed more than she could give, and she needed to get back to the things in her life she could be sure of. That meant going back to work. Only for the first time ever, her job actually did feel like work.

❖

The view from the press box was iconic, an early autumn night, the dark sky serving only to magnify the bright white stadium lights.

Duke felt like she was in some epic baseball movie with scenery built to heighten the overwhelming sense of urgency. If she were a director, she could've done no better a job of evoking those emotions. Busch Stadium literally vibrated with the collective energy coursing through her veins as a cast of forty-two thousand fans packed its every open space. The cool September breeze carried a teasing scent of autumn. Like the subtle perfume left in the wake of a beautiful woman, even the air itself seemed to hint at a path to October baseball.

Flashes of white danced across a sea of St. Louis red below her, and the stamp of feet echoed from the seats above. Concrete and steel hummed. A constant murmur of the crowd reverberated through the stands and spilled into the streets, but when the Cardinals scored a run, the roar deafened the city, drowning out the fireworks and rippling the waters of even the mighty Mississippi.

There had been more than a few of those earth-shaking cheers over the last two games. The Cardinals had pulled out a win off the arm of LeBaron and a single stroke of Molina's bat the night before, leaving them one game back of the Reds with two more to play. There had never been a more enjoyable math lesson than the one being taught all over St. Louis. Everywhere everyone ticked the magic number down from three to two and now itched to replace it with a one. The entire city had been swept into the excitement, with her report from last night's game having triple the readers she'd seen back in July. St. Louis couldn't get enough baseball and clamored hungrily for one more game, leaving Duke feeling like a stranger in her own home.

Even now with a one-run lead in the top of the ninth, she couldn't summon any faith. She waited for the inevitable error, the grooved pitch, the overthrow, or the defensive miscue to end it all. Even with victory and a tie for the National League Central division a meager three outs away, an air of defeat still permeated Duke's senses. It blew across her skin like a phantom mist and settled like a heavy yoke across her shoulders. She'd changed so much over the course of the season she hardly knew how to do her job anymore. She'd long since given up her lists of words to store for future use. She'd also passed on witty banter with her colleagues. She managed to keep score and tweet major announcements, but even her color commentary had dried up completely. As both the crowd around her and the blogosphere teemed with armchair coaches and catchers, she had no expertise left to share.

Now in the top of the ninth inning, all she looked forward to was the end. The first batter was easily dismissed with a ladder of incendiary fastballs. Outside, the crowd noise rattled the glass. Duke marked a K on her score-keeping app without comment.

The second batter wouldn't go down as easily. He crowded the plate, looking for a jump on the outside pitch, and got his reward in the form of a ninety-eight-mile-an-hour heater popped directly between his shoulder blades. The thud could be heard even in the third tier, followed by a collective wince and groan, leaving Duke the only one around unmoved by the blunt force trauma. The hitter spun dramatically and half hopped, half staggered toward first base. Every Reds fan in Ohio was, no doubt, glad to get their base any way they could get it, and maybe in a few minutes, the hitter might feel the same way, but Duke empathized only with the way he clenched his fists and jaw in an attempt to focus on the job ahead of him. She knew the struggle well. She even envied him the public and productive nature of his pain. At least he had something to show for his trouble. At least he stood the possibility of helping to build something better.

He'd also extended the inning, something Duke didn't thank him for. Why did the ninth frame always seem to last longer than the others combined? Finally, the third hitter dug into the batter's box. The All-Star first baseman had taken the lesson of the last pitch to heart and leaned away from another fastball, but this one caught the inside corner of the plate for strike one. The Cardinals closer wasted none of his momentum busting him inside again, but this time he got the bat off his shoulder, long enough to muscle the ball a hundred feet straight up. In one fluid motion Molina rose and tossed off his mask as easily as a normal person might remove a T-shirt. He trotted a quarter of the way down the third baseline, then seemed to will the ball's downward fall right into his mitt.

The crowd went crazy once more, and Duke felt a minor jump in her heart, not for excitement over the game, but at the thought of how close the catch had been made to the Grettanos' section. Were they screaming their heads off? She couldn't imagine Charlie in a crowd like this. Had his inner lion consumed him? Did Molly explain the play to him, or did he roar along with the rest of the mob even without understanding why? What about Joe? Had he been swept up into the frenzy as well? His hope had been rewarded up until this point. He should be ecstatic, but would he be able to relax until the final out flashed across the scoreboard? He always kept his optimism guarded, like his mother.

Molly—what did she make of all the high drama? Did she believe, like Joe, or did her own pain and expectation of disappointment prevent her from enjoying the moment? Was she smiling the radiant smile Duke longed to have directed at her once more, or did worry lines crease her forehead like they had the last time they'd spoken to one another? Duke wished again she was with them all. She wanted to see their reactions for herself but knew if she were down there, she'd likely wish she was back in the press box. She didn't want to be with Molly and the boys right now. She wanted to be with them three months ago, and that wasn't any more possible than willing a team into the post-season.

She typed a few notes on the game story she'd been writing since the third inning. Win or lose, she didn't feel like sticking around here any longer than she had to. She hoped to have everything but a few quotes already written before the game ended. She was so focused on finishing quickly she didn't even look up when Jordan Alverez stepped to the plate. The last great hope of the Reds to clinch the pennant tonight and render the final game of the season useless was a solid batter. He hit for average, he hit for power, and Duke fully expected him to do both against the Cardinals closer. From the changing sound of the crowd, tense and suddenly subdued, many of them expected, or at least suspected, the worst as well.

She never saw the pitch. With her head bowed over her tablet she only *heard* the ball strike the bat. The crack echoed crisp and clean through the cool air, a sound she associated instinctually with impending fireworks. Years of following baseball had produced a Pavlovian response to the sound, and she raised her head, her eyes immediately locking onto the ball as it shot toward centerfield. Cayden Brooks sprinted toward the wall, but Duke and everyone else in the ballpark could tell he was going to run out of room before the ball did. Its trajectory had it going almost a foot over the wall. All around her and out into the stands, people rose to their feet, silently willing it to drop a little lower, but the ball would not bend. It would not budge even an inch from its line.

Cayden Brooks, however, was not so unmoved. Running full speed across the warning track, his eyes trained on the ball, he leapt only in the final second, his cleats digging into the green pads of the outfield fence and his free hand pushing up off the top of the wall to accentuate his ascent. Extending his arm to full reach, he trapped the ball in the webbing of his glove. The force of the shot bent his wrist back at an unnatural angle, dipping it all the way below the outside of the wall, but when he snapped it back up, the ball was clearly still in place. He hung from the wall for the few stunned seconds it took him and the more than forty thousand spectators to realize what had happened. Then the explosion of cheers rocked Cardinals Nation, not just the fans, but also the coaches, the players, the camera crew and announcers. Even the reporters went wild. Everywhere around her, people screamed and jumped, hugging and high-fiving one another. Big, old, gray, and jaded newspaper men shrieked and pounded their chests, laughing like little boys.

Duke remained rooted in shock and awe amid the chaos. Her current mental state had no method for processing astounding feats of heroism. She simply lifted her tablet and typed, "Another elimination game tomorrow night," then hit "send" to share on a variety of social media platforms.

She probably should've said more, done more, felt more, but she didn't. She couldn't even pretend she wanted to play it cool, minimalist, classic. She'd just witnessed the biggest play of her career thus far, and all she could think about was having to go through everything again tomorrow.

"Holy shit," Cooper said, slapping one of his big paws on her shoulder and shaking it. "Ho-lee shit!"

She turned around to look at him but almost didn't recognize what she saw. He was smiling, a real, genuine smile. It stretched his cheeks tightly, making the stubble of his five o'clock shadow stand on end. The look was completely foreign, all beard and teeth. She'd sat beside him for 161 games, and she couldn't recall ever having seen his teeth. They were straight and even, if a little yellow. His joy made her feel strange, as if she'd shown up to a funeral only to find everyone else had come for a keg party.

"What's wrong with you?" Cooper asked with a laugh shaking his beer belly. "You've been vindicated. All your little Mary Sunshine predictions and annoying optimism about the team and Brooks and the post-season…Christ."

He stared at her, waiting for some answer to his convoluted question, but she had none to offer. She didn't know what was wrong with her. Well, she did, sort of. She missed Molly and the kids. She felt sad about coming up short for them. The sting of failure still clung to her, and the fact that she'd had to choose between them and baseball had put a damper on the end of the season. Still, she had chosen, and the decision in her wake had come down strongly on the side of the game. Everything happening right now should have only affirmed her choice and strengthened her resolve. The game had rewarded her with the stuff dreams were built and sustained on. Baseball had shown her the very best it had to offer, a beautiful gift for her devotion, and still she felt anything but blessed.

"I'm fine," she said, "just a little freaked out. I've never seen you so damn giddy before."

"What can I say? I'm in love." He laughed again and tossed a stack of score sheets and charts on the table with a dramatic flourish she wouldn't have thought him capable of. "I'm done hiding it. You showed me the error of my bitter ways."

"What are you talking about?"

"No matter how many times it hurts me, no matter how hard I try to guard myself against the letdown, no matter how crusty and jaded I become, this game always does something like *that*." He pointed to the outfield wall as if he could still see Cayden Brooks hauling the home run back over the fence. "And I fall in love all over again."

She stared at him in disbelief. How could Cooper Pachol be a grinning mess of sunshine and daisies at the prospect of a one-game, winner-take-all pennant race while she sat with her jaw clenched and her shoulders tensed for the same reason?

This wasn't how she expected her first season in the big leagues to end. This was her dream coming true. The culmination of her life's yearning, both on and off the field, couldn't really end in her complete disillusionment with the game, could it?

"It's flippin' grand," Cooper said, still grinning like a fool.

"What?"

"Being in love all over again, after all this time."

She eyed him suspiciously. Maybe he was screwing with her. Maybe he'd had a mental break, but his smile, as weird as it felt to her, seemed genuine. His eyes were clear and focused, his cheeks pink with life instead of red with alcohol. He even seemed healthier, as if believing in something else made him better or stronger than he'd been on his own. Hell, he looked younger.

The thought reminded her of Joe and his youthful exuberance. What if his belief wasn't the product of his innocence, but of love? What if it wasn't a pitching matchup, or a big bat, or a gold glove at the heart of this game? What if the heart of the game, really, was found in her heart?

There was no *what if* to the question. She knew the answer. She'd known it all along. Love had always driven this game for her, and as much as she tried to close herself off from that emotion, she couldn't. She was in love every bit as much as Cooper or Joe, only she was in love with Molly. She'd tried to convince herself she couldn't love them both, that somehow a divided love was a weakened one, but maybe the opposite was true. What if she couldn't be in love and closed off from it at the same time? Could love ever come at the expense of love? Or was it an all-or-nothing sort of game?

After seeing first Joe and now Cooper display all the love she lacked, she wondered if baseball didn't require a pure heart, a strong heart, a whole heart. Hers wasn't any of those things anymore. Without Molly her heart wasn't just broken, part of it was gone, and without that part the whole couldn't function. She'd given up the possibility of one great love in order to preserve another, and in the end she'd lost them both.

She'd worried all along she couldn't love Molly the way she deserved with baseball in the way, but now she realized she couldn't fully love baseball anymore either, not with part of her heart missing. She'd feared she couldn't have them both, but now she suspected she couldn't have either of them.

❖

Duke stepped out of the crowded tunnel of the main concourse and into the fading light of the September evening. As she neared the lower level of the stadium, she reached instinctively for her press pass, patting first her stomach, then her chest, and running her fingers up to her neck before realizing it wasn't there. Exhaling heavily, she slipped her hand into the back pocket of her jeans and pulled out the paper ticket she'd used to get through the main gate. She held it tightly until the sides of the card stock pressed a thin line into her palm.

"Ticket," she whispered, remembering the first time she'd held one in her hand. Even then she'd known it would lead to something amazing, but she could never have understood the cost of such an item. She had understood its magic, though. Looking out onto the field, she saw the scene again, the vast expanse, the vibrant colors, burnt orange to emerald green, dotted with a heavenly white of the home uniforms. She looked down at her own attire—the birds on the bat were still an exact replica of those on the field, but her mind no longer played fast and loose with those connections. Still, the same unnamable force that pulled her forward then guided her through the crowd tonight, only now she wasn't headed toward the players.

Turning toward the section that had become so entangled and embattled with the force of the field, she stopped short when she saw Molly. She was standing at the end of the row, and the crowd parted in some silent agreement not to obstruct any view of her. Duke froze and stared. Her dark jeans hugged the curves Duke loved to trace. Her fingers twitched and contracted at the memory of skin beneath the denim. Molly's white jersey covered a long-sleeved red turtleneck, and her hair was tucked under a navy blue ball cap before spilling out the back and down her shoulders. Their eyes met, and Duke watched the soundless intake of breath raise Molly's chest. Sadness, regret, and craving mingled quickly and shot between them, only to be returned in equal measure.

She stood, transfixed, for what felt like years before she sighed heavily, her shoulders sagging, and she forced a smile she knew everyone could tell was fake. Her heart beat a hollow bass drum through her chest and ears.

"Hi," Molly said.

Her muscles warred between the lethargic ache of their separation and the burning urge to pull her close once more. Instead, she stepped only close enough to be out of arm's reach. "Hi."

Would this awkwardness never end? How had they gone from making love and transforming lives to grasping vainly for basic conversation? Thankfully, the kids saved them once again.

"Hey, Duke," Joe said with a grin, "I told you we'd be okay."

Duke nodded and tried to swallow the lump of emotion choking her. She didn't feel okay. She couldn't even answer him. She looked away, down at her shoes.

Charlie scrambled onto his seat, standing so he could brace himself with one tiny hand on the back of the red stadium chair and reach out to her with the other. Putting his palm on her chest where her lanyard usually hung, he eyed her sadly. "Oh, Duke. You losed your necklace."

She always thought of Joe as the intuitive one, but Charlie's skills of observation were not to be underestimated. Few details ever got by him, and now that he'd brought them up, they wouldn't get by the others either.

She tried to sound as casual as possible when she cleared her throat and said, "It's not lost. I'm not working tonight."

"What?" all three of them asked in unison.

"I took the night off."

"How?" Molly asked.

"I called Beach and told him I couldn't do it. He's got some hotshot sportswriter out of Illinois State looking to get innings in. Who knows, maybe I gave the next Buzz Bissinger his big career break."

"What about your career? Isn't this suicide for you?"

"Well, he didn't fire me on the spot, so that has to count for something." She didn't want to think about Beach's reaction last night. She didn't want to think about the implications for next season either. If she got back on track, she'd be sure to make it up to him. But right now that didn't seem likely. "I know this will confirm to a lot of people that I don't have what it takes, but I had to do what's best for the team, and right now that's not me, I'm not much good to anyone right now."

"Don't say that," Molly said softly as she lifted her hand like she wanted to stroke Duke's hair. She longed to feel her touch, to feel anything other than the cold that stiffened her limbs, but she didn't. Molly dropped her hand and looked away. "I'm sorry. Maybe we shouldn't be here."

"No. This is the best place for you now, for your whole family." She nodded to the boys and dropped her voice. "Joe still believes. He's still got this game running through his blood. He belongs here."

"And what about you?"

Duke shrugged again.

Molly turned to Joe and said, "Keep an eye on your brother." They stepped out into the aisle behind their seats, far enough away to avoid little ears, but not enough for the kids to escape their eyes. The position put them between the constant stream of people pouring in and the field on which all their focus rested.

"You're scaring me. What are you doing?" Molly finally asked. "You could destroy everything you worked for." More softly she added, "Is this because of me?"

"I don't know."

"This." She held out her arms to the stadium, the field, and all it encompassed. "This is your passion, this is what you live for. Even I can see that now. Don't you feel all the excitement swirling around you?"

"No." She shook her head. "I don't feel anything. It's the biggest night of my career, everything I dreamed of, and I don't feel anything but cold and hollow."

"Then why are you here if it hurts so much, if the work is gone and the game is empty?"

"The game isn't empty. I am. I'm not who I was, but you are, and so are the boys. That's why I'm here, for you, and for them. I promised I'd be here always and I'd never let you down." She choked out the last part. "I mean, I know I let you down, but I'm not going to do it again."

Molly's eyes glistened, endless depths of emotion shimmering to the surface. "Even if it hurts you?"

"Even if it kills me."

"I never wanted that. Even when I was so mad at you, even when you hurt me, I never wanted to break a heart as beautiful as yours."

"My heart is broken, shattered even, but you didn't do that. I did," Duke admitted. "I wasn't the partner you deserved. I didn't give you my all. I didn't even give you my best. I didn't put you and the kids ahead of my job, and I was wrong, no matter what my job may be or how much it meant to me. I wasn't fair to you."

"I'm sorry. I wasn't completely fair to you, either. I know baseball's more than a job," Molly said. "Maybe that's what scared me most, or maybe I was jealous. You loved so freely, and I worried if I let myself believe in something that wonderful I'd only hurt worse when I lost it."

"You can't ever lose me, Molly."

"I know that now. I should have known then, too. I spent so many years shadowboxing my own demons I didn't know any other way. I shouldn't have pulled you into those fights, though."

"Yes, you should have. Your fights should've been my fights. We should've fought them together."

"No, we shouldn't have been fighting the past at all. You were something new, something bright and beautiful. I should've looked toward a future with you instead of pulling you into my past." Molly hung her head. "I was scared of being left again, and envious of how easily you opened up your heart, but I never should have pinned my issues on everyone else."

"*You* are my issue, Molly. I'm sorry I was so wrapped up in my own world, in this world." She indicated the field. "You were right to call me out, and I'm sorry you had to do so more than once."

"I don't get any satisfaction in being right if this is what it means for us."

"But you were right. I fell short of every ideal I professed to hold. You were right to say I wasn't giving you my best, and you were right about you and the boys deserving better." Duke rubbed her face. "You were right on absolutely every point but one."

Molly raised her eyebrows. "Which one?"

"The biggest one," Duke said, then bit her lip so hard it hurt. She wasn't sure how she'd get through the next part, but her heart forced her to try. "You said I'd never love anything the way I love baseball, and that's untrue, because that's exactly how I love you."

"Duke," Molly pleaded, "you don't have to do this here. Not tonight."

"What better place or time will we ever have? This is my sanctuary." She looked out at the field once more until tears blurred her vision. "But you're my soul." She shuddered, then plowed forward. "This is where I learned to love, but you're the true object of my adoration. This game taught me the meaning of sacrifice, perseverance, and faith, but you taught me how to live those virtues. You won me from game one. You taught me how lucky I was to be here. You showed me how to be the best, how to swing for the fences. You showed me how to keep my eye on the ball and how to work through a long season. And while it may have been too little and too late for us, you made me truly understand there's no 'I' in 'team.' Baseball offered me those life lessons, but you, Molly, you made all the lessons worth learning."

Around them, the crowds pushed past, the national anthem blared, the players ran onto the field, but for her there was only Molly. Taking her hand in both of hers, she had to shout to be heard: "Love is the heart of the game. It always has been, but my heart's empty without you."

"I don't want you to choose between loving me and loving baseball. I should've never asked that of you."

"Good, because I can't. It's all or nothing. The love is all wrapped up together. It's what makes me who I am, and it's what's built my capacity to love you the way I do. I know I wasn't the person you needed me to be before, but I can be if you'll let me. I think I've proven I have the ability to love one thing with a whole heart, with a pure heart, through good times and bad, for my whole life, but I can't do it without you anymore. Baseball built my heart, but I'm giving it to you."

"Please stop," Molly cried, tears spilling down her cheeks. "I can't stand any more. You have to stop."

The words knocked all the air out of Duke's lungs. She'd failed again. She poured out the tiny pieces of her broken heart, tangled, jagged, and raw, only to have them rejected. Molly didn't believe her, or didn't believe in her. She didn't want to hear any more. "I'm sorry. I didn't mean to bring this all up again. I didn't mean to bring up all the emotions and all the baseball talk. I just, I just—"

"You just can't help it," Molly said, her beautiful lips curling up at the corners. "You can't help but talk about love in sports terms any more than I can help falling in love with a sportswriter."

Duke nodded sadly. They were both victims of a cruel— "What?"

"I said, you can't change how you love any more than I can change the fact that I'm in love with you, too."

"But you said…you said to stop. You said you couldn't stand any more."

"I can't." Molly laughed. "You're too eloquent for your own good. You could've said you loved me, and I would've told you I loved you, too, but no, you have to give a heart-melting oration on the grand nature of that love tied to America's national pastime. It's not that I don't want to hear about your capacity for love and devotion, but I already knew those things."

"You did?"

"Yes, and I'm sorry I didn't realize them earlier. I should have, but you aren't the only one to learn big lessons this season."

"Really?"

"You got me back in the ballgame after years of losing more than

I won. You eased me in one game at a time. You taught me the games aren't played on paper, and I shouldn't let my fear of striking out keep me from swinging. You helped me see a person can be so much better than their box score, and home runs can come when you least expect them." She wiped a tear from her eye. "The only thing you couldn't teach me was that there's no crying in baseball."

Duke rubbed away her own tears before reaching out to caress one away from Molly's cheek. "That's because it's a stupid rule. Of course there's crying in baseball, what else is worth—"

"No more speeches, sportswriter." Molly hooked a finger through the belt loop of Duke's jeans and tugged her close. "Kiss me."

Their lips met in a rush of passion laced with sheer electricity, and the crowd went wild. Forty thousand people rose to their feet on a wave of exuberance as deafening cheers rocked Busch Stadium. Molly and Duke slowly stepped apart and turned toward the field in time to see Cayden Brooks cross home plate.

Molly wrapped one arm around Duke's waist and gave her a little squeeze before shouting, "Now, that's what I call a home run."

She laughed and looked from Molly to the boys, who were watching with wide, eager eyes so much like their mother's. They walked over together and pulled the whole family into their embrace. Duke rested her chin on Joe's head with one arm around Charlie and the other around Molly as she looked out across the familiar vista before her and saw her future once more.

Her understanding of baseball had grown, changed, and evolved over time, but some things remained constant. Like the child who'd first felt the magic of this sport so many years ago, this field, this team, this game had once again led her heart home.

About the Author

Rachel Spangler never set out to be an award-winning author. She was just so poor and easily bored during her college years that she had to come up with creative ways to entertain herself, and her first novel, *Learning Curve*, was born out of one such attempt. She was sincerely surprised when it was accepted for publication and even more shocked when it won the Golden Crown Literary Award for Debut Author. She also won a Goldie for her second novel, *Trails Merge*. Since writing is more fun than a real job, and so much cheaper than therapy, Rachel continued to type away, leading to the publication of *The Long Way Home*, *LoveLife*, *Spanish Heart*, *Does She Love You?*, and *Timeless*. She plans to continue writing as long as anyone anywhere will keep reading.

Rachel and her partner, Susan, are raising their young son in western New York, where during the winter they make the most of the lake-effect snow on local ski slopes. In the summer, they love to travel and watch their beloved St. Louis Cardinals. Regardless of the season, she always makes time for a good romance, whether she's reading it, writing it, or living it.

For more information visit Rachel online at www.rachelspangler.com or on Facebook.

Books Available From Bold Strokes Books

Twice Lucky by Mardi Alexander. For firefighter Mackenzie James and Dr. Sarah Macarthur, there's suddenly a whole lot more in life to understand, to consider, to risk…someone will need to fight for her life. (978-1-62639-325-7)

Shadow Hunt by L.L. Raand. With young to raise and her Pack under attack, Sylvan, Alpha of the wolf Weres, takes on her greatest challenge when she determines to uncover the faceless enemies known as the Shadow Lords. A Midnight Hunters novel. (978-1-62639-326-4)

Heart of the Game by Rachel Spangler. A baseball writer falls for a single mom, but can she ever love anything as much as she loves the game? (978-1-62639-327-1)

Getting Lost by Michelle Grubb. Twenty-eight days, thirteen European countries, a tour manager fighting attraction, and an accused murderer: Stella and Phoebe's journey of a lifetime begins here. (978-1-62639-328-8)

Prayer of the Handmaiden by Merry Shannon. Celibate priestess Kadrian must defend the kingdom of Ithyria from a dangerous enemy and ultimately choose between her duty to the Goddess and the love of her childhood sweetheart, Erinda. (978-1-62639-329-5)

The Witch of Stalingrad by Justine Saracen. A Soviet "night witch" pilot and American journalist meet on the Eastern Front in WWII and struggle through carnage, conflicting politics, and the deadly Russian winter. (978-1-62639-330-1)

Night Mare by Franci McMahon. On an innocent horse-buying trip, Jane Scott uncovers a horrifying element of the horse show world, thrusting her into a whirlwind of poisoned money. (978-1-62639-333-2E).

Pedal to the Metal by Jesse J. Thoma. When unreformed thief Dubs Williams is released from prison to help Max Winters bust a car theft ring, Max learns that if you want to catch a thief, you have to get in bed with one. (978-1-62639-239-7)

Dragon Horse War by D. Jackson Leigh. A priestess of peace and a fiery warrior must defeat a vicious uprising that entwines their destinies and ultimately their hearts. (978-1-62639-240-3)

For the Love of Cake by Erin Dutton. When everything is on the line and one taste can break a heart, will pastry chefs Maya and Shannon take a chance on reality? (978-1-62639-241-0)

Betting on Love by Alyssa Linn Palmer. A quiet country girl at heart and a live-life-to-the-fullest biker take a risk at offering each other their hearts. (978-1-62639-242-7)

The Deadening by Yvonne Heidt. The lines between good and evil, right and wrong, have always been blurry for Shade. When Raven's actions force her to choose, which side will she come out on? (978-1-62639-243-4)

One Last Thing by Kim Baldwin & Xenia Alexiou. Blood is thicker than pride. The final book in the Elite Operative Series brings together foes, family, and friends to start a new order. (978-1-62639-230-4)

Songs Unfinished by Holly Stratimore. Two aspiring rock stars learn that falling in love while pursuing their dreams can be harmonious—if they can only keep their pasts from throwing them out of tune. (978-1-62639-231-1)

Beyond the Ridge by L.T. Marie. Will a contractor and a horse rancher overcome their family differences and find common ground to build a life together? (978-1-62639-232-8)

Swordfish by Andrea Bramhall. Four women battle the demons from their pasts. Will they learn to let go, or will happiness be forever beyond their grasp? (978-1-62639-233-5)

The Fiend Queen by Barbara Ann Wright. Princess Katya and her consort Starbride must turn evil against evil in order to banish Fiendish power from their kingdom, and only love will pull them back from the brink. (978-1-62639-234-2)

Up the Ante by PJ Trebelhorn. When Jordan Stryker and Ashley Noble meet again fifteen years after a short-lived affair, is either of them prepared to gamble on a chance at love? (978-1-62639-237-3)

Speakeasy by MJ Williamz. When mob leader Helen Byrne sets her sights on the girlfriend of Al Capone's right-hand man, passion and tempers flare on the streets of Chicago. (978-1-62639-238-0)

Myth and Magic: Queer Fairy Tales, edited by Radclyffe and Stacia Seaman. Myth, magic, and monsters—the stuff of childhood dreams (or nightmares) and adult fantasies. (978-1-62639-225-0)

Venus in Love by Tina Michele. Morgan Blake can't afford any distractions and Ainsley Dencourt can't afford to lose control—but the beauty of life and art usually lies in the unpredictable strokes of the artist's brush. (978-1-62639-220-5)

Rules of Revenge by AJ Quinn. When a lethal operative on a collision course with her past agrees to help a CIA analyst on a critical assignment, the encounter proves explosive in ways neither woman anticipated. (978-1-62639-221-2)

The Romance Vote by Ali Vali. Chili Alexander is a sought-after campaign consultant who isn't prepared when her boss's daughter, Samantha Pellegrin, comes to work at the firm and shakes up Chili's life from the first day. (978-1-62639-222-9)

Advance by Gun Brooke. Admiral Dael Caydoc's mission to find a new homeworld for the Oconodian people is hazardous, but working with the infuriating Commander Aniwyn "Spinner" Seclan endangers her heart and soul. (978-1-62639-224-3)

A Spark of Heavenly Fire by Kathleen Knowles. Kerry and Beth are building their life together, but unexpected circumstances could destroy their happiness. (978-1-62639-212-0)

UnCatholic Conduct by Stevie Mikayne. Jil Kidd goes undercover to investigate fraud at St. Marguerite's Catholic School, but life gets complicated when her student is killed—and she begins to fall for her prime target. (978-1-62639-304-2)

Season's Meetings by Amy Dunne. Catherine Birch reluctantly ventures on the festive road trip from hell with beautiful stranger Holly Daniels only to discover the road to true love has its own obstacles to maneuver. (978-1-62639-227-4)

Courtship by Carsen Taite. Love and Justice—a lethal mix or a perfect match? (978-1-62639-210-6)

Against Doctor's Orders by Radclyffe. Corporate financier Presley Worth wants to shut down Argyle Community Hospital, but Dr. Harper Rivers will fight her every step of the way, if she can also fight their growing attraction. (978-1-62639-211-3)

Never Too Late by Julie Blair. When Dr. Jamie Hammond is forced to hire a new office manager, she's shocked to come face-to-face with Carla Grant and memories from her past. (978-1-62639-213-7)

Widow by Martha Miller. Judge Bertha Brannon must solve the murder of her lover, a policewoman she thought she'd grow old with. As more bodies pile up, the murderer starts coming for her. (978-1-62639-214-4)

Twisted Echoes by Sheri Lewis Wohl. What's a woman to do when she realizes the voices in her head are real? (978-1-62639-215-1)

Criminal Gold by Ann Aptaker. Through a dangerous night in New York in 1949, Cantor Gold, dapper dyke-about-town, smuggler of fine art, is forced by a crime lord to be his instrument of vengeance. (978-1-62639-216-8)